Also by Joyce Carol Oates

By the North Gate (1963)

Upon Sweeping Flood and Other Stories (1966)

The Wheel of Love (1970)

Marriages and Infidelities (1972)

The Goddess and Other Women (1974)

The Poisoned Kiss (1975)

Crossing the Border (1976)

Night-Side (1977)

A Sentimental Education (1980)

Last Days (1984)

Raven's Wing (1986)

The Assignation (1988)

Heat and Other Stories (1991)

Where Is Here? (1992)

Where Are You Going, Where Have You Been?

Selected Early Stories (1993)

Haunted: Tales of the Grotesque (1994)

Will You Always Love Me? (1996)

The Collector of Hearts: New Tales of the Grotesque (1998)

Faithless: Tales of Transgression (2001)

The Female of the Species (2005)

High Lonesome: New and Selected Stories 1966–2006 (2006)

The Museum of Dr. Moses (2007)

Wild Nights! (2008)

Dear Husband,

Joyce Carol Oates

ecco

An Imprint of HarperCollinsPublishers

for Susan Wolfson and Ron Levao

HarperCollins books may be purchased for educational, business, or sales promotional use. For information please write: Special Markets Department, HarperCollins Publishers, 10 East 53rd Street, New York, NY 10022.

Many thanks to the wonderful editors of the following magazines in which, frequently in different forms, most of the stories in this volume originally appeared: "Panic" in *Michigan Quarterly Review,* reprinted in *Detroit Noir* (2008); "Special," "Vigilante," and "Dear Joyce Carol," in *Boulevard;* "The Blind Man's Sighted Daughters," published in *Fiction* and reprinted in *The Best American Mystery Stories 2008*; "Magda Maria" in *McSweeney's;* "A Princeton Idyll" in *Yale Review;* "Cutty Sark" in *Salmagundi;* "Landfill" in *The New Yorker,* reprinted in *The Year's Best Fantasy & Horror* (2007); "The Heart Sutra" in *American Short Fiction;* "Suicide by Fitness Center" in *Harper's;* "The Glazers" in *American Short Fiction;* "Mistrial" in *Storie;* "Dear Husband," in *Conjunctions.*

A hardcover edition of this book was published in 2009 by Ecco, an imprint of HarperCollins Publishers.

FIRST ECCO PAPERBACK EDITION PUBLISHED 2010.

Designed by Cassandra J. Pappas

Library of Congress Cataloging-in-Publication Data is
available upon request.

ISBN: 978-0-06-170432-1

10 11 12 13 14   WBC/RRD   10 9 8 7 6 5 4 3 2 1

FT
Pbk

Contents

Part One

Panic

He knows this fact: it was a school bus.

That unmistakable color of virulent high-concentrate urine.

A lumbering school bus emitting exhaust. Faulty muffler, should be ticketed. He'd gotten trapped behind the bus in the right lane of the Chrysler Freeway headed north at about the exit for I-94, trapped at forty-five God-damned miles an hour. In disgust he shut VENT on his dashboard. What a smell! Would've turned on the A/C except he glimpsed then in the smudged rear window of the school bus, a section of which had been cranked partway open, two heifer-sized boys (Hispanic? black?) wrestling together and grinning. One of them had a gun the other was trying to snatch from him.

"My God! He's got a—"

Charles spoke distractedly, in shock. He'd been preparing to shift into the left lane and pass the damned bus but traffic in that lane of the Freeway (now nearing the Hamtramck exit) was unrelenting, he'd come up dangerously close behind the bus. Beside him Camilla glanced up sharply to see two boys struggling against the rear window, the long-barreled object that was a gun or appeared to be a gun, without uttering a word nor even a sound of alarm, distress, warning, Camilla fumbled to unbuckle her safety belt, turned to climb over the back of the seat where she fell awkwardly, scrambled then to her knees to unbuckle the baby from the baby's safety seat, and crouched on the floor behind Charles. So swiftly!

In a hoarse voice crying: "Brake the car! Get *away*!"

Charles was left in the front seat, alone. Exposed.

Stunned at how quickly, how unerringly and without a moment's hesitation, his wife had reacted to the situation. She'd escaped into the backseat like a panicked cat. And lithe as a cat. While he continued to drive, too stunned even to release pressure on the gas pedal, staring at the boys in the bus window less than fifteen feet ahead.

Now the boys were watching him, too. They'd seen Camilla climb over the back of her seat, very possibly they'd caught a flash of white thigh, a silky undergarment, and were howling with hilarity. Grinning and pointing at Charles behind the wheel frozen-faced in fear and indecision, delighted as if they were being tickled in their most private parts. Another hulking boy joined them thrusting his heifer-face close against the window. The boy waving the gun, any age from twelve to seventeen, fatty torso in a black T-shirt, oily black tight-curly hair and a skin like something smudged with a dirty eraser, was crouching now to point the gun barrel through the cranked-open window, at an angle that allowed him to aim straight at Charles's heart.

Laugh, laugh! There were a half-dozen boys now crowded against the bus window, observing with glee the cringing Caucasian male, of no age in their eyes except old, hunched behind the wheel of his metallic-gray Acura in the futile hope of minimizing the target he made, pleading, as if the boys could hear or, hearing, be moved to have pity on him, "No, don't!—no, no, God no—"

Charles braked the car, desperately. Swerved onto the highway shoulder. This was a dangerous maneuver executed without premeditation, no signal to the driver close behind the Acura in a massive S.U.V. but he had no choice! Horns were sounding on all sides, furious as wounded rhinos. The Acura lurched and bumped along the littered shoulder, skidded, began to fishtail. Both Camilla and Susanna were screaming. Charles saw a twisted strip of chrome rushing toward them, tire remnants and broken glass, but his brakes held, he struck the chrome at about ten miles an hour, and came to an abrupt stop.

Directly behind Charles, the baby was shrieking. Camilla was trying to comfort her, "Honey, it's all right! We are all right, honey! We're safe now! Nothing is going to happen! Nothing is going to happen to you, honey. Mommy is right here."

The school bus had veered on ahead, emitting its jeering exhaust.

Too fast. It happened too fast.

Didn't have time to think. Those punk bastards . . .

Had he seen the license plate at the rear of the school bus, he had not. Hadn't even registered the name of the school district or the bus company in black letters coated in grime at the rear of the bus. Hamtramck? Highland Park? As soon as he'd seen the gun in the boy's hand he'd been walloped by adrenaline like a shot to the heart: rushing blood to his head, tears into his eyes, racing his heart like a hammering fist.

He was shaken, ashamed. Humiliated.

It was the animal panic of not wanting to be shot, not wanting to die, that had taken over him utterly. The demonically grinning boys, the long-barreled object, obviously a gun, had to be a gun, the boy crouching so that he could aim through the cranked-open section of the window straight at Charles. The rapture in the thuggish kid's face as he prepared to pull the trigger.

Camilla was leaning over him, concerned. "Charles, are you all right?"

He was cursing the boys on the bus. He was sweating now, and his heart continued to beat erratically, as if mockingly. He told Camilla yes, of course he was all right. He was fine. He was alive, wasn't he? No shots had been fired, he hadn't crashed the car. She and Susanna were unhurt.

He would climb out of the overheated car as, scarcely more than a foot away, traffic rushed by on the highway, and he would struggle with the God-damned strip of chrome that had jammed beneath the Acura's front bumper, and then with mangled hands gripping the steering wheel tight as death he would continue to drive his family the rest of the way home without incident.

Camilla remained in the backseat, cradling and comforting the baby.

Comforting the baby she should be comforting *him*. She'd abandoned him to death.

He laughed. He was willing to recast the incident as a droll yet emblematic experience. One of the small and inexplicable dramas of their marriage. Saying, teasing, "You certainly got out of the passenger's seat in record time, Camilla. Abandoned your poor husband."

Camilla looked at him, eyes brimming with hurt.

"Charles, I had to protect Susanna. I only—"

"Of course. I know. It was remarkable, what you did."

"I saw the gun. That's all I saw. I panicked, and acted without thinking."

"You acted brilliantly, Camilla. I wish we had a video."

Camilla laughed. She was still excited, pumped up.

Susanna, eighteen months old, their first and to-be-only child, had been changed, fed, pacified, lain gently in her crib. A miracle, the baby who usually resisted napping at this hour was sleeping.

She'd cried herself into exhaustion. But she would forget the incident in the car, already she'd forgotten. The bliss of eighteen months.

Camilla was saying, in awe of herself, "Charles, I don't think

I've ever acted so swiftly. So—unerringly! I played high school basketball, field hockey. I was never so fast as the other girls."

Ruefully Camilla rubbed her knees. She was slightly banged
up, she would be bruised, she guessed. Lucky for her she hadn't
broken her neck.

Yet Camilla was marveling at what she'd accomplished in those
scant several seconds. While Charles had continued to drive the car
like a zombie, helpless. She had unbuckled her seat belt and crawled
over the back of the seat and unbuckled the baby and crouched with
the baby behind Charles. Shielded by Charles.

Charles understood that Camilla would recall and re-enact her
astonishing performance many times, in secret.

He said, "You hid behind me, which was the wise thing to do.
Under the circumstances. The kids had a target, it would have
been me in any case. It was purely nature, what you did. 'Protecting
the young.'"

"Charles, really! I didn't hide behind you. I hid behind the car
seat."

But I was in the seat. "Look, you were acting instinctively. Instinct
is impersonal. You acted to save a baby, and yourself. You had to
save yourself in order to save the baby. It must be like suddenly re-
alizing you can swim." Charles spoke slowly, as if the idea were
only now coming to him, a way of seeing the incident from a higher
moral perspective. "A boat capsizes, you're in the water, and in terror of drowning you swim. You discover that you can swim."

"Except you don't, Charles. You don't just 'swim.' If you don't
already know how to swim, you drown."

"I mean it's nature, impersonal. It isn't volitional."

"Yet you seem to resent me."

"Resent you! Camilla, I love you."

The truthful answer was yes. He did resent her, unfairly. Yet he
knew he must not push this further, he would say things he might
regret and could not retract. *You don't love me, you love Susanna. You love
the baby not the father. You love the father but not much. Not enough. The father
is expendable. The father is last season's milkweed seed blown in the wind. Debris.*

Camilla laughed at him, though she was wanting to be kissed by him, comforted. After her acrobatics in the car, after she'd demonstrated how little she needed him, how comical an accessory he was to her, still she wanted to be kissed and comforted, she was a wistful girl of about fourteen. Her smooth skin, her face that was round and imperturbable as a moon, maddening at times in its placidity. Charles had been attracted initially by the calmness of the woman's beauty and now he was annoyed. Camilla was thirty-six years old which is not so young and yet even in unsparing daylight she looked at least a decade younger, her face was so unlined, her eyes so clear. Charles, forty-two, had one of those fair-skinned "patrician" faces that become imprinted with a subtle sort of age: reminding Charles, when he had to consider it, of calcified sand beneath which rivulets of fresh water are running, wearing away the sand from within.

He was a corporation lawyer. He was a very good corporation lawyer. He would protect his clients. He would protect his wife, his daughter. How?

"Camilla, don't misunderstand me. Your instinct was to protect Susanna. There was nothing you could have done for me if one of those kids had fired the gun."

"If you'd been shot, we would have crashed anyway. We might all be dead now."

Camilla spoke wistfully. Charles wanted to slap her.

"Well. We're not, are we."

Instead, they were in their bedroom in Bloomfield Hills. A large white Colonial on a hill in Baskings Grove Estates, near Quarton Road. Leafy hilly suburb north of the derelict and depopulated city of Detroit sprawled choked in haze where, years ago as a boy, Charles had lived in a residential neighborhood above Six Mile Road near Livernois until his parents, fearful of "coloreds" encroaching upon them, had panicked, sold their property and fled. They were living now in Lake Worth, Florida. Charles thought of them as he tugged off his noose-necktie and flung it down. *Some of them, they'd kill you as soon as look at you. They're crack addicts, animals.*

In the car returning home, Camilla had tried to call 911 but the cell phone hadn't worked and now they were home, and safe, Charles debated whether to report the incident to Detroit police, now that the emergency had passed. No one had been hurt, after all.

Camilla objected, "But they—those boys—might hurt someone else. If they play that trick again. Another driver might really panic seeing the gun aimed at him, and crash his car."

Charles winced at this. Really panic. As if he, Charles, had panicked only moderately. But of course he had, why deny it. Camilla had been a witness. The swarthy-skinned boys laughing like hyenas in the rear bus window had been witnesses.

While Camilla prepared their dinner, Charles made the call. He spoke carefully, politely. His voice did not quaver. . . . *calling to report an incident that happened at about four-fifteen this afternoon on the Chrysler Freeway headed north at about the Hamtramck exit. A very dangerous incident involving a gun, that almost caused an accident. High-school boys, or maybe junior-high* . . . Charles spoke flatly describing in terse words what had happened. What had almost happened. Having to concede, he hadn't seen the license plate. Had not noticed the name of the school district. No distinguishing features on the bus except it was an old bus, probably not a suburban school bus, certainly not a private school bus, very likely an inner city bus, rust-flecked, filthy, emitting exhaust. No, he had not gotten a very good look at the boys: dark-skinned, he thought. But hadn't seen clearly.

In the kitchen, Camilla seemed to be opening and shutting drawers compulsively as if looking for something that eluded her. She was in a fever, suddenly! She came to the doorway to stare at Charles who had ceased speaking on the phone, which was their land-phone; he stood limply, arms at his sides, staring at the carpet at his feet. Camilla said, "Charles?"

"Yes? What?"

"Didn't whoever you spoke with have more to ask? Didn't he ask for our number?"

"No."

"That seems strange. You weren't on the phone very long."

Charles felt his face darken with blood. Was this woman eavesdropping on him? She'd left him to die, abandoned him to jeering black boys with a gun, now she was eavesdropping on his call to the police, staring at him so strangely?

"Long enough."

Camilla stared. A strand of hair had fallen onto her forehead, distractedly she brushed it away. "'Long enough'—what?"

"On the fucking phone. You call, if it's so important to you."

In fact, Charles had not called the police. Even as he'd punched out the numbers on his phone, he'd broken the connection with his thumb before the call went through. He hadn't spoken with any police officer, nor even with any operator. None of what had happened that afternoon seemed very important to him now. The boys (Hispanic? black?) were punks of no consequence to him, living here on Fairway Drive, Bloomfield Hills; his revenge was living here, and not there, with them; his revenge was being himself, capable of dismissing them from his thoughts. The gun had (probably) not been a real gun and whatever had happened on the Chrysler Freeway, after all nothing had happened.

"But I didn't get a good look at them, Charles. As you did."

There was nothing on the local Detroit news stations, of interest to them, at 6 P.M. But at 11 P.M. there came BULLETIN BREAKING NEWS of a shooting on I-94, near the intersection with Grand River Avenue: a trucker had been shot in the upper chest with what police believed to be a .45-caliber bullet, and was in critical condition at Detroit General. The shooting had occurred at approximately 9:20 P.M. and police had determined the shot had been fired by a sniper on an overpass, firing down into traffic.

Camilla cried, "It was him! That boy!"

Charles switched stations. Film footage of I-94 near Grand River Avenue was just concluding. "Why would it be I-94? An overpass? The boys on the bus were headed in the other direction. They'd have been off the bus, wherever they were going, hours before. And miles away. It's just a coincidence."

Camilla shuddered. "Coincidence! My God."

"You still do love me. Don't you?"

"Don't be ridiculous."

"*Don't* you?"

"Shouldn't I?" A pause. "I'm so tired . . ."

Knowing he wouldn't be able to sleep but he must sleep, he had an early meeting next morning: 8 A.M., breakfast. At his company's headquarters. Must sleep. They'd gone to bed, exhausted and creaky-jointed as an elderly couple, and Charles lay now stiff as a wooden effigy, on his back. He'd dismissed the incident (urine-colored school bus, smudged-skinned young punks, the ambiguous long-barreled weapon) from his mind, it was over. Beside him Camilla lay warm-skinned, ardent. Wanting to push into his arms, to make love with him, or wanting at least to give the impression of wanting to make love which, in a long-term marriage, counts for the same gesture, in theory. *See? I love you, you are rebuffing me.* Charles was polite but unreceptive. What pathos in lovemaking, in stark "physical" sex, when life itself is at stake! Civilization at stake! Charles's head was flooding with images like the screen of a demonic video game. (He had never played such a game. But he'd observed, in video arcades.) The ugly lumbering school bus he'd been trapped behind. The stink of the exhaust. How had it happened, had Camilla been speaking to him, he'd become distracted, hadn't seen the bus in time to switch to another lane, and if he'd done that, none of this would have happened. Seeing now the rear window of the bus: craning his neck upward, to see. What were those boys doing? The rear window was divided into sections and only the smaller panes at the sides could be cranked open. The pane at the left, directly in front of, and above, Charles, had been opened and it was through this window that the long-barreled revolver had been pointed. *No! Don't shoot! Not me!* Now Charles saw vividly, unmistakably, the faces of the boys: they were probably not more than twelve or thirteen years old, with dark, demonic eyes, jeering grins, oily-dark hair. As he stared up at them pleading with them the gun discharged, a froth-dream washed over his contorted face like an explosion of light. Was he already dead? His face was frozen. And there was Camilla screaming and pushing—at him—trying to get away from him, as he restrained her. *Brake the car! Get away!* He'd never heard his wife speak in so hoarse, so impatient a voice. For the baby was somewhere behind them, and nothing mattered except the baby.

Charles was alone now in the speeding car. A limping-speeding car as if one of the tires was going flat. Where was he? One of the freeways? Emerging out of Detroit, in a stream of traffic. And there was the school bus, ahead. He'd been abandoned by his family to die in their place. You are born, you reproduce, you die. The simplest equation. No choice except to drive blindly forward even as the gleeful boys, one of them pudgy-fat-faced, a faint mustache on his upper lip, knelt on the bus seat to aim a bullet into his head.

He heard the windshield shatter. He cringed, trying to shield his face and chest with his arms.

It is said that when you are shot you don't feel pain, you feel the powerful impact of the bullet or bullets like a horse's hooves striking you. You may begin to bleed in astonishment for you did not know you'd been hit. Certainly you know with a part of your brain but not the conscious part of your brain for that part of your brain is working to deny its knowledge. The work of mankind is to deny such knowledge. The labor of civilization, tribal life. Truth is dissolved in human wishes. The wish is an acid powerful enough to dissolve all knowledge. He, Charles, would die; must die at the hands of a grinning imbecile in a black T-shirt. Yet he seemed to know, and this was the point of the dream, that he could not allow himself such knowledge for he could not bear his life under such circumstances. In middle age he had become the father of a baby girl. He had neither wanted nor not-wanted a baby but when the baby was born he'd realized that his life had been a preparation for this. He loved his baby girl whose name in the dream he could not remember far more than he loved his own ridiculous life and he would not have caused such a beautiful child to be brought into a world so polluted, so ugly a world. As the bullets shattered the windshield of the car a sliver of glass flew at the baby's face, piercing an eye for she'd been left helpless, strapped in the child safety seat.

Charles screamed, thrashing in panic.

"Charles? Wake up."

He'd soaked through his boxer shorts, that he wore in place of pajamas. The thin white T-shirt stuck to his ribs and his armpits stank, appallingly.

"You've been dreaming. Poor darling."

Camilla understood: her husband had ceased to love her. He would not forget her behavior in the car, her "abandonment" of him. He was jealous of her acrobatic prowess, was he?—as he was jealous of her way with Susanna who would rather be bathed by and cuddle with Mommy than with Daddy.

It wasn't the first time in nine years of marriage that Charles had ceased to love Camilla, she knew. For he was a ridiculous man. Immature, wayward in emotion, uncertain of himself, anxious-competitive in his profession, frightened. He was vain. He was childish. Though highly intelligent, sharp-witted. At times, handsome. And tender. He had a habit of frowning, grimacing, pulling at his lips, that Camilla found exasperating, yet, even so, he was an attractive man. He was shrewd, though he lacked an instinctive sense of others. And yet Camilla herself was shrewd, she'd loved one or two other men before Charles and understood that she must comfort him now, for he needed her badly. She must kiss his mouth, gently. Not aggressively but gently. She must hold him, his sweaty, frankly smelly body, a tremulous male body, she must laugh softly and kiss him as if unaware that he was trembling. At first Charles was resistant, for a man must be resistant, at such times. For his pride had been wounded. His male pride, lacerated. And publicly. He'd been having a nightmare just now yet how like Charles not to want to have been wakened from it, by Camilla.

Panic can only be borne by a man, if there is no witness.

Charles's skin had turned clammy. Camilla could feel his heart beating erratically. He was still shivering, his feet and hands were icy. He'd had a true panic attack, Camilla thought. She was holding him, beginning to be frightened herself. But she must not let on of course. "Darling, I'm here. I've got you. You'll be fine."

Eventually, well before dawn when the baby in the adjoining room first began to fret and flail in her crib, this was so.

Special

oor child! But lucky to be alive, and not blind.

P One December evening in 1971, when Aimee Zacharis
was nine years old, she was the cause of a terrible accident in
the kitchen of her parents' home in Sparta, New York, and though
neither of her parents accused her, or indicated that she deserved
what had happened to her, staring at her reflection in a bathroom
mirror when she'd been brought home from the hospital, seeing
the ugliness there so bright-lit and exposed, Aimee knew that this
was so.

She looked like a plucked chicken! A scalded plucked chicken.
If the sight hadn't been so pathetic, and if the plucked chicken
wasn't her, she'd have laughed.

Quick little yelps of laughter. Like her sister Sallie Grace who
laughed when she was surprised, or anxious. Or angry.

Boiling water, in a large pot on the stove, salted boiling water in
which Aimee's mother was cooking spaghetti, had been overturned
onto Aimee when she'd stumbled into the stove. The boiling water
had scalded her right arm, her right shoulder, her neck, the lower
part of her right cheek and a considerable portion of her scalp. Like
frenzied worms the spaghetti had slithered over her. She'd thought
she was on fire! She fell to the floor, scalding water continued to

spill out of the half-gallon aluminum pot. The accident had happened so quickly, it had seemed to be happening to someone else: her older sister Sallie Grace was making her agitated cry *Nyah! nyah! nyah!* and her mother was screaming *No! no! Aimee no!* and there was another high-pitched cry like a wounded cat that must have been Aimee herself, before she lost consciousness in the puddle of hot water and spaghetti on the floor beside the stove.

Aimee's mother had called 911. Aimee had been carried off to the emergency room at Sparta Memorial Hospital. Aimee had not awakened until the next day and for a long time afterward floated in something billowy and white where you could shut your eyes and sleep immediately and such a delicious sleep it was, you wanted it never to end. On the insides of Aimee's eyelids were such fascinating faces, animals, cloud-shapes, vivid zigzag colors like rainbow-lightning, she wanted it never to end. At her bedside there came Momma to cry over her, and pray; there came Dadda to smile a wide glistening smile and to promise she'd be a "pretty little girl again, soon." And there came Sallie Grace to stare with shiny black beautiful eyes, jamming her fingers into her mouth.

Nyah. Nyah!

Dadda had taken Sallie Grace quickly away. Momma kissed her own fingertips and pressed them lightly against Aimee's nose that had been spared the terrible boiling water.

Now, Aimee's head looked so small. She had not remembered her head so small. Her eyes were small and damp and blinking and shone with an unhealthy lustre like a doll's eyes. In the hospital Aimee had had "skin-graft surgery" on her arm and shoulder but none on her face and head where the burns had been less severe. Somehow, her hands had been spared. All ten of Aimee's fingers! Most of her face had been spared which was very lucky, and her eyes had been spared which was even luckier, as people were saying. These were adults, many of them relatives. And nurses at the hospital. *Poor child but lucky to be alive, and not blind. So lucky!*

In the hospital Aimee hadn't been allowed to look at herself and had not wished to look at herself in the way that, in a delicious

dream, you don't think of who you are, for who you are isn't important in the dream, only the dream is important. So, coming home
was a surprise, like the cold stinging air outdoors. Like the smell of
snow, that made her nostrils pinch. Coming home meant having so
many opportunities to see herself in mirrors, there was an upstairs
bathroom and there was a downstairs bathroom, and there was a
mirror on the back of the door in her parents' room, and there was
a small mirror on the maple wood bureau in her room, that made
her face look scrunched together like a crumpled rag. The starkest
sight was in the downstairs bathroom mirror, that drew Aimee
like an evil thought, like Satan in the Bible, that Momma read
aloud in a thrilled quavering voice, though Momma and Dadda
would scold if they caught her staring at herself, touching herself, feeling sorry for herself which they said was unhealthy, and
morbid.

"Morbid" was Dadda's word. Often, Dadda used such words,
you had to figure out their meaning by the expression in Dadda's
face. Disdainful, disapproving. Dadda was such a good-looking
man with black wavy hair, black-gleaming eyes, a black mustache
always kept neatly trimmed, you wanted to make Dadda smile and
not frown. Dadda was a "certified public accountant" which meant
that Dadda was very smart and Momma's relatives were shy in his
presence.

Aimee stared in fascination at her small plucked-chicken head
and wizened face. This face wasn't the face of a nine-year-old girl!
Aimee's scalp showed through her hair that lifted in sad, silly curls
like damp string. There were not nearly enough of these sparrow-
colored hairs to cover the scalp that was scarred and bumpy. The
lower right side of Aimee's face and part of her throat looked like
mismatched pieces of skin that had been stitched together, worm-
like welts in the flesh she couldn't keep from touching. There was
Dadda's vague promise that someday there might be "cosmetic surgery" on Aimee's face and throat but this could not be for a while
for Aimee was still growing. Her bones were still growing, her
head. That silly head! She would wear a knitted cap in school until

her hair grew back. The cap made her head look even smaller. Aimee bit her fingers laughing at the sight of the sad-freaky little girl in the mirror so alone and so exposed. Aimee saw the little girl as the older, loud boys on the school bus would see her. They would be merciless when she returned to school in January for already they teased Aimee and her tall clumsy older sister Sallie Grace who was eleven and in special education at Sparta Junior High.

Special was always said of Sallie Grace Zacharis. *Special* had never been said of Aimee Zacharis.

Except now. She'd gone and made a freak of herself. *Brought it on herself. Provoked her sister. She's been told, and told.* Aimee wasn't sure if she'd overheard her mother say this or not. Maybe her mother had been speaking on the phone or maybe to her father in their bedroom with the beautiful pink satin drapes and matching bedspread which neither Aimee nor Sallie Grace was allowed to enter except when invited. The painkiller pills Aimee was still taking twice a day made her confused and groggy and sometimes she heard her mother scolding her but there was no one there. *Aimee! Bad girl brought it on yourself look what you've done.* Even before the boiling water and the hospital it was said of Aimee Zacharis by her fourth grade teacher Mrs. Halleron that she had quite an imagination.

Mrs. Halleron had meant her remark as praise. Aimee's parents weren't so sure.

Feeling sorry for yourself is a sin, Momma said. Touching your scars as if they are something precious is disgusting. If Aimee lingered too long in the bathroom staring at herself in the stark overhead light there would come a sharp rap on the door and her mother's stern voice: "Aimee. What are you doing in there." This wasn't an actual question but a command that meant Aimee must unlock the door and come out immediately.

Sometimes when Aimee emerged from the bathroom blinking and wiping at her eyes if she smiled up at Momma, Momma would relent and hug her, and brush her lips against Aimee's left cheek, which had not been scarred. But sometimes Momma pushed her away with a little sob: "Oh, that face of yours! I can't stand it. Go *away.*"

In the Zacharis household there were two daughters: Sallie Grace and Aimee.

Sallie Grace was the elder by two years and much taller than Aimee and going through any doorway, or on the stairs, Sallie Grace went first.

Sallie Grace had been born first and had sucked up all the oxygen in the household as she had sucked up all Dadda's and Momma's love in her greedy way of devouring food, lowering her head over her plate (so her hair sometimes fell into it, which Momma tried to prevent) and chewing noisily and rocking in her chair until all the glassware on the table vibrated and Dadda laughed and put a stop to it like a magician raising his hand: "Sallie Grace! Enough."

Only Dadda had that power. Only Dadda could wake Sallie Grace from one of her trances without throwing her into a rage and often, if Daddy said just the right thing, Sallie Grace would laugh.

"Da—*da.* Sil*ly.*"

Aimee's earliest memory was not of her parents but of Sallie Grace leaning over her crib staring and gaping at her. And Sallie Grace leaning over her crib to scream and laugh and jiggle the crib to wake her from a nap, and to scare her.

Aimee told Momma of this memory, and Momma said gently, "Nooou! You could not remember any such thing, Aimee. You were an *infant.*"

Though Sallie Grace could not have been much more than three years old at the time, Aimee remembered her sister as a giant.

Aimee thought *I do remember! I always will.*

Since her seventh birthday Aimee had begun to realize that she could think her own thoughts and neither Momma nor Dadda could "hear" them. And if she kept her face very still, neither Momma nor Dadda could "read" what was inside her head. This was an exciting discovery but scary, too.

"Your sister has a 'condition.' She is not retarded like those other poor children who are brain damaged and can never mature. In fact, Sallie Grace has a high I.Q., we've been told. Sallie Grace is being treated and Sallie Grace is 'making progress' and you will love Sallie Grace as we do." Momma paused, wiping at her eyes. Momma had fair, thin skin and limp brown hair nothing like Dadda's and her voice quavered when she was excited but you could not always tell if Momma was happy-excited or nervous-excited. "Sallie Grace is not a leper to be shunned."

Aimee nodded yes. Yes! Always, Aimee nodded *yes*.

Not needing to ask what "leper" meant, or "shunned." These were words like "morbid" you comprehended by the expression in an adult's face.

It was like wishing to please God. After God had caused the boiling water to pour over Aimee, and then God changed his mind and caused Aimee's eyesight to be "spared."

And Momma and Dadda wept: "Thank God!"

Sallie Grace did not weep though sometimes Sallie Grace's eyes shone like reflectors. Shiny dark-glass reflectors. Sallie Grace was eleven years old and five-feet-six and lanky-thin, "high-strung," "sensitive." The Zacharises had taken Sallie Grace to so many doctors, psychologists, therapists, family counsellors, they joked that their daughter was "beyond diagnosis." Aimee knew only that, when Momma took Sallie Grace and Aimee out, it was Sallie Grace who drew all eyes.

"Oh! What a beautiful girl."

Not seeing how Sallie Grace's beautiful eyes swerved to avoid theirs, or how her beautiful mouth sucked at itself. Not seeing the gnawed-at fingernails, and fingers. Sallie Grace looked nothing like Momma but only like Dadda with glossy wavy-black hair and a long straight nose and smooth olive-dark skin that looked as if it would be hot to the touch. (Except for Dadda, and sometimes Momma, no one dared touch Sallie Grace.) The Zacharis relatives saw that Sallie Grace was one of them and among them, and Dadda, who was called Ezra by them, there was a nervous smiling banter having to do with Sallie Grace (but never with Aimee) and how Sallie Grace was "doing" and Dadda would frown and say fine, fine! and Dadda would run his fingers over his neatly trimmed mustache, and Dadda would smile and say, "Well, that one, Sallie Grace, keeps us on our toes!"

Aimee felt a stab of jealousy staring at Dadda's feet. Dadda's shiny black shoes. She had never once seen Dadda on his toes. But there came Momma in high-heeled shoes and red lipstick on her mouth and it was easier to see Momma teetering on her toes, hoping to please Dadda's family.

Sallie Grace was enrolled in the special education class at Sparta Middle School where she'd learned to read though it was said that words were "scrambled" in her head. Unlike Aimee who read quickly, and silently, Sallie Grace had to shape each word with her lips as if tasting it and the effort was tiring and frustrating. Sallie Grace could do arithmetic "in her head" but had difficulty writing numerals down which was the opposite of Aimee who could only do arithmetic with a pencil and paper. The most special thing about Sallie Grace, which all the relatives admired, and Aimee envied terribly, was Sallie Grace's ability to play piano "by ear" after hearing Dadda play. Sallie Grace could imitate Dadda exactly, it was like magic! Side by side Dadda and Sallie Grace sat on the piano bench playing four hands together, sometimes laughing, singing. For Sallie Grace was very happy at such times. Sallie Grace was a lovable girl at such times. Aimee saw how at the piano her father and her sister were nearly the same height except Dadda was much broader-backed and Sallie Grace was thin with eager hunched shoulders and jutting elbows.

"Da-*da*. Love *you*."

But Sallie Grace could not learn to read music and so could not take piano lessons, as Dadda wished. Which was very frustrating to Sallie Grace and threw her into a frenzy of keyboard banging and gnawing at her scabby fingers, to punish them.

In the months before the boiling water and the upset that followed, it had been said that Sallie Grace was "making progress" at school as at home. Her new medication allowed her to sit in her desk at school for as long as fifteen minutes at a time without growing restless or anxious and allowed her for the first time to "interact" with other children without fear, aggression, or hostility. This fall there was a new special education teacher named Dana Stoat who excited the Zacharises by telling them that she saw "true potential" in their beautiful daughter who was one of her "star performers" and she believed that, locked inside Sallie Grace's mysterious brain, was a "high I.Q., possibly genius."

Genius! Aimee wanted to shrink away and hide. Nobody would ever say "genius" of Aimee Zacharis, she knew.

Except that, even with her medication, Sallie Grace was still susceptible to what Dadda called "spells." A kind of fury came over her if she fumbled doing something she badly wanted to do, or if someone (usually Momma, who was always home) told her *Sallie Grace: no* when she wasn't in a mood to be disciplined. Noises out-side (low-flying airplanes, sanitation trucks thundering past in the street, chain saws, barking dogs) could set her off moaning, whim-pering, rocking from side to side in agony, also "nasty" sights on TV (which Sallie Grace was not permitted to watch unsupervised, but did). Until recently, Aimee had been too small and inconse-quential to attract Sallie Grace's attention much, but lately she'd begun to notice her, and seemed resentful. "Don't provoke your sister," Momma was continually warning Aimee, "you know bet-ter." You could not hurry into any room ahead of Sallie Grace and you could not speak if Sallie Grace was speaking in her rapid breathless way that went on, and on, and on like a radio turned too loud, especially you dared not pass too closely behind Sallie Grace or stand behind her which made Sallie Grace very agitated. On the evening of the accident in the kitchen, something like this must have happened. Aimee did not remember provoking Sallie Grace but Momma insisted she had, so it must have been so. For Momma remembered so much more than Aimee could remember, and Momma was adamant. Sallie Grace had been in the kitchen help-ing Momma prepare supper and Aimee had wanted to help, too.

Momma had been at the sink, the big pan of boiling water was on the stove. Sallie Grace was in her trance of "setting the table nice" which she did for each meal in the same way, neat and exacting, to win Dadda's praise: blue plastic place mats wiped clean and positioned at each chair, blue paper napkins folded in half to the left, forks placed on the napkins and knives and spoons to the right, a space between for the plate which Momma would set down, and salt-and-pepper shakers (cut-glass, always filled to the top) in the center of the table. And there came Aimee into the kitchen, though Aimee did not brush against Sallie Grace, and Sallie Grace dropped a fork which was very upsetting to Sallie Grace for anything done "wrong" by her was a source of extreme anxiety, and suddenly Sallie Grace was whimpering, and Sallie Grace was muttering *Nyah! nyah! nyah!* and pushing Aimee at the stove, and the force of the collision caused the boiling spaghetti to overturn on her, as Momma cried what sounded like *No no! Aimee no!* in such anger, in even the confusion and terror of the moment, Aimee heard.

When Aimee returned from the hospital looking like a plucked scalded chicken, Sallie Grace could not keep from staring at her. Any kind of "ugly"—"nasty"—sight was alarming to Sallie Grace. If Aimee looked at Sallie Grace, even with a shy little smile, Sallie Grace became agitated and Momma had to hurry to calm her: "Sallie Grace, Aimee can't help it. Try not to look at her, if it bothers you."

Aimee overheard Momma saying, in a pleading voice, "Sallie Grace, you know who Aimee is, don't you? Your little sister?"

Momma was upset, her prayers to God had failed.

Momma began to insist that Aimee pray with her every day. Aimee usually liked prayer-time with Momma because it was just Momma and her (never Dadda, who didn't approve of "superstition"), a furtive half-hour while Sallie Grace, heavily medicated, had her afternoon nap, but Aimee didn't like kneeling on the hardwood floor which Momma believed was necessary now, to impress God. Before, they had knelt on the carpet. In January, Momma made a new friend from church whose teenaged daughter was so severely retarded she'd had to be "put in a home" and this woman gave Momma colorful "holy cards" of Jesus, Jesus' mother Mary, and others from the Bible said to be "saints." Aimee who was forbidden to buy comic books was fascinated by the cards and studied them closely. At first she thought they must be photographs but Momma told her they were drawings. Aimee asked Momma why there was no picture of God?—and Momma said that God was a "spirit." One of the cards showed a burning bush which was God—was it? But how could you pray to fire?

Momma said, "God looks into our hearts. He hears all our thoughts. If we pray for Sallie Grace with every breath, God will take mercy on us. *He will.*"

Momma spoke so vehemently, Aimee worried that God would become angry with her. Since the boiling water, Aimee did not trust God.

"Can we pray for me, too, Momma? For my scars to heal and go away? Just one prayer, Momma?"

Aimee knew it was risky when Momma was in such a mood to ask for any favor. Dadda had vaguely promised that Aimee's scars would "heal and go away" if she had patience and Momma seemed to believe this, too. Now Momma looked at her, frowning. Momma swiped at Aimee's fingers that were feeling the nape of Aimee's neck. "Oh, *you.* Always *you.* It's Sallie Grace who needs our prayers, Aimee. Sallie Grace's soul is in danger."

Aimee knew what "soul" was: "spirit." Something inside a person you could not see except, if you saw it, by a miracle, it was likely to be fire like the "burning bush" that appeared to Moses and scared him into acknowledging God.

Momma shut her eyes when she prayed, whispering to herself. She had to whisper quickly to get all her prayers said, all her wishes made, before Sallie Grace woke from her nap cranky and hungry and crept to the refrigerator to devour butter with her fingers, or leftover pudding, or ice cream out of a carton before Momma could stop her. Aimee pretended to pray but really she was looking at the Bible cards where the surprise was Jesus: Jesus Healing the Leper, Jesus and the Barren Fig Tree, Jesus Curing the Blind Man, Jesus Raising Lazarus from the Dead, Jesus with His Disciples, Jesus in the Garden, Jesus Crucified, Jesus Resurrected. Jesus had dark curly hair and a beard, a handsome strong face like Dadda's face except younger, and a mouth that was kindly and unusually red for a man's mouth, like Dadda, too. Jesus wore robes of many colors mixed together such as a woman might wear as a costume. Staring at Jesus, Aimee felt something warm and comforting in the area of her heart and when she shut her eyes and there came Jesus close as in the bathroom mirror and Jesus was smiling at Aimee saying *You can pray for your burns to heal, Aimee. That is your right.* Aimee was so surprised, she opened her eyes and Jesus was gone.

Later, Aimee asked her mother if Jesus was a spirit, too?—and Momma said vaguely, "Well, Jesus was a man. And Jesus was the 'Son of God.' All the other things Jesus was, I can't say."

"'Jesus was a man'? Like Dadda?"

"Like Dadda, yes. But more than Dadda. I think!"

Momma laughed. Momma had a wild rising way of laughing now, as if they were characters in a TV comedy.

After this, Jesus began to appear to Aimee whenever she shut her eyes in a certain wishful way. Even at school, even on the school bus, even at mealtimes when Sallie Grace began to hum loudly as she chewed her food and jiggled to make the table vibrate. Just inside her eyelids Jesus waited with his warm smile and warm brown eyes. *Aimee, hello! I am your friend, you don't need them.* At prayer-time Aimee only just pretended to pray for Sallie Grace, really she prayed for herself as Jesus had urged; and Jesus' advice was excellent for by March her hair had grown back feathery-brown like a bird's crest and she didn't have to wear the silly caps Momma had knitted for her any longer; and the most visible burn-scars were fading. Sometimes the pain returned, sheets and ripples of flame that made her whimper aloud, but this too seemed to be fading and Aimee was very careful not to provoke it with hot water. On the school bus the older boys had lost interest in teasing her now that she'd learned to defy them by shutting her eyes and hearing Jesus console her *Why should you care what these jerks say! Don't even listen*.

The boys still teased Sallie Grace, but she'd learned to mimic their nastiest swear-words, that no other girl would utter, which she didn't hesitate to shout at them. Also, Sallie Grace was learning to punch, claw, and kick at her tormentors. Sallie Grace seemed to be growing taller every week.

"Please God help my daughter. Help Sallie Grace to be a good girl, a normal girl, a girl to make us happy and proud, and help me to be a good mother and a good wife please God Amen!"—this was Aimee's mother's constant prayer now that Sallie Grace wasn't making so much progress as before. The prayer was like an old soiled towel too often used. The prayer was very boring, Aimee thought. Clearly God had a mind of his own and wasn't being swayed. Aimee smiled to think that she could pray to Jesus who would hear her and console her *Why should you care if they don't love you, just do your homework*.

Aimee did her homework. Aimee did extra-credit assignments. Aimee brought home a report card at the end of the year that was a column of A's and one A+ in communication arts. Mrs. Halleron said, passing out the cards, "Aimee, your parents will be very proud of you. I know I would be, if you were my daughter." But when Aimee showed the card to her parents it was in the midst of one of Sallie Grace's "relapses" and they were both distracted. Aimee hated it, Sallie Grace was forever "relapsing"—"going through a phase"—"having a bad spell"—and lately she was reluctant to go to school, refused to brush her teeth, take a shower or a bath, allow Momma to wash and comb out her long straggly hair that wasn't so beautiful now but a nest of snarls like spiders. The house rang with her shrieks and sobs. And Dana Stoat wasn't calling Sallie Grace her star performer any longer. When Dadda finally glanced at Aimee's report card he muttered, "Oh, fine," turning away with a sour look as if he had more important things on his mind than a fourth grader's grades. And Momma laid the card down absent-mindedly so that Sallie Grace who was sharp-eyed for destruction snatched it up and crumpled it out of meanness, and Aimee tried to snatch it back, and Momma said wearily, "Girls, girls!"—as if Sallie Grace and Aimee were the same kind of girl. And that night Jesus consoled Aimee *They don't know you at all, they are ignorant people and Sallie Grace is a mental case like the boys on the bus say, let them have her to love. You have me.*

During the summer, Momma ceased praying.

"Nobody's listening. Why should I keep trying!"

Momma seemed angry with God. Dadda was often angry, too. In their bedroom late at night Dadda and Momma argued. Aimee pressed her hands over her ears not wishing to hear. Yet she could hear Dadda's raised voice like a drum repeating *You will   you will   you will* and Aimee knew that Dadda was saying *You will love Sallie Grace as I love her, you will never give up loving Sallie Grace.* And Aimee felt a choking sensation in her throat, waves and ripples of terrible heat passed over her.

In the fall, Aimee began fifth grade at Sparta Junior High. Sallie Grace was expelled for fighting. Earlier, Sallie Grace had been suspended for getting into a scuffle on the school bus where she'd fallen or been pushed and lost one of her front teeth and Dadda was furious threatening to sue the school district. But the second time it was said that Sallie Grace started the fight herself in special education class, she'd "erupted" and "assaulted" another girl and when Dana Stoat quickly intervened, Sallie Grace turned on her, breaking the teacher's glasses; and when the principal Mr. Murdock came to escort Sallie Grace out, Sallie Grace became uncontrollable and attacked *him.* And so Sallie Grace was forbidden to return to school and would be home through the day and Momma said, "I can't. I can't care for her alone, I am so tired." And Dadda arranged with his employer to begin work at 6 A.M. three days each week so that on these days he could come home in the early afternoon to help with Sallie Grace.

In October, Aimee's tenth birthday was a day when Dadda and Momma were taking Sallie Grace to a "specialist" in Buffalo seventy miles away and after school Aimee went to Grandma Zacharis's house in an older neighborhood in Sparta. The house smelled of spicy foods, furniture polish, and the clear plastic coverings that were tight over the living room sofa and chairs like skins. Aimee did not cry but did her homework and read one of her many library books, she was in the habit of taking everywhere with her. When Grandma Zacharis asked about Sallie Grace in her sly frowning way that meant she hoped to hear some secret not confided in her by Aimee's parents, Aimee remembered that Jesus often cautioned her *Never speak your own mind, Aimee! Only what others wish to hear.* And so she said, "Sallie Grace is being 'home tutored' now and is 'making progress' again, Dadda says to tell you."

On the school bus, Aimee sat with Tamara Herkimer now. Her new best friend. *Thank you Jesus!* Aimee prayed.

Except: in November, Aimee's fifth grade teacher discovered that Aimee was squinting at the blackboard and so Momma had to take Aimee to the eye doctor at the mall where it was revealed that Aimee was "near-sighted" and needed glasses. Aimee wanted to cry, she'd known for some time that something was wrong with her eyes she hoped was not from the boiling water, she dreaded being made to wear glasses and look more freaky than she already looked. But at the mall Momma was in such a surprise mood, taking Aimee by the hand, laughing with the young woman who spread sample glasses frames on the counter for Aimee to choose among, and afterward Momma took Aimee for frozen yogurt, and Aimee began to feel less awful. Momma laughed and Momma was smoking a cigarette and Momma leaned over to kiss Aimee's nose saying, "Just you and me, Button!" for Aimee's nose was said to be a button nose not a long straight nose like Sallie Grace's. Leaving the mall,

Momma ran into a woman friend who called her Lizzie and asked her how was her family; which was a question everyone asked of everyone else, not to be avoided; and Momma said smiling, "Good! But it's good to get out sometimes, too." This was a strange reply but the woman gave no sign of noticing. Momma added, "Her father is tutoring her this afternoon. Sallie Grace, I mean. 'Home tutoring.' Ezra is the math genius in the family, not me." Aimee was embarrassed by her mother's nervous laughter, as if everyone in the world had to care about Sallie Grace! She tugged at Momma's arm, to escape.

At the eyeglasses store Aimee had wanted to select clear pink frames because her best friend Tamara's sister in ninth grade had clear pink frames and Tamara's sister was very pretty, but instead she selected clear blue frames, as she knew Momma would wish. For blue was Sallie Grace's favorite color and reds or deep pinks sometimes made her agitated. "What a good choice, Button! What a smart girl." A few days later when the new glasses were ready, and Momma took Aimee back to the mall, it wasn't the same feeling, for Momma had been scolded by Dadda for staying away so long the other time, today they had to return "straight home." And Momma was in a nerved-up mood as she called it, for Sallie Grace had been more difficult than usual lately, even with her new medication that was so expensive. When Aimee put on her glasses to wear out of the store, she was so surprised!—for everywhere she looked, objects were so sharp-edged and colors were so bright and you could see people's eyes if they lighted onto you, all these things Aimee had come to assume were blurred and fuzzy as in a dream and you didn't have to care about them, much. And on the drive home, Aimee couldn't keep from glancing at Momma's face, oh what a surprise that Momma's face that seemed such a glamorous face with a large red mouth, pink blushes on her cheeks and a way of looking happy always when she was out of the house, but now Aimee saw a net of wrinkles in Momma's face, creases between her brown-penciled eyebrows, and in her fleshy cheeks. And there were lines in Momma's throat, as bad as the sliver-like burn scars in

Aimee's throat. And Momma was smoking, which Aimee hated, and Dadda would be disgusted with, if Dadda knew. And Aimee thought she didn't love Momma after all and quickly there came Jesus' voice though Aimee hadn't closed her eyes saying *Of course you love your mother, Aimee, she is your mother too.* By *too* Aimee knew that Jesus meant Momma was her mother as well as Sallie Grace's mother and immediately Aimee felt better.

But oh! it was shocking to see, with the new glasses tight against the bridge of her nose, how Dadda's face was jowly and flushed and his eyes angry-shiny and the creases in his forehead deeper than Momma's, for Dadda looked nothing like Jesus after all; and there came Sallie Grace to peer suspiciously at Aimee, sucking at her fingers that were already scabbed, rocking back and forth and beginning to whimper at the sight of something so new, so strange and unexpected on her sister's face; though Dadda carefully explained to Sallie Grace that these were "glasses" and she knew perfectly well what "glasses" were, of course. Sallie Grace was apt to obey Dadda though not very often Momma and so Sallie Grace made a hissing sound, "Yesssss Dad-da, yessss Dad-da," but still Sallie Grace regarded Aimee with suspicion as if she wasn't certain who Aimee was. Her mouth was smeared with chocolate from treats that Dadda had given her during their math lesson at the dining room table: for each right answer of Sallie Grace's, a chocolate kiss.

Aimee was staring at her sister who was thirteen now and taller than their mother, her face coarse and doughy, her body thickening since she didn't go to school any longer but ate much of the day for it was too difficult for Momma to control her. Sallie Grace's thighs were heavy in the soiled slacks she wore constantly and her breasts were loose and straining against her soiled flannel shirt; she'd begun banging her head against walls in spells of frustration and fury, so she had to wear a shiny blue crash helmet on her head, tight-buckled beneath her chin. Her skin wasn't smooth any longer but blotched with pimples which Sallie Grace could not keep from picking at, as Sallie Grace could not keep from picking her nose

even at mealtimes, scratching and digging with all her fingers in all
the crevices of her body with a shameless grunting pleasure though
Momma and Dadda were forever scolding *Sallie Grace: no* and *Sallie
Grace: for shame!* The Zacharis family did not like to see Sallie Grace
behaving like this and so visits to Grandma's house were less frequent. And nobody wished to come to this house.

Aimee stood staring at her sister as if she'd never seen her before and though her eyes behind the new glasses were opened wide
there came Jesus to warn her *Don't say a word, Aimee! Your sister is a
freak to be laughed at by all the world but you must not say a word.*

Except when Aimee turned to go upstairs, to begin her homework before supper, Sallie Grace tried to snatch her glasses off her
face whining "Nyah! nyah! nyah!" as if in pain; and Dadda said,
"Aimee, take the glasses off for now. Till Sallie Grace gets used to
them. You can wear them at school. You know your sister is upset
by sudden changes." Aimee said, exasperated, "How can she get
used to them, if I can't wear them?" and Dadda pulled hard at
Aimee's arm, saying, "Just do as I say, Miss Smarty Pants," and
Momma intervened, "She's on her way upstairs, Ezra. Let her go."
But Sallie Grace was clawing at Aimee in a sudden frenzy and so
Momma tried to push Sallie Grace away, and Sallie Grace reacted
to being touched by screaming, and fumbled for the six-inch scissors she'd been using at the dining room table cutting geometrical
shapes out of construction paper at Dadda's instruction, and Sallie
Grace threw the scissors at Momma and one of its sharp points
struck Momma's arm, drawing more screams, and blood. And
Aimee was frightened and began to cry and Dadda said, "You! See
what you've done barging in here with those damned glasses"—but
it wasn't Aimee to whom Dadda was speaking so angrily but
Momma; and Aimee crept away upstairs to hide in her room where
Jesus consoled her *Just do your homework, Aimee. Don't even listen to them.*

Aimee didn't listen! Aimee wasn't going to listen. Except how
could she keep from hearing her parents when they brought their
quarrel upstairs to their bedroom shutting the door yet still Aimee
could hear Momma's voice pleading and plaintive saying she was so

tired, she could not keep caring for Sallie Grace, they could not keep Sallie Grace at home any longer and would have to find a place for her, and Dadda's voice was stronger saying Sallie Grace is our daughter, don't you ever forget Sallie Grace is our daughter, we will never give up on Sallie Grace not ever.

After this, scissors and knives were hidden away where Sallie Grace would not take time to search for them: in the backs of kitchen drawers, behind pots and pans in the cupboards. For Sallie Grace had not the patience to look for anything not visible. And Sallie Grace seemed sorry that she had hurt Momma. And Sallie Grace was on a new diet that forbade chocolate, cola drinks, iodized salt, sweet things made with white sugar and flour, etc.; and Sallie Grace began to be taken, by Dadda, to a new specialist in Port Oriskany, forty miles away, each Wednesday afternoon when Momma could have some time to herself which Momma usually spent resting with a wetted cold cloth over her face and the window blinds drawn in the bedroom. When Aimee came home from school the house was so quiet! Aimee would have liked Momma to hurry downstairs and swoop Aimee up in her arms—"Just you and me, Button!"—but Momma took one of the green capsules prescribed for Sallie Grace's nerves, so Momma could rest, and Momma needed to rest, Aimee understood.

Sallie Grace seemed to have forgotten Aimee's glasses for Aimee only wore them in her room and when she left the house for school in the morning. Aimee liked her blue glasses: several girls at school said they were "pretty." And Tamara Herkimer liked them. One morning on the bus Tamara asked Aimee where was Sallie Grace? Didn't Sallie Grace go to school any longer? and Aimee heard herself say that Sallie Grace had been expelled for stabbing the special education teacher with a pair of scissors and almost putting out her eye. Tamara was very surprised, Tamara had not heard this. Aimee said, "If Sallie Grace was older, the police would arrest her. She would be taken away in a 'straitjacket' and be put in a—" Aimee could not think where exactly Sallie Grace would be put, some kind of home, or hospital? Later, Jesus reprimanded Aimee for the first time, Jesus seemed shocked and troubled saying *Now Aimee! You are too special a girl to say such things* and Aimee was ashamed and told Jesus she was sorry and would never do it again. But a few days later when Aimee was invited to sit at a cafeteria table with three girls from her class she very much admired and one of the girls asked what it was like living with someone like Sallie Grace, Aimee said with a crinkled nose, "It's like living with a dog except a dog could be trained and Sallie Grace can't be trained." The girls were quiet. Aimee had shocked them! Aimee said, "She isn't housebroken. She bangs her head against the wall. I wish she'd bang her brains out. She's a mental case. My mother hates her. I hate her. She's like somebody took an ax and split her head open and her brains spilled out and got put back together all wrong." Aimee was laughing, and the girls were laughing, but uneasily; and Aimee said, "I hate her and wish she would die. Or they would all die. Then I could go live with—" Aimee's thoughts hit a blank wall, and stopped. She could not think what she'd been saying except the burns on her face and scalp were throbbing with heat and she'd begun rocking back and forth in her chair making the table vibrate and she was clenching her jaws together tight to keep from screaming or laughing in the wild rising way her mother laughed.

So ashamed, afterward! Sick-feeling and dizzy and her eyes burning behind the blue plastic glasses that fitted her nose too tightly, leaving red marks in her skin.

Jesus stayed away, Jesus was so disgusted. Aimee shut her eyes waiting for Jesus to come to her, but he did not.

"Momma, 'bye."

But Momma was busy with Sallie Grace and hadn't time to kiss Aimee goodbye or even notice she was leaving for school. So there was Aimee in the kitchen opening the drawer beside the stove where Momma kept pot holders and towels, and at the back of this drawer was the pair of six-inch scissors Momma kept hidden; and Aimee saw herself remove the scissors from the drawer and place them on what was called Sallie Grace's counter, where Sallie Grace kept some of her special things like her cereal bowl, her plastic cup, plastic forks and spoons. And Aimee ran outside breathless to the school bus and all that day at school she was shivering and distracted by Jesus' shocked voice *Aimee what have you done! Aimee what have you done! Shame, Aimee! Shame!* and by the time she returned home at three o'clock that afternoon she was sure that something terrible had happened to Momma but when she entered the house there was Dadda with Sallie Grace at the dining room table so engrossed in their math lesson, neither glanced up at her. Aimee might have been invisible, a silly little gust of wind.

Momma didn't seem to be home. Or maybe Momma was upstairs, resting. The scissors were gone from the counter. Aimee didn't check to see if they'd been returned to the drawer. Blindly she hurried upstairs. Every burn-scar on her body throbbed with heat. Jesus had been disgusted with her all day. *Aren't you lucky, your mother is still alive.*

And then, another day weeks later, it happened.

Aimee was upstairs in her room doing homework when she began to be aware of noises from below, from the kitchen where Momma and Sallie Grace were preparing supper. Aimee tried not to listen, she did not want to hear! Her father wasn't home yet from work, only Momma was with Sallie Grace and something must have provoked Sallie Grace for she was moaning in pain and indignation and Momma began to speak her name urgently: "Sallie Grace, no! No, Sallie Grace!" How like a dream this was, a bad dream Aimee had already had and had wakened from but must now experience another time, for each day was the same day for Sallie Grace, each day like the others, there could never be any change. Aimee was crouched beside her bed pressing her hands over her ears. There came a sound of something overturned downstairs, a sound of breaking glass. Aimee thought *If Sallie Grace hurts Momma she will have to be put away. If she kills Momma she will be punished.* This was not a new thought, Aimee had had this thought many times before and now it swept upon her fierce as scalding water overturned on her head and shoulders. She was holding her breath, she would count to twenty! Like holding your breath underwater in the school pool, you think you can't do it but you can do it. Downstairs the noises ceased abruptly. Calmly Aimee thought *Momma has fallen, Momma is bleeding to death.* There came a high wailing sound that meant that Sallie Grace was rocking from side to side in a trance, her red-splotched face contorted like a Hallowe'en mask.

Panicked, Aimee ran downstairs crying, "Momma! Momma!"

In the kitchen, Momma was pulling herself up from the floor, clumsy and stunned. Bright blood glistened beneath her left eye, and on her throat, and on her fingers where she was fumbling for a towel to press against her face. Aimee was whimpering now in terror helping her mother to her feet. On the floor was a paring knife wet with blood. Against the farther wall Sallie Grace was rocking from side to side, moaning. Momma was trembling but managed to speak calmly, "We are going to get help for Sallie Grace, Aimee. Your sister will have to go away, to be helped." Momma leaned heavily on Aimee, reaching for the phone which was a plastic wall phone beside the refrigerator. With her bleeding fingers Momma dialed 911, to report her thirteen-year-old daughter stabbing her. Calm at first and then not so calm—"We need help here, we need help here at this house, 728 Spruce Drive, we need help—"

Aimee's father would never forgive her mother for that call. For going outside the family.

"Just you and me, Button."

That weekend Momma moved out. Momma brought Aimee with her. Moving away from Dadda and Sallie Grace and they would not be allowed back if they left Dadda warned in his cold furious voice *If you leave this house. If you leave your daughter.* Momma had rented a station wagon, filled now with suitcases, boxes, clothes on hangers. Aimee had seen the new house just once, from the road: a large weathered-gray clapboard house like a mansion with stone pillars and a wraparound veranda, set back from the highway in a lawn of roughly mown grass. At the highest peak of the shingle roof was a copper rooster weathervane and beside the mud-puddled gravel driveway was a sign: APT'S FOR RENT. Aimee knew that "apt" meant "apartment"—she had never been inside one and thought it must be strange and exciting to live in a house, beneath a roof, with other people, strangers. And these strangers would know nothing of Dadda and Sallie Grace.

Mist rose in columns out of irrigation ditches beside the road. The fields glittered with cobwebs of frost. Only a few yellow leaves remained, swaths of sumac-red like paint. In a field horses were grazing. A lone horse close to the road, sleekly red-brown, lifting its long narrow head as if in anticipation of the station wagon, and Aimee. She had never seen any sight so beautiful. And in the distance were the Chautauqua Mountains, you could not see from the Zacharises' old house on Spruce Drive.

Aimee had been awake since before dawn. Too excited to sleep. Her heart beat quick and hard. She'd helped her mother load the station wagon and Dadda had not helped them, Dadda had stayed away and kept Sallie Grace away moaning and whimpering in another part of the house.

Jesus had told Aimee *Well, Aimee! You will be famous now.* Aimee had no idea what this meant. Was Jesus being sarcastic, like Dadda? Jesus' eyes were not so warm any longer, his features seemed to be fading. Aimee had never told her mother about Jesus though she had wanted to, many times. When she'd asked Momma if they should pray for Dadda and Sallie Grace, Momma said with a sad little smile they will have to pray for themselves.

Aimee would have thought she'd miss Jesus more—He'd been her friend, when she hadn't had any friend—but so much was happening in her life now, even at school she moved in a daze and her lips shaped questions. *Did I do this? Cause this to happen?* Meaning when Momma had called the police. When Aimee had removed the scissors from the drawer to lay on Sallie Grace's counter. The burn-scars on her scalp, her neck, her arm pulsed with a pleasurable heat. Momma said, turning the station wagon into the rutted driveway, that led uphill to the big house, "I am so afraid, Aimee," gripping Aimee's hand with icy fingers and squeezing, hard, "I am so happy." Aimee wanted to say she was happy, too. Wanted to say *Momma, I love you. I never wanted you to die.* A wave of such feeling swept over her, she could not have said if it was happiness, or terror, or astonishment at her own power. For she was, on this morning in November 1973, a girl of only eleven, who'd accomplished so much. And all her life before her.

The Blind Man's Sighted Daughters

Has he ever talked about it with you?"

My sister lowered her voice as if fearful of being overheard for our father's hearing had sharpened in his blindness. My sister who was fifty-two years old inclined her head in the disingenuous way she'd cultivated as a girl. *Don't tell me. I need to ask but don't tell me.*

Adding, unnecessarily, "He never has, with me. At least I wasn't aware if he had."

He, him were the ways in which we spoke of our elderly father in our lowered voices. *He, him* seemed more appropriate than such intimate words as *Father, Dad.*

Really there was no danger of him hearing us: we were in the front room of the house and the old man was at the rear of the house lying in a lounge chair facing a window through which winter sunshine streamed. He could not see the window, he could not see how dazzling white snow heaped outside the window as in a scene of Arctic desolation but he could probably see something of the light and he could feel the warmth of the sun on his face.

Sunning himself like a giant lizard. Almost, you could envy him.

He was eighty-one, he'd become almost totally blind over a period of years. A gradual dimming, fading. His condition was called macular degeneration: a hole in the center of his vision. Initially a pinprick, then it enlarges. You manage to see around it, as long as you can. By this time in the sixth year of his affliction the black hole had seemingly swallowed most of our father's vision but he hadn't entirely given up the effort of trying to see.

It was exhausting! For him, and for me.

Knowing yourself reduced to a blurred shape at the edge of a man's vision. The sudden panic of one about to step off the edge of the earth.

I told my sister no. Dryly I told her I'd have been aware of it, if he had.

We knew what we meant by *it*. This was a code between us, to be murmured with a kind of thrilled shame.

Abigail was watching me closely. She'd been shaken by the deterioration of our father and it was possible, she blamed me. Her nostrils were pinched as if against a bad odor. Her forehead was pinched, her mouth. I wondered what she was seeing. Living with a blind man you gradually become invisible.

"What does he talk about with you, then?"

"Stay with us for a while, Abigail. Talk to him yourself. Then you'll know."

I spoke warmly. Hearing me you'd think *A good heart!* But Abigail knew this was a reproach. Something hot swept up into her face, she smiled quickly to acknowledge yes, all right, she deserved it. But she would bear it for my sake.

Don't hate me! I had to save my own life.

I said, "He doesn't talk. He thinks out loud. I guess you'd call it 'thinking'—a stream of words like TV, if you switched from channel to channel. Old quarrels. People who've been dead for fifty years. Men he'd had business dealings with, who'd 'cheated' him. Not us. He has no interest in us. Anything he did, caused to happen, in this house or out, no memory of it. Sometimes he speaks of 'your mother.' The worst days, he confuses me with her. He never

asks about you. He never asks about me. He calls 'Hel-len! *Hel-len!*'
so he knows who I am. Though I could be a nurse's aide, I suppose." I paused, so that Abigail could laugh. Politely and nervously
Abigail could laugh. I'd missed my calling as a TV comic: the kind
who's angry and deadpan and provokes laughter in others that's
the equivalent of turning a knife blade in their guts. "He asks me
to read the newspapers to him, the worst news first, atrocities, suicide bombers, plane crashes, famines, killings and dismemberings
in New Jersey, anything lurid to do with politicians or celebrities,
he wants to be consoled that the world is a ridiculous hellhole,
people are no damned good and the environment is poisoned to
hell, only a fool would want to live much longer. I have to describe
for him what's on the TV screen, he can work the remote control
for himself. He falls asleep and I switch off the damned set and the
sudden silence wakes him and at first he doesn't know where he is,
maybe he's dead? had another stroke? then he's furious with me
saying he hadn't been asleep. 'Trying to put something over on me,'
he says, 'sneaky bitch like your mother—'"

"Oh, Helen. Stop."

We were laughing together. Jamming our knuckles against our
mouths like guilty children for if our father heard us immediately
he would know we were laughing at him.

"Helen, you turn everything into a joke. I wish you wouldn't."

"Everything isn't a joke, Abigail? Come on."

"You've even begun to talk strangely. Your mouth—"

"My mow-th?"

I felt it twist. Like wringing a rag. Had I been doing this unconsciously? Did I do it bringing our father to the medical clinic,
speaking with doctors, staff? Buying groceries, buying gasoline, at
the drugstore getting prescriptions filled? Mirrors had become so
leprous-looking in this house, I hadn't been able to see my reflection for months.

"*He's* the one who had the stroke, Abigail. Not me. My mow-th
is as normal as yours."

Earlier in the day when Abigail had arrived for her visit, she had looked extremely normal: the kind of woman, middle-aged but youthful, I sometimes observed, disliking, envious, in public places. She'd embraced me, the younger sister, with a cry like a stricken bird, hugged me tight against her as if she'd meant it. Oh she'd missed me, Oh I'd lost so much weight, Oh oh oh! she was sorry for having been out of touch for so long. She'd been an attractive well-groomed woman stepping into this house at 2 P.M. and now at 6:30 P.M. she looked as if she'd been bargain-shopping at Wal-Mart on Discount Saturday. She looked as if she could use a good stiff drink but I never kept hard liquor in the house, not even beer or wine. The old man would find it and drink himself into a coma. Or maybe, I would.

Abigail wiped at her eyes with a tissue. I was touched to see that coming to visit Sparta, driving the width of New York State from Peekskill, New York, she'd taken time to apply eye makeup.

"I wish you'd warned me, Helen. You might have."

Warned her about what? The old man wasn't so bad—was he?

"And I'm worried about you, too."

"Me! I can worry about myself, thank you."

"No. Obviously not. You don't look well, you must have lost twenty pounds. The way the house looks, and smells . . ."

Abigail's nostrils pinched primly. I was hurt, and I was offended. "Smells! It does not."

Though it was true: I'd tried to give our father a sponge bath that morning in preparation for Abigail's visit but he'd refused to let me near him. Couldn't have said when exactly he'd been bathed by me, or shaved. Or when I'd showered, myself. Or changed my underwear which I wore to bed in cold weather, with wool socks, beneath an old flannel nightgown.

But I'd wetted my hair and combed it. Smeared plum-colored lipstick on my mouth. In a shadowy mirror there was no face behind the mouth but the mouth was smiling.

". . . should be moved to an assisted care facility, Helen. That's why I've come, have you forgotten? Oh, please listen!"

I was listening. I saw my sister's mouth move and I was listening but somehow I seemed to have lost the knack of comprehending words in a coherent sequence as you lose the knack of comprehending a foreign language you have not heard or spoken in some time.

When Abigail called me and static interfered, I hadn't any choice but to quietly hang up. But when someone is speaking to you from a few feet away, you have not that option.

The power I'd been exerting over my sister just a few minutes ago to make her laugh against her will had faded rapidly. I didn't know how I'd lost it, I resented this too.

". . . six-month leave, you said? Unpaid? Aren't the six months up by now, Helen? Have you made new arrangements?"

I thought that I had, yes. I told my sister this.

I'd taken the leave because caring for our father had begun to require more and more time. There was the vague idea too, at least initially, that I would be preparing for the next phase of the old man's life which would be an assisted care facility. I had put off speaking to him about the prospect. Until Abigail mentioned it, I may have forgotten.

Scattered through the house were glossy brochures from such places. Deer Meadow Manor, Rosewood Manor, Cedar Brook Hall. Abigail had pushed some aside, sitting on the sofa.

She was saying in a brisk voice, having recovered some of her poise, that she would take time off, too. (My sister was a well-paid administrator at a science research institute in Peekskill.) She would help in the "move" of course. And after our father was "settled in" the new residence we would have the entire house cleaned, and painted, repairs made to the roof, then we'd put the house "on the market" . . . "Helen? Are you listening?"

Half-consciously I'd been listening for his uplifted voice at the rear of the house. It did seem time about now for him to call *Helen?* Sometimes the voice was raw and aggrieved, sometimes the voice was uncertain, wavering. Sometimes the voice was angry. And sometimes pleading like the voice of a lost child. *Hel-len!*

I lowered my own voice that had gone slightly hoarse from not being used much. I said, "Each day I think of it. Already when I wake in the morning the thought is with me."

"What thought?"

"'This day might be it. His last.'"

Abigail stared at me. For a long moment she seemed unable to speak. "And how—how—how do you feel, Helen? Thinking such a thought?"

"Anxious. Excited. Hopeful."

"'Hopeful.'"

Abigail didn't seem to be challenging me nor even questioning me only just trying out the word.

At the rear of the house the voice lifted querulously: "Hel-len?"

November 1967. In the night the temperature dropped below zero, the bodies had frozen together. Not in each other's arms but crushed together bloodied and broken in shattered glass in the front seat of the wrecked vehicle that seemed to have skidded off the road to plunge down an embankment above the Chautauqua River north of Sparta. The vehicle was a new-model Dodge sedan that had capsized in underbrush on the riverbank, thirty feet below the roadway. If the car hadn't capsized it would have rolled forward and broken through the ice to be submerged in fifteen feet of water, by morning a crust of ice might have formed above it. If snow had continued to fall heavily through the night the car's tracks might have been hidden from view, covered in snow.

The Dodge sedan was registered to the dead man behind the wheel whose name was Henry Claver. The dead woman was not Henry Claver's wife but another man's wife, a woman known to our father Lyle Sebera. She'd been his receptionist at Sebera Construction for several years and it would be said that she and our father had been "involved" for most of this time. Since her separation from her husband, the woman and her five-year-old son had been living in a brick row house in downtown Sparta that was one of several properties owned by Lyle Sebera and it would be said that on those occasions when her estranged husband came to take the boy away for the weekend, to Buffalo where he was now living, Lyle Sebera was a "frequent" visitor in that house.

The woman's name was Lenora McDermid. This was not a name that would be uttered in our house, ever.

That night he'd come home late. By eight o'clock our mother had several times called his office for it was her belief that he was working late. Though possibly he'd been traveling that day, and had neglected to tell her. Our mother was not a woman to ask very many questions of her husband who was not a man of whom a wife might comfortably ask questions.

By eight o'clock my sister and I had eaten dinner and cleaned away our places at the table. Our mother did not eat with us and afterward remained in the kitchen alone. She would call our father's number at Sebera Construction for this was the only number she had for our father. This was an era before voice mail when you called a number and when it rang unanswered you had no choice but to hang up and call again and later you might call again listening helplessly to a phone ringing unanswered.

Where is Daddy? was not a question my sister and I were in the habit of asking.

That night he was working late, very likely. He'd gone to check a building site. There were often business trips: Yewville, Port Oriskany, Buffalo. Lyle Sebera thought nothing of driving ninety miles round-trip in a single day. Possibly there were financial problems at this time in our father's business but we were not meant to know of such problems as we were not meant to know of any aspect of our father's life guarded by him as zealously as the large cluttered lot behind Sebera Construction was guarded by a fierce German shepherd inside a ten-foot chain-link fence. Some of the problems of which we weren't to know had to do with bank loans, mortgages on investment properties owned by Lyle Sebera in partnership with another Sparta resident whose name was not Claver but the man named Claver was a former business associate of Lyle Sebera's partner whose name was Litz.

McDermid, Claver, Litz. Names not to be uttered in our house.

Yet we knew of these names, that were not spoken in our house or in our earshot. Though no newspapers containing these names were allowed in the house and we were not allowed to watch TV news.

Abigail was thirteen and I was ten. We were in eighth grade and in fifth grade. Quiet girls, obedient, believed to be well-mannered because we were shy. We'd been trained not to test our mother's patience and we had hardly needed to be trained not to displease our father. Yet we scavenged neighbors' trash cans in the alley that ran behind our houses searching for forbidden knowledge. Eager, in fear of being seen, we pawed at newspaper pages smelling of garbage, damp pulp paper that left newsprint on our fingers. "Oh! Look," Abigail whispered pointing at a photograph on the front page of the *Sparta Journal*, of a dark-haired, squinting man with a familiar face.

LOCAL CONTRACTOR SEBERA, 44, QUESTIONED IN DOUBLE HOMICIDE

We were squatting beside trash cans in the alley. Dogs had de-filed the snow here. There was a rancid smell of garbage, we swallowed hard to keep from gagging. "'Double homicide.'" Our lips moved numbly. In the cold still air our breaths steamed.

"'Bludgeoned.'"

Bludgeoned! I seemed to know what this word meant. This was a word that carried its meaning in its sound.

On the same page were photographs of the dead woman Lenora McDermid and the dead man Henry Claver. The woman was smiling which seemed wrong because she was dead. She was younger than our mother and much prettier than our mother but her lipstick was so dark her mouth looked like a black wound. The man was our father's age and frowning the way our father frowned if he'd heard something he had not liked. *McDermid, Claver* had not died in the car wreck but had been "bludgeoned to death" with a weapon like a tire iron and Claver's car had been pushed over the edge of the embankment to make it seem like an accident.

I was staring at the blurry photograph Abigail had pointed out.

"Is that Daddy? No."

"Silly! Of course it's Daddy."

In those years we called our father "Daddy." We called our mother "Mommy." We must have been instructed in this, we could not have thought of such names by ourselves.

The picture was of a man like Daddy but I did not think it was Daddy. He had heavy eyebrows and a heavy jaw and he was squinting at the camera. His hair was thick and dark lifting from his forehead like a rooster's comb but Daddy's hair was not like that now.

"It isn't. Not Daddy."

"Stupid, it says 'Sebera' right there. *It is.*"

Abigail slapped the wet newspaper in my hands and ripped it. She nudged me with her fist to topple me over into the yellow-stained snow. Still I cried, "It is not *it is not him.*"

Other men were questioned in the double homicide. Other men had been involved with both the dead man and the dead woman and one of these was the dead woman's estranged husband Gerald McDermid whose photograph would also appear in the newspapers we were forbidden to see. Later, Gerald McDermid would be arrested by Sparta police and charged with the double homicide but by spring of 1968 these charges were dropped for insufficient evidence. McDermid's relatives insisted that he'd been with them in Buffalo, he'd brought the child with him for the weekend. No one else was ever arrested. Gradually the names *McDermid, Claver* disappeared from the newspapers and the name *Sebera* would never appear again, ever.

This was a fact: Lyle Sebera had been questioned by police and released. He had never been arrested like Gerald McDermid. Our mother's relatives meant to comfort her as they meant to comfort themselves pointing out this fact in murmured conversations just beyond earshot of my sister Abigail and me. *Yes but. Lyle was never. The other one, the husband. He was the one!*

Our mother had been questioned by police also, more than once. We had no idea what she told them. My sister Abigail and I were not questioned, we were too young.

When had we heard Daddy come home that night?—maybe we had not heard him at all. Maybe it was windy, snowy. Maybe we'd fallen asleep. Maybe it was some other night we remembered. Or maybe that was a night he'd come home for supper by six-thirty which was when my mother had expected him. Memories are confusing, when one memory is stronger than other memories it is the strong memory that prevails.

Daddy! Dad-dy. For there was this to remember, that Daddy could be impatient and angry but Daddy could make your heart lift, also. Daddy brought us presents, Daddy called me Funny Face. Daddy was gone, and Daddy came back, and Daddy whistled for us saying, Hey you two you're my girls, you know that, eh? in his two arms lifting us both so we squealed. Who's Daddy's special girl, Daddy would ask, who loves Daddy best, and Abigail would say, Me! and Helen would say, Me! Me, Daddy! until at last Abigail was too old and held back stiff and embarrassed but Helen was still a little girl, eager to hug and kiss Daddy for there was no one like Daddy, ever. The stubble-jaws he called The Grizzly, here's The Grizzly come for a kiss, and Daddy's sweet-strong breath, you shut your eyes feeling dizzy. So maybe it had been one of those nights and Daddy had come home in time for supper and was home all that night as Mommy said. For there were many nights. You could not possibly keep them straight. Our mother spoke sharply to us for it was a school night, we were not to watch TV but do our homework and at 9:30 P.M. go upstairs to bed. And she would check us there, to see. In our beds in the darkened room beneath the eaves except there came headlights against the blind drawn over the window and faint ghost-shapes moving across the ceiling in a way to be confused with crawling things in dreams and these dreams to be confused with wakefulness. *Are you asleep?* one of us would ask and the other would giggle *Yes!* Except not that night for we were frightened. Lying very still on our backs beneath the covers, arms against our sides and elbows pressed against our ribs to give the comfort of being held. Drifting into sleep that night and waking suddenly to see the ghost-lights and later to hear a car turning into the driveway and there was the sound of a door at the rear of the house being opened and then shut and if our mother had been waiting up for him there may have been an exchange of voices, muffled words we could not hear. And so *When had we heard Daddy come home that night* was not a question that could be answered even if it had been asked.

Has he ever talked about it with you my sister has asked. As if she has the right.

Back in December I had to take him for more urinary-tract and prostate tests, that had frightened him. By this time he had his way of turning his head to the side, the way you'd imagine a sharp-beaked predator bird turning its head, to fix prey in its sight. He sighted me in what remained of his peripheral vision so that I began to feel panicky, my breath began to quicken as if I were standing at the edge of a steep cliff. It was a dark time of year, winters are long and depressing in this part of the country and I'd taken six months off from work at the local community college where now I had to worry they'd give my job to someone else and wouldn't hire me back, and suddenly our father was asking if I remembered something that had happened when I was a little girl, a car found wrecked out in the country, a man and a woman were found dead in the car, and his voice was hoarse and faltering and I stood very still thinking *Maybe he can't see me, he won't know that I am here*.

I went away. I left him there. He was groping to find the edge of his bed. I was very upset, I had work to do. Vacuuming, housework. I hadn't time for this.

Next day he asked if I would take him to church. To church!

Long ago our parents had been married in St. John's Roman Catholic Church in Sparta. So we'd been told. From time to time our mother had gone to mass there but our father, never. Neither

Abigail nor I was baptized in any church. Our mother had never taken us with her to mass. She'd wanted to be alone, maybe. She'd become a nervous woman who wanted to be alone much of the time. Or maybe she hadn't believed that our souls were very important because we were children and we didn't require the solace of religion as we didn't, like our mother, require the solace of solitary drinking and painkiller pills. *But Mommy is there God?* once I asked my mother and she turned away as if she hadn't heard.

Now this elderly blind broke-back man who'd been Daddy long ago and was not recognizable as Lyle Sebera was saying, "I want—I want to go to confession."

I was stunned by this. Couldn't believe I'd heard right.

Fumbling I said I didn't think the Church had confession any longer.

"No confession? Eh? Since when?"

He couldn't see me—could he? Not when I stood right in front of him. He was quivering with strain, half-standing, the tendons in his elderly neck were taut as ropes. I feared those eyes that were glassy-hard and discolored like stained piano keys and the pupils the size of caraway seeds.

I tried to smile. I tried to speak reasonably. Observing this scene from the doorway you'd think *What a good heart, that woman!* "There have been 'reforms' in the Church. You know, there's a new Church now. The Latin mass has been gone for, what?—forty years. If you want to confess sins you say them to yourself, you don't involve others in your messes."

Was this so? I had no idea. Maybe it was so. Maybe I'd read it somewhere. I'd never been religious, it was like being color blind. *Messes* was to suggest childish behavior, not serious transgressions. *Messes* was to keep distance between him and me.

He was whining, "You can take me to church can't you? That church where your mother used to go? I want to talk to a priest. There must be a priest." He was breathing audibly, sweating. His face was drawn and anxious yet I knew that he was capable of suddenly slapping at me, clawing and kicking at me, even spitting at me if I dared to defy him. "I can't—can't—you know I can't—die without talking to a—priest."

"'Die.' You aren't going to die."

"I am! I'm going to—die! I want to die! God damn I want to talk to a—priest—a priest—I want to talk to a—and then I want to die."

I began to tremble. I was frightened but I was angry, too. How like Lyle Sebera to imagine that somewhere close by there was "a priest" to serve him. As, always close by, there was a daughter to serve him. And somewhere at hand there was God to forgive him.

"There aren't many priests today, either. Didn't I just read you that article in the paper, there's a shortage of priests. Remember you laughed, you said, 'Serves them right, assholes think they have all the answers.'"

My father seemed not to hear this mimicry of his voice. I'd thought it was damned funny, myself.

"I want to talk to —"

"—to God? You want to talk to God? That's what you're saying, isn't it, you want to talk to God, ask God to 'forgive' you. But there isn't any 'God,' either. It's too late." I was laughing, a sensation like flames without heat, flames of pure dazzling light passed through me. I was on my way out of the invalid's room leaving the old man gaping after me.

Invalids say things they don't mean. Invalids say things to test their caretakers who are likely to be the only individuals who love them and can endure them.

But often then he began to speak of dying. What I needed to do for him was get the right pills the kind that put you to sleep forever: "'Barbitch-ates.'" Or his own pills, damn-fucking pills, so many he had to take every day, at mealtimes, it was my task to sort out these pills and make sure that he took them, my task (as I'd promised his doctor) to cut the largest tablets into pieces so he wouldn't choke swallowing them. So why didn't I dump all the prescribed damn-fucking pills into a pile and pulverize them and dissolve them in a tall glass of gin, he'd lap down thirsty "like a dog." I listened to this, the pleading, whining, cajoling, the threat beneath, always the threat beneath, for this scrawny bent-back old man had once stood six feet tall and weighed somewhere beyond two hundred pounds and he'd been a man who had not needed to plead, beg, cajole you can bet your ass, he'd been a man who controlled his family with a frown, a glance, a sudden fist brought down flat on a table. So as I listened to my father's voice I understood that this was a test being put to me. I was expected to express surprise, alarm. I was expected to plead with him *No Daddy! Not when we love you.* Instead I mumbled something vague and conciliatory as you do when an elderly invalid is whining in self-pity and self-disgust spilling over you like a sloshing bedpan. But at the same time my heartbeat quickened. *He wants to die, I can help him die.*

He said, sneering, "You'd like that, eh! Get rid of the old man. You and—" His hoarse voice trailed off in befuddlement, he'd forgotten Abigail's name.

Not that this was flattering to me, for lately he'd been forgetting my name, too.

But now he'd trapped me: for I couldn't say "Yes" and I couldn't say "No." He laughed cruelly, baring his stained teeth. Stiffly I said, "You're not very funny."

"*You're* funny. 'Hel-len'-got-a-poker-up-her-ass."

Pronouncing my name as if it was a joke. Some TV comic inflection. When I didn't react, he snorted and threw the TV remote control at me, such a lightweight plastic thing it struck me harmlessly on my right breast and fell to the floor. (We'd been watching Fox TV, his favorite program was *The O'Reilly Factor.*) I went away, left the remote control on the floor where he'd have to grope for it partway beneath his bed if he wanted it.

Hel-len. I suppose the name was a joke.

So the subject of dying, wanting to die, how I might help him die began to surface in our life together in that house. It surfaced and sank from view and resurfaced like flotsam in a turbulent river. I thought that yes, my father was probably serious, I believed that he understood that his condition was terminal, he would never even partway recover his health before the stroke, yet of course I didn't trust him. He was feeling guilt for something he'd done years ago but he'd never once spoken of what he'd done to our mother. How he'd wrung the life from her. How he'd laughed at her, as he laughed at me, speaking her name in mockery. It was the way of the bully daring you to react with anger or indignation and knowing that you could not. Ovarian cancer had swept through my mother like wildfire and when after her first surgery she'd wanted to stay with an older sister to recuperate my father had said yes, that was a good idea, she'd taken his word on faith but after that he refused to see her, even to speak with her, he never allowed her to return to live with him, liked to say he'd washed his hands of her, she'd left *him*. Now he was elderly and blind and whining about wanting to die and yet he continued to eat most of the meals I prepared for him, except when he was actively sick his appetite was usually good enough, especially for ice cream. Elderly invalids frequently want to die and are aided in their deaths by sympathetic relatives and doctors, I knew this of course yet I would not have dared speak to his doctor about this wish of my father's, I would not even speak with my father about it thinking *I am not a daughter who wishes her father dead*. More truthful was the admonition *I must not be a daughter legally liable for her father's death*.

Would I have helped him to die, if I knew I wouldn't be caught?

Would I have held a pillow over his face until he stopped breathing, if I knew I wouldn't be caught?

" 'Hel-len.' Good daughter."

I laughed. Living with a blind sick old man who dislikes you, you become accustomed to talking and laughing to yourself.

Between us there was an undeclared war. In a distant part of the house I could hear, or believed that I could hear, the old man muttering to himself, laughing also, but meanly, as one might laugh stubbing his toe, and cursing *Damn! God damn! Fuck!* loud enough to hear if I wished. For years he had not been able to sleep for more than a few hours at a time, needing to use the toilet frequently, but now his nights were ever more restless, disruptive. I would be wakened in a jolt from my exhausted sleep hearing him prowling and stumbling through the downstairs. I dreaded him falling and injuring himself for already he'd sprained a wrist, sprained ribs, bruised himself badly. After a severe stroke at seventy-eight he'd had smaller strokes, all without warning. Years of heavy smoking, heavy drinking, heavy eating had weakened his heart that had now to be monitored by a "gizmo" in his chest—a pacemaker. And there was the macular degeneration that had begun years ago, to madden and terrify. Old age is one symptom after another, a doctor told me meaning to be sympathetic.

After the initial stroke I'd moved back into the house in which I had spent the first eighteen years of my life for I'd been shaken by my father's rapid decline and I'd been touched by his obvious need for me. For never had Lyle Sebera expressed any need for anyone, and certainly not for me. We'd relocated his bedroom downstairs and close to the bathroom in the hallway and I'd been cheerful and upbeat and he'd been grateful then, at the start. Before more symptoms emerged, that were not going to go away.

Later I would come to realize that my father's gratitude had been a trick to ensnare me. He'd been a man to seduce women, then to speak of them in contempt as "easy."

When Abigail called, I told her none of this. That our father was exactly the man he'd always been except now he was miserable and wished to die and that I wished him to die. That I was furious with her for her shrewdness in leaving Sparta to live hundreds of miles away. Instead I told her coolly, daring her to doubt my words: "Oh, you know Lyle. Hardy as hell, he'll outlive us all." Or: "He's doing as well as we can expect. Good days, not-so-good. Want me to put him on?"

Quickly Abigail would say no! For he seemed always to be agitated or annoyed by her, asking if she was "checking up on him"—"wanting money from him"—and seeming not to remember her name.

"But he asks after you, Abigail. All the time."

"Oh, Helen. He does?"

Abigail was doubtful yet wanting to believe. I had all I could do to keep from bursting into laughter.

Except one day when Abigail was questioning me too closely about our father's property investments, and his medical insurance, and his latest physical ailments, I did begin to laugh. I laughed, and I sobbed angrily. For it was the riddle of my life now, how I'd become our father's caretaker. I'd become the "good" daughter as our mother, before her cancer, had been the "good" wife. I told Abigail that it was some kind of grotesque mistake, these past several years. I wasn't a good person, I hadn't a good heart. She, Abigail, was so much the better person. Everyone knew that. I was selfish, cruel and indifferent to the pain of others, just like our father. My heart was shriveled and hard as a lump of coal yet somehow I was the sister who'd remained in Sparta, New York, while she, Abigail, had gone away to college and married and had children and never lived closer than three hundred miles away. While I'd never married, never been in love. I'd barely graduated from high school and remained in Sparta taking courses at the community college where now I worked in "food services" and had to be grateful for that. Now I was living in this house we'd both been desperate to escape. I wasn't a girl of ten, or nineteen, or even a woman of twenty-nine. I was forty-nine years old and how had that happened?

Abigail said, "Oh, Helen. Of course I'm coming there. We'll make new arrangements. I love you."

I love you would burn in my shriveled heart. Though I had not been able to mumble *I love you, too.*

"Helen, you must let *me*."

Yes I would let her. I smiled to think *Yes! Try.*

Through this second day of her visit my sister Abigail was suffused with energy, determination, good intentions. Reminded me of when she'd been, for a few ecstatic months in high school, a born-again Christian. She "aired out" rooms long pervaded with the stink of rancid food, soiled clothing and bedding, dried urine. With paper towels and Windex she washed window panes long layered in grime. She drove our father, sulky and anxious, to his morning medical appointment. In a voice pitched as if for a deaf or retarded child she spoke to the old man earnestly and cheerfully and tried not to be discouraged when he acknowledged her efforts only in grunts. I thought *He doesn't want your good cheer, he wants anger and hurt. He wants to be punished.*

Never would the old blind man speak intimately to Abigail as he spoke to me. I knew this.

"Why is he angry with me? Is he angry with me? Does he hate me, Helen?"

My sister's voice began to sound wistful, even resentful. She'd sent me away to take the afternoon off—"Spend some time on yourself for a change, Helen"—and when I returned in the early evening she was looking tired, baffled. The old blind man hadn't been grateful for her company but preferred to sulk in his room with the TV turned up loud. He hadn't even seemed to know, or care, who she was! The damned vacuum cleaner had gotten clotted with something gluey and smelly sucked up into the hose. The damned washing machine in the basement had broken down in mid-cycle. The first several "assisted-living facilities" she'd called had no openings, only waiting lists. Cleaning the kitchen cupboards that hadn't been cleaned for years she'd discovered roaches. Nests of spiders in all the corners of the house. I wanted to ask if she'd noticed how the rear of the old house had begun to sink into muck, to disappear. How the lead backing in the mirrors had begun to eat its way through the glass like cancer.

"How can you live in this house, Helen! How can you bear it!"

Because I am stronger than you. Like a roach.

The rest of the day went badly. I'd warned Abigail that the old man had sharp ears and so he'd overheard her on the phone calling "nursing homes" and he was furious saying he would never leave this house, he would die in this house, nobody could force him to leave this house which was his property, he knew his rights as a United States citizen and he'd go on TV to expose us, if we tried to cheat him. Abigail tried to explain which was a mistake, tried to apologize which was a worse mistake. He shouted, he spat, he threatened, he pummelled the air with his fists, there was nothing to do but assure him *Yes we promise no we will not ever, you have our word.* Abigail's next blunder was to try to feed the old man a "special supper" she'd prepared in place of the sugar-laced frozen Birds Eye suppers the old man was accustomed to eating and I was accustomed to preparing, the first mouthful of poached salmon he spat out onto the table: "Trying to choke me with fish bones, eh? That's why you're here, eh?"

Abigail protested, "Daddy, no. How can you think—"

Daddy caused the old man to snort in derision. He hadn't been *Daddy* in thirty years.

My afternoon away from the elderly blind man's house had been strange as a dream dreamt by someone not myself whom in some way I seemed to know, even to be bound with intimately, like a cousin not glimpsed in many years. Mostly I drove around Sparta. I drove out along the Chautauqua River. I stopped at a liquor store to bring back a bottle of scotch whiskey and this bottle like a shining talisman I brought upstairs with two freshly rinsed water glasses to share with my exhausted sister Abigail after—finally!—the house was darkened downstairs and the old man sunk into his comatose sleep in the hospital bed installed in his room. As we'd huddled together in our bedroom down the hall as girls so now we huddled together as adults in my bedroom which was our parents' former bedroom that still felt unnatural to me, that I'd dared even to enter this room let alone appropriate it. Sprawled on my back on the rumpled double bed whose sheets hadn't been changed in weeks, a soiled foam-rubber pillow scrunched beneath my head, I balanced my whiskey glass between my flat-sloping breasts and listened to Abigail speak in wayward feverish lunges like a marathon runner who has overexerted herself yet can't stop running, must continue panting and gasping for air until the collapse is complete. We had not undressed for bed. Our clothes were rumpled and smelled of a sickroom. This day that was meant to be my sister's triumph we'd been defeated by the old blind man yet—so stubbornly!—Abigail reverted to her subject of the assisted care facility we must find for him, as if finding the place was the task, the challenge, and not persuading our father to move into it. Abigail said adamantly that it wasn't possible for me to continue to care for him in this hopeless pigsty, he had to be moved immediately, for his own well-being as for mine, by which she meant, Abigail said pointedly, my physical and mental health. We would have to get power of attorney over his assets, there was no turning back. I told her yes but we'd just promised him, hadn't we: *No we will not ever, you have our word*. But Abigail seemed not to hear.

"If not in Sparta then somewhere else. Peekskill!—there are plenty of 'assisted living facilities' there."

Abigail was sitting on the edge of my bed sipping whiskey in small mouthfuls. Her weight felt heavy, leaden. Her hair that had been sleek-cut and glossy was nearly as matted now as mine and her skin exuded a sick clammy odor. I said, "He's serious, Abigail. He wants to die here. He wants to *die*." Abigail laughed angrily, "Well, he just can't *die*. Probably not for a long time."

I gripped the foam-rubber pillow with both hands, behind my head. I said, "We could hold a pillow over his face. He'd struggle like hell and he's strong but there are two of us and his heart will give out." I paused. I giggled. Inanely I added, "It's been done."

Abigail frowned. "Oh, Helen."

Abigail giggled. Abigail drained much of her glass and wiped her mouth with the edge of her hand. "Oh *Hel*en. The things you say."

Maybe in rebuke, or to comfort or console me, Abigail groped for my free hand, and squeezed. Middle-aged sisters gripping hands. That evening after our disastrous supper I'd overheard Abigail on her cell phone in the room she was staying in, our bedroom when we'd been girls, I stood outside the door listening hearing my sister's lowered voice, she was speaking with her husband back in Peekskill saying things were much worse than she'd expected, so much worse, *can't leave Helen, my poor sister I can't leave until* as quickly I turned away blinded by tears. My sister whose life was so rich and full and superior to my own cared for me! Another person cared enough for me to be anxious on my behalf, my name had been uttered in a tone of dismay. I was very moved though I could feel nothing much, I'd become anesthetized to sensation as a paralyzed limb.

I said, "Where I drove this afternoon? Out along the river? I was looking for where it happened—the wrecked car, the 'double homicide,' remember?" Abigail shuddered and seemed to stiffen but made no reply. She'd become drowsy, lying on her side on the bed, clumsily perpendicular to me, her nearly empty glass against her thigh. I said, "I don't think I found it. The exact site. I'm not sure," and Abigail said irritably, "Well, you'd never seen it, had you? *I* never saw it," and I said, "Supposedly they'd gone off the road, down an embankment. I mean, they were pushed off the road. It's very steep there, down to the river. There was a bridge there, I'd thought. Eventually I found an old iron-girder bridge so maybe that's where it happened. Not where I'd thought but farther out. It's desolate out there, a kind of swampy jungle along the river where the car must have capsized. I remember that word—'capsized.' Like 'bludgeoned'—a word that, if you hear it, you can guess its meaning. On my odometer I clocked it, where the wrecked car was found is seven point three miles from this house." Abigail made no reply. I heard her breathing in husky surges. Like depleted swimmers sinking slowly through the water, unresisting we settled in the warm black muck below.

We were wakened suddenly hours later by a noise downstairs of lurching footsteps. Helplessly we lay listening to the blind man make his uncertain way to the bathroom in the hall. I knew to wait for the toilet to be flushed (though sometimes he failed to flush it out of forgetfulness, or spite) and following this it was crucial that he return to his bed for if he did not return to bed, this meant he'd become confused and lost and I would need to go downstairs to guide him back to bed; but more upsetting was the possibility that he'd decided he did not want to sleep but preferred to prowl the house like a trapped animal searching for a way out. I was remembering how a few nights ago I had stopped him at the top of the basement steps, he'd opened the door and was about to pitch forward to break his brittle bones on the concrete floor twelve feet below. And there was the time I'd discovered him in the kitchen where he'd turned on four gas burners emitting a deathly hissing sound for of course (no need to tell me, I knew) the old man's wish to die might not be a wish to die alone. Abigail said, "How can you live like this, Helen!" but in the next moment she was up, slapping her cheeks to wake herself fully, saying, "We have to help him, he might hurt himself." Already I was at the door. I was practiced in such nighttime maneuvers and had no doubt that the old man downstairs was waiting for me and would be surprised that tonight there would be two of me, not just one.

We switched on lights. The downstairs was ablaze with light. A festive occasion here! We were not blind and so we required lights to see and in such dazzling light bracketing the vast and terrible night outside we did see: the old man barefoot and cowering in a corner of the living room, turning his head at an angle to sight us in his vision. Abigail spoke to him and he cursed her. I spoke to him and he cursed me. Though Abigail had cajoled him into changing out of his filth-stiffened flannel shirt and pajama bottoms to put on freshly laundered pajamas, yet he seemed to be wearing the same filth-stiffened things. "Oh, Daddy. Oh!" Abigail advanced upon him recklessly not knowing how quick his blows could come, surprisingly hard stinging blows and his nails were broken and sharp as a cat's, drawing a zigzag of blood in her cheek. We circled him, tried to head him off so he couldn't stumble into the kitchen. He was glowering, panting. He lunged at Abigail sensing she was the weaker of the two of us, he managed to thrust a floor lamp at her, striking her and hurting her, and he grabbed her, "Damn bitch! Want to suck my blood!" and they struggled together, I tried to pull him off her, loosen his talon-grip on her shoulders. He was fierce and writhing as a wounded snake. He fell and pulled Abigail with him, she straddled his bony thrashing body and grabbed a cushion from the sofa and pressed it against his face. Her eyes were bloodshot and triumphant. Her lips were drawn back from her glistening teeth. "Hate hate hate you why don't you die!" I grabbed my sister's wrists and managed to pull her from him. Her thighs were muscular, her bare feet curled with strain. The cushion lay on the old man's face, his body appeared headless. He was breathing feebly but he was breathing. When I tried to help him up he spat at me, he called me the vilest names. He could not have known who I was, he called me such names. On his belly then crawling, and I tried again to help him and was rebuffed and Abigail crouched above us dazed and affrighted as a sleepwalker wakened too abruptly, she seemed not to know what she'd done, what was happening except that it wasn't her responsibility but mine, and I would take charge. After some minutes of resistance the old man gave in, surly and still cursing, but I was able to get him back to bed, he was exhausted now and would sink back into his comatose sleep for a few more hours. "None of this has happened, Abigail," I told my sister, squeezing her icy hands, "he won't remember anything in the morning."

We made no effort to sleep that night. Already it was 4:20 A.M. I helped Abigail undress and ran a bath for her and shampooed her hair in the bath and treated the shallow scratch in her cheek and put a flesh-colored Band-Aid over it. By dawn she was prepared to drive back to Peekskill. She'd repacked her small suitcase, her eyes were socketed in fatigue yet she'd put on fresh lipstick and a bright smile flashed in her face. We thought it best for her to leave without saying goodbye to him. For very likely he wouldn't remember that she had even been here, let alone what had happened in the confusion of the night. Or if he remembered, he would blame

Helen. At the door Abigail hugged me tight and kissed me at the edge of the mouth. I held her for a long moment. "Call me, don't forget me," I said, meaning to be playful, and Abigail said, "Oh, Helen. I'm going to help you. I promise." Abigail could not hear what I was hearing, only just audible at the rear of the house: an elderly voice sounding weaker than usual, fretful and anxious. "Helen? *Hel-len?*" I shut the door after my sister and hurried back there.

Magda Maria

for Leonard Cohen

M agda Maria she was known to us in the early 1970s on River Street, in south Sparta. No one could have said what her last name was or where she'd come from. Magda Maria: the mysterious name. As Magda Maria's beauty was legendary even to those who'd seen her only at a distance, obscured by swirling clouds of smoke in the twilit River House barroom where she was first seen in the company of an older man known to us as Danto. (Though Danto had no corresponding awareness of us.) Danto was a massive man standing six feet four or five inches and weighing well over 230 pounds in hand-tooled leather boots. Danto wore his hair long, though receding at the temples, defiantly threaded with silver, hair like the plumage of a splendid male bird, and Danto wore stylish clothes, we coveted Danto's black leather coat with its sealskin collar and Danto's low-slung ruby-red sports car whose exotic name few of us would have dared to utter aloud: *Porsche*. Like *Magda Maria* and *Danto*, *Porsche* was a sound to be murmured in a low reverent voice in one or another River Street tavern where we drank away the hours like waders in a pounding exhilarating and exhausting surf, when we could afford to drink, or we bought drugs, or traded or dealt drugs, depending upon our desperation and recklessness and the shifting tyranny of our needs, at the mercy of shifting tides of availability (mysteriously, drugs appeared in south Sparta the way, for some citizens, newspapers appear on front stoops of houses) in accordance with laws as beyond our comprehension as the laws of higher mathematics. In the River House where time oozed, bent, collapsed into seconds, or looped back upon itself like rerun dreams, we had time to contemplate through the smoky twilight the beautiful doomed Magda Maria drinking at the farthest, shadowy end of the bar with her middle-aged companion Danto, it was a torment to us how Magda Maria was eclipsed by Danto's bulk as by Danto's intimidating personality, in silhouette unnervingly young, with the look both defiant and demure of a wayward schoolgirl, how was it possible, we wondered, that Magda Maria was served drinks at the River House?—had Danto secured a false I.D. for her, raising her age to an improbable twenty-one? Magda Maria was prized for her waist-long shimmering-black hair, her face often obscured by curtains of this shimmering hair at which from time to time Danto brushed with his fingers in a gesture of excruciating tenderness, that he might lean close to Magda Maria to whisper into her ear, or kiss the edge of her mouth. Magda Maria was shy: was she? Magda Maria was unaware of our interest: was she? Or was Magda Maria well aware of us, casting us glances of intimacy and scorn, her face suddenly exposed, pale, doll-like, delicately boned, and her mouth unexpectedly wide, fleshy, with the slightly swollen look of a mouth that has been much-kissed. There were few other girls or women in the River Street taverns but some were known to us, some of them were painfully known to us, we'd bought them drinks, we'd gone home with them or had believed that we were meant to go home with them except something happened to intervene, we'd given them money, or we'd stolen money from them, cheated them of drugs, nothing so precious as a few hours' happiness you've been cheated of, but these girls and women were of little interest to us now that Magda Maria had entered our lives for they were no longer beautiful enough or young enough or mysterious enough to be contemplated with yearning and lust. Instead there was Magda

Maria arriving at the River House with her companion Danto, Magda Maria who came only just to Danto's shoulder, Magda Maria in an ankle-length black fur coat (mink?) that must have been given to her by Danto, somehow it was known that Danto owned clothing stores in Sparta, or Danto owned properties that leased space to clothing stores, he was a man with money, a man with the power of money, surely he was a man with a family somewhere, perhaps even close by, a man who'd sired children now grown and bitterly jealous of Magda Maria, their father's love affair with a girl surely younger than his youngest daughter and it was for such reasons that Danto adored Magda Maria, as Magda Maria adored Danto. When Danto helped Magda Maria out of the black fur coat, tenderly he folded it beside them on a barstool where it seemed to drowse like a pampered beast, we saw then that Magda Maria wore clothes, or strips of cloth, that were layered, flimsy as cobwebs, black muslin and black silk and black lace, a black skirt with a jagged hemline and an unexpected slit at the sides that exposed her beautiful pale legs, a cobwebbed black-translucent fabric through which Magda Maria's small ivory-white breasts shone, and the shadows of her prominent collarbone could only just be glimpsed; and Magda Maria wore shoes with stacked heels, or boots with stiletto heels, that caused her to teeter like a little girl in an adult woman's footwear. It was believed that with Magda Maria's straight shimmering-black hair and something resistant and prideful, or arrogant, in her manner, that she was of Indian descent, she'd drifted down to Sparta from Rivière-du-Loup where there was a Seneca reservation, but no one could claim to know, no one could claim to have spoken with Magda Maria for invariably in the River House Danto leaned possessively over her, shielded her from prurient eyes, held her attention by speaking to her in a ceaseless whispered and seemingly one-sided conversation to which Magda Maria only murmured in response, smiled, nodded, inclined her head in acquiescence, and if other men approached them at the far, shadowy end of the bar, friends of Danto's, or men who wished to believe that they were friends of Danto's, Danto spoke grudgingly with them and blocked their view of his young-girl companion and did not introduce them. We observed Magda Maria drinking—was it whiskey? straight whiskey?—as Danto drank whiskey—and imagined that, should Magda Maria need to be rescued from her companion, it would be one of us to whom she turned.

Those years love festered in me like a wound. I have to think that I died then, what has survived is someone else.

Was Magda Maria alone? Staggering into the River House without Danto? For something terrible had happened to Danto and Magda Maria was rumored to have died in what the newspapers called a *suicide pact*, it would be said that Magda Maria had died for her heart had ceased beating, yet somehow Magda Maria had been revived, Magda Maria was living among us still, chalky-white-faced, thinner than we remembered, and more beautiful. Yet it seemed unnatural to us: that Magda Maria had returned to us from the dead not at night but in the late afternoon of a mild day in March when most of the ice in the Black River had melted and the place at the bar at which Magda Maria was standing wasn't the usual place to which Danto had invariably steered her but at the other end of the bar, where, so strangely, waning sunlight from a stained-glass fanlight over a door reflected in the long horizontal mirror behind the bar and the rows of liquor bottles arranged before the mirror as on an altar sparkled and shone with the innocence of Christmas lights; and this light fell across Magda Maria's face that was subtly ravaged from death and yet radiant with the memory of death like her eyes that shone with suffering. Now it was revealed to us why Magda Maria wore black: black is the shade of mourning, and Magda Maria was in mourning for her lost lover who'd died in her arms. Immediately the most aggressive of us, a man in his early thirties known on the street as Wolverine, stepped forward to buy Magda Maria a drink, a whiskey straight, and a whiskey straight for himself, already Wolverine whose oily-blond hair was pulled back into a ponytail and whose jaws were covered in silvery-blond stubble had fallen in love with Magda Maria, Wolverine would kill for Magda Maria, though Wolverine was notorious for his crude, cruel treatment of girls and women drawn to him like moths to an open flame, and it was known that Wolverine (who dealt drugs, pot and amphetamines for the college trade, cocaine and heroin for serious, seasoned users) had hurt certain of his associates and was the cause of others disappearing from Sparta and was a man to whom you did not wish to owe money unless you could repay it within twenty-four hours. In the slow dazed seductive voice of a debauched schoolgirl who lacks the fullest awareness of what has been done to her Magda Maria confided in Wolverine that Danto had insisted that she die with him for it was time for them to die together, Danto had poured whiskey into glasses for each of them to drink and Danto emptied a bottle of barbiturate tablets for each of them to swallow down, powerful sleeping pills that Danto had procured for their double suicide for it could not be that they could live together, their love would become contaminated, the truest love is doomed. Magda Maria had pleaded with Herkimer County prosecutors to understand: she had not wanted to die, she had not wanted her fifty-one-year-old lover to die, she believed that suicide is a sin, except she could not bear to outlive Danto who'd adored her, she dared not outlive Danto who would return from death to curse her, it was a holy act between them, it was their only possible marriage, Danto was Roman Catholic and all of his family was Roman Catholic and divorce was not possible for him, life had become an irritant to him, his brain was steeped in whiskey, his eyes were jaundiced from whiskey, his liver was enlarged and rode across the small of his back like a hard-rubbery leech, in Danto's six-room "luxury" apartment on the top floor of a high-rise building overlooking the Black River in the old-city center of Sparta miles from Danto's suburban colonial home, on Danto's enormous bed covered in black satin threaded with gold the doomed lovers lay together in each other's arms kissing and whispering together and their tears mingled as they lapsed into sleep, how much whiskey Magda Maria had been able to drink, how many barbiturates Magda

Maria had been able to swallow before her throat shut against them, and her bowels swirled with nausea, how close to death had Magda Maria come, lapsing into a twilight sleep that was not a peaceful sleep but wracked by coughing, choking, gagging, until at last Magda Maria began to vomit helplessly, vomiting up whiskey sour-tasting as acid and barbiturate tablets in chalky clumps and as Danto sank ever more deeply into unconsciousness, his breathing erratic, stentorious, Magda Maria thrashed in a delirium of physical distress, misery, unaware of her (soiled, befouled) surroundings, Magda Maria sank exhausted into unconsciousness and wakened twenty hours later to a stench of vomit and excrement and there was a dead man heavy and stiffened in her arms and she could not move for a long time partly crushed beneath the dead man's body, faintly she called for help uncertain if in fact she was alive or dead and, if dead, in an interim state not clearly the afterlife yet as clearly not life, for what seemed a very long time trapped in this state as in a paralysis, her throat was raw, she was crying for help, but there was no help, she could hear voices down on the street, she could hear traffic, she prayed, tried to pray, tried to work herself free of the dead man's embrace, his muscled arms gripping her, his heavy head, clammy-skinned face with eyes like mashed grapes oblivious of her, until at last she was able to work herself free dazed and not knowing where she was on her hands and knees crawling across a patch of carpet calling for help and now someone outside in the corridor heard what sounded like a cat mewing piteously and finally then she was discovered and an ambulance was called. But Danto was already dead, Danto had been dead for hours, Magda Maria pleaded she had not wanted Danto to die, she believed that suicide is a sin and she had not wanted Danto to die and yet if Danto died, it had seemed necessary for her to die, for she could not betray her lover even at the risk of condemning her soul to an eternity of hell, did he believe her?—Magda Maria's thin fingers outstretched and pressed against Wolverine's chest in a gesture of childlike appeal and her dark-bruised eyes brimming with suffering lifted to his face so Wolverine was suffused with the happiness of

new, young love as more often Wolverine was suffused with the
wish to do harm to another person stammering to Magda Maria
she was safe now, all that sick Danto shit was over.

Locust season! Panic hit me like a wave of filthy water, the things
were everywhere and yet I could not assume that they were not
inside my head and spilling out as other hallucinations had done in
the past. And I'd been sick then, and was possibly sick now hearing
shrieks out of the trees, the things were falling onto my head and
into my matted and unwashed hair. Hearing that Magda Maria
had died—how, finally, one of her lovers had killed her, over a
weekend—I was staggering along the riverbank kicking a path
through locusts that lay an inch thick on the ground. I tried not to
be frightened of them, I tried to feel pity for such accursed creatures, some were only just shells, some were still alive and crawling
over one another and others were in trees screeching with the desperation of the damned. *Seventeen-year locusts* it was explained to us by
our elders for we were not old enough to have lived in Sparta at the
time of the last locust eruption in the mid-1950s, the most tragic
of God's creatures born with no capacity for eating, lacking a
mouth and an alimentary track, possessing only rudimentary eyes
and sex-organs encased in a shell awakened (why? our elders could
not explain, though we could see that the question had engaged
them) from seventeen years cocooned underground, frantically
digging their way to the surface of the earth to fly into the lower-
most branches of trees careening like drunken pilots, crawling on
tree trunks and tumbling over one another, blindly mating in a
pandemonium of deafening shrieks after which the male locusts
began to shrivel and die almost immediately and the females lived
a few hours longer in order to lay their eggs in the earth that the
seventeen-year cycle might begin again immediately and then the
females too began to die and by the next day the earth was strewn
with the husks of locusts like discarded souls barred even from
Hades this raw-aching morning after the news came to me that

Magda Maria had died and where Magda Maria had not loved me in the past it was only now that it became impossible that Magda Maria would ever love me and in this way redeem me from the wreckage of my life bitter as bile in my mouth.

. . . in the Black Bass Tavern, I saw her: Magda Maria! For rumors of her death were false, confused with the crazed din of the locusts, my jaundiced eyes and skin, a collapse, "rehab" and release. And then I was back, though more frequently in the Black Bass where some of us were made welcome who weren't any longer at the River House where the bartender had taken an irrational dislike to us, and had threatened us. I wept to see Magda Maria still alive, returned to me though in the company of a shaved-headed man known as D.G. who was a former associate of Wolverine, in some quarters believed to be Wolverine's murderer though D.G. had not been arrested for the crime only just taken into police custody and "interrogated" and in fact Wolverine's body had never been found. It had been printed in the newspapers for all to see, Magda Maria's surname was *Huet*, her age was given to be twenty-five, *Maria Huet* had been taken into custody by Sparta police as a "material witness" in a "suspected homicide" and when she was unable or unwilling to cooperate with police she was remanded by a judge to the Herkimer County Women's Detention where voluntarily she entered a drug rehab program (alcohol, heroin) and after six weeks was released and abruptly then disappeared from Sparta only to reappear months later in the Black Bass in the company of the shaved-headed D.G. who sometimes spoke harshly to her, twisted her wrist or shoved her, causing tears to spill down her geisha-white face. Still Magda Maria was perceived to be young and beautiful if not so young and beautiful as she'd once been with her long loose black hair coarser now, and her skin dead-white as if bloodless and her crimson mouth that looked perpetually hungry. Magda Maria's laughter was high-pitched and uncertain as the cries of woodland birds and Magda Maria's bruised-looking eyelids were often heavy, hooded as if sleep tugged at her, the most exquisite oblivion tugged at her, Magda Maria folded her arms on the bar, lay her head on her arms in dreamy exhaustion and D.G. might irritably prod and pinch her awake or with gentle whimsy stroke her shoulders bent like broken wings, or her hair, fanning her black hair about her head as if to hide her from inquisitive eyes. By this time it seemed to be known among us that Magda Maria's family (whose name had to be Huet, a disappointment to us, who had not wished to believe that Magda Maria had any surname and, like ourselves, "family" to define her as a net might be said to define a creature trapped and struggling inside it) had disowned her years ago, French Catholics from Quebec who'd settled north of Plattsburgh, Magda Maria was a Catholic schoolgirl when she'd begun seeing an older man, no more than fifteen years old, already she'd begun drinking, she'd begun using drugs, ran away with her lover or with another lover in a succession of lovers who vied with one another for her, living in Messena, in Ogdensburg, in Watertown reappearing then in Sparta where, in one version of her story, Magda Maria enrolled in the nursing school, for Magda Maria's wish was to become a nurse, or, in another version of her story, Magda Maria posed as a (nude) model in the university's art school, ravishingly beautiful, very young, naively trusting and vulnerable, willing to pose naked before strangers, or in such need of money forcing herself to pose naked before strangers, and all of her (male) students fell in love with her, and one of her (male) instructors seduced her, a sculptor who also dealt drugs to undergraduates and was arrested and dismissed from the university. These years!—in which a doomed yet pitiless war was being "waged" in the cause of "democracy" on the far side of the earth by soldiers who were former classmates of ours, cousins, brothers who despised us, young Appalachian men, blacks who'd been drafted out of high school, we were shamed and exhilarated by our own moral rot like the rotting teeth in our jaws, we were captivated by the prospect of early death, yet at the same time in a permanent state of paranoia believing that though some of us had minor criminal records or were recovering from hepatitis or jaundice or were alcoholics whose brains had begun to shrink or drug addicts whose forearms were riddled with needle tracks yet we might be drafted into the U.S. Army as the Army became increasingly desperate for soldiers, we would be forced to march in platoons in the zombie-uniforms of dead heroes who'd despised us. There must have been a time when we'd been students, and "promising": some of us had had scholarships, we'd been valedictorians of our high school classes. Why we'd washed up in the shabby urban neighborhood south of the shabby campus of the state university at Sparta, an under-funded and generally reviled campus formerly a teachers' college, long since expelled from our dorms, evicted from rooming houses and living with friends, if we had friends, or living on the street, we could not have said. Some of us had been poets, artists, "intellectuals." We were musicians, composers. Some of us had been graduate students and some of us had in fact earned Ph.D.s in such hopeful subjects as literature, philosophy, "humanities," we'd been adjunct instructors at the university whose contracts had not been renewed. And yet a kind of hypnosis held us here in Sparta, a rain-washed city on the Black River, for here was the wreckage of our early promise. As in Hades visited by Odysseus and subsequently by Aeneas we were spirits of the dead and the damned clamoring for our lost lives in a perpetual trance of longing and there was Magda Maria we were in love with, Magda Maria who (we believed this) would forgive us our cowardice, Magda Maria who'd once been (we'd come to believe this) a nurse, like Dido who'd nursed the wounded Aeneas, saved his life and surrendered her very soul to him. And the River House was awash with expelled and exhausted souls, everywhere underfoot you kicked them inadvertently. These years!—yet they were happy years, though it was a matter of shame to the more sensitive among us that Herkimer County like most of rural America was filling up with war veterans not much older than we were, in some cases younger, and more tragic, shipped back from the far side of the earth maimed and broken and garlanded with glittering medals and their eyes demented with chagrin, hurt, bafflement, rage. *Why? Why so many deaths, for this?*

You would expect the vets to hate us, as we hated ourselves, and some of them did hate us, but others unexpectedly became our friends and allies, drinking with us in the Black Bass, scoring drugs, buying drugs from us or providing us with drugs, trading girls among us, trading wives, in the Cloverleaf down by the wharf, in Dunphy's on Quay Street that was partly burnt-out but open for business, and, as tides shifted, at the River House again where Magda Maria drank ever earlier in the day and less frequently with D.G. who'd been arrested, out on bail and re-arrested and badly beaten by another drug dealer unless by the Sparta police who were notorious for punishing "hippies"—"junkies"—"pimps"—in their energetic, practical way. D.G. suddenly vanished, sent away to the men's maximum security prison at Follette where, eventually, he was killed by other inmates unless by guards and Magda Maria, whose coat was now clearly not mink, not even fur, but something synthetic and glossy like Formica, had been commandeered by a Vietnam vet named Ike with the baby-boy face of a battered Robert Redford, pitted skin and a patch of dirt-colored whiskers and endearingly shaky hands and a voice permanently hoarse from a war injury to his upper thorax. Ike was a serious drinker and storyteller easy to befriend for Ike was careless in his friendships like a spendthrift, Ike behaved like a man under a sentence of death or perhaps like a man who has already died, not so proprietary of Magda Maria as her former lovers had been, in fact careless of Magda Maria like any spendthrift and it was known (it was rumored, whispered) that Ike was living with Magda Maria in a house shared by others and Magda Maria was herself "shared" if circumstances veered in that direction. Close up I saw that Magda Maria gazed at me, or toward me, with dark, bruised eyes, Magda Maria had herself been sick for a while, at the time of D.G.'s beating, her skin was now sallow and her eyes just perceptibly jaundiced, yet beautiful eyes they were, with thick lashes, and there was the shimmering-black hair that had been cut in one or another medical facility, now beginning to grow out again but not so profusely, brittle at the ends, and giving off a rich, rankly oily odor of unwashed hair, that aroused me to such longing, it was as if a demon had slipped inside me, down through my throat, into my body, pulsing at my groin. It was believed by some that Magda Maria's mouth was no longer so beautiful, ringed with reddened sores, but I could not look away from that mouth, I was transfixed. Because Ike was present we could not speak to each other but had to communicate in more subtle ways and so I was spared the stammering banality of *I love you, I've loved you since the first time I saw you Magda María please will you love me?* For there was a part missing somewhere inside me, only in Magda Maria could this missing part be retrieved like a jigsaw puzzle piece fallen onto the floor, kicked beneath a table into the grubby shadows. *Not this man, not this brute but I am your lover Magda María, I would die for you.* Within months Ike would become my enemy, Ike would take my money, each crumpled bill precious to me, Ike would sell me diluted goods, like you'd sell undergraduates, coke laced with talcum powder if not something worse, Ike daring me to confront him, Ike Balboa was his name, friendly-seeming guy, big-whiskered guy with a quick smile, eyes leveling with yours, so you're led to think, think you can trust a guy like Ike, it's a shock to discover differently, when Sparta police banged me around, began to kick, beat me in the rear of the station house where they'd brought me "on suspicion" (drugs, breaking-and-entering, loitering "with intent") at first I was determined not to give anybody up, I wasn't that kind of person, I was one to be trusted, yet somehow, five seconds into the beating, possibly less than five seconds, the pain was unbelievable, I'd been living for so long numbed and not-feeling even cold, certainly not hunger, it was a shock and a revelation to me that pain exists, such pain exists, immediately I gave up Ike Balboa's name, a name already well known to Sparta police, sobbing, so shamed, frightened of being hurt even more, I'd have given up the name of my closest friend if I'd had a close friend, I'd have given up my brother's name, my older brother who despised me as a draft-dodger/junkie waiting for years to hear news of my death so he'd shrug, make a face of commingled grief and repugnance consoling our mother *He's been gone from us for years, it was his choice*. That evening at the River House none of this would have seemed possible to me, who'd lost the capacity to imagine beyond the next few hours, the next drink, the next drug-score and high, impossible to believe that I would betray Ike Balboa whom I admired, wanted to be my friend, though you expected Viet vets to be more taciturn than Ike, not blustery-sweaty loud-laughing crackheads but tragic clammy-skinned death-in-life heroin users, there is something soulful about a heroin user while a crackhead is only just dangerous, lacking a soul. Even as Ike was talking and laughing loudly at the bar it happened that Magda Maria was looking at me with her beautiful bruised eyes, Magda Maria understood my plea as clearly as if I'd spoken aloud *Magda Maria! Love me, we can save each other*. I leaned toward her inhaling the oily-rank odor of her hair, her body, seeing how her cobwebby clothes were thrift-shop items, castoff and mismatched clothing once owned by strangers, a filmy black-translucent shawl wound about her upper body had been sprinkled with glitter, tiny moons or mirrors, there were cheap clattering bracelets on Magda Maria's thin wrists, and her small ears glittered with gold piercings, and around her neck was a meager gold chain and on her breastbone a small gold cross. To be damned you must have faith, Magda Maria had never lost faith in her own damnation. Magda Maria was lifting her whiskey glass with a slow shaky hand, I saw that her fingernails had been polished red but were now chipped and broken, I wanted to kiss her fingers, instead I lifted my glass to click against hers, a gesture of sudden intimacy, sudden collusion, knowing that Ike was too drunk to observe, such love for Magda Maria pumped in my heart!—and Magda Maria smiled quickly and shyly as if I'd spoken her name, smiled at me with her beautiful wounded lips *Yes I can love you, I have been waiting for you, we will save each other*. Ike was joking about the steel plate in his head, saying how his skull had been cracked in an explosion and some of his brains had leaked out, you could rap on Ike's skull, in fact you could see a shallow, slightly discolored indentation in Ike's forehead like the place where a third eye might have been now sunken and the skin grown over mysteriously scarred and ridged.

Save me, we can save each other was the promise in Magda Maria's eyes and I was determined not to fail her, if only I had the strength.

. . . so close to the country you had only to drive over the Quay Street bridge and within a mile or two you were outside the city limits, following the Black River into a steeply hilly landscape of ancient glacier fields, small mountains, hills strangely shaped as if the earth had been bulldozed to no purpose other than to disfigure it. Along the river was more level land, farmland, reputedly the most fertile soil in Herkimer County yet the old farms were for sale, in some cases farms appeared to be abandoned. Farmers had moved on. Or they'd worn out and died and their heirs who were of my generation had no patience for the labor of farming and no faith in the spiritual worth of farming and no skills if they'd had either the patience or the faith. Some of the woodframe farmhouses stood vacant, boarded-up, but others scattered in the countryside south of Sparta were rented by drug dealers and their girlfriends and associates. It was a shifting population of individuals not native to Herkimer County some of whom were said to have died abrupt and mysterious deaths and their bodies buried back behind the old barns or in the woods where their bones moldered amid the tangled roots of trees. Through our long Adirondack winters winds howled in the trees but these were not the spirits of the damned, the damned were very quiet and often we envied them.

A terrible story circulated of Magda Maria beaten to death by a jealous lover or possibly at the bequest of Ike Balboa who'd been remanded to the county house of detention without bail awaiting trial. For it seemed that Magda Maria had been living in the country in one of these houses a few miles beyond the Quay Street bridge. We had not seen her on River Street in months. On River Street where the bars opened at 10:30 A.M. each day except Sunday and closed at 2 A.M. we pined for Magda Maria but had not the courage to seek her out where we had reason to believe she might be living. It was late winter, a treacherous season for herds of white-tailed deer that were said to have overbred the previous year and were now starving, their ribs showing stark against their dun-colored winter coats. They grew exhausted with the effort to live, they lay amid remnants of snow and froze to death in the night. Or they were struck by vehicles on country roads, too weak to escape, their eyes widened and piteous in our headlights. In death their graceful bodies were swiftly dismembered by scavengers. It was a sobering sight to see black-feathered creatures (turkey vultures, crows) picking at raw flesh in the roads, flying low across fields clumsy with the weight of bloody organs, chunks of meat, sometimes entire legs gripped in their talons.

... evicted from my room in the Empire Hotel I'd been sharing with a friend and collapsed on the street in the rain, maybe it was later that my brother Mike showed up, or maybe it was a dream that Mike who was now a sheriff's deputy in Beechum County had been summoned to drive to Sparta to help me but must've seen something in my face to piss him off, there was Mike beating me, kicking me where I'd fallen and guys riding high in the cabs of trailer trucks, dump trucks on Railroad Avenue pausing to look on bemused, these were guys who hoped you might stagger out into the street so they could run you over and be blameless. An adult man shouting the way my brother shouted at me is a sound to tear the nerves like silk *Junkie-bastard! Why don't you die!*

And so maybe, yes I did. What has survived is someone else.

My name is _____. I am a _____. In rehab at Watertown. In long twisty snarls your guts are pulled out. Twenty-nine years old incarcerated in the (locked, medium-security) facility and thirty years old when discharged as "clean"—"sober"—seven months later and for the first time my thoughts were so clear and crystalline I was able to weep for my lost youth—"promise"—though very likely to be realistic the loss of my youth/promise could have been of no more significance than litter blowing in the street. And yet: *We have faith in you, your talent. All that you have to live for and to give the world.* It was so, in rehab after the hallucinations faded, after taken off the anti-convulsive drug that mashed my soul flat as roadkill, I'd begun writing again, lyric poetry in the vein of *Un soir, j'ai assis la Beauté sur mes genoux.—Et je l'ai trouvée amère.—Et je l'ai injuriée* you would not believe it (would you? who imagine you have peered into my heart?) for once I'd known French fluently enough to have read Rimbaud, and this long before the romance of Magda Maria whose people were from French-Quebec, such lyric poetry flashing like iridescent flame from a cheap lighter and of the fleeting nature of that flame some mistake for the deeper illuminations of the soul. Into the autumn I lived again at home—"at home" like a child returned to safety—in the gas-heated two-storey box-house of my middle-aged parents, muted anxiety in their raddled faces, helpless love in their bifocal-eyes and these good people continued to have faith in me, their younger son whom they'd never ceased to love as my brother Mike who'd cursed me had long ago ceased to love me, my parents' faith was smothering as pancake mix poured like liquid putty down your throat, yet the fact was: I was regaining the weight I'd lost as a junkie, a "living skeleton" I'd been when my brother found me in the street discarded like trash, I was regaining my old ability to reason, to speculate and to imagine the future, not *the* future but *a* future maybe, beyond the next few hours a future comprised of weeks, months, and even years—but could I bear to contemplate years, in my weakened state?—like shining a flashlight into a darkened building, might be a wreck of a building, might be a building in good repair, might be a vandalized building, might be a building that beckons, you must see into the building to determine whether it is wise to enter and where you must step if you wish to enter in safety.

The most elementary facts of our lives as adults but new and exciting discoveries for me, as my muscles had atrophied and were now regaining tissue, the effort of regaining such strength like armor was exhausting, my parents' pancake-batter love for me was suffocating and ridiculous like clothes I'd outgrown, old posters in my room yellowed and tattered on the walls, and there were claims *But we love you! you are our son!* that sickened me but I could not tell them *This is my season in hell, in this house* could not tell any of them *To live a day longer in this house is not possible* and so I fled taking with me what would fit into a duffel bag, what loose bills from the house it was reasonable to believe would not be missed, or would not be much missed, and I returned to Sparta and to the ugly iron bridges spanning the Black River and to River Street where the wish is always to think *Nothing has changed* except the corner where Dunphy's had been was now a weedy and trash-strewn vacant lot nominally a parking lot, and there were more barges on the river, and more trucks including tractor-trailers clattering along the narrow waterfront streets, certainly there were more shrieking gulls swooping and darting out of the sky in flashes of soiled white feathers and on the river riding the choppy waves like painted decoys and their cries harsher than I recalled, more plaintive.

Enfin, ô bonheur, ô raison—d'or de la lumière nature my heart was filled with joy, an almost unbearable happiness flooded my veins, how happy I was to be back falling to my knees to kiss the filthy paving stones of River Street.

In the River House there were strangers drinking in the twilit smoke haze, more women than in the past, but none of these women in any way resembled Magda Maria. Beside me in the long horizontal mirror behind the bar drinking with me was one of the Vietnam vets who'd been cheated by Ike Balboa speaking now with bitter satisfaction of what had happened to Ike, that the cruel bastard deserved, and of Magda Maria it was said that she'd been injured in a fall down a flight of stairs, another time left outside unconscious in the backseat of a car where she'd nearly frozen to death, still Magda Maria was alive and if she had not yet showed up at the River House (it was only 10 P.M., the tavern wouldn't close until 2 A.M.) possibly she would, unless she was at the Cloverleaf, or the Black Bass, or with someone at the Empire Hotel. In the Cloverleaf there was no one at the bar who resembled Magda Maria, in the Black Bass there was no one at the bar who resembled Magda Maria, except when I drew closer, staring at a woman slumped at the bar in the company of a thick-necked bald man with glinting eyeglasses suddenly I recognized Magda Maria, her beautiful face now ravaged as if corroded, enormous eyes in shadowy sockets and deep circles beneath the eyes, and the wide fleshy crimson mouth, and her hair loose and matted falling past her shoulders not so shimmering-dark now but dull, threaded with gray. This woman was my age perhaps or older and seemed at first not to see me, as I approached her staring and blinking, asked was she Magda Maria?—and now the woman took note of me startled and uneasy yet smiling, a quick mechanical smile with pursed lips as if she did not wish to bare her (stained? rotted?) front teeth. Ignoring the thick-necked bald man I asked again was she Magda Maria, now a wary expression like a gauze mask came over her face, finally she said *Maybe. Once.*

. . . *could die together* Magda Maria whispered and the thought came to me immediate and helpless *Yes this is meant to be.* I'd brought Magda Maria back to the hotel with me, a night and a day and another night we lay together on the bed or in the bed sprawling naked and heavy-limbed with sleep, the torpor of love overcame us, kisses that drew blood, I loved the taste of Magda Maria's blood she warned was poisoned, I loved her small white maimed feet covered in grime, the two smallest toes of her feet missing for both had had to be amputated after freezing, to prevent gangrene. And it was so, Magda Maria's teeth were stained and rotted. So lonely!—Magda Maria gripped me with her stick-arms tight around my neck, we slept, we woke, we drank from the bottle I'd brought back to the hotel, we shot up with heroin I'd bought on Union Street, Magda Maria's breasts were small and slack and her little belly protruded hard as a drum, I could feel her ribs, the delicacy of her rib cage, Magda Maria was telling me a disjointed story of a rich man who'd wanted to take her to Montreal with him, or was in fact planning to take her, and Magda Maria was telling me a disjointed story about her mother who'd died of a wasting-away disease a long time ago when Magda Maria had been a schoolgirl at the Catholic academy and terrified at the change in her mother, the change in her mother's personality caused by her sickness, except Magda Maria spoke of her mother's soul, I could not follow the convolutions of Magda Maria's stories for I was very sleepy, so very happy in Magda Maria's arms kissing, biting, whispering and laughing together plotting *D'you know what would be lovely?—to fall asleep with you and never wake up, just the two of us.* Magda Maria was wistful, yearning, like a little girl you wanted to protect from her own evil. And so with a tarnished spoon and a blue-tinged flame I prepared a liquid medication with the most beautiful name—"snow"—and steadying my hand, I injected this magic balm into a vein on the inside of Magda Maria's bruised knee, for other veins of Magda Maria's were too small, or too rubbery, or had dried up like shallow riverbeds in late summer; and when the liquid hit her heart, Magda Maria's beautiful bloodshot eyes swooned—*Oh! I love you.* And next I injected myself, in a ropey vein on the underside of my left foot that was encrusted with dirt, an awkward shot since there was bone just beneath the skin, the needle kept striking. *Love love love only you.* In our lumpy swaybacked bed with soiled sheets in room 408 of the Empire Hotel where (we believed) we would be found dead in a day or two by a housekeeper who would claim she had never seen a couple so rapturous in death, a doomed couple OD'd on heroin and liquor and such tales would be told of us how we'd died to consummate our love for there was no other way. I could not clearly recall the name of Magda Maria's middle-aged lover of long ago but I did recall my youthful envy of him. Very sleepy now, we were sinking into darkness. In our embrace in our naked fever-skinned

bodies and on the river the mournful horns of the freighters and
when I woke hours later I was blind, I could not open my eyes for
my eyelashes were stuck together, a woman's brittle hair smelling
of chemicals lay across my mouth. Was Magda Maria alive?—
sleeping heavily, sprawled and moaning in her sleep, sweating, an
oily musk-smelling sweat, in her throat layered in grime there were
pulses beating feebly beneath the skin, I lay beside her in the
wreckage of our love holding her as she began to breathe more la-
boriously, making a guttural sound *Uh-uh-uh* like a sexual moan,
unless it was the sound of my own harsh breathing, phlegm in my
throat, a taste of black bile at the back of my mouth, like heavy
slumberous snakes our limbs were coiled together, only a little
more, I thought, only a little more for each of us, before we could
slip into the comfort of oblivion, not much more, an inch, another
few seconds *Magda Maria I will never abandon you* but I lost consciousness and sometime in the night Magda Maria must have ceased
breathing, must have slipped over the edge without me, this second
time when I awakened Magda Maria was utterly still, unyielding
in my arms, my lips brushed against her cold lips evoking no response, her skin was clammy-cold, I could find no pulse in her
throat, I could find no pulse in her wrist, I could find no heartbeat
inside her fragile rib cage, in mounting panic I called her name but
I could not revive my darling Magda Maria and so I slipped from
our filth-stiffened bed and barefoot and naked and with shaking
fingers groped for my scattered clothing, groped for my water-
stained shoes, left twilit room 408 of the Empire Hotel smelling of
our love, dried semen-mucus and vomit and death, and fled.

Still she's waiting for me. In Sparta. I know this. Any time I
return. Stepping into the River House. Approaching the bar. Not
the farther end but the nearer, near the door with the stained-glass
fanlight. Magda Maria alone, with her whiskey. My love. Waiting.

Lines from Arthur Rimbaud's *A Season in Hell* quoted in this work of fiction are trans-
lated by Louise Varèse.

A Princeton Idyll

661 Covenant Avenue #14
St. Paul, Minn.
March 8, 2005

Dear Muriel Kubelik,

Hello! I am Bertrand Niemarck's granddaughter Sophie whom you last saw in March 1969. Forgive me for writing to you "out of the blue"—after thirty-six years.

Last time you saw me, Ms. Kubelik, I was a chubby little dimple-faced girl of seven. Now I am a chubby big dimple-faced girl of forty-three. I wonder, would my Niemarck grandparents who so doted on their little Sophie recognize her now!

I have your Moore Street address from a Princeton acquaintance who discovered "M. Kubelik" in the phone directory. So I am writing brashly and blindly with the assumption that 1) You are indeed "Murll" who worked for my grandparents Elizabeta and Bertrand Niemarck at 99 Olden Lane, Princeton, in the 1950s and 1960s; and 2) You will have the time and inclination to reply to me, Sophie Niemarck, after so long.

Hoping to hear from you soon, eagerly—

Sophie

661 Covenant Avenue #14
St. Paul, Minn.
March 19, 2005

Dear Muriel Kubelik,

Forgive this (second) intrusion! It's been almost two weeks since
I wrote to you and I'm afraid that my brashness must have
offended you, I am so sorry. Should have enclosed a stamped
self-addressed envelope for your reply as I will now.

And if I offended you by calling you "Murll" which you
probably haven't heard in thirty-six years (but which seemed to
make you smile in those days, I'd thought) please forgive me for
this blunder, too.

I am appealing to you with a certain urgency. At the Institute
for Advanced Study in Princeton where my grandfather
Dr. Niemarck was a renowned logician it was variously argued that
1) Time is infinite, 2) Time is finite, 3) Time is "flowing," 4) Time
is static: a "fourth dimension." Which it is, I don't know, but I do
know that, for some of us, time is RUNNING OUT.

This is a melancholy season for me. Late winter when the
snow looks like used Kleenex. Late winter when my grandfather
died that sudden and mysterious death.

Anything you can tell me about Dr. Niemarck's death, and
the events leading up to it, would be so appreciated, dear Ms.
Kubelik! As my grandparents' housekeeper you were an intimate
of their lives, and must have known much that was happening,
though discreetly (like most housekeepers, I'd guess) you would
not say a word to violate your employers' privacy. But now, so
many years have passed. I guess I'm becoming desperate, my
father recently died, and I am not on easy terms with my mother.

My father was Andre Niemarck, my mother is Lydia. Do you
remember us, Ms. Kubelik? Or has it been too long?

Surely you remember the distinguished Bertrand Niemarck, I
hope!

I've asked my parents about Grandpa Niemarck, many
times. They'd told me—vaguely, evasively—that he had "medical
problems" and died of a stroke at the age of seventy-eight, in bed.
My grandmother Niemarck would speak of a "mental illness"
crinkling her face as if the subject gave off a bad odor. Always
there has been secrecy, subterfuge among the Niemarcks!

You loved my grandfather, too, Muriel, I think? As we all did?

"Murll"—this was all I could manage as a little girl, of your
beautiful name "Muriel." Many times you watched me at my
grandparents' house when we came to visit. I remember your
dark, deep-set eyes that seemed to see so much, yet disclosed
so little. Your hair that was thick and springy and always
wrapped in a kind of roll, or coil, at the back of your head.
When you polished my grandmother's silver in the gloomy
dining room, at the long table, light reflected upward onto
your face in little ripples; you took such care, my fussy grandmother couldn't find fault. And when I stumbled through my
piano lessons on my grandfather's Steinway, propped up on a
cushion, always I hoped that you would hear, you would smile
to hear me hitting the right notes, but you never said a word,
not even of praise.

You were a young woman then, I have to realize. (Everyone
in my grandparents' household seemed "old.") After my grandmother sold the house, you surely moved on to other employment
in Princeton. How I wish I'd kept in touch with you, somehow!
But I was such a young child when my grandfather died,
and as I was growing up (a nomadic academic life in New
Haven, CT, Ithaca, NY, Columbus, OH, at last in Minneapolis
where my professor-father had teaching positions) I had reason
to believe that many things pertaining to Princeton were kept
from me.

So much more to say! But I will break off now.

Awaiting your reply in the enclosed envelope or, if you prefer,
my e-mail address is sriddle@earthlink.net.

Sophie

38 Moore St
Princeton NJ
3/25/05

Dear Sophie Niemark

It is a surprise to hear from you. It was a long time ago. "Little Sophie" grown up now. As you say its too bad you & the Niemarks did not wish to keep touch. Now I am 71 yrs old & very alone but not a bitter woman like some others.

 My memory is not so good of those years. I do not think of them much. After Dr Niemark passed away it came out in the papers how famous he was, I had only a small idea of, like Mr. Eintsein who came to that house sometimes when I was new to the Niemarks, this was long ago in 1953 or 1954. And other men who came to the Neimark house who were at the Instute, some of them were foreign but mostly they were gracious gentlemen like Dr Niemarcks & Mr. Eintsein who is so famous everywhere, his picture known even by the ignorant.

 Your grandmother was not so nice. Did you know Mrs Niemark should not fulfil Dr Niemarks wish for me after his death as he had promised.

 Maybe it is a joke that you give "e-mail address" as if I would have a computer here.

Muriel Kubelik

661 Covenant Avenue #14
St. Paul, Minn.
March 28, 2005

Dear Muriel Kubelik—

Thank you THANK YOU for writing to me. That is so kind of you, Muriel, and I am so very grateful.

But embarrassed, to speak of e-mail to you. Why would you wish to have a personal computer, mine is always giving me trouble except for me it's a professional necessity! I am a (moderately successful) author and illustrator of children's books who has won a few awards & you could say (if you wished to be kind) is "famous" in her field but would not expect you to have heard of me. My writing name is SOPHIE RIDDLE.

Dear Muriel, I am so sorry about Grandmother behaving in such a way. Perhaps you will be more specific about the "promise" Grandpa made to you. Please excuse my grandmother who was not well at that difficult time. I hope you will not judge too harshly.

How a "perfect" family can fall to pieces! And so quickly.

I am remembering the last time we saw each other which was on the sad occasion of my grandfather's funeral it must have been March 10 or 11, 1969. For he died on March 8, 1969. My memory of that time is confused and fractured like a broken mirror. My parents insisted that I was too young to attend the funeral service with the family and so I was made to stay behind in the gloomy old house on Olden Lane with a neighbor girl to look after me. I was so upset, I kept asking *Why isn't Grandpa here? Is Grandpa coming back?* You would have stayed with me except of course you went to the funeral with the others for you were mourning my grandfather like the others. I remember that you returned early from the funeral, Muriel, while the others went on to the cemetery, because you had to help set up the luncheon. I'd slipped away from the neighbor girl and was waiting out in front of the house, in the snow, behind the privet hedge, and when I saw you, I saw your eyes were reddened and raw from crying, and your mouth looked as if it had been hurt, I started to cry, too. And you stared at me as if you didn't know me, what a little troll I was hiding in the privet hedge with chocolate on my mouth, *Oh Sophie* you said and quickly you brought me back into the house to wash my face saying what if someone had seen me eating chocolates at such a time! and later you said something so strange, Muriel, I remember it to this day, *That chocolate on your face, Sophie, for a moment I thought you'd hurt yourself and it was blood.*

Up to Christmas 1965 (I've calculated) when I was three years, ten months old, I was Grandpa's little girl; after that, Grandpa seemed hardly ever to be home when my parents brought me to visit, and our visits were less frequent. And I was never allowed to be alone with Grandpa. (As I came to realize, later.) Muriel, why was this? Was there something shameful about my "distinguished" grandfather, that only the family knew?

Anything you might tell me, Muriel, would be SO APPRECIATED.

Sure, I've read all the Princeton memoirs and biographies of that era I can get my hands on as well as those few books of Bertrand Niemarck's that are comprehensible to the layman. (My grandfather was a logician with a "soft humanist streak" as he called it, apologetically.) He was writing a memoir titled *A Princeton Idyll* over many years, sections were published but the book was never completed and—so frustrating!—the manuscript wasn't found among his papers after his death. Once I asked my father if the memoir had been destroyed and my father became angry with me for it was their way—my parents' way—their strategy—to become angry with *me*, their misfit daughter. No wonder I write silly "riddle" books for children aged zero to eight, is it?

Not that they are so very silly. I've won a few awards.

Muriel, I am deeply sorry/mortified to learn of my grandmother's selfishness. Please provide details!

This time, I enclose a stamped envelope for your reply. Also, one of Sophie Riddle's more popular books. (If you're curious!)

With much, much hope across the miles/years—

Sophie

38 Moore St
Princeton NJ
3/31/05

Dear Sophie

Thank you for the book. It is so amazing to me little Sophie has
become a successful author. I am not surprised, you were so smart
& had so many questions. Do you remember Dr Neimarck called
you my little chikadee. This is a very nice picture book, wish I had
grandchildren to give to. The big woolly dog is like your grandfathers dog Oskar that was a "sheepdog" and the little girl is
meant to be you? I have not heard the name "Sophie Riddle" it is
a strange name, I see you have written many books. At the library
I saw 8 books on the shelve by "Sophie Riddle." Dr Neimark
would be so proud.

It is a good surprise to hear from you. Thank you. I was very
happy to work for such a distinguished family. I left home at age 15,
I did not look back. My family was in Paterson NJ, there were 11
children that is like a joke now. When I came to the house on
Olden Lane I was 19 & when left I was 36 & a matur woman. I was
very respectful of your parents also. Mrs N gave me a good refer-
ence I think for I was hired by the Strunks on Battle Rd where I
was housekeeper for 14 yrs. I have been asked sometimes to be
interviewed about the "old days" at the Instute what I remember of
Dr Niemarck & Mr Eintsein & some others for they were all
famous genises, the men I mean not the women. Always I say it was
a happy time working for such people, of course housework &
cooking in those days was not so well paid as now but you could be
made to feel "one of the family" though of course you were not.

It is a sad time to think of. I believe that a fair sum of
rennumeration owed to me after 36 yrs would be $15,700.

Sophie you will be very kind to remember "Murll" in such a way.

Truely yours,
Muriel Kubelik

38 Moore St.
Princeton NJ
4/6/05

Dear Sophie

I have had opportunity to rethink my estimat of a "fair sum"
& think that $15,700 is too high, that I quoted to you. I would
not wish to be ungrateful for any sum you would wish to
send me.

Here is a good memory of those days before Dr Neimarcks
trouble when you were a little girl but walked holding his hand. I
would dress you for outdoors, even in winter & your grandfather
& Oskar went out walking in the Instute woods in the snow. In
summer you would walk to town & Dr. Niemark would do his
erands & drop by the smoke shop for his cigar he had to have fresh
& afterward he would treat you to ice cream at the Nassu Inn, do
you remember Sophie, Dr Niemark would ask me to come along
sometimes. Mrs N did not like this, I think!

Later when Dr Neimark had his spells you could not be
allowed to be with him, that was why. Especially Mrs N was
disgusted with him for she had not married such a man to be his
nurse. Nor did a lady like Mrs N have the strength to nurse a
disturbed man like Dr N in those years. Some days he was very
sick but other days better, he would tell me my kindness to
him would one day be renumerated so Sophie you see, I loved
Dr Neimark as you did. But I knew him as you did not.

I knew him as the other genises did not.

Well there is more to say but not now. I am very tired. My
heart is beatting hard enough to hurt. I hope that I will hear from
you soon. I am in need of Coumadin pills, Medicaid does not
reumburse the full sum.

When you are alone & old you become a begger.

Truely yours,
Muriel Kubelik

661 Covenant Avenue #14
St. Paul, Minn.
April 6, 2005

Dear Muriel Kubelik,

I have your letter of March 31, I have not known how to answer. I
am so grateful that you would write to me with such warmth and
I long to hear more but the sum you have suggested is a shock to
me, I have to confess.

I wish that I had such a sum of money that I might freely give
to you but a children's book author does not make much money,
Muriel, I'm afraid. I have drifted through my life after leaving
college in one rented apartment or another and have not saved
much money though my expenses as a single woman are modest. I
did not wish to live with my parents as I might have, not at my
age. I did have an "entanglement of the heart" in my late twenties,
it was a mistake I did not make a second time.

Muriel, I am so lonely sometimes! I wish that I lived closer to
you, I would come to visit you.

I have a terrible homesickness for Princeton, that I have not
seen in twenty years. It would break my heart to drive by the
Institute where Grandpa would take me hiking in the woods with
his sheepdog Oskar and for lunch in the cafeteria where he had so
many friends and colleagues who clearly loved him: and young
men who revered him, wanting to shake his hand. It would break
my heart to see the old English Tudor house at 97 Olden Lane,
probably "renovated" by strangers . . . It was a dark gloomy house
by day yet at night with lights on, so warm and festive. In the bay
window at Christmas there would be a ten-foot evergreen with so
many lights and beautiful glittering ornaments, and so many presents beneath! This time I'm thinking of, it was meant to be a
happy time but something had happened, my mother was upset
pulling me upstairs to where our rooms were when we visited, in
the kitchen there were angry raised voices. No one ever raised his

voice at the Niemarcks'—this was so strange. I was crying, Momma was saying over and over *You shouldn't have done that! Oh why did you do such a thing!* It was my father's voice that was angry, I could not hear my grandfather's voice. Why I was crying, I don't know.

After that, everything was changed. Our visits to the Niemarcks were never the same again.

What was it, Muriel? Why?

Enclosed is a token of my esteem for you, and my affection across the years. I realize that it is far below the sum you believe to be "fair" but I hope that you will accept it. And I hope that you will write back to me, in the enclosed envelope.

Thank you!

> With a hopeful heart,
> Sophie

661 Covenant Avenue #14
St. Paul, Minn.
April 9, 2005

Dear Muriel,

Our letters crossed in the mail! Yours of April 6 just arrived. Thank you Muriel THANK YOU. I was worried that I'd offended and disappointed you, but I should have known better.

That is indeed a precious memory of my grandfather taking me and his sheepdog Oskar walking—he called it "tramping"—in the Institute woods. And our long "hike" into Princeton which was always an adventure. Sometimes we made purchases at Hinkson's Stationers and Urkin's Hardware, sometimes we dropped by the public library on Witherspoon, there was the "Five and Dime" as Grandpa called it on Nassau, and there was the underground restaurant—the Annex—where the food, Grandpa said, wasn't very good but anyway was cheap. At the Nassau Inn there was the Garden Room with all the glass, you could look out onto Palmer Square and, at Christmas time, at the enormous evergreen glittering with lights. There was a smoke shop on Witherspoon where Grandpa bought his special cigars and sometimes newspapers and magazines and a comic book for me—"Donald Duck" was my favorite.

Yes, the "big wooly dog" in my picture book is based on Oskar. He had such a coarse fur, that grew over his eyes! He loved to chase squirrels. (In Princeton, there were such unusual black squirrels!—like the seventeen-year locusts, you don't find such Princeton novelties anywhere else.)

Muriel, I wonder if you remember a trick my grandfather's young friend Richard Feynman taught Oskar? It was so unexpected and comical—to retrieve a stick thrown across the lawn but not directly, in the usual way, for Oskar was trained to set off all excitedly at a 180° angle, and to work his way back to the stick, with all sorts of detours, before he earned his reward. The trick always took observers by surprise, they laughed and laughed . . .

Strange to realize, Feynman is dead now. No one had been more full of life. I wonder if you knew, my grandfather's handsome young friend went on to become a great physicist?

You'd mentioned Albert Einstein, you'd seen at the Niemarcks' house. He'd died in 1955, long before I was born, but my grand-parents and their friends still spoke of him as if he was alive. He'd lived in a white clapboard house on Mercer Street, much smaller than my grandparents' house, we passed all the time. Of course Einstein is a "legend" in the world but in Princeton there were other men almost equally esteemed, like the philosopher Jacques Maritain, my grandfather was close friends with, and the composer Roger Sessions, and his fellow logician Kurt Gödel, and the Hungarian physicist Wigner, and the man who was building a computer, von Neumann. These are names I came to know long after my grandfather's death, when I was old enough to appreciate my family legacy, so to speak. But I do remember the Nietzsche translator and philosopher Walter Kaufmann who came by on his bicycle to introduce himself to Bertrand Niemarck and who became one of my grandfather's good friends. So boyish-looking, people mistook him for an undergraduate at the university. "Uncle Walter" he wished me to call him for he seemed to love children. He took my picture with Grandpa and Oskar, many times. These photographs he gave to me, I remember holding them in my hand, but later they were "lost."

Amid the Niemarcks, so much was "lost." But I am bent upon retrieval.

Dear Muriel, I am hoping that my check for $500 was not an insult to you. Perhaps I can send another soon. I know that when a woman is alone in this world of "couples" and "family values" no matter her age it's a hard lonely life. Believe me, there are many types of beggars!

I look forward to your reply, Muriel. Envelope enclosed.

> Your Sophie Riddle with her Hopeful Heart—
> Sophie

38 Moore St
Princeton NJ
4/14/05

Dear "Sophie Riddle"

Maybe it is a riddle you are telling me, or maybe it is a joke, what I am meant to think I dont know.

If it is a joke it is not funny. No I am not "insulted" by $500. If you are a woman of 71 a "domestic employe" all your life now living alone in two rooms & without family or anyone to speak my name & not in the best health & forced to beg for crumbs you are not "insulted"!!!

Your letter is so proud! You are a "Niemarcks" & so you are proud telling me of the "great men" of your grandfathers life. Dr Niemarcks was a good man & a kindly man & it did not matter

to me that he was one of the genises of that time like it means
to you.

It is very sad "a childrens book author does not make much
money" I am very sad for you. Of course you are poor as me, &
you think you are lonely like me. Oh yes.

There is some trick hidden in your letter. Please to tell me why
you speak of "Walter Kaufmann." I will not write to you again
unless this is explained.

Muriel Kubelik

661 Covenant Avenue #14
St. Paul, Minn.
April 17, 2005

Dear Muriel Kubelik—

I have been baffled—shocked—by your letter of April 14 which
seems so angry and sarcastic. I read and reread it—there must be
some misunderstanding, Muriel.

There is no "hidden trick" in my letter, Muriel, truly!

I will enclose here another check with the apology that it is
far, far less than you deserve.

If somehow I have offended you, in my typical clumsy way, it
was surely inadvertent and unintended. I try to keep my "upbeat"
(i.e., annoying) children's-book voice from intruding into my
adult relations but often fail. So I'm told!

Why did I mention Walter Kaufmann? The memory of him
came to me so vividly. Of Grandpa's many friends "Uncle Walter"
was the nicest. I think that my father was somewhat jealous of
him, for my grandfather took so warmly to him, as to a son; and
there was always the feeling, I learned later, that my father had
"disappointed" my grandfather in his career. When I was older I
read many books by Walter Kaufmann but never found any
mention of Bertrand Niemarck which was disappointing.

One day I read an obituary, Walter Kaufmann had died at a young age of an aneurysm, not yet sixty, in the early 1980s. Such a shock, I was depressed for days . . .

Truly, Muriel, there was no trick or riddle in my letter. I am the least "riddlesome" of people. A glance at me and you know all there is to know of me. Sophie Riddle doesn't wear her heart on her sleeve but tattooed on her forehead for all the world to see. In fact she hates riddles.

Hates hates hates the hypocrisy and subterfuge of the (adult, fallen) world. Hates liars.

So Muriel, will you have pity on me?

Sincerely,
Sophie

661 Covenant Avenue #14
St. Paul, Minn.
April 24, 2005

Dear Muriel,

Awaiting your reply with some anxiety. Maybe our letters will "cross" again in the mail. Somewhere above the wilds of western Pennsylvania.

Have read & reread your letter of April 14. I am feeling so damned guilty, & such a hypocrite. Enclosed here is a check for $1,200, exactly half my royalty statement for this quarter. You are quite justified in being sarcastic about my Niemarck pride. There is an odor of vanity & self-esteem even in acknowledging how far below Bertrand Niemarck's world I have settled for. Below even the career of Andre Niemarck who was forced into early retirement by his sociology colleagues at the University of Minnesota. There is pride in abject wallowing oh yes! Bertrand Niemarck who was a gentleman as well as a genius would feel pity for his only grandchild, and sorrow, but not, I hope, blame.

For I have worked hard—so very hard!—for the meager "success" that I have.

My grandfather would often quote his friend Einstein—"The Lord God is subtle, but malicious He is not."

I want to believe this. I must believe this.

Would you call me, Muriel? My number is (651) 373-9462, I am always home. Of course, please call collect.

I have tried to call you but a record comes on announcing that your number is "no longer in service."

Awaiting your reply, with hope—

Sophie

38 Moore St
Princeton NJ
4/29/05

Dear Sophie

Well I am sorry too, my letter written too fast. Maybe there is no trick to either of us except tricks are played on us of cruelty and scorn because we are so trusting.

You are generous to send these checks. THANK YOU. I am very grateful and will hope to tell you some things precious for you, to know.

Your grandfather Dr N always loved his little Sophie & did not turn from you but became a sick man, an alcohollic in those last years. He would not pity you I think for he would not judge you like himself & would be proud of you, such a career is a wonderful thing.

Yet some things about Dr N you did not know. Tho' a good-hearted man he was not a fool. When that saying of Eintsein was remarked that the Lord God is not "malicious" Dr N would laugh & say his old friend was just silly, like pretending he was on good terms with the "Lord God" & knew the first thing about the universe, Dr N said was a "dice throw but lacking dice & a thrower" that was Dr Niemarcks wisdom.

Dr Niemarks was a handsome man, until the end. In his sickness his skin turned yellow, thats a sign of cirrosis of the liver. His face was lined & there was a sorrow in his eyes. Before the sickness he was always laughing & joking in a quiet way & he said to me, he was a logic-man because the world was not a logic-world. In his study I would see so many pieces of paper, covered in numbers and "equations" it made me dizzy to see. Most of them on the carpet, or in the waste basket crumpled. He had another study at the Instute, I never saw. Such a clean man, bathed each morning & wore only fresh-laundered clothes & Mrs N was strict with me, how to starch & iron his white cotton shirts for he would not wear any others. Mrs N was vain of her genise husband. I had to smile at that woman thinking anyone would care for her, for her silly opinions, without *him*. All the ladies of Princeton must have know this, how little they counted for except through their husbands.

The "ax-face lady" the hired help spoke of your grandmother. The italian men who did the grounds, their name for Mrs N was not so nice as this.

Mostly Mrs N was fair with me, I think. Until the last year or so. Maybe you are right, the old woman was not well in her head, either.

Mrs N used to say, If Muriel is in charge things will be done well. Houseclean & cook, polish furniture, silverware etc. scrub floors, tubs, toilets smeared with the shit of the rich etc. Loads of laundry, & ironing. And later, tending to the poor sick old man such a lady would not wish to touch nor especially to smell for Dr N lost habits of cleanliness in his last months.

I would bathe him, when necessary. I would shave his trembling chin & clip hairs from his ears & nose. I would massage his back that seemed broken, his sallow skin. He would cry like a great helpless baby, that I would touch him in kindness & not in rebuke.

Yes it was Christmas 1965. When your parents & Mrs N were so upset. That time that Dr Niemark ran from the house at night to his office at the Instute, out of shame. The family did not know where he was for hours. Later, your parents asked me to take you to Christmas Carol to get you out of the house. You were such a scared little girl for once not chattering like a chikadee to give me a headache. I held your hand that was so little in your white angora glove and tried to think what to say to you but I could not.

It was later after Dr N's funeral, you were waiting out by the hedge & youd been eating chocolates, you were older then, and bigger, and it was not so easy to like you, I think as it is not so easy to like any child that becomes older. I saw the fear in your face & I said not to be afraid, Sophie. What happened to your grandfather will never happen to you.

It makes me sad to tell such things, I think that I will stop now.

Truely yours
Muriel Kubelik

661 Covenant Avenue #14
St. Paul, Minn.
May 3, 2005

Dear Muriel,

Your letter is astonishing to me. I am stunned and enraptured and have no words except to plead with you, *please continue.* Enclosed is an envelope for your reply. (I wish that you would call me, collect. I have so many questions, my mind races & churns, I couldn't sleep much of last night.) I will enclose also another check, not so generous as I wish it could be, dear Muriel!

(I remember the white angora gloves. I remember *A Christmas Carol* at McCarter Theatre. I remember my grandparents' house so quiet. We left early that year to return home.)

Urgently yours,
Sophie

661 Covenant Avenue #14
St. Paul, Minn.
May 4, 2005 3 AM

Dear Muriel—

In the afterglow of your haunting & mysterious letter my brain is
rushing too rapidly for sleep. I've been remembering how in a
selection from *A Princeton Idyll* my grandfather wrote with wry
humor of a colloquium at the Institute in 1951 called "Is Time's
Arrow Reversible?" in which he'd participated along with his
colleagues Einstein, Gödel, von Neumann, and others whose
arguments were too abstruse for me to follow, even as my grandfather summarized them. Now I am thinking: *is* time reversible? If
the universe is finite, it might be run backward like clockwork, yes?
(Or no?) But through you, I seem to be traveling backward into
time into that lost world of Princeton so precious to me. Thank you
THANK YOU dear Muriel for entering my life that has been such a
riddle!

Wishing that we might meet sometime soon, your

Sophie

38 Moore St
Princeton NJ
5/11/05

Dear Sophie

Thank you for the new check. What a good kind lady you are
grown to be. The Neimarcks would be proud of their grandaughter
so generous like them.

Such a small town Princeton was in those days. The "domestic
help" would shop for food at Davidsons grocery on Nassu, now
there are two food stores but then only Davidsons where you saw

everybody. The aisles so narrow you could barely push a cart past another cart. Boxes in the aisles. Many forign men and women. Among these I moved in my dark rayon clothes like a uniform, Mrs N liked for me to wear. I was a neat young woman shy to speak with strangers and my teeth were not good, I did not wish to smile. Yet there were men who looked at me in a certain way. I was not eager to be anyones wife for I knew from my mother what that would mean, a man rutting on you as he wished & making babies in you etc that was not for me. Wet slap-slapping of skins, groaning & carrying-on it disgusted me, what "sex" is. Now I am an old woman, almost no hair & its white, a hump to my back from so many years of stooping over scrubbing the toilets of the rich. Now nobody looks at me, I see couples on the street, so many retired people here in Princeton, I want to laugh in their faces like this is some kind of masquerade. You don't love each other, its a joke that anybody would love you, just you could not do better & now you are stuck together like glue.

When I came to the Neimarcks house I felt different, for a while. I worked hard but was young & had a strong back & it made me happy, to be praised by such people as your grandparents. I was shy in that house, the rooms were so dark with heavy drapes and lace curtains between. Every room was beautiful to me, silk wall paper & such furniture, & beautiful "Oriental" carpets like what you would see in a castle. When I first came there I was a cleaning girl not yet cook or housekeeper but I thought if I worked hard & did not ask for much money, I would be kept on. Dr Neimarck was always kind to me but very particular about how his study would be cleaned & "aired." I must not move any papers except to dust or polish beneath them, then to replace them exactly. Sometimes I would look at Dr Niemarcks writings, I could not make sense of them no more than if they were a forign languge.

Many visitors to the Niemarks house, I came to know their faces & some of them were forign speaking. Mrs N said they were genises. I thought, You are as stupid as I am in knowing what such genises are. One of them came alone on his bicycle, I thought he was a student but this was "WK" who was so kind to me, he would call me Muriel & did not seem to act like I was "help." Mrs N saw us laughing together, there was a flush in my face I knew. I had to hide my mouth, my teeth were not good. Once on Olden Lane I was walking & WK stopped his bicycle to walk with me. He wore cordroy troussers and a V neck sweater like a boy. His hair was very dark and his eyes were dark and lively. He was not much older than I was. He was not married, I thought. Later he found out it was my birthday, he would take me to the french restarant on Witherspoon street he said, I think he was serious. I would wear my best dress which was black tafetta. I would wear stockings & high heels. I was so excited! WK had talked to me of how he was the first jew in the philosophy dept at the university & very lonely. He told me that Dr N was a "polly-math" which was a danger for a genise, because you are drawn to many things, & that was his danger, too. WK talked to me of poetry & recited a poem in German he said was by a poet named "Gerth" & later he recited a poem in English, he said it was his own. I wish that I could remember it but I forgot it at once. I was in love with WK, I will tell you this. Now he is dead & I am an old woman. But I was in love with Dr N too like you would love your father wanting to please him. When WK came to the house to take me to the french restarant the Niemarcks were there & Mrs N stared at me, very angry. Dr N smiled but was not pleased. He took WK in his study & shut the door & they were there some time & Mrs N said to me, Muriel go change your clothes. So WK went away, he was embarassed.

WK was not in love with me, I know. He meant to be kind. They were often kind to me. Its bad times you remember when you are angry but truely they were kind to me. Yet I hated them so, it was like a fire inside me. Even your parents, I did not know well, I hated that they could "boss" me if they wished & when they came to stay, there was extra work. Even you, when you were born, the Neimarks were so excited to be grandparents, even this little baby Sophie with blue eyes & fat cheeks sometimes I hated & wished in my heart would sicken & die.

I had to push you in your buggy. In your stroller. There were nannies in the park, we looked at each others babies. I liked to tell how I worked for the Neimarcks, for Dr Neimarck was at the Instute. Only the most important men were at the Instute. You were a fat baby & very beautiful. You were so blond. In the sun, I would lift the screen so the firey sun came into your eyes then I was afraid, what if you were blinded & I would be blamed! One of my little sisters in Paterson, she died in her crib in a hot spell, she was 5 months & "stopped breathing" nobody knew why.

I thought, Even a rich baby can stop breathing. But you did not.

It happened that sometimes when I came into Dr N's study if he had not heard me knock, he would be surprised & hurry to push some papers over what he was looking at. Saying, Muriel please knock before you come in here. I said that I had knocked but he had not heard me & so I had thought nobody was there, I was sorry.

Mrs N never went into Dr N's study, nor anybody else except if he was there. Except I would clean there, vacum the carpet etc but never touch anything on the desk. On a bookshelve were bottles of whisky & brandy Dr N might serve to visiters sometimes. I would never touch this of course.

Later when WK came to the house, he did not talk with me so much. There was a day, I saw he had forgoten my name. I did not hate WK, I told myself, He will marry one of his own kind. I accepted this.

A while later it happened again that I came into Dr N's study & he had not heard me & he was annoyed at me & embarassed at something, pushing papers over a magazine with a picture cover. I told him I was sorry & went away. When the

Neimarks were gone then I returned & was very careful looking
through all the drawers of the big desk. I was patient till I found
what I was looking for: a magazine hidden inside a folder of
notes.

I could not believe what I saw. On the very cover of this magazine was a naked woman with breasts so heavy she had to hold
them in her hands, & red nipples like plastic, & her legs were
spread, you could see hair at her crotch. In a sweat of disgust I
opened the magazine seeing many naked females, some of them
laying down with legs spread wide, fingers stuck into their
vaginas, mocking smiles on their faces like snouts. Ridiculous
bodies you would not believe are real but made of rubber. SUCK
OR FUCK? I SWALLOW CUM & LOVE IT.

I put away the ugly magazine, I was sick with disgust. For
some time after that it was hard for me to look at Dr N for I
could not believe that such a gentleman would wish to see such
filth. I was very sad about this but had to laugh, if Mrs N should
know! You would not say that Mrs N looked much like the naked
females in such a magazine.

When your parents came for christmas that year, I thought
what I would do. I planned this laughing to myself but I was
scared, that I would be caught. The day before christmas, at
breakfast time, the Niemarcks were downstairs & your parents &
you were looking for one of your books, it was a picture book of
baby elephants & inside was a page from the magazine of a naked
woman sprawled to show her cunt & her fingers stuck inside & her
lipstick mouth open & the words were SUCK ME TILL I SCREAM
BIG DADDY I LOVE IT.

You came in the breakfast room holding the magazine page
like a chikadee chattering & your mother asked what you had in
your hand, I was in the doorway carrying a tray of french toast &
bacon & coffee taking care not to be watching your mothers face
seeing what you had in your hand, it was like a knife was stuck in
her, & turned. Fast as she could she pulled the page from your
fingers saying, Oh. Oh my God. Your father looked up from the

paper he was reading. What is it, he asked. Your mother was saying Oh oh oh God. Where did she find this!

I did not seem to be watching, setting down the tray. Your father took the magazine page from your mother's hand saying, Jesus Christ. What is this.

Dr N & Mrs N had been looking out the window at the busy bird feeder, now Dr N saw what his son Andre had in his hand, so shocked. At the table Dr N held a coffee cup in his hand & I saw that the cup was shaking, & spilled coffee onto the white table-cloth. Now Mrs N was wishing to see what her son was holding but he would not allow it, his face was firey also & he was staring at Dr N & by this time your mother was taking you from the room you were scared & beginning to cry & I was frightened thinking that I should come with you asking your mother what was wrong for now it was upsetting to me also like a boat capsize & what had begun could not be stopped. I followed you & your mother but your mother snapt at me saying, Go away, Muriel, & pulled you upstairs & back in the breakfast room your father was angry & his voice sharp & loud as I had never heard it & how this would end, I didn't know I ran away to my room on the third floor to hide.

I was excited & scared, & I was laughing hiding my face in my pillow. Ever after that hour, Dr N was a changed man. You could see it in his face he was older & his eyes damp with shame. Your grandmother was so disgusted with him she would not eat with him often. After the christmas time she went away to visit with relatives for three weeks, during that time Dr N started his drinking, that he would never stop for years.

Between Dr N and your parents, there was never any good feeling again. Of course they would not allow Dr N to be with you. Your parents did not often come to visit. Sometimes I saw Dr N downstairs in the house alone & the rooms darkened & he seemed like he was lost for he could not do his work very well any longer, he had lost his spirit, I think. He would not speak of himself as a "logic-man" again, that I knew. I would help him to the back bedroom where he slept now, for Mrs N would not allow him upstairs with her. I was sorry for Dr N but smiled to myself thinking, Now you know. All of you, now you know. In my heart it was like a needle pricked me, of happiness.

You will ask, Sophie, why did I do such a thing? Did I hate you & your family? What was the hurt, the Niemarcks had done me, that I would wish such revenge? & truely I would say, There is no reason.

Truely yours
Muriel Kubelik

661 Covenant Avenue #14
St. Paul, Minn.
May 16, 2005

Muriel Kubelik:

I don't believe your vile story. I don't believe a word you have told me. You are a slanderer, a liar, a mentally ill depraved old woman. Please will you never write to me again!

SN

38 Moore St
Princeton NJ
5/26/05

Dear Sophie

I am surprised, I had thought you wished memories of the Neimarks & so I have told you. If you wish me to lie to you, it will

not come so cheap as the truth. If you wish my story changed, that
I have not yet told to any "interviewer" you will have to pay for it.

Truely yours,

MK

661 Covenant Avenue #14
St. Paul, Minn.
May 29, 2005

MK:

Now are you blackmailing me? I don't believe your cruel &
vindictive story & if you slander my family, I will take legal action
I promise you.

How could you defile the memory of this man who was so
good to you, so beloved by all who knew him. Bertrand Niemarck
who is listed in the *Columbia History of Western Philosophy* and was a
beautiful and noble human being while you are vile as a
cockroach. I hate you & ask you *please not to write to me again.*

SN

38 Moore St
Princeton NJ
6/17/05

Dear Sophie

A cockroach! I am not a stranger to cockroaches. You would be
surprised, the roaches in those big old houses of Princeton, in
those days. Your bitch-grandma made me spray DDT till I was
sick, in the kitchen & bathrooms of that old house.

You will not believe, I did love your grandfather & was very sorry sometimes, how his cruel family would not forgive him tho many times he wept & begged for this, I heard him. He would not forgive himself & became alcohollic, & later would not eat for fear of "poisons" in his food & lost so much weight he was like a skelton at his death. You did not know that Dr Niemarck died at the Instut, not at home. He would stay in his office there & drink & sometimes sleep there for Mrs N did not like him at home & he was found in the morning one day fallen down some stairs, his skull was broken on the concrete. Then they were sorry in your cruel family, it was too late.

Muriel help me, I am so sick, Dr N would say. I was the one to come to him, where he was vomiting & nothing would come up & then a gush of something yellow & pus-colored splattered on the bathroom floor. Once I was washing Dr N & saw how his old-man belly was loose & yellow like old piano keys. His old-man pennis hung down between his legs like a chicken neck. His skin was grizzled, his chest was caved in & you could see the ribs. His breath was sour, like something rotted. He said, Muriel, will you touch me? His voice was weak & shamed for he knew how none of the fine Princeton ladies would touch him now nor even look at him for the disgust they would feel. I told him yes I would touch him, I washed him with a sponge & dried him in soft towels as you would a baby not wanting to chafe his sore skin. I massaged his shoulders that were covered in liver spots & his back that was bent like a bow, the hump of his spine. He groaned & began to shake & to cry. He said, You are so good to me, Muriel. You are the only one. He would have given me any sum of money then, that I asked, but Mrs N had the control of all money, by that time. He said he would remember me in his will, he promised this but even at the time I thought, probably this would not be so. For I would be cheated by the Neimarks, always one like me is cheated by the bosses & I did not care. I thought, I am strong enough. I am not weak like you, as a nurse would not be. Feeling happiness then, like a bride.

Since you have written, these memories are with me more. Dr Niemarks voice is with me more saying Thank you, Muriel. Its a happy memory when Dr N wept to be touched by me. All these years it was lost, now I have it again.

For this I thank you.

You dont owe me a penny.

Truely yours,
MK

Cutty Sark

You are the love of my life. Only you!

He was seventeen. He woke from sleep with the abruptness of a rifle shot. These past months his sleep had become a stupor, a torpor, a warm suffocating black muck that was his only solace. By day he was suffused with shame for his very name *Smartt* and for what was crudely whispered and scorned and laughed-at that accrued to *Smartt* but by night he slipped from that identity like a young snake shedding its first crinkly skin, no longer *Smartt* but a no-name being of coarse appetites and raw emotions inhabited him, and this was his solace. At such times he did not even dream. If he took his meds as prescribed, he did not dream. Yet even without his meds if he'd worn himself out at lacrosse practice, if he'd been working at his computer late into the night often he didn't dream in any normal way, his stuporous sleep was too deep for dreams descending into that zone of the ocean known as the hadal as his hot-skinned adolescent body sweated through T-shirts and boxers and sheets and mattress covers and his mouth that was a soft mouth, a bruised-looking mouth, a boy-mouth his mother used to kiss became unhinged at the jaws and leaked drool down his chin and when he woke he was swallowing compulsively for the interior of his mouth was dry as baked sand. *Love of my life. Only you!* If he'd been banged-up on the lacrosse field at practice the day before now these muscles and joints began to ache. Here was a return to who he was. Panicked trying to recall where he was—not home, on East 72nd Street, for he was rarely home—had to be a residence hall, in a narrow lumpy bed—but which school?—he'd had to transfer twice in three years—not West Ridge School in the hills of northwestern Massachusetts but, this fall of his junior year, New London Academy, Connecticut—feeling that kick of shamed apprehension, anxiety. In his sticky tangled sheets he whimpered, groaned. His back teeth ached from nighttime grinding. Waking was a physical effort: you had to reassemble the scattered parts of yourself, force them back together.

For maybe she was coming today, to see him. Maybe today, he'd have to see her.

Fully awake now and his eyes open and staring and now the ignominy of the day began, he must plug into his life as *Kit Smartt* for he had no other option.

Except: his uncle he'd never known. His mother's younger brother. This ghost-uncle, this boy—seventeen, in fact—at the time of his death in 1970—had killed himself. Long before Kit was born.

So it was in the family, so to speak. A gene for killing yourself.

And at this school as at Kit's previous boarding schools there had been suicides. Rumors of suicides. More common were suicide attempts—"cries for help" as pious adults called them. Kit Smartt professed scorn for mere "attempts"—as a second-string lacrosse midfielder Kit Smartt could appreciate the distinction between "attempt" and "succeed" and it was considerable. Kit's six-foot hulking roommate Gervais from Montreal professed a grim Catholic repugnance for suicide which was both a "mortal sin" and a "coward's way out." Kit could not share his roommate's belief in sin nor did he believe that there was anything cowardly about suicide but he would not kill himself, ever.

Vowing *Someone else, first. Not me.*

Her recent calls he had not answered. Her e-mail messages he'd deleted without reading. He had come to resent her so bitterly, furious at her and shamed by her and could not bear to hear her voice in his head though it was a beautifully poised voice in which even pleading bore a hint of flirtatious reproach, seduction. *Kit please! At least we can talk—can't we? I will come to New London and take you to that Inn. Your father says there is an Inn. You won't have to be seen by your class-mates with your mother if that's what you most dread, darling.* And somehow he knew, this was the week. His mother—that is, Quincy Smartt—as the world knew her, Quincy Smartt—would arrive at Kit's school someday this week, driving back from Boston to New York City. Unless she was driving to Boston from New York City. Or she was in the area, she was visiting a friend/former lover in New Haven. Kit's father who must have been as deeply shamed by the publication of his (former) wife's memoir quaintly titled *Memoir of a Lost Time* had told Kit that it was up to him, to Kit, if he chose to see his mother, or chose not to see her; but Kit had to know that the custody arrange-ment was still in effect, after four years. (Of course, Kit was now seventeen: you can't expect to manipulate a moody seventeen-year-old as easily as you'd been able to manipulate a confused and heart-broken thirteen-year-old. There was that to consider.) *But I don't love her. I hate her* Kit had wanted to protest but thought better of it, Kit Smartt was a stoic of a kid you could count on to limp off a playing field biting his lip to keep from crying and maybe he has a hairline fracture in a femur and/or a bleeding nose but he will decline even to acknowledge having been fouled when the referee was looking elsewhere. It had been a shock to Kit to discover how bearing the name *Smartt* could be a disadvantage: Kit *Smartt* as an appendage of *Quincy Smartt*, or, like his mother's Prada handbags, an accessory. It was soon after Kit's parents' divorce that the name *Quincy Smartt* first began to accrue something of its present-day notoriety. Since Quincy Smartt was a writer who traveled frequently it had seemed a practical matter, that the child custody arrangements favored Kit's father; no one among Kit's relatives had been tactless enough to remark in his hearing that Quincy Smartt hadn't pressed very strenuously for fuller custody of her son; and so it happened, when Kit wasn't away at one or another of his boarding schools or at one or another of his summer camps, which was most of the time, you could say that he "lived with his father" on East 72nd Street, New York City, in the three-storey brownstone overlooking a courtyard in which he'd always lived; Kit's father Lloyd Smartt was a neuro-surgeon on the staff at Columbia Presbyterian. From earliest child-hood Kit had been made to know that his father was highly respected in his field and so Kit learned young the sobering fact that there can be achievements that matter to some people but to others scarcely at all. "Your mother became restless with just us," Kit's father had told him with a clumsy smile. *Just us!* No one to blame but themselves.

Thirteen when his parents had separated, and soon after di-vorced. Though he'd prided himself on being precocious and brainy and knowing much more than most of his classmates Kit had never quite recovered from the news—unexpected, rudely blunt—that for some time his mother had been involved with another man, or with men; worse yet was the revelation that his mother had a life—a "professional life"—that meant more to her than any merely com-monplace domestic life could mean. *Just us! Not enough for her.*

The last time Kit's father had spoken with him at length had been in early September. "Your mother seems to have a—a need"— Dr. Smartt searched for the precise, tactful word with the air of a neurosurgeon probing an exposed brain with a scalpel that has begun to tremble—"to do these things. These 'public' things. The need may be increasing as your mother gets older."

Kit wondered if *gets older* was meant to be mean. It wasn't like his father to be mean, intentionally.

As Dr. Smartt talked, Kit listened politely. Long ago he'd learned not to attempt to converse with his father except in the most superficial and breezy of ways for Dr. Smartt's forte was the unhurried uninterrupted monologue that revealed so much, like a medical dictation into a machine. "You must wonder how much I knew, Kit—if your mother had ever told me about—what's in the memoir. I'm not sure if you've read the memoir all the way through, Kit, I have to confess that I have not, and we need not discuss that. But no, she did not. Your mother had not told me, and I had not known. But possibly"—here Dr. Smartt paused another time, frowning, proceeding then with the now bloody scalpel that was the instrument to reveal deadly brain malignancies or harmless cysts with equanimity—"I had a sense from time to time that something might have happened when your mother was a girl since she never spoke of her brother Oliver, or very much of her parents, except in joking ways. That is, angry-joking ways. And so much seemed to have happened to Quincy of a 'traumatic' sort already in her life, before I'd met her . . ." Dr. Smartt's voice trailed off like a fading radio station.

Kit wasn't looking at his father. He was furious thinking *Is he apologizing to me? For what?*

A phone began to ring in the next room. Kit heard the housekeeper answer: Dr. Smartt would now be summoned. Quickly Kit excused himself to run upstairs to his room on the third floor taking the steps two at a time.

Cutty Sark. The name had intrigued him, initially.

He was eleven when he'd fallen under the spell of the clipper ship. And that name had intrigued him, too: *clipper ship*. Those nineteenth-century sailing ships with long narrow sleek hulls, sharp bows, great sails billowing in the wind . . .

Looking through photographs in a massive book displayed on a table in his grandfather's study in Tuxedo Park. Christmas it had been. Just Kit and Daddy for Kit's mother wasn't with them, away "traveling on assignment" in a distant part of the world. "Beautiful, eh? *Cutty Sark* is the most famous of the grand old clipper ships." Kit's grandfather had sat heavily beside Kit on the leather sofa to leaf through the book. Kit was fascinated by the dignified old ships with their astonishing sails, as many as twenty sails he could count, their tall vertical masts, upright in a way modern ships were not. Here was romance, adventure! As Kit's grandfather spoke of having visited the *Cutty Sark* Museum in Greenwich, England, when he'd been Kit's age, suggesting that maybe some summer he could take Kit to the museum, Kit stared at the photographs thinking he'd never seen anything so beautiful.

His mother had not left them yet. Had not moved out of the brownstone on East 72nd Street, yet. But more and more often she was away and spoke in hurried snatches to Kit on the phone from distant places—Japan, India—promising Kit she'd bring him back gifts though frequently it seemed she forgot, or her return was delayed by another trip for Quincy Smartt's life had become so complicated the very effort of explaining it to a thirteen-year-old would require too much time.

Just know I love you darling! Always know that.

Cutty Sark had been built in 1869 by a master Scots shipbuilder. Fast-sailing clipper ships were needed to bring to England, from China, the "first tea" of the season. In the famous race with the rival clipper *Thermopylae*, in 1872, both ships sailed out of Shanghai in the same hour but *Cutty Sark* lost her rudder en route and docked in England a week after *Thermopylae*, a journey of many thousands of nautical miles covered in 122 days. Yet *Cutty Sark* was to acquire a fame beyond that of *Thermopylae* for *Cutty Sark* had persevered despite a devastating handicap. In time, clipper ships were replaced by steamships that were more reliable as oceangoing vessels though not capable of the speed of the clipper ship, and lacking its beauty.

Kit's grandfather surprised him with one of the great gifts of his childhood: a *Cutty Sark* modeling kit. Together they constructed a reasonably realistic-appearing model ship measuring twelve inches to the top of its tallest mast. The sails were of canvas and every rosewood-plank in the deck had to be glued in place by hand. There was a copper-plated miniature hull and every minuscule detail of the rigging was authentic. Constructing so intricate a ship was not an easy task. Concentration and patience were required. And there was a battery to insert in the hull, and there was a remote control, for the model clipper could not be a true model of course, its sails were too small to pick up wind and be propelled by it.

One Sunday morning Grandpa Smartt drove Kit to a nearby park to launch their beautiful *Cutty Sark* on a pond amid other battery-driven model boats, most of them sailboats. How thrilled Kit was, and how anxious, seeing their *Cutty Sark* moving across the rippling surface of the pond as if wind-driven . . . He'd have liked his mother to see this spectacle for she was one to exclaim at beautiful and unusual sights, but this was not to be. Through that summer and the following summer Kit's grandfather continued to take him to the park but eventually it happened that the outings ended at about the time Kit's parents separated and Kit was too confused and distracted to care about such a childish hobby.

And Grandpa Smartt became elderly, and infirm, and could no longer drive a car.

Now Kit was seventeen, and his grandfather had been dead for two years. Still prominently displayed in his room was the model ship, on Kit's bureau. At a distance of several feet the miniature *Cutty Sark* took your breath away, so beautifully intricate and airily floating on its pronged pedestal, but up close you could see how the graceful canvas sails that had once been white were now discolored, the rigging and the deck were covered in a fine scrim of dust. Kit would not allow any cleaning woman or housekeeper to touch his model ship, even to dust it carefully. He would have flown into a rage if anyone dared to touch his special things—CDs, DVDs, video games, R. Crumb comics, paperback books. Kit Smartt's cache of special things that were not for adult eyes.

Dr. Smartt would never have thought of entering Kit's room. When she'd lived in the house, Kit's mother had rarely entered the room. Quincy Smartt hadn't been the sort of mother to poke about in her son's bedroom looking for forbidden things for Quincy Smartt had not time for such things. Placing her hands on Kit's shoulders she'd spoken to him as if they'd been equals and not as if he'd been a deeply wounded boy of thirteen and she his thirty-nine-year-old mother: "If there's anything in your life that I should know, I'm taking it for granted that you'll tell me, Kit. We don't need to depend upon your father, even. You tell me." But Kit had never told for Kit had had nothing to tell.

Now Kit was going away to school again, to this new school in eastern Connecticut his father had located for him. Another time he'd be leaving the model *Cutty Sark* behind, to gather dust.

Downstairs Kit's father was calling him. Maybe they'd made plans to go out to dinner around the corner on Lexington. Maybe the housekeeper had prepared a meal for them. Whatever. Kit stepped into his bathroom and flushed the toilet. In the mirror above the sink were damp-accusing eyes and reddened eyelids that looked weirdly scratched or scaly. *Just us! Not enough for her.* Another time Kit flushed the toilet. No chance of hearing his father's strained voice—"Kit? Kit?"—way up here on the third floor.

Kit Smartt? Are you related to—?

Since the memoir that had been published in June, and the storm of controversy following. Seeing that look in the eyes of strangers of quickened interest, curiosity. Kit had come to dread such looks as he dreaded such questions put to him with infuriating frequency. With a shrug he turned away, biting his lower lip to keep from muttering *Fuck no! I am not.*

Strictly speaking, Quincy Smartt's shame was not hers since she seemed not to acknowledge it, but Kit's. Since Kit was her son—her only child, as she often spoke of him wistfully, in the interviews he'd seen. Her shame was a septic field that had overflowed its confines and was spilling out for all to smell.

On the Internet, you would not want to type in QUINCY SMARTT. MEMOIR OF A LOST TIME. A heaving-up of sewage, Kit was appalled and sickened and could not bear to return to West Ridge School where *Smartt* was known and so he'd begged his father to send him to a school far away from New York City, there had to be good prep schools in Montana, Idaho—certainly in Oregon, Washington, California—but Kit's father insisted that his son who was his only child attend a boarding school no more than a few hours' drive from home.

What the fuck, Kit wanted to say. You won't drive up to visit me anyway.

What had been promised at the New London Academy was anonymity, privacy. What had been promised was a place where *Smartt* wasn't likely to be known. New London Academy wasn't Exeter, Andover, Columbia Prep: a Gothic red-brick campus a scant mile beyond the New London city limits, a second-tier boarding school charging first-tier tuition. Of course the headmaster Skelton (a name presumably chosen to provoke sniggering laughter in boy adolescents) had to know that the new transfer Christopher Smartt of New York City was the son of the writer/memoirist Quincy Smartt, and Mrs. Skelton who had a way of smiling with such exuberance her small eyes disappeared into the fleshy ridges of her face had to know; it must have been that some of Kit's instructors knew, or suspected. Kit was certain! His English instructor observed him covertly, Kit thought. As if memorizing his features. Did not ask *Are you related to*—? because the headmaster had warned him not to.

Age twenty-one, Kit would change his name. Move far away.

It was a vengeful fantasy, he'd enlist in the U.S. Army, get shipped to Iraq and be transformed into a killer zombie, unless a brain-damaged spastic, or "remains" in a body bag. Quincy Smartt could write a "searingly frank"—"corrosively unsparing"—memoir on this subject.

Kit was desperate to make himself muscled as with armor and so he'd begun to work out in the school gym as well as at lacrosse practice but he couldn't seem to build muscle or put on weight and he was in terror of having ceased growing. His lean body was

covered in a faint fair down very different from the wiry pelts of
the most developed boys. His penis was a fleshy stub resembling
one of those deep-sea worms that unfolds and contracts: unfolds to
a startling length, and glowers with phosphorescence, or contracts
ignominiously into a tight little knot, swallowing itself up to elude
predators. Anxiously Kit weighed himself in dread of discovering
that since arriving at New London, he'd lost several pounds: at five
feet seven and a half inches he weighed 130 pounds which was
puny set beside the school athletes Kit most admired. Yet Kit took
care to carry himself publicly like a jock with a jock's carelessness
for physical mishaps, injuries and pain and even humiliation on
the lacrosse field where, to the surprise of observers, he never hesi-
tated to risk hurt in the effort of proving himself a team player—not
gifted, never outstanding, but reliable, steadfast, good-natured and
uncomplaining. The coach would never put Kit Smartt into a game
unless the New London team was winning by a comfortable margin but if the coach did Kit played as fiercely as his small frame
allowed him. Dazed with pain, limping yet thinking *This is where no
one knows me. Where she can't follow.*

"You are the love of my life. Only you."

That last time he'd seen her. Kit's birthday in March, he'd been
home for spring break from the school in northwestern Massachusetts and she'd called him and insisted upon taking him out for a
"birthday luncheon" at an expensive and very crowded French restaurant in TriBeCa. And she'd been very beautiful, and very spir-
ited making such extravagant and playful remarks to her taciturn
son who didn't entirely trust her. Yet, lifting her wineglass in a
toast to him, fixing her dark eyes on his with myopic intensity,
wasn't Kit's mother sincere? "Only you, Kit. Please know that.
One day, maybe you will understand."

Always there was something wistful about Quincy Smartt, at
her most brazen. You felt yourself in danger of being drawn in,
another time.

"At your age, you judge harshly. No one more puritanical than an adolescent boy vis-à-vis his mother."

Kit's birthday but she hadn't asked him where he'd have liked to go for lunch knowing it wouldn't have been L'Auberge on Chambers Street where clearly Quincy Smartt was known and admired and drew the eyes of strangers. Eager to show off her handsome son she'd said, seventeen years old and you could see the two were related, the sharp cheekbones, the shape of the face, the deep-set ironic eyes. Kit squirmed in embarrassment on the verge of saying, "For Christ's sake, Mom, lay off," but it had been a long time since he'd called his mother "Mom," still longer since he'd called her "Mommy." He wasn't comfortable calling her "Quincy" as she'd requested and so most of the time he called her nothing at all.

"Smile, Kit! This is your day."

"Sure."

It was a time when you'd have thought that Kit would be proud of his mother, or at any rate not embarrassed: for Quincy Smartt was known and admired for her glib, corrosive yet lyric prose pieces—"Portraits Up Close & Personal"—that appeared in the *New Yorker*, *Vanity Fair*, *Vogue*, the *New York Times Magazine*; her several novels, travel books. Kit resented her beauty, an ugly sort of beauty he thought it, aggressively "elegant," her long straight hair that had turned silver in dramatic streaks and fell like liquid past her shoulders, kept in place by antique tortoiseshell combs. Expensive perfume wafted from her, Kit's nostrils pinched in distaste. His mother was in her early forties—an age so advanced, Kit shuddered to think of it—yet she dressed like a girl half her age and from a short distance, Kit had to concede, you might mistake her for a girl half her age. Her makeup was elaborate, meticulous. Her naturally sallow skin was made up to appear creamy-pale and her sensuous, fleshy mouth was a chic dark-maroon. She was very thin, with bony shoulders and wrists. Always she wore striking clothes and today she was wearing a very short taffy-colored suede skirt studded with metallic starbursts that Kit supposed must be expensive designer apparel and a twisted-looking satiny-black tubular crepe top with a V-neck exposing the shadowy crevice between her breasts, and extravagantly high-heeled shoes. Around her neck carved amber beads the size of almonds, on her pale bare arms a cascade of bracelets that clattered gaily. On her left wrist and only just visible in the descending V of her neckline were crimson-orchid tattoos, Quincy had acquired in—had it been southern India? Indonesia? Kit knew from a photo spread in *Vanity Fair* of his near-nude mother that Quincy Smartt had elaborate exotic tattoos elsewhere on her body.

As long as Kit could recall, when he'd been growing up, it had not been uncommon for people to stare after his mother in the street at a time when "Quincy Smartt" had not been known; there was the expectation, seeing so striking a woman, and one who clearly thought so well of herself, that she had to be *someone*. At such times Kit's mother had rarely acknowledged such attention—"Kit, c'mon! It's rude to stare"—but in L'Auberge she'd reserved a table at the front of the restaurant and not, as Kit had expected, in a quiet corner. She'd told Kit that they had "significant matters" to discuss and yet: how like Quincy Smartt to display herself publicly on even a private occasion; how like Quincy Smartt to glance up repeatedly through her meal with Kit with an expression of startled surprise and pleasure when someone, usually female, and of Quincy Smartt's age, paused in passing to smile at her, or even to speak her name: "Excuse me, are you—Quincy Smartt?" More egregious yet when Quincy Smartt felt obliged to shake hands with an admirer and turn to sulky Kit with a smile of bare-gummed rapacity, greed: "And this is my son Christopher. Today is his seventeenth birthday."

Kit laughed. Surprised himself, blushing and laughing and sure he was pissed at his mother, but that was Quincy Smartt for you.

"Kit, don't scowl! You're only seventeen once."

"I'll be seventeen for three hundred sixty-five days," Kit said. "If I live that long."

Disconcerting to Kit, how raw and defensive his voice was. Whiny, snotty. So quickly his mother whom he did not much love and did not at all respect could reduce him to this rich spoiled prep-school Manhattan kid which truly Kit Smartt *was not*.

"Sweetie, don't be trite."

This wasn't flirtatious. This was a rebuke. Kit felt the sting. For Quincy Smartt was one of those individuals who were in terror of *trite*. She could be rude, she could be cruel, she could be shameless in her vanity but she could not be *trite*.

Foreseeing embarrassment at L'Auberge, Kit had asked his mother several times to please not tell anyone at the restaurant that it was his birthday but of course she'd done this for how could a mother resist?—a festive occasion was desired, and festive occasions require orchestration. At least Kit hadn't had to endure a Happy Birthday serenade by waiters. L'Auberge wasn't the sort of restaurant for such maudlin displays but the chef had prepared an exquisite little French chocolate layered tart for the birthday boy and his doting mother, a cursive *K* in cream and a single silver candle for Kit, now fiercely blushing, to blow out.

Next came a present for Kit to unwrap as Quincy looked on, a sleek new BlackBerry Pearl—"To help us keep in better contact, darling"—and Kit must have murmured thanks in a way to nettle his mother, his voice lacked sufficient volume and enthusiasm. Sharply Quincy said, "Maybe you already own one? I asked your father and he'd assured me . . ."

Kit said no, he didn't own a BlackBerry Pearl. Thanked her again, with a forced little smile.

"And I have another surprise for you, I think." Quincy spoke slowly as if the words were awkwardly sized in her mouth. "Back at the loft. Which you've never seen."

The surprise or the loft? Kit wondered. He was feeling uneasy, for his mother had managed to eat only a few forkfuls of her expensive crab-stuffed sole while she'd put away several glasses of red wine. The chic dark-maroon lipstick on her fleshy lips was eaten away and her normally throaty/seductive voice had become thin and shrill. "Not all surprises are pleasant ones, Kit. But the truth is more important." Pausing now like a skier at the top of a treacherous ski run who can't see her destination below but is determined to set out nonetheless.

How long it had been since Kit's mother had presented him, or his father, with a "pleasant" surprise of any kind and so the prospect of a less-than-pleasant surprise held little attraction for him.

"Kit, come! We will go through with this."

Leaning on Kit's arm as they left the restaurant, glamorous Quincy Smartt in her ridiculous high-heeled shoes. Though the loft was only a few blocks away it wasn't possible for Quincy to walk in such shoes, Kit had to hail a taxi.

Even then, he was thinking he could escape. Shut the taxi door as Quincy sat inside, wave and walk away.

The loft was on the seventh floor of a former industrial building on windy Greenwich Street looking toward the Hudson River a few blocks away. The space was airy and chill and flooded with a sharp sort of light that looked artificial. Through ten-foot windows Kit could see the steely glitter of the river in the near distance. The loft appeared to be sparely furnished like a museum with bare hardwood floors and a high hammered-tin ceiling painted a glaring white but Kit knew, or seemed to know, that the back rooms of his mother's loft would be very different, her work-room and her bedroom would be very different, rooms in which Quincy Smartt lived intimately, articles of her clothing lying about, drawers and closet doors partway open, in the bedroom a sumptuous unmade bed smelling of the woman's body . . . How Kit knew this he couldn't have said, he had not stepped inside any bedroom of Quincy Smartt's for years.

"You've never visited here until now," Quincy said in a tone of flirtatious reproach in which, Kit well knew, there was a sharp steel pin of genuine reproach as Quincy's pleasant smile masked an angry bared-gum smile, and so he said, "So? I've been other places, Mom. I've always been someplace." Intended as a defiant remark, a clever-kid remark, Kit's words sounded lame and his mother stared at him uncomprehending. What had he said?

As soon as she'd entered the loft Quincy had rummaged in her leather handbag for a cigarette, lit it and was now fouling the air which annoyed Kit but provoked him to smile thinking *She's smoking, I can leave soon.*

Like a restless athlete needing to be in motion Kit drifted about the large living room/dining room among his mother's striking things as if despite himself he was fascinated by where she was living now, how she lived, with whom she was living. (But she seemed to be living alone now. Kit was grateful for this!) Here were spare minimalist furnishings offering little conventional comfort: low sofas covered in dust-colored burlap, matching chairs shaped like praying mantises. Coarse woven wall hangings from—Morocco?—Nigeria? An enormous coffee table made from a single slab of green-tinted glass that must have weighed as much as Kit and spindly halogen floor-lamps you wouldn't readily identify as lamps but as weirdly ugly sculptures. Quincy Smartt's loft had been featured in *New York* the previous year, Kit had leafed through the pages with both pride and repugnance. For always Quincy Smartt must be admired, envied. Artfully she'd created a private life to be presented to the public to evoke admiration and envy in others for what was the point of a private life, otherwise? When she'd lived with Kit and Kit's father in the dignified old brownstone on East 72nd Street she'd rarely been home more than a few days in succession; you were made to sense how, elsewhere, where Quincy Smartt was becoming known and celebrated, her soul dwelt. She had not begun a serious writing career until after her thirtieth birthday, and had long resented what she called, in interviews, her "veiled years"; she'd married too young, and naively—married an older man, a neurosurgeon, for his money and social position . . . Frankly she'd conceded as much for in interviews Quincy Smartt had a disconcerting habit of suddenly speaking the truth: "It's just something that 'jumps' in me. Like a nerve. Like a worm. 'The imp of the perverse.' If I try to lie it backs up on me like bile . . ."

On the glaring white walls of the loft were framed covers of Quincy Smartt's books and photographs of the glamorous author and in each Quincy Smartt stared moodily and enigmatically into the camera. Her long straight striking hair went from jet-black to silver as her distinctive face seemed scarcely to age; in some poses, Quincy was smiling faintly, and wistfully. Such yearning and vulnerability that drew you to her, every time. You wanted to trust her, protect her. Though you knew better, this was so. In the corner of his eye Kit saw his mother nervously smoking and eyeing him in that way of calculated wistfulness that enraged him, like a mean low foul on the lacrosse field. He'd fallen for it so many times.

In her brief but spectacular career Quincy Smartt had published just eight books so far of which one, originally serialized in the *New Yorker*, was a profile of a celebrated avant-garde Italian filmmaker and two were "erotic travel" books and the others were slender works of fiction with attention-grabbing titles: *Envy, Pride, Lust, Despair, Appetite*. Kit had never read any book of Quincy Smartt's but he'd skimmed her magazine pieces; he'd seen interviews with her in the *New York Times*, and on local television; growing up in Manhattan he'd been aware that his mother was a celebrity of a kind, in some quarters. Not "famous" as pop musicians, film and TV personalities were "famous" but yes, in some quarters Quincy Smartt was "known." She'd acquire a reputation for frankness in sensuous/sexual matters; her off-the-cuff remarks outraged feminists, as well as the more conventionally minded; her politics were "radical," but not predictable. As Quincy Smartt lived in terror of *trite*, so Quincy Smartt lived in terror of *predictable*. She was a woman of intense passions who'd become, over the years, obsessed with Japanese music, Indian erotic art, European avant-garde artists and filmmakers. Kit had been astonished to learn, years after the fact, from an article in *Vanity Fair*, that his mother who he'd been told was "away, traveling" had been living with the elderly Italian filmmaker in Rome for most of the year Kit had been in sixth grade in a Manhattan private school. On a wall of the loft was a moody portrait of Quincy Smartt and the gravely handsome old white-haired filmmaker, taken just before the filmmaker's death;

close by, a more festive full-color shot of Quincy Smartt swathed in white like a girl-bride seated with a dark-skinned youngish man atop an enormous elephant: *Pārvatipuram, India 2003.*

"I miss that person. I was younger then. Fleeing my past but blindly. What I *did* was a way of not confronting who I *was*."

This declaration, made to Kit as he examined a wall of photos, sounded brave, defiant. A sound bite from an interview, Kit supposed.

Quincy stubbed out the cigarette, seeing how it annoyed her priggish son. Asked him if he'd like a drink, maybe a beer?—since he hadn't been able to drink in the restaurant, being under-age. Kit looked at his mother to see if she was serious. A drink? Beer? No adult had ever asked Kit Smartt such a question before. Dismayed he thought *She wants to drink, but not alone.* Shook his head no, he didn't want a drink.

"Yes. You do."

It was a club soda Quincy got for him, from the kitchen. Poured the fizzing liquid over ice. And Kit took it from her and drank, thirstily. Drained the glass in three or four swallows. On an elaborately carved mahogany sideboard with a mirrored back were numerous glittering bottles of liquor and from one of these Kit's mother poured herself a half-glass of a warm amber liquid: Cutty Sark.

Cutty Sark! Kit stared at the bottle.

Quincy drank. Quincy laughed. Quincy was feeling excited, nerved-up.

"D'you remember, Kit? When you were little, you were so taken with the clipper ship label on this bottle. I taught you to say 'Cutty Sark.' This was years before your grandfather bought you the modeling kit."

"No. I don't think so."

"You were so little, darling! Maybe three years old. I washed out an empty bottle so that you could save the label."

Blood pounded in Kit's cheeks. He knew it hadn't been that way. The first he'd seen of any clipper ships had been in his grandfather

Smartt's house but he wasn't going to argue with a drunken woman.

"Your father doesn't want me to show you this, still less publish it. But I must."

Quincy had led Kit into her work-room, beyond the kitchen. Here was another high-ceilinged room with a ten-foot window overlooking rooftops and in the near distance the river reflecting an overcast March sky. On the table was a black lacquered box with what appeared to be Japanese characters on its cover, in gilt. "You don't have to open this box, Kit. If you don't want to. There is something inside crucial for you to know but if you don't want to know it, you don't have to. We don't even need to discuss it afterward. I'm going out now because it's too hard for me to remain in the loft while you're here. I'll be back in about an hour and we can discuss this if you want to—what you've discovered inside the box—but if you don't want to, darling, whether you've opened the box or not—you don't have to, of course." Kit's mother spoke rapidly and breathlessly and seemed confused, unsure what she meant to say. Nor did Kit follow all that she'd said. Lightly she touched Kit's wrist. A faint stale smell of perfume hung in the air. "I—I hope that you will be waiting for me, Kit. When I return. That's all I ask."

She left. Kit was alone. Kit's heart had begun to pump harder. How like his mother to dramatize a situation, he thought. Probably this was some elaborate joke, a part of Kit's birthday surprise but she'd made him uneasy, and he resented it. Those evenings when he and his father had waited for his mother to return, and at 11 P.M. a call might come, or might not. Kit forced himself to sit at the table. If this was a game, Kit Smartt liked games. He drew his fingers over the black-lacquered box, that had to be an expensive object. Maybe it was an antique. Maybe Quincy Smartt had smuggled it back from Japan. On the table lay a number of ballpoint pens, pencils. To Kit's left, a laptop computer, its lid closed. On a just-perceptibly grimy window sill in front of the table were small framed photographs of glamorous Quincy Smartt alone and with individuals whom Kit didn't recognize. And there, framed in

mother-of-pearl, was Quincy Smartt as a happily smiling young
mother with her son Kit at about age nine, youthful mother and
dimple-faced child smiling into the camera from out of a sunny
patch of what appeared to be a sandy beach, in a long-ago time
on—Nantucket?—at Kit's grandparents' house on the water?—Kit
could not recall.

If this was a game, what was inside the black-lacquered box?
Photographs? Documents? Blood pounded in Kit's temples but he
wasn't going to become frightened. His birth certificate was
inside—was that it? For seventeen years it had been kept secret
from him, he wasn't Quincy Smartt's son, nor was he Lloyd Smartt's
son, but an adopted child. Was that it? Kit thought *I don't need to
open this. I don't need to look.* But already his fingers were prying the lid
open.

He thought *It will be something terrible. Nothing in my life will be the
same again.*

Was his mother gone? Could you trust Quincy Smartt, to have
actually gone away at such a time? Kit listened, the loft was silent.
Seven floors down on Greenwich Street was a hurtling vehicle,
flashing lights and a wailing siren. The shrill combative sound of
the city was consoling to certain of its inhabitants, signaling danger elsewhere, serious injury and harm elsewhere. In this chic furnished loft there could be no danger. Kit was seventeen, he'd led a
ridiculously sheltered life. He knew this, he was a rich doctor's son.
He scored high on tests, he was of a generation geared to take and
to excel at tests. He could not be hurt, really. He was untouched by
the emotion that swept over others with the power to destroy,
something in his soul was mineral-hard and unyielding, even the
woman could not touch it.

Inside the lacquered box was a stack of pages: a manuscript.

A manuscript! A manuscript could not hurt him.

Aloud Kit said, sneering: "I don't have to read this."

He read the title page: *Memoir of a Lost Time* by Quincy Smartt.
He said, "I don't have to read more. This is bullshit." He turned to
the Prologue. He read:

When I was fifteen and my parents were divorcing I set out to seduce and corrupt my twelve-year-old brother who was their favorite because he was "high-strung"—"sensitive." This is my story of how I succeeded and how when he was seventeen and a high school dropout my brother committed suicide and all these years I have borne the secret guilt . . .

Kit let the pages fall. Kit shut the black-lacquered box.

By the time Quincy Smartt was scheduled to return to the loft, Kit was gone. He'd reopened the lacquered box and dumped out the manuscript of 212 neatly typed pages and with a ten-inch steak knife from the kitchen he'd cut and slashed many of the pages and others he'd kicked and torn underfoot. He'd smashed the lacquered box. He'd yanked the laptop out of its several sockets and smashed it on the floor. The framed photographs of smiling people he'd swept off the windowsill. The work-table he'd overturned. With the knife he'd cut and slashed those clothes in his mother's bedroom closet he could reach easily and in the front room he cracked a mirror with his fist, overturned and smashed the precious bottles of whiskey, vodka and gin on the sideboard and he ran from the loft leaving the heavy door swinging open behind him.

2.

"Kit? Give me a hug."

He would not. At the foot of the stairs he made no move toward her. Regarding her as if without recognition and after a moment's hesitation she came to him, and laid her gloved hand tentatively on his arm. "Well! If you won't, I will."

Her arms closed around him. Her arms were unexpectedly strong. He held himself stiff, resistant. He held his breath against her cloying perfume, that made his nostrils contract. Female animals release such smells, to attract males. But there were smells that repelled, too.

That morning she'd called him at his residence hall and left three messages and he had not replied and yet, here she was. Through the day he'd been distracted and anxious in his classes, aware that Quincy Smartt had checked into the New London Inn which was less than two miles from campus and it was her plan to arrive on campus in the late afternoon, to seek him out. He'd thought of running away. He'd thought of hiking out into the birch woods beyond the playing fields and returning late that night when his mother would have to be gone but how ridiculous that would be, how Kit's classmates would laugh at him, a seventeen-year-old frightened of his own mother! Kit could not bear the thought of Gervais laughing at him . . . And so she'd arrived at Kit's residence hall at 4 P.M., and she'd asked for him. And he'd descended the stairs unsmiling. He hadn't shaved. He hadn't showered in two days. He'd pulled on his maroon lacrosse jersey sweat-darkened beneath the arms and he was carrying his grungy down jacket.

"Kit, darling! You look gaunt. You've lost weight, I can see."

With a show of motherly anxiety she framed his face in her hands. It was a gesture meant to inspire Kit to bend to her, to accept her kiss like a supplicant, a smear of dark-maroon lipstick on his cheek she'd have to rub away, but Kit did not bend.

They went out. He was going with her. For she would make a scene otherwise, her arrival on the school campus would become an Event. And he, Kit Smartt, would become a participant in the Event, and would be subsequently defined by the Event, through the remainder of his time at the New London Academy. And so he went with her, and he was being seen with her and there would be witnesses *This woman Kit Smartt was with, had to be his mother.* In high-heeled black leather boots she was nearly Kit's height. She leaned on his arm, she was laughing nervously. The long straight silver hair spilling past her shoulders. The ivory-white face, heavily made up as a geisha's. Her coat was black sable, her eyes outlined in black. There was something frantic in her eyes, that wistful yearning Kit hated. He felt a revulsion for the woman that was purely physical.

It was the first time he'd seen Quincy Smartt in person, since

his birthday. That windy March day, the loft on Greenwich Street.
Kit could not recall precisely what he'd done that day after skim-
ming the pages of *Memoir of a Lost Time* and she had never accused
him of trashing her things and had not reported him to his father
so far as Kit knew, for which Kit felt not the slightest gratitude but
despised her all the more.

Outside in the chill November air she continued to chatter in
her bright brittle way as he'd heard her speak in television interviews. She was asking Kit about the school, in which buildings
were his classes held, what was he studying? In the distance Kit
could make out running figures on the lacrosse field, too far away
for Kit to be glimpsed by any of his teammates should he have
lifted a hand to wave to them. Bitterly he resented this glamorous
perfumy woman, he'd had to miss practice that afternoon.

Coach had asked Kit if it was a family emergency? Seeing the
look in Kit's face.

Quickly Kit said no. Not an emergency. But it was family, he
could not avoid.

"'Josiah Cobb.' I've been reading about him—your 'Founder.'"

Quincy had stopped Kit in front of the quaint old red-brick
chapel. Asking him about the school's founder—she'd been reading in a school brochure—who the hell Josiah Cobb was, Kit had
no idea. Old railroad billionaire who'd donated land and money to
establish the New London Academy for Boys with the provision
that his gravesite would be on campus, beside the chapel and facing
the green; Kit was being made to look at the raised grave now, that
was made of hoary old weather-worn granite topped by a rugged
cross and of about the size of a barnyard trough. "So he wouldn't be
lonely! The old man must have loved young boys, to want to spend
eternity among them." Quincy laughed, you couldn't have gauged
whether in sympathy, or scorn.

Please would Kit come to her hotel room, she was saying. She
hadn't eaten since early that morning in Boston and she was
light-headed with hunger and could Kit have an early dinner with
her, a meal at the Inn, in private. She wanted to speak with him in

private. She'd taken a suite at the Inn, overlooking the river. She was chattering nervously, brightly. Kit did not intend to have a meal with his mother but with his lacrosse teammates in the dining hall at their usual table, maybe they would ask him about who'd come to visit him that afternoon but maybe not. Maybe no one would ask. Kit must've given in, climbed into Quincy's car and she drove to the Inn in a state of fevered excitement so he had to wonder if she'd been drinking before she'd come to get him, beneath the flowery scent of her perfume was a sharper smell of alcohol. She was telling him about her car which Kit had had to admire, a bottle-green Jaguar XJ she didn't own but was leasing by the month and naturally a seventeen-year-old kid would be intrigued by the luxury car, a thrill in the gut just to climb into such a vehicle and to feel the power of the near-inaudible engine and to wish—for just this fleeting moment—that some of the guys on the team had seen him get into the car and drive off campus. And this thrill in the gut seemed ignoble to him, contemptible. Quincy was asking if he had a learner's permit to drive yet and when Kit mumbled no she said, "Well, too bad! You could try out this amazing car," and a moment later, glancing at him sidelong with her wistful dark gaze, "—maybe next time."

At the Inn, they entered from the rear parking lot. The single time Dr. Smartt had driven to New London to visit with Kit and to stay overnight they'd had dinner in the Yankee Doodle Tap Room seated in a wood-plank booth of the size and proportions of Josiah Cobb's gravesite. But Kit's mother took him directly to her suite on the fourth floor of the Inn where as soon as she shed the soft-shimmering black sable coat and, with a grunt of relief, her tight-fitting high-heeled boots she placed an order with room service: Cutty Sark, imported Belgian beer, club soda with lemon, a platter of Room Service Deluxe sandwiches. In a vehement-bemused voice she was telling Kit about a "mistake" she'd made recently, becoming "too deeply involved" with an individual, a man whose name Kit wouldn't know; she'd met this individual on her book tour to California, she'd allowed this individual to "exploit" her mentally and physically but finally she'd had enough, she'd called Malibu police to "report an assault" and the man had been arrested and she was not going to drop charges; the incident had been picked up on cable news and "wildly distorted" but she didn't regret any of it for from now on, Quincy Smartt intended to reclaim her rights as a woman. "And that's why I am here, with you, Kit: to reclaim my rights as a mother." To this torrent of words Kit listened dazed and distracted. He was staring at his mother's unexpectedly fleshy legs, her somewhat thick ankles, her small pudgy feet in sheer stockings the shade of smoke, her toes inside the smoke-hued fabric that wriggled with the vehemence of her voice. Initially, Kit was drinking club soda. So thirsty!—his mouth felt parched. He'd been diagnosed with a "sleep disorder" which was why he was prescribed to take medication but medication made him sleep so heavily, in that exhausting stupor-sleep he hated, when he woke his mouth was dry from having been open during the night and that morning early in the dark, Kit was remembering now, his roommate Gervais had nudged his shoulder saying for Christ's sake Kit was grinding his teeth so, moaning in his sleep, must've been having a nightmare . . . Kit shook his head clear seeing that that time was past now, had to be later in the day though twilight outside the windows of his mother's suite in the New London Inn. Why he'd come here with his mother, when he'd vowed he would not, Kit could not have explained. His mother had pushed one of the sandwiches in Kit's direction urging him to eat but Kit refused. Kit ate with his friends in the dining hall, at the table reserved for the lacrosse team. That was where Kit Smartt ate dinner unless there wasn't a chair for him, but if Kit got there early enough, or if Kit came with Gervais, there was always room for him yet still Kit felt a clench of apprehension, anxiety in the pit of his stomach and so he had no appetite for food here, now. "You look so gaunt, Kit! I hate the idea of something 'eating' at you—your father refuses to take responsibility." They were sitting together on a sofa, closer than Kit would have liked. Quincy's perfume filled his nostrils but also the rich warm amber smell of Cutty Sark. In her wistful-girlish voice Quincy was saying that she understood and respected Kit's wish to "distance yourself emotionally" from her but she hoped that he would see how "unnatural and self-destructive" that was. Did Kit know, the river outside was the Quinebaug River?—had to be an Indian name, she'd never heard before. Kit could stay the night and in the morning they could drive up along the river and "explore." A quick call to the school, and arrangements could be made, a drive up along the river to—where?—it was a scenic countryside of many waterways and small lakes.

To this, Kit mumbled "Yes ma'am"—"No ma'am"—in robot politeness. Knowing that nothing so annoys a glamorous woman than to be called "ma'am." Kit's mouth still felt parched, he'd begun drinking the Belgian beer. And Quincy had urged a sandwich upon him, moist ham, Swiss cheese, a crusty baguette he'd begun to eat though he would have said he wasn't hungry, yet he took a tentative bite, and then an enormous bite, and ate. Kit disliked the taste of beer, disliked even the smell of beer, he'd had beer a few times at parties and he'd gotten a buzz from it but hadn't liked the taste, for it was an acquired taste, as people said. Seeing at such close range that Quincy Smartt was not a beautiful woman truly but so carried herself, so meticulously made herself up, and lavished such attention upon herself, you were led to acquiesce, you would see her as beautiful, desirable. The ivory-white skin in which thin white lines were just perceptible at the corners of her mouth and eyes, and a tiredness beneath the eyes, and in the fleshy throat, yet you were distracted by her animation, her daring. Here was a woman utterly open and frank and vulnerable. And willing to ignore her adolescent son's rudeness. Though in fact rudeness excited her, male cruelty excited her. Female masochism, male cruelty were Quincy Smartt's usual subjects. A female is a sort of receptacle into which the male discharges himself. In interviews Quincy Smartt had said. You can access these interviews on the Internet but Kit Smartt would not, no longer. To provoke she'd said a woman has only her will, her "cunt-cunning." A man has strength. A man desires through the eyes. The primary male sex organ is the eyes. A woman must be sexually attractive or she is nothing. In her beautifully modulated girlish voice Quincy Smartt made such pronouncements meant to enrage, and attract. And arouse. And bring hundreds of thousands of readers to her books. For Quincy Smartt could be relied upon to speak frankly of intimate things others would not speak of, out of hypocrisy. Yet she was a charming woman, soft-voiced and seductive. See how Quincy Smartt shrewdly ignores her son's hostility! Her son's obstinate silence. No prig like an adolescent boy incensed over his mother's sexual life, that was the key. Why the many e-mail messages she'd sent to him he had deleted without reading. (How did Quincy know this? Quincy knew.) Phone and text messages she'd left for him he had not answered. On the very BlackBerry Pearl she'd given him, her son had snubbed her. But she forgave him, he had to know.

Now she was asking him about "your father" as you might ask after an invalid for whom you felt pity but hoped never to see again. "Your father should remarry, Kit! There must be many women on the Upper East Side who'd adore to be the new Mrs. Lloyd Smartt. Is he seeing anyone?"—a way of asking *Is your father sleeping with anyone?* and Kit irritably shrugged no, how'd he know. Nothing so offended him as Quincy asking about his father in that smug-solicitous way of hers for it was shameful to Kit, the thought that his father still loved Quincy who'd betrayed him and made a fool of him and had even written about him obliquely, in unkind ways.

"Kit, why are you looking at me like that? You make me uncomfortable."

"I don't want to talk about Dad with you, O.K.?"

"Well!—'Dad.' How cozy."

In his grip the baguette splintered, ingredients spilled out. Kit's mouth was greasy and the tart Belgian beer was causing him to belch. There came a stir of nausea in the pit of his belly, he had to think how wrong this was, how fucked-up, why was he here? why with her? eating when he wasn't hungry, drinking beer when he hated the taste, and her knee nudging his, as if by accident; and her black silk shirt falling open at the throat, a shirt lacking buttons, a shirt that was a kind of wraparound garment fastened shut with a tie, and in the hollow between her breasts a crimson-orchid tattoo you might mistake for a birthmark. Kit had told himself he would not see her again. He didn't want this, whatever it was. Yet, he was here. He was in terror that she would telephone the school and say *My son will be staying with me tonight, don't expect him back even tomorrow. We are going on a family trip on the Quinebaug River*!

Unexpectedly Kit's mother was saying that she'd made an appointment to see the headmaster of his school the next afternoon, she hoped that Kit wouldn't mind. She would stay another day, perhaps. She would make appointments to see all of Kit's teachers for she was concerned for his welfare, she said. She had not heard very much that was encouraging about the New London Academy, a place for students who'd had to leave other schools, a place for the "learning disabled," she'd spoken to Kit's father questioning his decision to send Kit here instead of Andover, Exeter, Groton—"It's heartbreaking to see the exit sign for Groton, and not be going there to see my son. Why couldn't your father have gotten you into Groton!"

Kit stammered that he'd applied late, to transfer. Groton wouldn't have considered his application.

"What about next year, then? Is your father looking ahead to next year?"

"My friends are here, Mom. I—I have friends here."

Kit's mother stared. Her dark-maroon mouth puckered in disdain. "Friends here? How can you have friends here? You've only just transferred here."

Kit opened his mouth to speak, but could not. His heart was beating hard and pulses beat in his temples and he could not bring himself to look at his mother. He'd made a mess of the sandwich, baguette-crumbs and bits of shredded lettuce on the carpet beneath his feet. Not wanting to reach over for a napkin, to lean close to his mother, he'd wiped his hands on his trousers and on the brocaded sofa.

After a moment Kit's mother said, in a softer voice, "Your behavior is to spite me, is it? Yours, and your father's? But why? Why are you angry with me? What I wrote—my memoir—had nothing to do with either of you. My life as a girl, long before you were born. You never knew Oliver, he had nothing to do with you." Truly she seemed perplexed. Pressing the heel of a hand against her breast, as if she'd been wounded there, a random strike of Kit's.

Stunned and silent Kit could not reply. He was fearful of her touching him. She had drained her glass of Cutty Sark. Out of a decanter she poured more whiskey into her glass, and drank. In her wayward mood she might be tender, or accusing; she might turn on him suddenly, or she might begin to cry. He did not trust her. He could not predict her. He hated it that she was wearing another of her short skirts, of some satiny-cashmere black material, that fitted her much too tightly. It had slid past her knees, up her thighs tightly encased in the sheer smoke-colored fabric. The long silvery hair was disheveled, where a tortoiseshell comb had come loose. There was a flush in the ivory-pale face across her cheeks, a thickening at her jawline. Though Quincy was thin as an anorexic girl in her shoulders and arms she was fleshier elsewhere, her thighs, legs and ankles, as if gravity were tugging her down, inexorably. The black silk shirt had fallen open to reveal a small flaccid sallow-skinned breast cupped in a black lace brassiere. Kit wanted to yank the shirt shut.

Sensing Kit's disapproving eyes on her, Quincy shut her own eyes and recited: "'The writer writes his letter to the world and when the world replies it is like the sorcerer's apprentice. She cannot control what she has summoned.'" She paused. She was breathing quickly. When Kit made no reply she said, opening her eyes: "The words of Anaïs Nin. Whom the world persisted in misunderstanding, too."

Kit laughed hoarsely. Kit took a clumsy swig from the beer bottle, and belched.

With unexpected belligerence he said: "So you're saying,

'Quin-cy,' no one can be blamed for anything? It's no fault of anybody's, what happens?"

"In a way, no." Quincy spoke slowly not wanting to slur her words. "For we can't predict."

Again Kit laughed. It was the tart Belgian beer speaking. "Know what, Mom?—I don't like you. 'Quincy'—don't like. No fault of anybody's, is it? See, if you weren't my . . ." Badly wanting to say *my fucking mother*.

"If I weren't your mother, Kit darling, know what?—you would not exist. 'Kit Smartt' who imagines he's so smart exists solely by way of 'Quincy Smartt.'" Gaily she laughed, clapping her beringed hands together like a malicious child.

Kit opened his mouth to rebuke this but could not. Had to concede, Quincy was right.

Kit heaved himself to his feet. His head swam, he liked the sensation. He'd come out of the woman's cunt, that was the biological bottom line. That could not be rebuked. What you despised about Quincy Smartt was, she was so often right.

"'Cunt-cunning.'"

Kit made his way to the bathoom on unsteady feet. Collided with a chair, he knocked out of his way. She was calling after him sharply, "Kit? What did you say?" but inside the headachey-bright bathroom Kit fumbled to unzip himself, urinating into the sparkling peach-colored porcelain toilet bowl not very accurately and with such urgency he hadn't had time to completely shut the door. It was the Belgian beer he'd acquired a taste for, that had flushed through his kidneys. In the enormous mirror Kit's teeth were bared in an angry-dog smile. Unless it was an abashed-boy smile. His face seemed to him painfully ugly and his skin was flushed and mottled and his eyes unexpectedly bloodshot, glassy-bright. At the back of his skull a beer-buzz like hornets and behind his eyes a weird numb sensation as if he'd been part-lobotomized and liked it. While he was pissing something edged sideways into his head like a lateral play on the lacrosse field, he'd lunged to net the ball but somehow the ball whipped away from him rushing along the grassy field like something alive . . . He recalled an interview he'd seen on late-night cable TV alone in the floor lounge and there was Quincy Smartt being interviewed by a man with dyed-dark hair and droopy cartoon mustache acknowledging yes, she'd been a "deeply disturbed and perverse" girl at the time of the "incest" but that didn't excuse her behavior, of course. Because she'd been older than her twelve-year-old brother by three crucial years and she'd set out deliberately to seduce and corrupt him knowing that he was "emotionally unstable"—"terrified of being touched." In a grave sympathetic voice the interviewer asked how long had the affair with her brother lasted, and Quincy said, "Five years, but intermittently. I went away to boarding school when our parents were divorced, and Oliver went away, but when we returned home at breaks and summer vacations we started again, it wasn't just revenge on my part. I loved my brother, and he loved me. It was a solace to us, our love." The interviewer asked what did Quincy's family think of *Memoir of a Lost Time* and Quincy said, "You would have to ask them, I think," as if this were an answer she'd given many times before; and the interviewer said, "But your brother actually had a breakdown, and committed suicide?" with an air of unscripted surprise, and Quincy said, more slowly now, wiping at her eyes, "Yes, Oliver killed himself. It was hushed up in the family of course but he'd died a hideous—calculated—death drinking Drāno and burning out his insides. But our closeness"—uttered with the delicacy of one lifting a tiny sliver out of a wound with a tweezers—"was a solace for him, I will always believe that. Oliver was a strange unhappy boy, part autistic, I think. He had 'eating disorders' and 'sleep disorders' and a phobia about being touched but at the same time he was desperately lonely and wanted to be touched. Our intimacy was good for him," and the interviewer said, with a skeptical smile, "'Good for him'—if he committed suicide?" and Quincy said defiantly, "Well, no one ever touched Oliver, much. He was this 'musical prodigy' paralyzed by phobias, he had a kind of curvature of the spine, I was the only one who cared for him."

A sharp knock on the bathroom door, that was partly ajar. She was asking if Kit was all right and Kit told her to go away, he'd be out in a minute.

Fumbling now to zip himself up. Fumbling to flush the toilet. Unsteady and weaving Quincy pushed into the bathroom in her stocking feet, shorter than Kit would have imagined her. The ivory-white cosmetic mask was smudged, the eyes leaking moisture. "Kit? Kit? Darling." She came to him, and held him. Capturing him in her thin strong arms that put Kit in mind of a spider-crab's legs, a sea-creature that would be monstrous on land. Kit stood very still. Kit did not dare to breathe. Though wanting badly to raise his elbows against her, body-check her with all of his weight and thrust her from him. She had hold of his head, clutching at his damp hair. She was clutching him to her, sobbing. It was a rapturous sobbing, a kind of laughter. She was whispering she'd never loved anyone until him. She had married his father without loving him and other men she'd lived with, and had believed she'd loved, she had not. She had only loved him: "You are Oliver returned to me but more beautiful than Oliver, far more beautiful. And this time chastely, a chaste love." Her breath smelled strongly of whiskey. Kit was revulsed by her but could not summon the strength to push her away. A wave of darkness rose in him, like something foul, choking. He would burst, he could not breathe. He said, "'Oliver'—was my age when he killed himself—wasn't he—" and Quincy said, "Please don't speak of that, Kit! That was years ago, before you were born. All that was years ago and we are now."

His first blow struck her on the shoulder. It was not a hard blow but Quincy cried out in pain and astonishment and stumbled away from him.

He tore at the black silk shirt. He was tearing at the lacy black brassiere. He saw that a strap had left a reddened mark on her shoulder. He gripped her bony shoulders and shook her. He was speaking to her but had no idea what he was saying nor would he recall afterward what she said, what words she uttered, to him. She

struck at him, clawed at him. Though he seemed to know that she
wanted him to hurt her yet she was clawing at him, and screaming
at him. He shoved her away and she stumbled backward against a
dazzling-white tiled wall. He backed away from her, panting. His
hands were uplifted, he wanted her to see that he was leaving:
wasn't going to hurt her: wasn't going to strangle her, or smash her
skull against the wall: why was she continuing to scream, hysterical
now, furious now calling "Help! help! help!" like a crazed woman
in terror of being killed though she could see that Kit was harmless
now, Kit was leaving, not entirely wakened from his beery trance
but knowing he had to run away, with the presence of mind to grab
at his down jacket that lay flung across a chair beside the
shimmering-black sable coat, beautiful sable coat she'd flung down
partly on top of Kit's grungy jacket; as his mother continued to
scream behind him he found himself running along a corridor,
through a door marked FIRE EXIT STAIRS and down the stairs taking the steep antiquated steps two at a time, and then he was at the
rear FIRE EXIT and a white-uniformed man carrying a tray gaped
at him with the comical surprise of a TV character who has walked
into a dangerous scene and Kit pushed past him, Kit might have
shoved him or even struck him backhanded in his need to escape,
the tray fell to the floor with a deafening clatter, blood sprang from
the man's nose in the instant that Kit pushed out of the door and
found himself outside, in the fresh cold air, what a relief to be outside in this cold damp air, walking swiftly from the inn whose
name he could not have said in the exigency of the moment, in a
parking lot and gravel crunching beneath his feet. His breath was
steaming, his face pounded with blood. She'd stabbed him with
her sharp fingernails, from a half-dozen little wounds blood oozed
stinging. She would report him, he knew. She would summon police. *I want to report an assault* she would tell them making an effort to
speak calmly and not hysterically or drunkenly and in this way
convincingly *The assailant is my own son.* Though in the next instant
Kit was forgetting this, he would forget most of what he'd done in
the bathroom uncertain if he'd torn off all of his mother's clothes,

or only the black silk shirt. And the lacy black brassiere, that so offended him.

Adrenaline pumped in his veins, he was excited, dangerous. He
liked the feeling. There was simplicity here, forward-motion. He
was not running back-and-forth, side-to-side, in cramped circles
on a playing field being struck at by other plunging figures, he was
running and sliding down an embankment he'd never seen before,
yet opened before him like magic, and felt right. Near-dark now, a
faint quarter moon shone overhead like a winking eye. Somehow
he'd left his jacket behind after all, dropped his jacket at the FIRE
EXIT door. He wasn't cold but he seemed to be shivering, his teeth
chattering. The sprawling old house out of which he'd run had
been built at the top of a hill and this hill dropped to the river that
had no name Kit could recall, along this river there was an over-
grown gravel path he could follow by moonlight. On the grass close
by were ugly unwieldy wooden chairs, picnic tables hunched like
malevolent figures in the shadows. Quickly it came to Kit, he could
hide beneath one of these. Or—there was a bridge a quarter mile
away, on the river—he could wade out into the river and hide beneath the bridge for often beneath bridges there are mounds of
concrete rubble, the water isn't deep. This he knew: he could not
return to his residence hall, just yet. For he would be apprehended
at school. The dorm proctor would accompany the police officers
to his room, he knew. And so he'd suddenly changed course not
headed for the bridge but ascending the embankment, toward
the highway. He would follow the highway that led to—was it
Norwich?—in the underbrush beside the highway. Except the underbrush was too thick, littered with papers and debris, thorns cut
at his legs and exposed hands. He ran, on the shoulder of the highway. He was short of breath, his heart ached inside his ribs, he began to walk, he was walking and panting and it seemed to be later,
as headlights of oncoming vehicles swung onto him shrewdly he
hid in the underbrush like a wild creature. All this while his head
was filled with thoughts rapid as heat lightning and yet these
thoughts were not coherent and could not help him. He was like

one struggling with a language he'd never heard before. His gut was clenched in nausea. He'd stuffed himself with greasy food, he'd swigged bottles of beer. He was dazed and light-headed and fighting nausea. He had not the right footwear for a long run on pavement. He yearned to confide in his roommate Felix Gervais. How he yearned for Felix Gervais to squeeze his arm above the elbow as a few rare times Gervais had done after Kit had played passably well on the lacrosse field and now Gervais would assure him frowning and wishing him well *It's cool, Smartt. You're going to be all right.* Though it was a lie, yet Gervais would lie for Kit's sake. This was all Kit wanted, that Gervais lie for his sake. He was stumbling now, on the shoulder of the highway. His damned face bled from her nails. One of her nails had nicked his right eye, that was flooded now with tears. The cold air stung his wet face. When vehicles swept past him from behind he had not the strength to avoid them but stood hunched and stiff until they were gone. No one slowed to offer help though Kit was wearing his lacrosse jersey in the school color maroon. In the near distance there was a siren, he panicked and ran, slipping and stumbling down an embankment. Branches struck at him, he was bleeding from his mouth. Vehicles braked to a stop on the road. A spotlight swung onto him, he could not escape. He was crawling, he could not escape. Uniformed officers shouted at him. Strangers approached him, sliding down the embankment. There were shouts, commands. He saw that they were aiming guns at him. Never would he forget, uniformed men, adults, had aimed guns at him. He was being instructed to lie down, to extend his hands so that they could be seen. Blindly he scrambled to his feet, he was desperate to escape. A uniformed officer who could not have been more than a few years older than Kit seized his arm and swiftly and blindly Kit turned to strike at him and in that instant he seemed to be lifted into the air, struck by more than one officer and lifted and thrown and wrestled to the ground as if at 130 pounds Kit Smartt offered no more resistance than a young child. He struck the ground face-first. His breath was struck from him. There came a knee against the small of his back hard enough to snap his spine, and there came a gloved hand against the nape of his neck, and his face that was raw and torn was forced into the dirt. His arms were yanked behind him, his wrists tightly cuffed so that pain shot through his arms to his shoulders. Wildly his young heart beat to contain his terror. His bladder seemed to split in two, he'd wetted himself. The police officers were shouting at him, these were deafening commands he could not obey. There were drawn guns, Kit knew. Badly Kit wanted the guns to be fired at him so that he could die but he had not that power, he had lost all his strength. Yet his arms were being pushed up higher, the pain was excruciating. They wanted him to cry, he thought. He would not.

Landfill

Tioga County landfill is where Hector, Jr. is found. "Remains" buried in rubble, trash, raw garbage. Battered and badly decomposed and mouth filled with trash. Couldn't have protested if he'd been alive, buried in trash. Overhead, shrieking birds. In the vast landfill, dump trucks and bulldozers and a search team from the Tioga County Sheriff's Department in protective uniforms. Three weeks missing, in all the newspapers and TV. Most of his teeth broken at the roots but those that remain are sufficient to identify Hector Campos, Jr. of Southfield, Michigan. Nineteen years old, freshman engineering student, Michigan State University at Grand Rapids reported missing by his dormitory roommates in the late afternoon of Monday, March 27, but said to have been last seen around 2 A.M. of Saturday, March 25 in the parking lot behind the Phi Epsilon fraternity house on Pitt Avenue, Grand Rapids. And now in the early morning of April 17 Mrs. Campos who never sleeps answers the phone on the first ring. These terrible weeks her son has been missing, Mrs. Campos has answered the phone many times and made many calls as her husband has made many calls and now the call from the Tioga County Sheriff's Department they have been awaiting and dreading *Mrs. Campos? Are you seated? Is your husband there?* after these weeks of being no longer Irene Campos but Mrs. Campos of Southfield, Michigan, the distraught mother of Hector Campos, Jr. missing for an estimated twenty-three days to emerge now in this windswept season of pelting rain and vivid yellow forsythia blooming beside the Campos house at 23 Quail Circle in the brick-gated community Whispering Woods Estates. Mrs. Campos is not seated but standing uncertain and barefoot only partly clothed, shivering and her hair matted and eyes glazed, mouth tasting of scum from the hateful medication that has not helped her sleep yet Mrs. Campos smiles into the plastic portable phone receiver as she has learned to smile these many days as if to placate whoever is addressing her, whoever is bringing news to her, as, hurriedly descending the stairs close by, heavy-footed, in rumpled boxer shorts and sweated-through undershirt, unshaven, bloodshot-eyed Mr. Campos says *Irene, what is it? Who is it? Give me that phone* rudely prying her icy fingers off the receiver, snatching it from her. Tioga County landfill, medical examiner, morgue. Identification, death certification. Approximately eighty miles from the Campos home: how quickly can Mr. and Mrs. Campos drive to the morgue to corroborate the identification?— except of course the body has "badly decomposed" and so at the morgue Mr. Campos views the body alone staring through a plate-glass partition that emits no smell while Mrs. Campos in a state of terror waits in another room. *Remains!* What is this strange, unfathomable word—*remains!* Mrs. Campos whispers aloud· "*Remains.*" She seems to have stumbled into a restroom, white-tiled walls, door locked behind her and the light switch triggering a fierce overhead fan releasing freezing antiseptic air. Why is Irene Campos here, why has this happened? Is this a public restroom? Where? The stark settings to which, on a weekday morning at 10 A.M., emergency brings us. Elsewhere, Mr. Campos observes the "remains" laid upon a table beneath glaring lights, most of the body shielded by a sheet so that only the head, or what remains of the head, is exposed. How is it possible, these "remains" are Hector, Jr. who'd once weighed 175 pounds of solid flesh just slightly soft at the waist, like his father Hector, Sr. squat-bodied, short-legged, with thick thighs, a wrestler's build (except Hector, Jr. who'd wrestled for Southfield High in his senior year had not made the wrestling team at Grand Rapids), five-feet-nine with wiry dark hair growing forward on his head, a low forehead, what remains now of Hector, Jr. could not weigh more than ninety pounds yet at once his father recognizes him, the shock of it like an electric current piercing his heart, the battered and mutilated and partially eaten-away face, the empty eye sockets, Oh God it is Hector: his son. Mr. Campos can barely murmur yes, turns away hunched and quivering with pain, yes that is Hector, Jr. Never the same man again, a man who has lost his son, his soul catheterized telling his anxious wife *Don't ask, don't speak to me please* even as Mrs. Campos loses control despite the medication she has been taking *Are you sure it's our son, I want to see him, what if there's a mistake, a tragic mistake, you know you make mistakes, you forget things, you've given up hope and you forget things, you didn't love Hector as I did, why would Hector be in that terrible place, how has this happened, how has God let this happen, I want to see our son.* Hector, Jr.: called by school friends "Heck"—"Scoot." Within the Campos family, sometimes called "Junior" (which the boy came to hate, as soon as he was old enough to register the indignity) and sometimes "Little Guy" (until the age of twelve when Hector, Jr., chubby-solid at 120 pounds, five feet five, wasn't any longer what one would call little), more often just "Hector" even as his father was "Dad" within the family, or, less often, "James" (his baptismal name was Hector James Campos). Away at college Hector, Jr. was called "Hector" by his teachers, "Scoot" by his friends, "Campos" by the older Phi Epsilons he so admired and wished to emulate. *Campos was an O.K. guy, a good guy, great sense of humor, terrific Phi Ep spirit. Of the pledges, Campos was, like, the most loyal. Seems like a tragedy, a weird accident what happened to him but it didn't happen at the frat house, for sure.* On the Hill partying begins Thursday night, mostly you blow off your Friday classes which for "Scoot" Campos were classes he'd gotten into the habit of cutting: Intro Electrical Engineering taught by a foreigner (Indian? Pakistani? whatever) who spoke a rapid heavily accented English that baffled and offended the sensitive ears of certain Michigan-born students including Hector Campos, Jr. whose midterm exam was returned to him with the blunt red numeral 71, translating C−; and Intro Computer Technology in which, though the course was taught by a Caucasian-American male who spoke crisp clear English and though Hector, Jr. never got less than A− in his computer classes at Southfield High, here he was pulling C, C−, D+. *Probably yes Scoot had been drinking that night, maybe more than he could handle, not in the dorm here but over at the frat house, weekends he'd come back to the room here pretty wasted and, yes that was kind of a problem for us, but basically Scoot was a good kid just maybe in over his head a little, freshman engineering can be tough if you don't have the math and even if you do.* His roommates in Brest Hall reported him missing, finally late Monday afternoon they'd guessed something might be wrong, called the frat house but no answer, Scoot's things exactly as he'd left them sometime Saturday afternoon, it wasn't like Scoot to stay over at the frat house on a Sunday night, or through Monday, he was only just a pledge and didn't have a bed there, and he had four classes Monday he'd missed, had to be something was wrong. And weeks later signing forms in the Tioga County Morgue as through the twenty-two years of their marriage Mr. and Mrs. Campos have signed so many forms, mortgage papers, bank loans, home owners' insurance, life insurance, medical insurance, their son's college-loan application at Midland Michigan Bank. Hector Campos, Sr., one of the reliably high-performing salespersons at Southfield Chrysler, at least until recently, lies sleepless in his king-sized bed in the white-gleaming aluminum-sided Colonial at 23 Quail Circle, Whispering Woods Estates of Southfield, Michigan as his wife sleeps beside him warmly fleshy and oblivious of his misery as by day Mrs. Campos is oblivious or in any case indifferent to her husband's misery, thoughts racing like panicked ants, his head hot and heavy ringing with the crazed demand for money, more money, always more money, more than you've computed, Mr. Campos!—more than the sum quoted by the university admissions office for tuition/room-and-board/textbooks, "fees" for fraternity rush, for fraternity pledging, a startling high fee (payable in advance, Hector, Jr. has said) for fraternity initiation upcoming in May. *Send the check to me, Dad. Make it out to Phi Epsilon Fraternity, Inc. and send it to me, Dad. Please!* Mrs. Campos, lonely since Hector, Jr. has gone away to college if only seventy miles away, has taken up the campaign, excited and reproachful. Mrs. Campos is fierce in support of her son, pleads and argues, if you refuse Hector you will shame him in the eyes of his friends, you will break his heart, you know how hard he worked this summer, it isn't Hector's fault he couldn't earn as much as he'd hoped, you know how much a university education costs these days, even a state school like Grand Rapids, if you refuse him you will destroy him, this fraternity Pi Episom, Pi Epsilom?—this fraternity means more to Hector than anything else in his life right now, more even than the wrestling team, more even than that girl from Bloomfield Hills, this is Hector's new life, if you refuse him he will never forgive you *and I will never forgive you.* Yet: Mr. Campos gave in only when Mrs. Campos threatened to borrow the fifteen hundred dollars from her parents, suddenly then Mr. Campos gave in, disgusted, defeated, as so often through the years of a man's marriage, if he wishes to preserve the marriage, he gives in. *Married for love, does that mean for life? Can love prevail, through life?* Six months later in the chilled antiseptic air of the Tioga County medical examiner's office Mr. and Mrs. Campos are co-signing documents in triplicate that will release the "remains" of Hector Campos, Jr. for burial (in St. Joseph's Cemetery, Southfield) after the medical examiner has filed his final report. Still, Mrs. Campos is stunned slow-speaking and her eyes shadowed in exhaustion blinking tears appealing to whoever will listen in a reasonable voice *Must be some terrible mistake, a terrible accident, how did this happen, God help us to understand, why?* The police investigation has yet to determine: had Hector died in the early hours of March 25 in the steep-sided Dumpster behind the Phi Epsilon frat house at 228 Pitt Avenue a few blocks from the university campus where stains and swaths of blood (identified as the blood of Hector Campos, Jr.) were discovered in the interior of the trash bin as if made by wild-thrashing bloody wings or had Hector died hours later, as long as twenty-four hours later, deeply unconscious, possibly comatose from brain injuries dying as late as Monday morning hauled away unseen amid mounds of trash, cans, bottles, Styrofoam and cardboard packages, rancid raw garbage, stained and filthy clothing, paper towels soaked in vomit, urine, even feces, dumped into the rear of the thunderous Tioga County Sanitation Dept. truck at approximately 6:45 A.M. of March 27, from 228 Pitt Avenue hauled sixteen miles north of the city of Grand Rapids to the Packard Road recycling transfer station to be compacted amid tons of trash, rubble, raw garbage and subsequently hauled away to be dumped in the Tioga County landfill, a gouged, misshapen, ever-shifting landscape of trash-hills, ravines and valleys, amid a grinding of dump trucks, bulldozers, cries of swooping and darting birds. These long-winged birds, some of them gulls, some of them starlings, red-winged blackbirds and crows, graceless turkey vultures, in a perpetual frenzy of appetite and plunder. "Foul play" is not at the present time suspected the Tioga County sheriff has said, carefully the sheriff has explained that "foul play" has not been entirely ruled out as a possibility, though the medical examiner has determined that the "massive injuries" to the body of Hector Campos, Jr. are "compatible" with injuries that would have been caused by the trash-compacting process. Yet a more complete autopsy may yield new information. Yet the police investigation will continue. And the university administration will convene an investigating committee. As many as one hundred college students have been interviewed, Hector's roommates, classmates, Phi Epsilon pledges and brothers, even Hector's professors who take care to speak of him in neutral terms befitting one who has suffered a terrible but inexplicable—and blameless—fate. *Jesus! You have to hope that the poor bastard died right away, smashed out of his mind diving down the trash chute into the Dumpster like breaking his neck on contact and never woke up.* Had Hector Campos, Jr. been "compacted" while alive no one wished to speculate, except police investigators. No one wished to contemplate. Before the discovery of the body in the landfill and the identification of the "remains" during the strain, anxiety, insomniac misery of the three-week search it was perceived how the mother of the missing boy never gave up hope, fierce and frantic with hope, a model mother, prayer vigils at St. Joseph's Church, family, relatives, neighbors, parish members, lighted votive candles, for God is a God of mercy as well as wrath, hiding her face in prayer, *God let Hector return to us, send Hector back to us, Hail Mary full of Grace the Lord is with thee blessed art thou among women pray for us sinners now and at the hour of our death Amen.* Angry that the medical examiner has released the autopsy report, "elevated" level of alcohol in Hector, Jr.'s blood, "more than twice the legal limit" for driving a motor vehicle, both Mrs. Campos and her husband deny that their son had a drinking problem, not once had they seen their son drunk, if something happened to Hector at the fraternity party where were his friends, to help him? Why did his friends abandon him? Mrs. Campos is angry too with Mr. Campos who betrayed their son by giving in, after bloodstains were discovered in and near the Dumpster, Mr. Campos is too quickly resigned to the worst, most terrible news a man can bear, in Hector, Sr.'s face that look of defeat, fury turned inward like cancer. *Why'd they wait so long. That call. Why hadn't anyone at the fraternity seen that Hector was missing, or might have needed help, where were his friends, why hadn't the search begun earlier!* Hector might have been still alive in the Dumpster, those hours, injured and unconscious, but living, breathing, his life might have been saved. Mrs. Campos lives, relives, will forever relive the shock of that call out of nowhere: a male voice, identifying the caller as an assistant dean at the university. And Mrs. Campos says *Yes? Yes I am Hector's mother* drawing a quick short breath *Is something wrong?* In weak sick moments reliving the possibility of a phone call, bearing different news. The possibility of subsequent phone calls, bearing different news. For it is crucial, these days, these interminable stretches of (insomniac, open-eyed, exhausted) time, to believe that Hector is alive, our son is alive, *he is alive!*—having only to shut your eyes to see him, Hector as he'd looked when he'd come home for a few days the previous month, his frowning smile, such a handsome boy, Mrs. Campos must always tell him how handsome he is, Hector has hated his "fat face" since puberty, his "beak nose," his "ape forehead, taking after Dad," Mrs. Campos winces at such words, pulls at Hector's hands when, unconsciously, he digs and picks at his nose, any serious discussion between them must be initiated by Mrs. Campos and then apologetically for her son so quickly takes offense, *Jesus Mom lighten up will you, you and Dad bugging me all the time, must've missed your call, what's the big deal, this crappy cell phone you bought me.* And Mrs. Campos cries *But I love you! We love you* but her words are muffled, she's sweating and thrashing in her sleep the nightmare has not lifted. Must keep the flame alive these terrible days, weeks. At Easter Sunday mass kneeling at the communion rail shivering in anticipation, shutting her eyes tight but this time seeing Hector, Jr.'s grimace, how he'd hated going to church, in recent years he'd refused altogether, even midnight mass on Christmas Eve he'd refused, Mrs. Campos had been so ashamed, so hurt, now kneeling at the communion rail hiding her hot-skinned face in her hands that feel like ice, ice-claws, blue veins on the backs of her hands like the hands of an elderly woman, Mrs. Campos's numbed lips are moving rapidly in prayer, dazed and desperate in prayer, snatching at prayer as you'd snatch at something to clutch, to grasp, to grip to keep your balance, the tranquillizers she's been taking have affected her balance, her sense of her (physical) self, numbness in her mouth, in her head, buzzing in her head *Please help us please help us please do not abandon us in our hour of need,* blindly she lifts her head as the elderly priest makes his way to her, Mrs. Campos is next, craning her neck like a starving bird opening her beak-mouth to take the doughy white communion wafer on her tongue, how dry Mrs. Campos's tongue, how dry Mrs. Campos's mouth, scum coating the interior of Mrs. Campos's mouth *This is my body, and this is my blood.* Half-fainting then in ill-chosen patent leather pumps staggering away from the communion rail, into the aisle, all eyes fixed upon the heavily made-up woman with so clearly dyed-dark-red hair, a middle-aged fleshiness to her face, bruise-like circles beneath her eyes, quickly there comes Mr. Campos to help the dazed-swaying woman back to the family pew, fingers gripping her arm at the elbow. Hector Campos, Sr.! Father of the missing boy! Swarthy-skinned, with dark wiry forward-growing hair, low forehead crisscrossed with lines, large oddly simian ears protruding from the sides of his head, a grim set to the man's mouth, a flush of indignation, impatience as Mrs. Campos confusedly struggles with him as if to wrench her arm out of his grip, as if Mr. Campos is hurting her, making her wince, in the car driving home Mrs. Campos will dissolve into hysteria screaming *You don't have faith! You've given up faith, I hate you!* For it's crucial to believe, as Mrs. Campos believes: nearly three weeks after Hector, Jr. has "disappeared," he might yet be found, unharmed; might yet call his anxious parents, after so many days of (inexplicably) not calling; might turn up at home, you know how adolescents are, returning to surprise them on Easter Sunday, waiting in the house, in the kitchen, eating from the refrigerator, when they return from St. Joseph's; or, somehow Hector has been injured and is "amnesiac"; or, has been "abducted" but will escape his captor or be released by his captor; has been wandering, drifting, who knows where, hitchhiking, left the university without telling anyone, quarreled with someone, he's upset, problems with a girl, a girl he'd never told his parents about as he'd never told them much about his personal life since sophomore year of high school, since he'd put on weight, grew several inches, became

so involved with weight lifting, and then with wrestling, the
fanatic weight-obsession of wrestling, fasting, binge-eating,
fasting, binge-eating, and maybe the Phi Epsilons were putting pressure on Hector, maybe he was made to feel inferior
among the pledges, calling his mother to say how crappy he
felt never having enough money, the other guys had money,
he didn't, how shitty he was made to feel, if the fraternity
dropped him, didn't initiate him with the other pledges,
he'd kill himself, he would he swore he'd kill himself!—and
Mrs. Campos pleading *Please don't say such terrible things, you don't
mean what you are saying, you are breaking my heart.* Mrs. Campos
blames Mr. Campos for coercing Hector into engineering,
such difficult courses, who could excel at such difficult
courses, it's no wonder that Hector has been so lonely, away
from home for the first time in his life. None of his Southfield High friends were at Grand Rapids. His classes were
too large, his professors scarcely knew him. Twelve thousand
undergraduates at Grand Rapids. Three hundred residents
in ugly high-rise Brest Hall where poor Hector shared a
room with two other guys—"Reb" and "Steve"—who in
Hector's words "didn't go out of their way" to be friendly to
him. In turn, Hector's roommates spoke vaguely, evasively,
cautiously of him, when interviewed by Tioga County sheriff's deputies *Didn't know Scoot too well, kind of kept to himself, kind
of obsessed about things, like the wrestling team last fall, he tried out but
didn't make it but the coach encouraged him to try again he said so he was
hopeful, you had to care a lot about Scoot's interests that's all he wanted to
talk about in kind of a fast nervous way and he'd be like laughing, inter-
rupting himself laughing, and, like, it was hard to talk to him, y'know?
Fraternity rush was a crazed time for Scoot, he was really happy when he
got a bid from the Phi Ep's, he'd had his heart set on that house and was
really proud of his pledge pin and looking forward, he said, to living in the
frat house next year if his dad O.K.'d it. Because there was some money
issue, maybe. Or maybe it was Scoot's grades. He was having kind of a
meltdown with Intro Electrical Engineering, also his computer course,*

*some of the guys on the floor he'd ask for help which was mostly
O.K.—you had to feel sorry for him—but then Scoot would get kind of
weird, and sarcastic, like we were trying to screw him up, telling him
wrong things, there were times Scoot wouldn't speak to us and stayed
away from the room and over at the frat house, hanging out there, Phi
Ep's are known for their keg parties, kind of wild-party guys, there aren't
many engineering majors up there on the Hill, anyway not in the Phi Ep
house.* At 228 Pitt Street is a large, three-story Victorian
house, a small mansion with peeling gunmetal-gray paint,
moss growing in rain-gutters, rotting turrets, steep shin-
gled roofs in need of repair. The Phi Epsilon house dates
back to the early decades of the twentieth century when
the Hill was Grand Rapids's most prestigious residential
neighborhood, now the Hill is known as Fraternity Row,
and Phi Epsilon exudes an air both derelict and defiant, its
enormous metallic-silver Day-Glo Φ ε above a listing por-
tico. Scrub grass grows in the stunted front yard. Vehicles
are parked in the cracked asphalt driveway, in the asphalt
parking lot at the rear, in the weedy front yard and at the
curb. Often, the Dumpster at the rear of the house over-
flows and trash lies scattered at its base. It's a feature of the
Phi Epsilon house that, warm weather or cold, its windows
are likely to be flung open to emit high-decibel rock music,
particularly at night; and that, out of the flung-open windows, begrimed and frayed curtains blow in the wind. Inside the house there's a pervasive odor of stale beer, fried
foods, cigarette smoke, vomit and urine. The high-ceilinged
rooms are sparely furnished with battered leather sofas
and chairs, the decades-old gifts of alums. On the badly
scarred hardwood floors are threadbare filth-stained carpets, on the walls torn and discolored wallpaper. Brass
chandeliers have grown black with tarnish. There are rick-
ety stairs and bannisters, gouged wood paneling, in the
dining room a long battered table gouged by initials like
fossil traces. In the basement is the enormous party room

running the width of the house, with a stained linoleum floor, more battered leather furniture, leprous-green mold growing on the walls and ceiling, intensified odors. Scattered through the house are filth-splotched lavatories, in a room beyond the party room is an ancient, rattling oil furnace. For several years in the 1990s Phi Epsilon fraternity had been "suspended" from the university for having violated a number of campus and city ordinances: underage/illegal drinking on the premises, keg parties in the front yard, "operating a public nuisance," sexual assaults against young women and high-school-age girls and even, during a secret initiation ceremony in 1995, against a Phi Epsilon pledge who'd had to be rushed to a local emergency room with "rectal hemorrhaging." Bankrupt from fines, lawsuits, and a dwindling membership, the fraternity had gone off-campus until in 1999 a group of aggressive alums led by a Michigan state congressman campaigned to get it reinstated, but by 2006 the fraternity hadn't yet regained its pre-suspension numbers, with an estimated twenty-six actives of whom one-third were on academic probation. In the rush season that Hector Campos, Jr. became a pledge, the fraternity had needed at least seventeen pledges; instead, only eight young men accepted bids: Zwaaf, Scherer, Tickler, Tuozzolo, Vreasy, Feibush, Herker, Krampf, and Campos. Of these only the first three were first choices of the fraternity, the others were accepted for practical, pragmatic reasons: to help fill the membership. Hector "Scoot" Campos knew nothing of this of course. None of the pledges knew of course. Though drinking, you know how guys are when they're drinking, it might've been, nobody can recall exactly, might've been Herker's "big brother" who was pissed off at Scoot Campos falling-down drunk belligerent and more than usual asshole-behaving, who'd told Campos he wasn't anybody's first choice, for sure. *Fuck fuck you fuckhead* the guys yelled at each other, lurched at each other, or maybe none of this happened, or didn't happen in this way, interviewed by the Tioga County investigators none of the guys would remember, or would say. *First we knew Scoot was missing, it's the dean calling. Nobody knew he was missing here. Must've gone back to his dorm and something happened there or maybe he never went back. But whatever happened to him didn't happen here.* Mrs. Campos tries to take pride in this fact: Mr. Campos brought his family from Detroit to live in the suburb of Southfield, in a white aluminum-sided four-bedroom Colonial at 23 Quail Circle and no one in Irene Campos's family has so beautiful a house, not her sisters, not her cousins, and no one in Mr. Campos's family has so beautiful a house, living out their lives, on lower Dequindre, in mostly black Detroit where for thirty-five years Cesar Campos worked for Gratiot Construction & Roofing, squatted and stooped on roofs in the blazing sun and drove a truck for the company, cement truck, dump truck hauling rubble from construction sites until his back gave out, died of heart failure at only sixty-seven, Irene Campos is terrified seeing in her husband's face the defeated look of the old father, resigned always to the worst, it's the peasant soul, bitter in resignation, dying before his time. *He has given up, he has lost hope we will see our son again, I will never forgive him.* But Mrs. Campos continues to have faith, just look at her! How many times she has called her son's cell phone though knowing Hector, Jr.'s cell phone was no longer in operation, no one knew where it was. (In the vast Tioga County landfill amid tons of rubble. Very likely. Where else?—Hector, Jr. kept his cell phone in the back pocket of his jeans, and that part of his clothing was torn from him.) *Mutations are the key to natural selection* he'd learned in Intro to Biology, his science-requirement course said to be the easiest of the science-requirement courses but Hector, Jr. wasn't finding it so easy, barely maintaining a C average. *Natural selection is the key to evolution and survival* he'd written in wavering ballpoint fighting to keep his eyelids open, so very tired, wasted from the previous night, hanging out with the guys, he was trying to concentrate, unshaven and fattish smelling of his body, a taste of beer and pizza dough coming up on him even now hours later, *genes are the key to change, evolution is only possible through change, species change not by free will but blindly.* No idea what this meant, what any of the words meant. What the lecturer was saying. If words were balloons these words were floating up to bounce against the ceiling of the windowless fluorescent-lit lecture hall, collide with one another and drift about, stupidly. Would've used his laptop except his fucking laptop wasn't working right. E-mail seemed to be frozen, why's that? *No purpose only just chance, the pattern of scout-ants seeking food would look to a viewer like "intelligent design" but is really the result of the random haphazard trails of ants blindly seeking food.* Ants? No idea what the hell this guy's droning on about like it matters Jesus he's so bored!—thirsty for a beer, his throat is parched. Checks his cell and there's the text message sinking his heart PLEASE CALL MOM DARLING and with a stab of annoyance erases the message *What looks like "intelligent design" is merely random. Instinct and not intelligence any questions?* Meant to call his mother but Jesus why doesn't that woman get a life of her own, it's pledge-party weekend, Scoot Campos has other priorities. The girl he'd been planning to take to the party sent an e-mail something's come up, bitch he knew he couldn't trust, a girl one of the Phi Ep guys hooked him up with last time says thanks but she's out of town starting Friday, Scoot is damned disappointed, depressed, what's he going to have to do, pay for it? *Kind of earnest and boring when he was, like, sober, you got the impression Campos hadn't a clue how totally uninterested people were in things he'd talk about, the frat house, wrestling, his opinions on his courses, girls, me and Steve liked him O.K. at first it's cool we got a Hispanic roommate, or, what's it—Latino?—that's cool. But Campos, he's just some guy, nothing special about him you could pick up on, except he wanted to hang out with the frat guys, thought we were weird not to sign up for rush, after he pledged he'd start coming back to the room really late, stumbling around drunk like an asshole, mess up in here, piss on the toilet seat and the floor and next day act like it's some goddam joke, that last weekend he didn't come back, truth is that was great. That poor guy you have to feel sorry for but we didn't, much. It's a shitty thing to say, can't tell any adult but we don't miss Scoot. Can't tell anybody, it's, like, speaking ill of the dead, but we're fed up answering questions about him, we told all we know. Fed up with everybody assuming we were friends of his involved somehow, or responsible, fuck it we are not involved, and we are not responsible! And seeing his parents, Mrs. Campos is so sad and so pathetic, trying to smile at me, hugging me, and Steve, like we were Scoot's best friends, it's totally weird to real- ize that a guy like Scoot Campos, so pathetic, a loser, is somebody that is loved, by somebody.* At the party things were going O.K. in spite of the red-haired girl ditching him first chance she had hooking up with one of the older guys, O.K. Scoot could live with that but later there's some exchange of words, he's hot-faced trying not to show he's pissed at the guys taunting him, O.K. he's laughing to himself crawling—where? Upstairs, where? Can't think, his head is bombarded by deafening rock music, heavy-metal/industrial so high-decibel almost you can't hear it. Some kind of a joke, eager to make the guys laugh to show he isn't hurt by, who was it, that girl, blond girl, little-bitty tits, skinny little ass in jeans so tight it's all you can do not to trace the crack of her ass with your forefinger, maybe in fact somebody did just this, braying with laughter, so somebody slaps him, punches, kicks and he's on his knees, on his hands and knees crawling, needing to get to a toilet, and fast.

Maybe it isn't funny, or—is it? Scoot Campos has fine-honed a reputation at the Phi Ep house as a joker, funniest God damn pledge, the other pledges are losers but Scoot Campos is a wrestler and he's witty, and wired. And good-looking, that kind of swarthy-sexy Hispanic way, thick oily hair, thick solid jaws and fleshy mouth. Funny like somebody on Comedy Central except Scoot makes it up himself, improvised. A few beers, tequila, Scoot isn't tongue-tied and sweating but witty, and wired. Chugging beers with the guys, must be the ninth—tenth?—hour of the annual pledge party, by coincidence it's Newman's Day the twenty-fourth of the month named for the actor Paul Newman, Scoot doesn't know why, nobody knows why, the challenge is to chug twenty-four beers in some record time, except at the party there's tequila, too. Scoot has acquired a taste for tequila! If he'd known about tequila in fucking high school, might've had a God damn better time. Trying to remember what it was, a few weeks ago, some crappy thing, humiliating, hurt his feelings, middle of midterms he'd fucked up the engineering exam, he knew, couldn't concentrate studying for his next exam drinking with some of the guys over at the frat house and (somehow) fell down stairs somewhere, he'd been puking, and sort of passed out, and somebody disgusted dragged him into a bathroom and turned on the shower and left him, and after a while one of the guys came back and turned off the shower and by this time Scoot had crawled out onto the floor flopped over on his back and the guy kicks him *Hey Campos, hey man how'ya doin* like meaning to wake him, or turn him over, but did not so Scoot slept off the drunk soaking wet and shivering in the cold and next morning when he woke groggy and dazed with a pounding headache, a taste of vomit in his mouth, dried vomit all down his front, he'd been lying flat on his back and had to think with the cruel clarity of stone-cold sobriety *They left me here, to puke on my back and choke and die, the fuckers.* His friends! His fraternity brothers-to-be! Had to think *Never again! Not ever.* Meaning he'd depledge Phi Ep, and he'd stop drinking. But somehow, next weekend he'd come trailing back, couldn't stay away. These guys were his friends, Scoot's only friends. Except tonight, there's some kind of bad feeling again, Scoot's feelings are bruised, fuck he isn't going to show it, of the pledge class "Scoot" Campos is possibly the alums' favorite, he's been given to know. *Ethnic diversity! An idea whose time has come for Phi Epsilon.* At the top of the stairs he's out of breath, can't hold it back God damn is he pissing his pants?—can't help it, can't stop it, how'd this happen, if the girls downstairs learn of Scoot's accident they will be totally grossed-out and who can blame them, the guys are going to be disgusted, not the first time Scoot has pissed his pants too staggering-drunk to lurch to a toilet, or outside on the lawn, or too confused about where he is, if he's awake or in fact asleep, maybe this is a dream, one of those weird dreams it's O.K. to piss, nobody will scold it's O.K. to piss into some receptacle or crack in the floor, that hot wet sensation spreading in his groin, soaking his underwear and down his legs, strong-piss-smelling, quickly turning cold. A piss-trail following Scoot Campos up the stairs soaked into the carpet, he's laughing like a deranged little kid soaked his diaper on purpose, hell the carpets at the Phi Ep house are already (piss?) stained, what's the big deal? *Fuck you* he's saying, defending himself against some guy, or guys, stooping over him, cursing him calling him names, Scoot Campos is wired tonight, he's

laughing in their faces, somebody dragging him
where?—toward a window?—wide-open windows
and curtains sucked outside and blowing/flapping in
the wind, and there's a moon, Jesus!—glaring—white
moon like a beacon, some kind of crazy eye peering
into Scoot Campos's soul *How'ya doin Scoot hey man know
what?—you're O.K.* This is God's eye, Scoot thinks.
(Or maybe a street light? Outside on Pitt Avenue?)
Cursing him somebody is lifting him he's thrashing
and flailing his arms, laughing so any remaining
dribble of piss is eked out and whoever it is grabbing
Scoot in a hammerlock, one of the older-guy wres-
tlers, built like a tank and taut-jawed and giving off
heat and that strong pungent smell of a male body
meaning he's in fighting mode, cursing Scoot calling
him asshole, dickhead, fuckhead, Scoot is being lifted,
pushed into an opening in the wall, it's the trash
chute, or maybe the drunken pledge is crawling head-
first into the chute of his own volition, and one of the
guys grabs his ankles to pull him back, and Scoot is
kicking, and yelling, and laughing, at least it sounds
like laughter, with this wild-wired spic anything is
possible. *Hey guys?—help me?—help me guys?* kicking like
crazy so whoever has hold of his ankles has to let go.
God-damned dangerous Campos when he's been
drinking, and Scoot's thick stocky body lurches down
the trash chute, sounds like a pig squealing, a kid
shooting down a slide in an amusement park,
down-the-chute, down-the-chute into something
soft to break your fall, at the end of the pitch-black
stale-air chute there should be something soft except
there isn't, with the impact of 175 pounds Scoot Campos strikes the edge of the trash bin, his forehead
strikes the sharp metal edge of the bin, immediately
he's bleeding, dazed, a terrible pounding pain in his

head, his neck has been twisted, his spine, his legs
are twisted weirdly beneath him, too dazed to be
panicked not knowing what has happened or where
he is feebly he pleads *Hey guys?—help me?* amid a confusion of rich, ripe, rotting smells, something rancid, trash and garbage, upside-down trying to turn,
to twist his body stunned and quivering like a mangled worm, trying to lift his head, to breathe, to
open his mouth, a terrible throbbing pain in his
neck, in his upper spine, like a gasping fish he opens
his mouth but no words, no sounds are uttered,
can't call for help his mouth is filled with trash, his
brain shudders, and is extinguished. For sure the
guys will check on Scoot, make their way downstairs shouting and laughing like hyenas, craziest
damn thing this drunk pledge smashed out of his
head slid down the trash chute, not the first time a
drunken pledge or active at the Phi Ep house slid
down the trash chute, down into the Dumpster,
anyway there's the intention that the guys will check
on the pledge in the Dumpster, but amid party
noise, a swarm of people including high-school-age
girls heavily made-up and costumed in hooker
mode, high-decibel music pounding the ears, there's
too many distractions. Later it will be claimed that
a couple of guys did in fact check the Dumpster but
Campos wasn't there. Possibly Campos had been
bleeding but couldn't have been hurt seriously because evidently he'd crawled out of the Dumpster
and gone away, back to the dorm maybe, anyway
nobody was in the Dumpster when they checked,
they swore. Yet, the guy had a weird sense of humor,
everybody would testify to Scoot Campos's weird
sense of humor, he might've returned and crawled
back into the Dumpster, like a little kid would do,

like hide-and-seek, except he fell asleep there, or he'd hurt his head and passed out, and got covered in party trash, had to be some freak accident like that, what other explanation is there? As Scoot's brain is bleeding, as Scoot's mouth is filling with trash, as Scoot's heart beats and lurches with a frantic stubbornness like the heart of a partly dissected but still living frog seventy miles to the east in Whispering Woods Estates, Southfield, Irene Campos lies awake in bed uncomfortably perspiring, hot flushes in her face, in her upper chest, her thoughts come confused and slow and have something to do with the moon veiled by curtains, or by high-scudding clouds, the full moon is a sign of good luck and happiness or is there something disquieting about the full moon so whitely glaring, unless it's a neighbor's outside light, Mrs. Campos isn't fully awake nor is she asleep planning how next day she will insist to Mr. Campos that they drive over to Grand Rapids to visit with Hector, Jr. who hasn't been answering her calls, hasn't even answered e-mail messages recently, beside her Mr. Campos is sleeping fitfully on his back, twitches and thrashes in his smelly underwear she'll find, sometimes, kicked beneath the bed or in a furtive mound in a corner of Mr. Campos's closet—why? Why would a man hoard soiled underwear? And socks? Mr. Campos snores, snorts, sounds like a drowning man, careful not to wake him Mrs. Campos pokes and nudges him until he rolls off his back, now grinding his back teeth but facing away, at the edge of the bed. That day Mrs. Campos sent Hector, Jr. a pleading text message PLEASE CALL MOM DARLING for text messages are all the rage now, Mrs. Campos's woman friends tell her, it's how young people communicate with one another but hours later Hector, Jr. has not communicated with his mother, she has become seriously worried. Oh, if only that college hadn't been so aggressive sending brochures, pamphlets, even a phone call, recruiting students from Southfield High, not that the university was going to offer Hector, Jr. a scholarship, not a penny, his parents would be paying full tuition/room-and-board/fees, if only Hector, Jr. had decided to go to Eastern Michigan University at Ypsilanti, no more than forty miles away, there's an engineering school at Ypsilanti, too, and fraternities, but Hector, Jr. could live at home, at least, and Mrs. Campos could take better care of him. Unconsciously caressing her left breast, clutching her left breast in her right hand, lying on her side clutching her large, warm, soft breast, how like a sac of warm water it is, or warm milk, on the brink of a dream of surpassing beauty and tenderness Mrs. Campos shuts her eyes, why does Mr. Campos never caress her breasts any longer, why does Mr. Campos never suck her nipples any longer, Mrs. Campos runs her thumb over the large soft nipple stirring it to hardness, like a little berry, she is driving back from the city, driving back from ugly Detroit to Whispering Woods Estates, such joy, such pride, turning into the brick-gated subdivision off Southfield Road, making her way floating along Pheasant Pass, Larkspur Drive, Bluebell Lane and at last to Quail Circle where, in the gleaming-white Colonial at number 23, the Campos family lives.

Vigilante

In late October he returned home for several days. The sky was not the clear porcelain blue of autumn but the color of wet slate. The river—this was the Delaware—at that scenic conjunction of New York State, Pennsylvania, and New Jersey called the Delaware Water Gap—was swollen from recent rains, ochre-colored, debris-laden, with a look of something live and sinuous and obscenely jocular like a great translucent sea worm. He had not wanted to come home so soon but it had happened and he found it difficult to speak to his mother without betraying the anger he felt, that had backed up in him like raw sewage. The few people he still knew from public school, when he'd gone to public school here, who might've been back for October break if they were still in college, weren't home when he called, or weren't available to see him. He thought *They're avoiding me! I can't believe this.* Though in fact, he could.

Old yearnings he'd believed he had outgrown, childish wishes he'd extracted from his inflamed flesh as you'd extract shrapnel piece by piece, swept over him again, but he did not give in: he remained sober. He was twenty-two years and five months old and he'd been sober for the past four months, two weeks and sixteen days.

All that he really missed was that thing they'd done together. That thing which he shrank from naming.

All that he really missed was his life! Of that, he wasn't going to think.

This week was called October break, an abrupt and seemingly purposeless recess in the fall term at certain private universities, upscale liberal arts colleges and prep schools. "October break"—falling at the end of the month, continuing into November and through Election Day. The idea having been, in the long-ago 1960s and early 1970s, when American university students had been galvanized by idealism—civil rights demonstrations, anti-war, feminist—that energetic young people would volunteer to help with voter registration in "racially tense" regions of the United States. But by the time J.J. was an undergraduate, several years into the twenty-first century, few recalled such idealism let alone had the energy or goodwill to act upon it.

"'October break.' We truly did try to 'get out the vote.' I went with a minivan of friends from Penn out to Chester, to help at the polls. We'd pick people up in these ghastly tenements, elderly or sick people, or single women with no transportation, and drive them to the polls. We were accused by Republicans of telling them how to vote but we did not! As if they were such fools they wouldn't have known." J.J.'s mother spoke with that air of regret tinged with mockery that had come to be her predominant mode of speech in recent years, that made J.J. uncomfortable. Were these black voters?—J.J. didn't have to ask. Who else but "black voters" had to be helped by rich white Ivy League college kids in minivans? J.J. did ask where was Chester, not that he was much interested but he'd wanted to appear interested, assuming it was somewhere in the south, for vaguely he'd known that his mother had been a civil rights activist in Mississippi, Alabama, Georgia in that long-ago and unfathomable time before his birth when she'd been approximately the age J.J. was now; but his mother said no, Chester was in Pennsylvania, just west of Philadelphia by about thirty miles. "It's said to be even worse now. More poverty, more drugs."

J.J. had annoyed his sensitive mother, asking a careless question. For of course J.J. knew, or should have known, where Chester, PA was. As he should have known the noble tradition behind "October break" that was now just a few days off following midterm exams for students to show up back home when they'd only just left in September.

"Well, Mom, I'm here. Not in Chester. Sorry you're disappointed."

The exchange with his mother, on the first night of his visit, left him unsettled, annoyed. He'd driven nonstop for four hours from Hanover, New Hampshire, to Port Jervis, New York, to return home and there was the specter of Thanksgiving looming in three weeks and his mother would want him back then, too. For he was her only child, and she'd almost lost him. And he felt that sensation of yearning and despair wash over him, murky water against his mouth. Couldn't breathe, couldn't open his mouth to protest. On the phone she'd made her usual sardonic jokes hinting at her son's "social-sexual life"—"the life of a normal healthy young unmarried male"—but he'd understood that for all her sophisticated banter she was anxious about him, and anxious about herself, and he'd said, "Look, Mom, if you want me there," with the easy laugh he'd cultivated as an adolescent, to disarm and placate his elders, "I'm *there*."

So he was. Four days, three nights. They would see a few elderly relatives, he would track down some former classmates who hadn't moved away and weren't yet married, who remembered him in mostly flattering ways: Jon Quinlan—"J.J."—whose father owned Quinlan Heating & Cooling, Inc. and whose mother was an administrator at Port Jervis Community College. He wouldn't call his father, who was living just six miles away. J.J. knew that his mother was expecting him to ask about his father, from whom she'd been divorced for nearly a year, but he didn't ask; he wanted never to see his father again.

His mother framed his face in her small, cool hands that held him firm, as one might hold firm a panicked bird that freezes in the face of danger: "You're happy, J.J.? At school? You're all right, are you?" *Happy* and *all right* were code words. Meaning was he sober, not-using. Was he clean. J.J. laughed to reassure her. "Sure, Mom. Look at me: poster boy for clean living."

Thinking *You want me to take a urine test? No problem.*

Frankly he missed being high. That thing he'd learned to do, that a girl had taught him, especially he missed but he could not tell his mother who looked at him with such searching eyes, sick-brimming with love that almost—almost!—he could not bear. Not just being high but the anticipation. On your way to score if you're driving you can feel your foot on the gas pedal and the fuel propelling the vehicle is a part of the high, a tidal wave lifting you warm and engulfing and protective of you, that was lost to him now. This was the great loss of his life, more even than the wreck of his parents' marriage. More than the protracted divorce of which his mother had remarked it was like an autopsy performed on a living subject. And his father telling him that last time *You know you're not just killing yourself, God damn you you're killing your mother and me you know that don't you you sorry little prick.*

His life now was a plateau flat as a sidewalk. Thinking of it his mouth twisted like a living thing.

"When I think of you, honey—I mean, of the future—and you—the one thing I want so badly is for you to be happy."

"'Happy.' That's a grim prognosis, Mom."

"Don't be sarcastic. And don't do that juvenile thing with your mouth, please."

"My 'mow-th,' Mom? What juvenile thing?"

J.J. laughed. Inside his head, his laughter sounded like metal being crumpled. "My 'mow-th' is my own 'mow-th,' Mom. In case you didn't know, it isn't yours."

He drove back to New Hampshire early, and in the near-empty residence hall he thought of killing himself. He thought *You can do anything you want, at any time.* There was that solace. In fact he was doing reasonably well in his courses. The difficult part had been being re-admitted into the university, after withdrawing for an indefinite medical leave. J.J. was making up his sophomore year that had ended in a wreck two years before. He was one of those on "academic probation" but after another semester, if he continued to do well, high B's, low A's, his name would be removed from the list and his record would be "expunged." All very legal, for universities fear litigation. Though at a remove, J.J.'s father continued to oversee what you might call J.J.'s public, official life. For there would be a time—and not in the distant future—when prospective employers would be vetting J.J.'s undergraduate record, and J.J.'s father meant this record to be free of obvious blemishes.

Mr. Quinlan was a successful businessman. He was a bastard, J.J. had to admire. Unlike J.J.'s mother who could not keep any resolution that involved ultimatums put to her son, Mr. Quinlan had a strong and unyielding will. *If you don't clean yourself up you are dead to me. Nobody is going to plead with you ever again.*

Strictly speaking, this wasn't true. J.J.'s mother had pleaded with him numberless times.

Last time he'd seen his father, before he'd gone into rehab at Harrisburg. There'd been some difficulty there and J.J.'s mother had had to transfer him to a rehab clinic in Philadelphia where "security" was higher. During these weeks—in fact, months—maybe a year—lost track of time, lobotomized and eviscerated—Mr. Quinlan had not visited his son. Reports were sent to Mr. Quinlan and very likely Mr. Quinlan conferred with the medical staff but Mr. Quinlan had not conferred with his incarcerated son. Now J.J. was out of rehab and allowed under the terms of his probation to resume his university education, his father wanted to see him again. Wanted J.J. to call him Dad. Sent him checks, which J.J. tossed into a drawer.

He'd cleaned himself up. Still, he was dead to the old man. It was easier on the nerves, having just one parent.

At twenty-two J.J. was still of an age when "fresh starts" are encouraged and are, in some quarters, epidemic. In his last prep school everyone he'd known had been an ex-addict—except those who were still addicts, or had relapsed; it wasn't cool to inquire too openly about the status of others, but somehow you knew. Nor was it cool to express hope. Though you might cherish hope as J.J. did, the way you hoarded those precious OxyContin tabs in your most secret stash at the rear of a drawer of jumbled underwear.

Not now, though. Since rehab, J.J. didn't keep a stash.

It was the great change in his life. It was like not having any money in the bank—it was like not having a bank.

Instead, J.J. was *all right*. You could live like that indefinitely, he'd been told. Not happy exactly but *all right*. You could.

Thanksgiving: Constance wanted J.J. home.

"Constance" was J.J.'s mother's name, which she did not like shortened and "cute-ified" into "Connie."

For you could see, Constance Plummer (she'd taken back her old, maiden surname) was not a "Connie."

Though wanting her son home for Thanksgiving. Her phone messages airy and casual for this was not a mother to exert pressure on her son only just telling him she was planning for him, and the others she'd invited for Thanksgiving were expecting to see him, and so—he was coming, wasn't he?

That lift in her voice—so vulnerable! J.J. shut his eyes in resentment seeing his mother's beautiful faded face like something on an old coin, worn smooth by careless handling.

Constance didn't "do" e-mail except for professional purposes. Constance "did" voice transactions solely. Saying defensively, "I need to hear a human voice. I need to hear my own voice. I need a reply—I need to laugh. E-mail makes me sad."

J.J. squirmed to hear such revelations, intimate in his ear. J.J. had come to dislike speaking to his mother on the phone, even leaving messages for her, knowing that his living voice could betray him.

Don't love me so much, hey? Find somebody else.

With the air of one who'd only now just thought of it, J.J. told his mother that he'd been invited to a friend's home for Thanksgiving. He'd gotten himself into "a kind of predicament" and maybe couldn't get out.

See, I'm sleeping with a girl. You can figure that. Right?

In fact there were two girls: the rich girl from Hilton Head, SC, and the rich girl from Beverly Farms, MA. He'd been irresponsibly vague with each girl allowing her to think that maybe he'd come home with her though in fact J.J. would've greatly preferred going home with one of his rich-boy roommates whose Thanksgivings involved skiing in Jackson Hole, Wyoming. ("We can hunt, too. You like to hunt? We have plenty of guns at the lodge. We can tramp out in the woods. My granddad owns like five hundred acres. There's fantastic scenery. We can hunt white-tailed deer, geese, and pheasants. They're all in season. Last Thanksgiving me and my cousin shot an elk. A buck! We couldn't follow it all the way to kill it, but I guess it died. You know how to use a rifle? That's cool.") For in this phase of his life, J.J. had emerged as a popular guy. Weird how you can wreck your life, drown, re-surface and somehow you don't look the age you feel inside, you don't even look like what you were when you'd crashed. At college where Jonathan—"J.J."—Quinlan was older than most of his classmates by two or even three years but did not appear older, he was what you'd have to call, without irony, a social success. Friendship came easy to him, like scattering paper money. Sex was no problem for him, though remembering girls' names was.

Finally he decided sure, he'd come home. Thanksgiving was the day you returned home, even if you'd only been home three weeks before and had slipped away early unable to breathe otherwise.

Even if there was something dangerous at home. Something waiting to happen, that could happen only through you.

For, on the phone, his mother had sounded dangerously cheerful. Here was a woman who'd overdosed on sleeping pills at least once of which J.J. knew, during the protracted months of the divorce. The overdose had been "accidental"—of course. But there were blackout episodes, as well. Driving her car, managing to get to the community college parking lot and—whatever happened then, J.J. hadn't ever been sure. Probably he hadn't been told. J.J.'s father had left Constance to marry a young woman employed at Quinlan Heating & Cooling, Inc. and there'd been things said at court hearings, some of which had found their way into print in the Port Jervis newspaper, deeply wounding to Constance, deeply humiliating, and so J.J. didn't trust his mother's unwarranted cheerfulness. When you're depressed you don't have the energy to do harm to yourself. That requires good cheer, optimism. That requires a clear and sober vision of the future awaiting you.

She was overjoyed to see him. She was too damned happy to see him, it tore his heart, that was a flattened-mummified-roadkill heart, to see how happy his mere presence made her. Sure he'd hug his mom, sure he'd let her reach up to grab him, and kiss his stubbled cheek. Tears in her just-slightly-bloodshot eyes, she brushed away laughing and embarrassed. "Sweetie, I am so relieved to see you! I've been listening to the weather report. Thinking of you on the Interstate. There's a 'storm watch' for later tonight—"

Crazed winds howling in the trees. Gigantic oaks surrounding the house on High Post Road. In the night he'd used to lie awake hearing screech owls. The thrill of their cries which returned to him, when his guts were ripped out of his belly hand-over-hand unless the cries he'd recalled were those of rabbits in the field just beyond the house, as the talons and beaks of the screech owls tore into them.

She'd ordered a twenty-pound tom turkey. She'd "gone a little crazy" inviting relatives, friends. Strays who had nowhere else to go for Thanksgiving, from the community college. A couple from church—this was new, and ominous: "church"—who shook J.J.'s hand with an excess of warmth and called him "J.J." with a familiarity that offended him. He became sulky, sarcastic. He was—maybe—jealous: all these people including strangers he'd never glimpsed before, plus a fretful four-year-old girl cousin seated close beside him at the enormous dinner table. (With extensions—he'd had to help his mother enlarge the table, grunting with effort—the familiar table had grown grotesque to accommodate eighteen!) Why'd Constance have to invite so many people, when she'd been begging him to come home? J.J. had nothing to say to these people, even his relatives. Except for the little-girl cousin, he was the youngest person at the table. Had to endure questions about his classes at the university, his professors, political views, what did "your generation" think of x, y, z as if anyone whom J.J. knew had views worth repeating and it would matter if they did. Affably he said, "'Global warming'—it's some cyclical kind of thing. Tidal waves, tsunamis, comets crashing into the earth, Ice Age, shrinking polar caps, flesh-eating microbes. What's to worry? There's gonna be an 'immortality' gene in the next few years."

In the perplexed looks of the others J.J. saw that his attempt at—whatever it was—Comedy Central stand-up humor—had fallen flat.

Only Constance was laughing: "Jonathan, really! At twenty-two, you can afford to be cynical."

An unattractive flush rose into her face, to indicate her dismay. "At forty-two, Mom, what'll I be? A 'Christian'?"

In fact, Constance was forty-eight or -nine. He thought so. His clever reply, if that was what it was, rolled along the lengthy table like a meandering marble that came to rest midway.

There were elderly aunts of his mother's at the table. These were good Christian women you'd call them. And the couple "from church" with their pink-gummed smiles and glistening teeth. J.J. hated it that his so-rational mother with her Ph.D. in psychology, a professional woman to whom religion had seemed to count for very little while J.J. was growing up, had been drawn to some sort of predictable religious solace now, in the wake of divorce.

He thought that had to be the reason: the divorce.

The male half of the pink-gummed church-couple pointedly asked J.J. about "religious belief on campus" and J.J. shrugged saying he didn't know. Still the man persisted: "But there is a revival of religious belief among college-age people, isn't there?—it's in the media."

J.J. said politely that must be right then, if it was in the media.

So bored! Wanting to shove his chair away from the table. Wanted to flee upstairs to his old room.

Wanted—what?—what did he want?—to grasp a rifle. His own rifle, he hadn't touched for years. Maybe his mother had gotten rid of it. Maybe his father had taken it when he'd moved out. This was a handsome .22-caliber Winchester deer rifle his father had given him. Years ago when his father had taken J.J. hunting in the Poconos hoping to reassert himself in his son's life. For already by the age of fourteen, J.J. had begun to drift.

Like a balloon drifting over the familiar rooftops, treetops. Up and away and lost in the sky and never look back.

He'd been a precocious kid. Already by age twelve he'd been smoking dope, drinking beer. His first drunk-fumbling sex with an older, high school girl.

The outing in the Pococnos with Dad had not been successful. But J.J. had liked the rifle, in itself. Not enough to go hunting with his father ever again—nor had Mr. Quinlan suggested another expedition—but he'd liked the feel of the gun, its promise. Except why would you have to trek for miles into the snowy woods with the rifle, when you could examine it, fondle it, sight along its barrel right here at home.

J.J. said, "In my next lifetime maybe I'll be a 'Christian soldier.' Like in, 'Onward, Christian Soldiers.' That's a hymn, isn't it? Or maybe I'll enroll at the police academy. Train to become a New York State trooper."

The others laughed uneasily. J.J.'s mother was staring at him, from her end of the table.

Five months, three weeks and six days he'd been sober.

". . . call police? We think . . ."

". . . have you told . . ."

". . . Connie, please! Harold knows what he is . . ."

". . . all right, then. For tonight. But tomorrow . . ."

An exchange at the front door J.J. wasn't meant to hear. As Constance was saying goodbye to guests. It was the couple from church—whose names were Harold and Ev, or Evvie: in lowered voices speaking to J.J.'s mother who stood with her back to J.J., a few yards away.

Mysterious lowered voices, urgent and intimate. At this moment J.J. was lifting his little-girl cousin in his hands, making the child giggle. And the child's mother, an older cousin of his, not a girl with whom J.J. had ever been particularly close, was telling J.J. some news of—whatever it was—to which J.J. wasn't listening—distracted by trying to overhear what was being told to his mother, she seemed resistant to hearing.

Afterward J.J. would recall how forcibly the church-couple had spoken to Constance. How Ev, or Evvie, had hissed a warning into Constance's ear, like a pushy older sister.

When all of the guests were gone, he'd cornered his mother in the kitchen. "So what was that about? 'Call police'—why?"

J.J.'s mother stared at him in surprise. He saw that she would lie to him, and he didn't want to hear it.

"It's him? My father? What's he doing—calling you again? Making threats? Is he?"

"No."

She spoke quickly, her eyes were evasive. She'd been wrapping turkey leftovers in cellophane wrap, now she carried a heavy platter to place in the refrigerator pushing past J.J. who stood in her way.

"'No'—what? He isn't—what?"

"He isn't—what you said. Threatening me, or—"

"Mom, I thought this was ended. Like, a year ago. You said it was over. You got that—from the court—" In his excitement J.J. couldn't come up with the legal term—injunction?—seeing that his mother, who was several inches shorter than he was, was frightened of him, and she was lying to him, and anger rose swiftly in his throat like bile. He wanted to slam the refrigerator door shut and confront her. Wanted to shake her by the shoulders as once—more than once—he'd seen his father shake his mother by the shoulders;

at a distance he'd seen, from the stairs; though at whatever age he'd been he had not been meant to be a witness, and he had not remembered, until now.

"It isn't what you think, honey. Whatever you overheard. I don't care to discuss it now."

"Mom, if he's threatening you, I need to know. That son of a bitch."

"Honey, no! It's a misunderstanding."

"What's a 'misunderstanding'?"

"I said, I don't care to discuss it now."

"Fuck that! You tell me, Mom."

She winced. She pushed past him. She was headed for the stairs, J.J. wanted to pull at her arm but dared not touch her.

"You're protecting him? That fucker? That tried to fuck us both? That—son of a bitch?"

Though sober J. J. was feeling stoned, suddenly. A roaring in his ears like a cocaine rush. But it was a bad trip, an evil dose. Impurities in the high, like sand in his teeth. Air-bubbles in an artery, rushing to the heart to kill it with an embolism.

There was this thing they'd done. They'd done together. He never thought of her now and even her name was not a name he wished to recall and he could not have said if she was alive yet, or had died and he'd been informed but had not wished to process the information at just that time. You could ruin a high, processing the wrong information. You could ruin the last pure high of your life.

She'd been older than J.J. All his best girls had been older. *Booting* she'd called it. She'd taught him, though he'd never been able to *boot* with her skill. Like a nurse she'd been. Maybe in fact she had been a nurse. Carefully you draw the blood back up into the syringe once the heroin is partially injected in the vein, back and forth like the sweetest sex-teasing to prolong and intensify the high she'd taught him, done it to him how many times and he'd never forget, there was no high like it.

He'd been crazy for her, he remembered. Not her name but that, he remembered.

Now the sex he had wasn't like sex but something else. Like an old silent black-and-white movie. It was sex, but not sex. It was the kind of sex that, if your cell phone rang, you'd answer.

Howling wind! He loved it, high in the old oaks.

After she'd gone to bed and the house was darkened. After he'd been released knowing she had to be asleep. You can sense it, going off Mom's radar. That good feeling.

Too restless to stay indoors. The grease-smell of turkey, congealing gravy. At the table he'd wanted to laugh in all their faces. He'd wanted to tell them *Not a one of you knows. All of you dead and not a clue.*

By midnight he was cruising the strip. Beyond the Miracle Mall at the intersection with I-84. Some of the landmarks were changed but there was Friday's, and there was Galloway's Go-Go, and there was the Truck Stop, and there was the snow-swept desolation of the vast parking lot beside the shuttered Kmart where they'd smoked dope, and later "ice"—that had scared J.J. Quinlan, it was a high that blew off the top of his skull.

He'd never tried ice again, after that first time. Tonight he scored just a few nickel-bags of dope, high-school stuff. His hands shook, even so. His mouth had gone dry with anticipation. He'd had to have known that, starting off that morning from Hanover, easing his car onto I-84, he'd end like this at the strip beyond the Miracle Mall.

Cruising along the river. On full deafening volume was his Juice tape. Smoking he could breathe, finally. Deep into his lungs. He could feel his freeze-shrunk brain opening at last, like rose petals opening, the kind of roses his mother tried to grow—"multifoliate"— with such obsessive ardor and frustration.

Could've driven this stretch of the River Road with his eyes shut. All those summer nights he'd been too restless to stay home, headed out to score at the strip, with a girl sometimes but most often alone, he'd looped back along the river liking to see it by moonlight except tonight the moon was shrouded in mist or cloud and his eyes were flooding with moisture stinging from the smoke he wasn't accustomed to, after so long.

Sixteen he'd been, when the spell first came upon him. He'd found a new religion! In an explosion of light like shattered ice he saw how things must be, and are; the justice of the universe; anything that happened was meant to happen and could not have happened in any other way. The knowledge was so excruciating, he'd have to kill himself—it was like one orgasm following another, you couldn't bear it. Or he'd kill a few others, and then himself.

"Two for the price of one. Or three."

His speaking-aloud voice was both sardonic and wistful. Speaking aloud when he was high signaled that he, J.J. Quinlan, was on camera and being observed. He was being videotaped. He'd be downloaded from the Internet long after he'd died.

"Bargain. Prices slashed. Storewide sale."

He thought, if he killed enough of them, he would be justified then in killing himself. Otherwise, suicide was a show-offy gesture. Meaning you took yourself too fucking seriously, how's that cool?

Must've been, he'd changed his mind. Coming down from the high, and feeling like shit. In which state you'd never see the angel Moroni in a blaze of light unfurling a scroll the way Joseph Smith did though J.J. had to figure, from what he'd read about the founder of Mormonism, that Joseph Smith had been a kid not much older than J.J. high on—what?—maybe he'd been smoking jimson weed.

That night—this was still Thanksgiving—he'd taken the rifle with him in the Volvo. Out to the mall, to score. Exactly why he'd taken the rifle with him he could not have said. He wasn't sure the gun would even fire, after so many years. Wasn't sure he'd loaded it correctly. Smoking dope he'd been talking and laughing and you could say he'd been enjoying himself so the rifle was part of that, playful and not intended to be—whatever else a rifle might be misunderstood as.

After his mom had gone to bed. After she'd taken her nighttime medication. He'd located the rifle in a closet in the basement exactly where he'd last seen it and he'd located a box of ammunition that had been opened and only a row of bullets used. His excitement had mounted, his mouth was dry and he'd been swallowing compulsively knowing now that his anger and disgust at dinner, his choked-up fury at the pink-gummed smiling strangers his mother had invited into their house, had been aimed at this: the moment of lifting the rifle, and seeing that the handsome maple wood stock was still shiny, and the bluish steel was not pocked with anything like rust.

This is a sign, he thought. In the right place, at the right time.

All the sacred visions had that in common: the seer through whom the visions flooded had to be in the right place, at the right time.

"'Christian soldier.' Maybe it isn't too late."

Opening his eyes—wide-open—the sudden surprise of seeing where he was—on the River Road?—recalling then how he'd gotten here; and figuring that he was waiting for the moon to pierce through the soiled shreds of cloud. How many months it had been since he'd smoked a joint—really smoked a joint—though what was in this exactly, J.J. didn't know—there was a weird delayed kick like a bomber—was this some kind of meth?—some new mix, everybody knew about except him?—feeling his life quiver inside him, like something inside a cocoon, stirring to emerge. Like in that movie *Alien*.

"You are dead to me"—gravely his father had decreed.

Unless it was: "I am dead to you."

J.J. laughed. "'I am dead to you.'" He liked that. Like in some old tragic play of Greek times, a figure still as a statue with a mask—overlarge, with exaggerated features of grief—hiding the human face; so you lost the connection, a human face is behind such a mask, and human eyes are inside the hollowed-out sockets for eyes.

At Milford, PA, he turned the Volvo around. It was nearing 2 A.M. His headlights were picking up a swirl of snowflakes frenzied as lice. Why he'd driven into Pennsylvania he wasn't sure. Maybe he'd planned to look up someone . . . Couldn't remember any name, or any face to go with any name. He drove back to Port Jervis and north to the I-84 intersection, the strip beyond the Miracle Mall where no time seemed to have passed since he'd been there, again at Truck Stop where this time he picked up a nickel bag of blues—sodium Amytal tabs—since the other, the dope, was a weird mix of something he couldn't identify, though he liked—to a degree, he guessed he liked—he liked the effect it was having on him—clearing up his thoughts—razor-sharp, his thoughts—though maybe he was risking—wasn't sure what he was risking—unless, having the .22 with him, in his car, carelessly hidden on the floor in the rear, was some sort of—what'd you call it—violation of probation, was it? Not academic probation but the other.

For when he'd smoked all the dope. Wouldn't want to crash, he'd have the rest of the weekend to get through: Thanksgiving meant Friday/Saturday and Sunday morning he'd drive back north to Hanover.

Break this down into hours, you could see J.J. would soon run out.

The blues, he thought he could trust, more. He'd had good experiences with blues since his heart was a good strong heart, unimpaired by experience. His heart wasn't going to burst. The hairs on the nape of his neck stirred, it was like the promise of sex: anticipation.

Through the high-pitch volume of the Juice tape he was hearing—was it a siren?—police or ambulance, fire engine—and his heart clutched, guessing it had to be him they were pursuing—the guy he'd just scored from was an undercover cop—trying not to panic seeing in his rearview mirror coming up swiftly behind him—now passing him—not one but two Port Jervis police squad cars—sirens, red lights flashing—in pursuit of some luckless fucker not J.J. Quinlan, not just yet.

Last time he'd been home, at October break, he'd cruised streets near the high school, no reason but for the hell of it: Port Jervis Senior High he'd attended only for a year and a half, abruptly then his parents had withdrawn him and he'd transferred to Basking Ridge Academy, a private prep school in north-central New Jersey; from Basking Ridge, to New London School, CT. But he'd kept in touch with certain of his friends from this high school, and from middle school, and there were girls, there was one girl in particular, that night he'd driven past her parents' house on Elm Ridge Avenue and in the cul-de-sac at the shadowy end of the street he'd parked the Volvo, and stared at the part-lighted house: the upstairs rooms, visible from the street, and one of these rooms was the girl's room, or had been—they'd gone there, afternoons when no one was in the house: stoned and eager to make love, however many times and however long they could. Later, they'd had some misunderstanding. She'd betrayed J.J., or J.J. had betrayed her, or maybe both. And this time he'd returned home, he'd called her number, the number he still had for her, and somebody there, had to be the girl's father, said she wasn't home and J.J. said his name and the man said with more emphasis *My daughter isn't home, she doesn't live here anymore.* And J.J. said in his best affable-American-kid voice, Let me give you my number, you can tell her I called. (For he'd remembered then, this girl had gone away to college in California, by now she'd have graduated. Maybe she was married. Maybe she had a kid. Maybe she was dead. Maybe, if her father told her Jon Quinlan had called, she'd have laughed in scorn saying *That loser? He's still alive?*)

Not that the fucker had written the number down, J.J. knew.

Some people, you see how it's only just, somebody should put a bullet through their skulls.

If he'd had a clear silhouette, Mr. Leary at a window: how cool would that be, leaning out his car window, with the rifle, to take aim, and to fire?

Except, that night, J.J. hadn't had the rifle with him. But he'd thought of it, belatedly.

Tonight, he had the rifle. But he wasn't driving on Elm Ridge, he'd turned off onto Delaware which would take him into the neighborhood where his father now lived—alone, J.J. had reason to believe—for Mr. Quinlan hadn't remarried after all; that, J.J. knew though he'd never made inquiries, and he was sure that his mother hadn't told him. The house was a two-storey stucco and this too, in a cul-de-sac at the end of the narrow residential street. Properties on this street backed onto a township-owned nature preserve of many acres. J.J. felt a pang of longing, if he'd grown up in this house, if his parents had lived in this house, and not in the other with its showy front lawn and truncated back lawn, facing houses with similar showy front lawns, if he'd grown up on Highland Street and not Old Post Road maybe his life would have turned out differently.

By now, he'd have graduated from the police academy. He'd be a state trooper. He'd look good in a uniform, his heart would be at ease behind an identifying badge. He guessed you always knew who you were, in such circumstances. If you had to shoot, you shot to kill: two shots. You shot to protect yourself, and others. You shot in the cause of justice. You never drew your gun without being prepared to shoot and to die in the line of duty and that was why you were allowed to continue to live.

He'd cut his headlights. He was parked at the end of the narrow tree-lined street, where there was a wooded area, what appeared to be a wood chip trail filling up with snow. Still the motor was running, he was listening to Juice he'd turned down so no one in the sleeping houses was likely to hear; he thought *I need to clear my head. There is something wrong with my head.*

The shit he'd been smoking. Laced with crystal meth, was it?— he hadn't known what the dealer was saying, mumbling into his dyed-looking black biker goatee, and it hadn't seemed cool to ask.

He cut the motor, climbed out of the car. Trying to walk without slipping on the ice—his smooth-soled boots on the icy pavement—

and his breath steaming in anticipation—his pulse excited, fast—which he liked—you had to go with that feeling. In stealth making his way in the soft-snowy earth alongside the darkened stucco house, avoiding the driveway where he might be seen, if there was anyone to see at this hour of the night; for it seemed J.J. wasn't going to ring the doorbell at the front door shrewdly knowing that this wasn't a time of day—wasn't a time of night—when his father might reasonably expect someone to ring his doorbell, and hurry to answer it.

Except if his father knew it was him: Jon. His father had said *Will you return my call, please?* E-mails his father had sent, in his in-box identified as URGENT PLEASE OPEN but in disdain he'd deleted these messages without deigning to open them.

At the rear of the house there was a raised redwood deck, and the land below fell away into what was nearly a ravine, rocky and filled with snow, and beyond was the township-owned property, tall straight pine trees, beautiful and silent in the falling snow. Above was a faint tarnished-looking moon, just visible through the low cloud ceiling. Summer furniture still remained on the redwood deck, layered in snow. Almost J.J. could recall he'd been here before, on this redwood deck, and his father had grilled steaks and hamburgers on the barbecue, but he knew this could not have happened, such a "memory" was a trick of his father's: as in a sci-fi movie, parasite-thoughts could slip into an unwitting brain.

J.J.'s blunt boot prints were the first prints in the new-fallen snow on the deck. The house was still darkened upstairs and down. With the butt of the rifle, J.J. knocked at a door. It was a screened door, that rattled when he struck it. Behind it, a solid windowless door.

He struck the door again with the rifle-butt. His father had wanted to see him, next time he returned to Port Jervis: here he was.

"Hey Dad: it's me. 'Jon.'"

Not raising his voice. He knew, don't raise your voice. Neighbors might hear. This was a private transaction, no one else was to hear.

A light came up, upstairs. A shadowed figure at the window, peering down.

J.J. waved a hand. Not the rifle, he'd slung in the crook of his left arm so it wasn't immediately visible.

Shortly after, lights came on, illuminating the redwood deck from four corners. It was both a harsh glaring light and a light that cast disfiguring shadows. The door opened and a tall thick-bodied man stood in the doorway squinting through the screen door with an expression of such surprise and bafflement, J.J. had to laugh.

"Who'd you expect, Dad? It's 'Jon.'"

The man stared. Without smiling, he stared. Pushed the screen door open, and stepped outside. You could see how he'd been wakened rudely from sleep and in haste he'd thrown on clothes, a parka. He'd shoved bare feet into canvas shoes that resembled yachting shoes. His thinning gray hair was disheveled and his heavy face resembled a fleshy tropical fruit whose ripeness is indistinguishable from the first stages of rot. His eyes narrowed in alarm, disapproval.

"Jon? You?"

The closeness of his father, the familiar stricken-incredulous-disapproving tone of his father's voice, provoked in J.J. a familiar thrill of loathing.

"You're—here? Now? At three in the morning? Is this one of your jokes? Is this your idea of—"

Seeing the rifle, then. Though J.J. had only just shifted it inconspicuously in the crook of his arm.

"Is that loaded? Why have you brought that rifle? Is that—the rifle I gave you? What do you—"

"Just thought I'd stop by, Dad. I was in the neighborhood."

Mr. Quinlan was making fumbling gestures with both hands as if trying to zip up the parka. As if he feared he might be naked inside the parka.

In fact, Mr. Quinlan was wearing trousers, and what appeared to be a flannel pajama top.

This was funny: Mr. Quinlan's thin slit of a mouth. It was a fish-mouth, engaged in the effort of smiling. The eyes—not that J.J. could see his father's eyes in the harsh blinding glare of the outdoor lights very clearly but J.J. recalled them to be the color of mold—were fixed on J.J. as on an unwanted revelation.

The mouth moved. The mouth issued some kind of declaration.

Disgusted-Daddy voice. The thrill of loathing stabbed harder, in the region of J.J.'s groin.

"Just in the neighborhood, Dad. See, it's Thanksgiving. Maybe you forgot Thanksgiving?"

"Are you staying with your mother? Does she know you're here?"

"Sure! Mom sent me."

Mr. Quinlan had given up fumbling with the zipper, now with both hands he fumbled to clutch the parka shut. With a forced laugh he said skeptically he doubted that Constance knew where J.J. was at this hour of the night and J.J. shrugged saying sure: probably that was right.

Mr. Quinlan said he was sorry that J.J. hadn't called, to say he was coming. He'd have invited him over. For the next day.

J.J. said he was here now. Technically speaking it was the "next day"—it was the early morning of the day after Thanksgiving.

They were standing approximately three feet apart. J.J. observed that he was fully his father's height, now: six feet three. Except J.J.'s father outweighed him by thirty or more pounds.

Mr. Quinlan had never struck his son with more than an opened hand. He had never struck his son with a clenched fist. He had never knocked his son to the floor and stood over him, trembling with rage. Yet J.J. recalled these sights. In the movie of J.J.'s life these sights would fly past his widened entranced eyes like the crazed moons of Jupiter in *2001*.

"What'd you want to say to me, Dad? Now I'm here."

Mr. Quinlan smiled. Not the mold-eyes, that were watchful and wary, but the thin-slit mouth, a thin smile. This was a smile to placate, and to distract.

"I just wanted to speak with you, Jon. It's been a while. We can plan for tomorrow, if—"

"Hey Dad: I'm not drunk. If that's what you're worried about."

J.J. laughed, affably. Now he'd lifted the .22 Winchester with the handsome still-shiny maple wood stock, to show his father what good condition it was in, kept in that closet. Though he had yet to pull the trigger, he seemed to know that the bullets would fire.

"You're 'using'—I suppose? You've started again?"

"'Using.'" J.J. laughed. It was funny, everybody thought it was funny, embarrassing to the point of making you wince, parents trying to mimic their children's speech.

"Why are you laughing, Jon? This is funny? To you, it's amusing?"

Mr. Quinlan had been a high school athlete. Football mostly. J.J. had heard all about it, to the point of wanting to puke. Yet, J.J. had had to admire the man, he'd never lost that high-school-football confidence. Overweight and saggy-jowled and probably half-hung-over from all he'd had to drink that night, yet he was pressing forward, advancing on J.J. who was twenty-two years old, and holding the rifle. Had to hand it to the old bastard, he had guts.

And not that old: maybe fifty-two, -three. Older than J.J. would live to be but not, J.J. thought, *old*.

Mr. Quinlan saying, more aggressively now, "There is nothing amusing about this, Jon. Showing up here like this, 'high'—'stoned.' What are you—'wasted out of your mind'? That's funny, is it? 'Wasted out of your mind' is funny? Your mother has no idea, of course—where you are, and what you've been doing. Out buying drugs, 'using' as you'd promised her you would not, ever again—this is funny, isn't it? Your poor blind deluded mother—"

J.J. was snorting with laughter. Wiped his eyes, his nose on the sleeve of his jacket. "I wouldn't, Dad. If I were you."

"Wouldn't—what?"

"Wouldn't go there, Dad. 'Your mother'—shit like that."

"Are you threatening me, Jon? You're here, threatening me?"

"Fuck no, Dad. I am not."

J.J. squinted at the rifle. Was the safety lock on, or off? There was a red dot on the lock, he couldn't see in the harsh glaring light if the red lock was on, or off; but it was a crucial matter, to a hunter: *on, off*. You couldn't pull the fucking trigger if the safety lock was *on*. And if it was *off*, you couldn't touch the trigger, it might discharge the bullet.

To make sure, J.J. pushed the little button. There was a gratifying click.

"Are you trying to frighten me, Jon? That's why you've come here, waking me up, out of a sound sleep, to frighten me?"

"Fuck no, Dad. Didn't I just say."

J.J. was laughing. Trying not to laugh. Something had been said a minute before, his father had been saying—what? Something ugly, his father ought not to have said.

Mr. Quinlan began speaking rapidly, "reasonably." He was speaking to a small gathering of employees, possibly. The fish-mouth smiled but the mold-eyes were wary, calculating.

"What we will do, son, is: you will hand that rifle to me. You will hand that rifle to me and we will come inside the house where it's warm, and private, and not-snowing, and—we can talk. We can talk quietly. How does that sound?" The smile gripped tighter, the mold-eyes shone with goodwill. "I think that I should call your mother, Jon, to let her know where you are—to warn her, I'll be driving you back home. Because I don't think that you should be driving just now. In your condition, if you were to have an accident—if police arrested you—that would be unfortunate. And if your mother wakes up and discovers that you're gone, she'll be— you can imagine how upset she'll be—very upset. By nature, your mother is an emotional woman. Your mother is prone to hysteria. She hasn't been a well woman. You have taken advantage of her, a mother overly willing to believe what her beloved son tells her." Again there was a pause. J.J. observed his father's steaming breath: how fleeting, the visibility of a breath.

"Jon? Are you listening?"

"Fuck yes, Dad. Who else'd listen to your bullshit." J.J. laughed, not unpleasantly.

"Jon. There is no need to be rude."

"Just stay back. Don't make that move, Dad."

With his remarkable new vision—like laser, it was—J.J. clearly saw what his father was contemplating! As in a movie you see in an actor's eyes what he is preparing to do, and you see—it's a weird kind of movie-premonition, that grows on you, the more movies you see—what the outcome will be: the shot-in face, blood bursting from the mouth, the exploded nose. So swiftly it would happen, before the deafening retort of the gunshots even registered. And once the man had fallen, onto the blood-splotched snow on the redwood deck, there'd be nothing to prevent the rifle barrel from striking his head like a tire iron, or an ax. Until the skull caved in, like a melon.

Overripe, close to rot. Spilling rot-seeds like brains.

In anthropology lecture you might learn that in "aboriginal" cultures the brains of revered elders are devoured by the young. Exclusively male: father-son.

It was the meth J.J. must've smoked, that gave him this fantastic insight. The shit fries your brain—no contesting that!—but in exchange for supernatural powers.

"Jon? Son? Let's go inside, shall we? You're shivering—so am I—this isn't—ideal—"

It was true, J.J. was shivering. This wasn't his heavy quilted jacket he was wearing but the other one. Snowflakes were swirling, blinding. Melting on J.J.'s heated face and on Mr. Quinlan's heated face.

J.J.'s mistake was—only afterward would he realize: mistake—he'd been too close to his father, he'd allowed his father to approach him, and now he was standing too close to lift the rifle and to sight along the barrel in that way he'd anticipated. His mistake was, he'd seen in his father's face what he had believed to be guilt, and the implicit defeat of guilt; he'd seen concession in the shrewd mold-eyes; and in that instant, his father was on him.

They fell, grunting. Mr. Quinlan had thrown himself onto J.J. and his weight brought J.J. down. On the slippery-snowy redwood deck they struggled for the rifle, Mr. Quinlan had taken hold of the barrel with both his hands and meant to wrench it out of J.J.'s grasp. So surprised was J.J. by the attack, at first he couldn't comprehend what was happening. His instinct was to squirm out of the heavier man's grasp, to become wiry and sinuous as a snake except that would mean surrendering the rifle, he dared not let go of the rifle!—he was desperate to keep hold of the rifle. Clumsily the men wrestled together, grunting, panting. Mr. Quinlan's doughy face was contorted with rage, and determination; J.J. understood that his father meant to overcome him, and he would show no mercy if he did; he would murder J.J. Veins like livid worms swelled on Mr. Quinlan's forehead. There was a smell of sweat, animal panic. The man was a demon! There could be no release from a demon except death. Yet somehow—J.J. would recall this afterward, its strangeness—the rifle did not discharge—as if (possibly) he'd clicked the safety lock on, and not off. The men struggled grunting, cursing but did not lift their voices. Apart from their struggle all was silence amid the falling snow in which time was curiously protracted though no more than a few minutes would pass. J.J.'s father was trying to force J.J. down onto his back pressing the length of the rifle against his chest; desperately J.J. flailed out at him, sinking his teeth into his father's left ear, and his father yelped in pain, and released his hold; and J.J. overcame him, straddling him like a wrestler, gripping him with both knees as wildly he struck at his father with his fists, his bare and soon-bloodied knuckles striking his father's face, his throat and exposed upper chest, beating the older man into submission and so exhausting himself, J.J. could barely stand, groping for the rifle where it had skidded on the snowy deck, and backing away.

"You—'Dad'—go to hell, see? Don't you call her again—or me—ever again—see?"

He staggered down the redwood steps, made his way to his car parked in the cul-de-sac. His heart was beating so hard it felt like bursting and his eyes leaked tears of hurt and indignation and when he wiped his damp face on his jacket sleeve, he saw that he was bleeding but what a good feeling this was!—climbing into his car, driving away.

Thinking elated *I could have killed him. But I didn't.*

Thinking *He won't reveal this. Not ever.*

He laughed, he'd shamed the old man. Broken and humiliated the old man and the knowledge would prevail between them, forever.

On the way home he stopped at a darkened gas station. Discarded what remained of what he'd purchased that evening. He was coming down from the high, but he didn't yet feel like shit. He felt pretty good. A balloon into which hot crazed helium gas has been pumped, pumped to near-bursting and now the helium was leaking out but not quite yet, the balloon was still aloft, adrift. He wouldn't risk waking his mother, entering the house. In the driveway he parked his car where approximately he'd parked it earlier, you could see the tire tracks, not quite obscured by fresh snow. Behind the wheel he slept, his head flung back against the headrest and his mouth open and agape and leaking drool and watery blood and hours later—somehow it had become daylight, a wary thin-looking very cold but windless daylight—and he was being wakened by a sharp rapping against the window beside his head and it was his mother stricken with alarm, and now he must explain in a reasonably coherent and convincing voice where he'd been, what he'd done, unable to sleep after the heavy Thanksgiving meal and so hiking in the nature preserve and he'd fallen on some rocks, cut his face, his lip, scraped his knuckles, he was God-damned sorry to be upsetting her; and he saw in her dazed eyes how she doubted him, for how could she but doubt him, who lied so extravagantly, so recklessly; he saw in her dazed just-slightly-bloodshot beautiful dark-lashed eyes how she made the decision, quick as a heartbeat, and irrevocable, to believe him; laughing with sudden relief, clutching at him saying thank God!—he hadn't injured himself seriously, behaving in such a way. And staggering beneath the weight of his

arm slung around her shoulders she helped him make his way into
the house, and to the downstairs bathroom where tenderly with
trembling hands she washed his battered face in warm water, she
examined his numerous cuts and bruises and his skinned and swollen knuckles, impulsively she kissed the knuckles of his right hand
exacting from him the promise he would never behave so recklessly
again.

He was overcome with love. He said, hey Mom: sure.

The Heart Sutra

It has not happened yet. This most exquisite moment of equipoise, equilibrium.

The moment between heartbeats. The moment between breaths. The moment of quick sharp terror before the plunge into orgasm, the body's helpless convulsing as the soul is extinguished like a flame.

Sometime before dawn of March 31. Though Serena has no sense of the date as she has but the vaguest sense of the season: this teasing New England stasis between late winter and early spring. She is certain she hasn't been sleeping—not since Andre has left her and the child—yet her eyes spring open alert and dilated. Someone—it must be Andre—has unlocked a rear door, has entered the house quietly and is approaching in the hall. Serena's heart pounds like a terrified bird beating wings in her chest, she clutches the fifteen-month little Andre in her arms hearing his father's footsteps in the corridor—

"Andre? We're in here."

He will know where to find us. I have left messages—so many messages! His assistant knows. His friends know. He knows that I am waiting, and that I am not going to go away.

This raging insomnia! The sixth night of Serena Dayinka's vigil in the borrowed house—the Nichelsons' "big-open house" the child calls it, so many skylights, floor-to-ceiling plate glass windows, sliding glass doors overlooking a hilly late-winter terrain of drained and etiolated and curiously depthless pine woods—on rural-suburban Edgehill Lane three miles north of the village of Tarkington, Massachusetts. Serena has had phases of insomnia in the past—since the age of thirteen, when her father *went away*—but none has been so virulent as this, raging like wild fire, dry brush, furious crackling flames rushing over the glassy walls, the high white ceilings and the hardwood floors whose high gloss has been dulled by boot prints (she, the grateful occupant of the borrowed house, *de facto* homeless until her June first residency begins at Breadloaf) has been careless about tracking damp, mud, gravel in and out, indifferent to stains from the child's spilled food and leaky sodden underpants where in one of his more robust moods he has played at pushing himself across the floor like a little monkey) as other parts of the beautifully furnished house will be discovered to have been defiled by the recent occupants, some more willfully than others. *How could this horror have happened! We welcomed her into our house to help her out, she was in such a predicament. We did it to help out Andre. We had no idea the poor woman was so*—Wiping the child's runny nose on a paper cocktail napkin she then crumples and tosses aside—much of the house is strewn with wadded stiffened tissues—mother and little Andre are lying in a patch of sunshine on the high-gloss living room floor, the several bedrooms in the Nichelsons' house have become too smelly.

Serena laughs to think how such superior individuals as Gerald and Danielle Nichelson—he, Andre Gatteau's poet-critic pal who publishes so frequently in *The New York Review of Books*, she, a "celebrated" Renaissance art historian—will be obliged to stammer the inevitable clichés, how scripted their reactions will be, like those of TV performers. All of Andre Gatteau's friends, acquaintances, admirers—everyone who has known both Andre and Serena—and those who knew Andre's son—will be forced to stammer in the days, weeks, months to follow *But where was Andre, how could Andre have allowed such a horror to happen!*

She laughs, to think.

Well, where *is* Andre Gatteau? In the early-morning of March 31?

Andre is in retreat. Andre has gone away for an indeterminate period of time—it might be a few days, a week, two weeks. Very likely, it will not be longer, nor has he traveled abroad, for, as his assistant knows, he has not taken his passport; she has reason to suspect, since she'd made hurried arrangements for him just the previous week, that Andre Gatteau is at the Lost Lake Mountain Zen Retreat in the Adirondack Mountains, eleven miles west of Schroon Lake.

Several times in the past twenty-three years, Andre Gatteau has retreated to Lost Lake Mountain. In the exigency of personal crises, Lost Lake Mountain has become his solace, his spiritual home. *That place where, when you come there, they have to take you in.*

Here, in the mist-shrouded Adirondack dawn, so cold in the barely heated *sesshin* room overlooking leaden-glass Lost Lake that his breath is steaming, Andre Gatteau, fifty-three years old and feeling his age, is sitting *zazen* with a dozen other seekers of enlightenment under the tutelage of a revered Zen monk. They were wakened in the dark at 5:45 A.M., it is not yet 7:30 A.M., and already Andre Gatteau is feeling the strain of the intense Zen meditation. Though Andre has been sitting *zazen*—in the classic lotus position, buttocks on the bare pine floorboards, ankles tucked beneath (sinewy-muscled) legs, knees raised and hands in loosely gripped fists on his knees—for little more than an hour, already his bladder is pinching with a need to urinate; there have come mocking little jabs of arthritic pain not only in his legs but in his wrists, and in that tenderly vulnerable spot at the base of his spine; he is assailed by distracting thoughts, hornet-thoughts, obsessive thoughts—all that Zen meditation forbids. *Observe your thoughts. Observe your thoughts as they emerge, as they arise, as they fill your consciousness, as they clamor and howl and fade and vanish, observe your thoughts knowing always that your thoughts are not you: your thoughts are not your Zen-mind.*

This is true! He knows, this is the one true fact.

And so he is determined, this time at Lost Lake Mountain he will not fail. As he did not fail in the several heroic endeavors of his life, the first of these being a re-invention of his life, a scouring and a cleansing and a re-making of his soul, as an African-American boy of fourteen, in Lakeland, Florida.

The eastern sky above Mt. Hood is veined and mottled like a tumorous growth, curious streaks of shadow, crevices of sunshine and rain-swollen cumulous clouds. *Here is the beauty of the world, without humankind to name it.*

With the exception of a flush-faced porcine white man in his sixties and an older, emaciated white woman with a starved-hawk look of sheer desperation—*Help me! help me!*—the other Zen-seekers embarked upon this twelve-day *sesshin* retreat appear to be considerably younger than Andre Gatteau. At the silent breakfast Andre had taken care not to look at anyone very closely—Andre Gatteau isn't a man who wishes to exchange smiles, greetings, handshakes with strangers—certainly Andre doesn't want anyone to look closely at *him*. Known for his shyness, or his willful passivity, Andre is one to speak only when directly addressed and then often in a near-audible murmur. (Though he reads his poetry on stage, as a performer, in a voice of astonishing emotional nuance, power, and beauty.) Andre is a stocky dark-skinned man with a wrestler's build: muscled shoulders, large hands and feet, slightly foreshortened legs. His face looks as if it has been battered, as in a car wreck; he is ugly-handsome, with unusually large alert almond-shaped eyes aslant in his stolid face; on his forehead just beneath his hairline is a sickle-shaped scar, that catches the light like a winking third eye. His graying nubby hair is trimmed short. Not a tall man, at five-foot-nine, Andre carries himself with an almost military bearing, he has a dread of stooped shoulders, a drooping head; he has a dread of aging, as he cannot imagine a future in which, by an effort of will, he will not be able to control the circumstances of his life utterly.

At Lost Lake, Andre Gatteau is *incognito*. In any case no incoming calls are accepted here, and no uninvited visitors. The effort of *sesshin* is intense meditation: sitting *zazen* seven to ten hours daily, in the late afternoon walking *zazen* on the trails circling the retreat. There are interludes of work *zazen*, Zen instruction, brief breaks for meals, bedtime promptly after sunset.

Andre relieves some of the stress of the *zazen* meditation by going for a run of two to three miles before the evening meal and already by mid-morning his body yearns ahead to that interlude of release, and freedom: always Andre has gone on solitary runs, often in the early morning, or in the early evening after a day of highly concentrated work. *Take me with you, I'm a runner too, I promise I won't talk to you Andre please take me with you* she'd pleaded before pregnancy distended her small supple body and there was no possibility of Serena joining him.

It was nothing personal: Andre had never wanted anyone to accompany him, running. Since he'd begun seriously writing poetry in his mid-twenties running—solitary running—has been sacred to him, a time of intense meditation: his model is the blind John Milton who'd purposefully spent much of his time alone, developing his remarkable memory as one might develop muscles through sheer exercise and repetition; Milton could retain as many as fifty hendecasyllables of blank verse in his memory at a single time and then dictate these to whoever was available. In this way the entirety of the magnificent *Paradise Lost* was composed.

No living poet can be said to be "famous" in America—nor even "known"—yet in some quarters, predominantly east-coast, urban, and academic, Andre Gatteau has become a famous name in the past fifteen years: his photograph has appeared in the *New York Times* (National Book Award, Pulitzer Prize, MacArthur award, et al.), he has been the subject of lengthy profiles in the *New Yorker* and *Harper's*. Such attention has made Andre even more self-conscious in public. Serena teased *Poor Andre! He resents being recognized when he doesn't want to be recognized and he resents not being recognized when he isn't recognized.*

Serena! His heart contracts in pain, he will not think of her.

Nor of the child: his child.

Hers, and his. He cannot think *Ours*.

Andre? Please call me.

I am so sorry, I did not mean to be so emotional.

Did not mean to accuse you, it's just I am so exhausted.

Andre, forgive me, you know I didn't mean the ridiculous things I said.

Little Andre is missing you, darling. Here, I will put him on the line, say hello to Daddy, honey, c'mon sweetie Daddy is listening—

Call my cell phone, Andre. It's never turned off. I am staying at Gerald's and Danielle's as you know, I am expecting to see you here maybe this weekend, please call and confirm will you, I will leave their number another time in case you've misplaced it.

As the Heart Sutra is being chanted by Zen devotees, young Caucasians in coarse-woven monk-robes like a PBS documentary: this continuous lulling chant like slabs of water cascading down a rocky mountain stream.

The Heart Sutra of which it is claimed that somewhere in the world at all times without ceasing the Heart Sutra which is the oldest and most beautiful of all the sutras is being chanted.

No color   sound smell taste
Touch   object of mind

No realm of eyes   no realm of mind
No ignorance   no extinction of ignorance

No old age   death   no extinction of old age and death

The great bright mantra   the utmost mantra
Gone   gone beyond
Gone all the way   beyond
    Bodhi Svaha!

Serena surprised him stealing up behind him barefoot and naked except for wispy black panties sliding her small hot hands inside his shirt, kneaded and stroked his fleshy chest, tickled the taut
little nipples, kiss-sucked that special spot just below his ear that
never failed to arouse him sexually whispering *All that Zen can tell
you, darling, is what you already know: you are perfect. And—I am perfect!
So—come to bed!*

Mum-my! Mum-my.
    The child stirs and frets in her arms, his skin is flushed with
fever. Premature by nearly five weeks the child is prone to respiratory ailments, for several days he's been sneezing, nose running
and that tight barking little cough that tears at her heart like a
reproach. *Mum-my! Mum-my! Why doesn't Dad-dy love us anymore!* As the
Tarkington pediatrician has recommended Serena has been giving
little Andre children's aspirin dissolved in fruit juice, she's been
urging him to eat the hot oatmeal with raisins that has been his
favorite, but the child hasn't much appetite, spits and chokes up
what he manages to swallow, pushing the spoon irritably away
whining *Mum-my no! Don't want.*
    Even whining like a sick puppy, hair stuck to his forehead like
seaweed and a powerful stench of baby-filth eking from him, little
Andre is a beautiful child. No Caucasian child so beautiful as
Andre Dayinka Gatteau. Exquisite thick-lashed dark-brown eyes,
silky cocoa-colored skin distinctly lighter than his father's
burnished-dark skin but darker than his mother's creamy-tawny
skin, and those perfect little sculpted lips Mummy likes to kiss,
suck-suck-kiss, as playfully Mummy suck-suck-kisses little Andre's
wriggling monkey-toes. It has been a while since Serena has bathed

little Andre, she intends to bathe him this morning while there is still time, no later than 11:30 A.M. she must bathe him, he must be prepared.

In the bath, the tiny penis. Flesh-knob penis, miniature penis, so unlike the penis of an adult man she stoops to kiss it lightly, not a suck-suck-kiss in the tub (for that would be wicked, perverse)— such a Mummy-kiss is forbidden. *God help us. God O God help us. Help me not to do this God help me send me this child's father O God.*

It is a fact, a legal fact: the child's name is Andre Dayinka Gatteau.

On the birth certificate this is so. There is no questioning the paternity of the child, Serena Dayinka and Andre Gatteau had been sharing a residence for more than a year in Amherst, Massachusetts.

You can laugh at such legal formalities, such bourgeois convention, of course flamboyant young poets like Serena Dayinka laugh at such things but there is a time (Serena knows, recalling the distraught example of her mother after her father died without leaving a legally executed will) when these may be the only words that matter.

And they are to be married, Serena had begun to tell a few friends. Impulsively she'd called her mother with whom she had not spoken in months and had not seen in more than a year. Her mother's voice had been eager, thrilled. You could not predict Phyllis Ferguson's behavior: though she and her youngest and most mutinous daughter had not spoken in a long time it was as if, in this matter of marrying the *great man* they'd been conspiring like girls on the phone every day. Will it be a public sort of wedding, Phyllis asked shamelessly, reporters, the press? Andre Gatteau was very famous, Phyllis said, she'd looked him up on the Internet and people had heard of him where she lived. (In Bethesda, Maryland. With Serena's elderly grandmother. In the stolid-brick house in which Phyllis had grown up in the long-ago 1950s that held very little interest for Serena since it fell beyond the scope of her poetry.) When was the wedding scheduled, Phyllis asked and Serena said, Late October.

Almost shyly Phyllis asked where. Serena said Chapel Hill, North Carolina.

Chapel Hill! North Carolina! But why, Phyllis asked, confused.

Because she and Andre had a *joint appointment* at the University of North Carolina at Chapel Hill, Serena explained patiently. Because they were moving to Chapel Hill at the end of the summer after they returned from the Prague literary festival.

Prague! Phyllis did not even ask about Prague.

Phyllis had not yet seen her beautiful cocoa-colored grandson in person. Phyllis had not yet held her fifteen-month grandson in her arms. So strange Serena thought it, a stab of pain between her eyes, a quick jolt of her old furious hatred for this woman, Phyllis seemed scarcely to respond when Serena spoke of her son. She'd inquired after his skin color, initially. She had not asked after him since.

Mum-my?

Little Andre has heard the sound, too—a man's footsteps in the rear of the house—his eyes spring open, glassy yet alert. Is it *Daddy?* It seems to be a promise—Mummy has promised?—that the child's father will be coming to see them very soon. There has been the wonderful tiptoe-Daddy game, Daddy returning late at night and tiptoeing into the child's room to lean over his bed and kiss him solemnly on the forehead.

Don't wake up, little-Andre. Bless you, in sleep.

Often it has happened, for Daddy travels frequently. It is Daddy's complaint that he hates to travel, yet there is a pleasure in Daddy returning home, sometimes surprising Mummy; or sometimes in the night there is a call, and the child is wakened to hear his mother's girlish voice catch in surprise. *Oh darling! It's you, where are you?*

This raging insomnia! Its advantage is, Serena sees so very clearly.

One of the Zen poems she'd copied into her journal, that Andre had shown her

> Nothing in the cry
> of cicadas suggests they
> are about to die

Nine glittering knives on display in the Nichelsons' kitchen! Nine Japanese-made stainless steel knives with carved black handles, magnetized against a metal bar above the blond wood butcher block table. Why so many knives? Several appear to be nearly the same size, and similarly shaped; the differences are near-imperceptible. One, the longest, at a wicked ten inches, must be a carving knife; there is a chef's knife, with a specially weighted handle; there is a knife for the left hand; there is a deceptively ordinary-looking paring knife. *But razor-sharp. A serious cook keeps his knives razor-sharp.*

Serena felt a touch of vertigo. These instruments of savage beauty taunting Serena Dayinka to look, to see. Lurid as pornographic images, obscene in display as chattery Danielle Nichelson insisted upon showing Serena through the dazzling Mexican-tile-floored kitchen as if she, Serena, were a prospect buyer, and not a desperate homeless squatter clutching at her whimpering cast-off son.

Gently Danielle kept touching Serena's thin bare arm in a way meant to give comfort that felt like mockery.

You and little Andre will be very comfortable here, I think! There's plenty of food and the village is only five minutes away and friends at the college will be looking out for you. Say yes, Serena! Gerald and I would be so happy if you stay here until—things are sorted out with Andre.

Quickly Serena looked away from the knives. Not a second glance, that Danielle Nichelson would recall.

Winter sunshine! There is something stark and cleansing about it.

She wonders if, driving to Tarkington this morning, early-morning on the Interstate, Andre has been wearing the Gucci sunglasses she'd given him.

These were very chic very expensive steel-rimmed glasses with a dark amber tint, of which Andre had been disapproving of course. But how handsome he looked wearing these glasses, Serena understood that he was secretly pleased.

Lying with little Andre in her arms in a patch of wintry sunshine on the floor of the glass walled living room—opening her legs to the sunshine—naked legs, beneath her soiled flannel nightgown—this raging insomnia has gutted the inside of her skull, it is what is called *rebound insomnia* for she'd been taking an anti-anxiety medication called lorazepam which a Tarkington doctor had prescribed for her with but a single refill for he'd wanted her to come back within a week to see him but this Serena will not do. As Dr. Bender wanted her to bring little Andre back within a few days for fear the child might develop bronchitis or pneumonia but Serena has no time for such things, Serena's mind is blazing. Like the Heart Sutra which is a continuous chant Serena's mind is a continuous chant. Strange how she is lying here on the floor gazing up at floor-to-ceiling bookshelves crammed with books—so many books—too many books!—Serena who has published just three books of poetry of which the first has already gone out of print looks away wincing. After her father *went away*—such terms as *death, self-inflicted* were never uttered—Serena's grief-stricken and furious mother summoned a secondhand bookstore proprietor to haul away her father's books; when Serena and her sisters returned from school that afternoon every shelf in their father's study had been cleared, no sign of the man they'd called *Papa* remained.

Never has Serena told Andre Gatteau such shameful details of her childhood in College Park, Maryland. It has been Serena's strategy to present herself as *utterly bourgeois, suburban* despite the fact—the novelty-fact!—that her parents were mixed-race: her father Indian, born in Delhi; her mother Caucasian, from Bethesda. Rarely does Serena tell anyone the fullest truth about herself except in her poetry in which, in meticulously crafted stanzas, she *tells the truth slant* as Emily Dickinson has prescribed. *Never reveal what can be flung back into your face* Serena's mother warned her daughters. Serena hasn't been telling the Tarkington pediatrician that she has been keeping little Andre with her at all times; night, day, even using the bathroom she is determined not to let the high-strung child out of her sight for a moment, in terror that the child will suddenly begin to vomit and choke to death on his vomit, in terror that on his skinny wobbly legs he will fall and strike his head on one of the sharp-edged chrome-and-glass tables in the borrowed house; he will begin to convulse, he will lapse into a fever-coma, he will simply cease breathing. Andre had seemed to blame her, the child's mother, for little Andre's perpetual sniveling and runny nose. For the way in which, in Andre's words, the beautiful cocoa-skinned child *did not seem right*—his fussiness with food, his frequent temper tantrums, his fits of screeching and babbling at a deafening volume. (Often, Andre simply fled the premises. Nor could Andre abide what he called a "messy" household.) Had not Serena's own mother reacted with disbelief when Serena called her to inform her of the pregnancy *You? Pregnant? Having a child? Oh Serena I don't think that is a good idea and will this man—the father—marry you?*

At 9:13 A.M. the phone rings but it is not Daddy and yet it is early enough, there is plenty of time.

Noon, Serena has decided. She will bathe the child at 11:30 A.M. for lately there has been a struggle getting the child into the tub, Mummy must not lose patience with little Andre, but Mummy must be firm. A line from Nietzsche that has always struck her *It comes, it is nigh, the great noontide!*

The call was from one of the *mutual friends*. Checking up on Serena and the child, expressing *concern* for Serena and the child, asking if Serena and the child would like to come for supper that night, gladly he—Hugh—would come over and pick them up, bring them back to the house, Serena politely murmurs *No thank you* making no effort to recall who the hell Hugh is, one of Andre's professor-friends from Tarkington College, or could be from Amherst—Amherst is just fifteen miles away—maybe this is the pushy man, with his wife, who'd approached Serena in the Tarkington Market the last time she'd ventured out a few days ago alarming and upsetting Serena in her state of nerves and at an embarrassing moment when the child was behaving badly, kicking, whining, precarious in a child-seat attached to Serena's shopping cart *No please thank you leave me alone I am busy I can't talk now thank you so much goodbye.*

How Serena has come to hate these people! Pitying her, condescending to her, Andre Gatteau's rejected woman and her brattish child, Serena Dayinka has become a figure of scorn, ridicule, contempt and her child an unwanted bastard as in the most brutal and horrific of Grimm's fairy tales Serena had appropriated for her use as an ambitious young poet.

Powerful poetry. I like this voice. This is good poetry Serena.

Softly he'd spoken, and sincerely. It was not Andre Gatteau's way to speak other than softly and sincerely and when Serena's poetry did not please him, or when Serena herself did not please him, it was silence with which he responded, from the very first it has been silence with which he has responded, there can be no reply to silence, there can be no defense against silence, what power have the most persuasive, heartrending, carefully chosen words against silence and so it came to Serena months ago, as long as a year ago the terrible thought *If I can't make this man love me I will make this man hate me, I will pierce his stony heart.*

Of the Japanese knives Serena has selected just three to bring with her into the living room, to the spreading patch of sunshine on the rug. An eight-inch steak knife, a long-handled bread knife, and the practical little paring knife. But it is the longest knife, with its wicked-sharp blade, its sly-winking-steely-*masculine* authority, that most captivates Serena in her mood of heightened awareness. Thinking *An instrument like this wields its own justification.*

The child knows not to play with knives—or with forks, either—but has been fascinated by the flash of knife blades in the sun. Is this one of Mummy's games? That leave Mummy and little-Andre squealing with laughter, gasping for breath? Mummy says *No!* lightly slapping away the child's inquisitive fingers.

Sometimes when Mummy says *No* it is really *Yes.* And sometimes when Mummy says *Yes* it is really *No.*

"If your Daddy loved you better. If your Daddy loved *me.*"

Serena isn't speaking reproachfully but playfully. For she and the child are embarked upon a game. Serena will think of it as a game. Mummy and little-Andre in the borrowed house on Edgehill Lane and Daddy making his way to them on the Interstate: he is traveling at just the speed limit for this is Andre Gatteau's way of caution in all matters. Not even the pressure of time—it is 10:48 A.M., by 12:08 *it will have happened* in this patch of sunlight on the hardwood floor of the Nichelsons' borrowed house—can force him to behave otherwise.

Serena wipes the perspiring child's face, brushes his sticky hair back from his forehead. Brightly Serena kisses the little pug nose.

"He knows, you know. What will happen. If he doesn't love us. I've told him in my poetry, he has read my poetry and *he knows.*"

When you are the lover of a famous man his friends become your friends except when you are no longer the lover of the famous man and he has abruptly departed from your life you discover that these friends are no longer your friends but his.

Please tell me where he is! Henry? Catherine?

This is Serena. Are you there—please pick up the phone. Anthony?

I am so sorry to be bothering you—again—but I need to speak with Andre, I need to leave a message for him, this is urgent and I don't think his assistant is passing my messages on to him, please help me, I haven't heard from Andre for almost two weeks, he hasn't returned my calls and I don't know why I swear I don't know why please help me don't do this to me—Jeanne? Steve?—don't do this to me, you will regret it.

How humiliating for Andre Gatteau, the most private of men! How mortified Andre will be when he learns that the distraught and vindictive mother of his child—his youngest child—younger than his (estranged, scattered) adult children by more than thirty years—will have contacted, or tried to contact, as many as forty people in the several harried days leading to noon of March 31: Andre's New York editor—his publisher—his agent—the very nice woman who arranges for Andre's lucrative public appearances (who has begun representing Serena Dayinka, too, on a smaller scale); Andre's poet-friends, Andre's most valued poet-friend Nobel Prize–winning Derek Walcott who "isn't available" to speak with her (Serena carefully spells out her name to Walcott's assistant identifying herself as *The fiancée of Andre Gatteau and the mother of his baby*). With these people Serena is initially courteous until she understands how they are lying to her, protecting Andre; then she becomes angry, sarcastic, abusive. With mounting desperation she contacts former colleagues of Andre's in the graduate writing program at NYU, some of whom have not glimpsed Andre Gatteau in years; she swallows her pride to call one of Andre's former lovers—a black woman lawyer associated with the Children's Defense League in Washington, D.C., who doesn't return her call; one frantic morning after a terrifying insomniac night she calls the dean of Arts and Sciences at the University in Chapel Hill where she and Andre have joint appointments to teach poetry in the fall. *Yes but you must have a number for him, a way of getting past his assistant I think so, you were speaking directly with him last fall, Andre was negotiating his salary you must remember! Please help me this is a matter of life and death!* A wave of fury, nausea, shame sweeps over her, Serena breaks the connection and begins to cry.

"Mum-my? No—cry."

Serena hugs little Andre, kisses him wetly on the lips. This child is her salvation.

Until her damned laptop developed a glitch Serena has been sending e-mails as well. Dozens—hundreds?—of frantic messages like deranged and rabid bats flying out blindly into the void. Many bounce back, Serena doesn't have the correct addresses for these strangers.

When she was nine, Serena and her two older sisters were informed by their mother in a furious quavering voice: "Your father has gone away, to be sick. Your father is a sick selfish man. Your father is a bankrupt, d'you know what a 'bankrupt' is? You will know! Soon enough, you will know!" Their mother was a nervous woman with a fair, thin, flushed skin, a high-pitched voice, faded-red hair falling past her shoulders in a style too youthful for her age; she was alternately over-protective of her daughters, or withdrawn and hostile to them. What Serena could remember of her father—her gentle, melodic-voiced father!—Papa with his tawny skin, his beautiful thick-lashed eyes so dark as to appear black, a scent of something like cinnamon on his breath—was that he'd been a fastidious man who dressed with care, at five foot seven inches no taller than his Caucasian wife and smaller-boned than she, with glinting wire-rimmed eyeglasses that were always crooked on his delicate nose; born in Delhi, India, Serena's father had come to the United States to earn a Ph.D. in psychology at George Mason University; he met Serena's mother in a section of Psych 101, an enormous lecture course in which she'd been enrolled. Phyllis imagined herself an intensely spiritual person, in opposition to her secular-Protestant parents; impulsively she married soft-spoken Shahid Dayinka who'd been smitten with her golden-red crimped hair, her fair freckled Caucasian skin and dazzling toothpaste smile. Each would turn out to have made an irrevocable error. To Phyllis's astonishment, Shahid Dayinka suffered from myriad health problems—he was irritable, anxious, prone to "nervous stomach upsets" and "respiratory ailments"—an insomniac, he was addicted to barbiturates; to get through a lengthy teaching day (now at the University of Maryland in Baltimore, where he'd been hired as an assistant professor) he took amphetamines. Preparing his classes he became increasingly anxious and short of breath, he had difficulty communicating with undergraduates, his powerful medications left him groggy and dazed; his students wrote cruel evaluations speaking of his *sub-literate English*—his *biased grading*; it was Mr. Dayinka's failure to amuse his undergraduates that sealed his doom, undergraduates will not forgive you for boring them. Brazenly reading the student newspaper, yawning, talking to one another, even sleeping, though Profssor Dayinka pleaded with them *Attention please! Let us have quiet in here please! For those who are trying to hear me*—

He could not continue. He took a medical disability leave. Without tenure, Mr. Dayinka would not be kept on at the University, his contract was voided. One day when Serena and her sisters returned from school, a day that had not seemed so very different from any other day after their father had ceased working at the University, their mother told them, "Your father has gone, your father has gone away to be sick. Your father has left us and will not be returning." Phyllis's greeny-amber eyes shone with tears of righteous anger. Her mouth was a thin bitter line. She never wept. She never wept that Serena observed. She never explained the circumstances of Serena's father's departure though years later Serena would learn from her sisters the astonishing fact that he'd killed himself with an overdose of barbiturates, dying alone in a motel twenty miles away. Never a drinker, Mr. Dayinka had managed to drink a quarter-bottle of whiskey which alone would have had the authority to stop his heart. Serena's mother would never forgive such a despicable act, she told her daughters that weakness in a man is the most shameful thing, The Fergusons had been adamantly opposed to their daughter marrying a dark-skinned foreigner—Delhi-born, a Hindu!—what had she been thinking? And now these three daughters, unmistakably *mixed-blood*.

Serena's mother took money from the Fergusons to send Serena, the smartest of her daughters, as she was the lightest-skinned, to a "posh" private school in Baltimore. "You need to meet people who can help you. You will need help, from such origins "In this private school, Quaker-affiliated, Serena Dayinka thrived: like a young filly running her heart out, desperate to excel she began a model student. Art, poetry, music, journalism, theater. Everyone's favorite. Most of her friends were Caucasian girls. Their parents adored her. Very pretty and petite and sharp-tongued she intimidated the Caucasian boys, though they were drawn to her creamy-pale skin, beautiful eyes and "exotic" features and long shimmering dark-glossy hair. Serena was influenced in her art by the savage unabashed narcissism of the Mexican painter Frida Kahlo, her poetry was "deeper" and "more spiritual."

It was her poetry that had drawn Andre Gatteau to her, of course. And Andre Gatteau's poetry, that had drawn Serena to him.

Andre had asked Serena only politely about her family. Andre Gatteau was not one to invite confidences, even in circumstances of physical intimacy. In her bright bemused voice Serena told him that her parents had been "nice enough" but "utterly bourgeois" with the "usual middle-class pretensions"—though her father was from Delhi and had a Ph.D. in psychology he'd become "hopelessly Americanized."

He'd died—of a heart attack—when Serena was just nine, she said. She'd scarcely known him. And she and her mother were "not on easy terms." So calmly Serena spoke, so without self-pity, Andre squeezed her hands, in sympathy. Both Serena's small child-hands in one of Andre's enormous hands. How she loved him, then! How love passed between them, in that vulnerable moment! It was the very start of their relationship, their first week as lovers. "Sometimes it's for the best, Serena," Andre said. "Not to be on easy terms with one's parents." Gently he'd cradled her in his arms, kissed the tremulous vein at her forehead. In turn, Serena had not asked Andre much about his background for what she wished to know, what was essential in Andre Gatteau, was contained in his sparely crafted elegiac poetry. *All poets secret their deepest selves in their art. The person you are likely to meet is but an imposter.*

Because it is happening continuously without end as the Heart Sutra is forever being chanted *it has not happened yet in the borrowed house on Edgehill Lane.*

Has to uncoil his legs! Can't bear the posture another moment, his body is wracked in pain. Like great benumbed snakes his sinewy-muscled legs have been coiled together for nearly ninety minutes. And his bladder aches, he must stumble out of the *sesshin* room quickly and get to the drafty closet-sized lavatory just outside.

Urinating into the ancient stained toilet, what bliss! The truest bliss of the long strained morning, Andre thinks.

He has been distracted, thinking of the woman. And of the child. He had not wanted Serena to have a child, he'd made it clear to Serena from the start that his life could not include a second family, Serena had assured him yes she understood, of course. And yet: Serena had become pregnant. And yet: Serena had convinced him, they must have this child.

Your last-born child, Andre. Another son! But this one you will love, your life is settled now. Everything has fallen in to place now. I promise, I will be as exemplary a mother as I am a poet!

> Come here, go away poor raggedy Papa
> Nothing in my hands but crumpled old paper

A refrain from one of Serena Dayinka's mock-elegies for her past mesmerizing to the audience at the Waterloo Arts Festival. And how captivating Serena's presentation of herself, understated, yet impassioned; coolly restrained, yet sensuous; she wore a crimson silk shirt and black silk trousers, black leather lace-up shoes on child-sized feet, her skin was creamy-caramel and her lips plum-colored and her long glossy black hair shimmered nearly to her waist; on her head a man's black fedora hat tilted at a rakish angle. The crowd was wild for her: of the "emerging" poets on the program that evening, Serena Dayinka was the star.

In the audience was Andre Gatteau. And afterward at a party there was Andre Gatteau brought to meet Serena Dayinka by friends of Andre's, knowing he'd wanted to meet the young woman but was reluctant to approach her. They'd shaken hands, they'd stared and smiled at each other—how much shorter Andre Gatteau was, than Serena had envisioned: yet how powerfully built how luminous a presence, rich dark-ebony skin, broad flaring nostrils, deep-set almond eyes, the shy curve of his mouth. On his forehead, a small sickle-shaped scar. His nubby graying hair was trimmed short as a cap, in the earlobe of his right ear he wore a small gold stud.

Serena had been reading Andre Gatteau for years. Since her early twenties as an M.F.A. student at Johns Hopkins. Of the poets a generation or two preceding hers, Andre Gatteau was the most acclaimed. His work appeared frequently in the *New Yorker*. Linked sonnets, ingeniously orchestrated sestinas, ballads, beautifully crafted work like iron filigree exploring the poet's past as a descendant of slaves coming of age in the 1950s in Lakeland, Florida. You could surmise from the poetry that Andre's father had been a construction worker who'd died young; the family had scattered, but Andre had been singled out for a scholarship to a Jesuit school where naturally he'd thrived. Like a young eagle soaring high over Lakeland, Florida, he'd left the home of his birth on scholarships, fellowships, residencies at distinguished universities, his was a singular American-literary success story, the more remarkable in that Andre Gatteau avoided outright racial themes in his work, political stridency, overstatement; he explored his slave-heritage, and the identity-conflict of black Americans—is one essentially *black*, or *American?*—the question first brought to public consciousness in the 1960s by the activist-visionary Malcolm X. These were powerful themes but so delicately and ironically presented, in Andre

Gatteau's poetry, the effect was of a glass rod tapped against crystal, not a raised voice, still less a howl of execration. Here was a brilliant black poet whose heritage was more clearly Wallace Stevens than Langston Hughes; whose predecessors were Donne, Herbert, Marvell.

For such poetry, Andre Gatteau was widely acclaimed. By the Caucasian literary establishment particularly.

Here was poetry to engage the brain, not merely the groin.

Here was poetry *we will all want to read and discuss*!

Here was poetry we will want to reward.

Still Andre had been insulted. Plenty of times. Sometimes subtly, sometimes not-so. Though he'd done all he could do to distinguish himself from black political-activist poetry still there were those who wished to reduce him to the color of his skin. Serena herself had witnessed an extraordinary incident at the annual luncheon of the American Academy of Arts and Letters when an older Caucasian poet, white-haired, drunk and swaying on his feet, remarked to Andre, "You people win all the prizes now. Sure, I know—it's your turn. God knows we can't begrudge you. We had a good long run."

Her refrain from "Raggedy Papa" he'd quoted to Serena, that first night. After the party, in Serena's hotel room. *Poor ragged Papa like crumpled paper.* He'd said, "You've been reading Roethke, little Serena."

Serena blushed. It was true! Andre laughed, and kissed her.

The first time, so sweet. Their mouths tasted of wine. Serena thought *This is the happiness of my life. This is why I have lived.*

Three years, seven months. Serena Dayinka and Andre Gatteau have been together.

Though, Serena must concede, they have not always lived together. For Andre had at all times to have a separate residence, where Serena, and then Serena and the child, were not really welcome.

A place to which he could withdraw, when he needed to be alone.

You might say—in fact, this is plausible—that Andre hasn't left Serena even now, he has just gone away to be alone.

This is what some of her friends have suggested. Serena knows better, she knows what has passed between them, still Serena wishes to believe.

"Daddy will be here. Daddy is on his way."

She has managed to feed the child a few spoonfuls of cereal. A small quantity of orange juice in which aspirin has been dissolved. The child sniffles, shivers. That hacking little cough. Gently Serena strokes little Andre's feverish skin—at the doctor's he'd had a temperature of 101°F but it must be higher now, his skin burns.

Recalling how she'd once seen Andre lifting the baby, when little Andre had been just a few months old. With an expression of such pained tenderness, she'd loved the man passionately, though knowing even then that she could not trust him, that he could not love her as she loved him nor even as he wished to love her, there was something in him wounded, raw and unhealed; yet love for Andre Gatteau and for his infant son came so strong, Serena felt that she might faint. *If he would look at me that way* she thought. *Only then.*

She does not want to hurt her child! She isn't a deranged woman, still less a vindictive woman. It is entirely up to Andre: the choice isn't hers.

Andre isn't one to quarrel, Andre never raises his voice. On the contrary Andre lowers his voice when he is most furious, you cannot know what Andre is saying.

Andre's stony face, stony silence. The absence of Andre Gatteau even when the man was present.

Even when the man lay beside Serena in their bed.

Even when the man made love to Serena in their bed.

Already it is 11:09 A.M., Serena stares at the clock. How is it so late? Are their lives passing so swiftly? Panicked she gropes for her pen. A letter she'd been writing in a desperate scrawled hand

Dear Gerald & dear Danielle please forgive me but I know you can't you won't you will hate & despise me you should not forgive me for I have defiled your beautiful home you'd so cared for, this property with such scenic views 39 Edgehill Lane how grateful little Andre & his mother are to be here homeless otherwise truly I am sorry to defile your precious house, sorry to stain the polish of this hardwood floor where little Andre & I are basking in the sun it's a chill cleansing sun I have opened my legs to the sun & the sun has pierced me & that is the risk I have taken, I do not regret. Do you think that I don't know that you have been in touch with Andre you knew where he'd gone & you lied to me, I think that all of you have lied to me from the start & I was naïve enough to believe you. What has happened is necessary, I know you won't believe me. When the truth is revealed. When Andre Gatteau is exposed. His cruel stony heart. He has fled to his Zen retreat, I think. He is hiding in the mountains. Where I can't follow him, I am too exhausted. You will ask Andre why this is necessary, he will tell you. (Of course he won't! He will never speak of this. Andre Gatteau is the most vicious of liars: the one who refuses to speak.) You will beg him as I have done & he will turn from you. You know he refused to see me since Feb. 16. Now it is March 31, this is the end. The child & I are so very tired. The child is sick, his breath smells sour. Andre refused to see his son unless he could see his son "unaccompanied" by the son's mother—brought to him by a designated "neutral party"—nor would he answer my calls. So many calls! It isn't money we want from him, it is his love. It is Daddy's love the child wants. Which is why the child is ill, Daddy has ceased to love him. Daddy has ceased to love his mother. There must be some reparation. There will be reparation. I am too exhausted now to make the drive into the mountains & they would turn me away, I am not one of them. Forgive me I have no choice. Andre has cursed us. The child is flawed, & I am to blame. There will be reparation. The justice of the sharp blade, the flashing light that cuts through all subterfuge.

Your grieving but not vindictive friend S.D.

Young she'd learned. Soon after her father *went away*. That look of desire in a man's eyes. The thrill of the involuntary, the not-willed. Her pleasure was increased by this knowledge, she was taking from the man something he would not have freely given. For Andre Gatteau had not wanted to love her, he had not wanted to desire her so passionately, she was so much younger than he: seventeen years. "People will think that you're my daughter. My beautiful 'mixed-blood' daughter." Especially it troubled Andre, that his oldest daughter was nearly Serena Dayinka's age and would surely think of him with contempt.

Serena was never to meet this daughter, who lived in San Francisco and from whom Andre was estranged. Serena was never to meet any of Andre Gatteau's relatives.

In triumph thinking *I will be his only family* she thought. And when she was pregnant *The child and I, we will be Andre Gatteau's family. Only us!*

It was so, as an ambitious young poet Serena Dayinka could not help but think of her radically elevated position in the literary world: the lover of Andre Gatteau. In time, the *wife*.

In time—for Serena's love for Andre did not preclude such shrewdly pragmatic thoughts—the literary *executrix* of Andre Gatteau's estate.

It was Serena who, once they were living together on a more or less daily basis, when Andre was poet-in-residence at Amherst College and Serena taught part-time at the University of Massachusetts, insisted upon organizing Andre's papers: more than a dozen boxes of carelessly filed manuscripts, letters, documents dating to the 1970s. "Your papers are valuable, Andre. Your archive. You must know this."

He knew. He was not a vain man but he'd acquired a sense of his own worth as a poet, the quality of his achievement set beside most of his contemporaries. But his sense of himself was one of struggle, embattlement. His slave-ancestry heritage, his working-class background. His sympathy for those of his *own kind*, though rarely now his life intersected with theirs.

And it was Serena, when she was pregnant, who urged Andre to draw up a will. "I mean a 'real' will, Andre. Executed by a lawyer. Not something you've scribbled on a piece of paper."

Andre shuddered, and looked away. His eyes were large, mournful, frequently threaded with fine broken capillaries, with curious thick-skinned eyelids, like a turtle's; strange haunted beautiful eyes, in which there was a glisten of panic. Serena understood that the prospect of drawing up a *last will and testament* terrified this man who wrote with such elegant stoicism of death in his finely crafted poems.

She said, laying her hand on his arm, "My father died without leaving a real will, Andre. It was a terrible thing to have done, my mother was devastated."

"We can't have that, darling. We can't have anyone devastated by a man dying."

Andre spoke quietly, dryly. Serena laughed uneasily, and kissed him.

And so, too, in the matter of Andre Gatteau's will, drawn by an attorney in Amherst, Massachusetts, shortly before the birth of his son, Serena triumphed. Except—was this ominous?—Andre failed to share with her any of the details of the will, to whom he was leaving his estate, only just the fact that yes, he'd named Serena Dayinka *literary executrix*.

Serena thought *And next, we will be married.*

"Baby? Daddy is on his way."

The child is feverish, fretting. Pushing irritably at Mummy's hand as Mummy wipes his runny nose.

As the Heart Sutra chant continues *Gone gone beyond   Gone all the way beyond   Bodhi Svaha!*

The beautiful razor-sharp Japanese knives she has laid reverently on the hardwood floor. The steak knife, the chef's knife, the paring knife—instruments of surgical precision. The child has ceased to be distracted by the glittering blades for the child's eyelids are drooping with fatigue and his scant child-breath has a curious orangey-sharp odor. *He is ill, he will never be right. Andre is right. This is for the best.* She is not a vindictive woman but reparations must be made. There is shame here, the flawed child, the cast-aside female, an old story that requires retelling. In a sequence of engagingly colloquial villanelles—for which she'd received an award from the Poetry Society of America—Serena Dayinka had brilliantly retold the tales of Rapunzel, Thumbelina, The Ice Maiden, The Beggar Maid, for these are tales of female hurt, exploitation, and reparation that require retelling. Andre Gatteau had much admired the linked villanelles, he'd praised the young woman poet and Andre Gatteau's praise was not readily forthcoming.

Except he'd chided her, for appropriating lines, images, cadences from certain predecessors. His was a sharp unsparing ear. He'd recognized immediately the lines she'd owed to Roethke. *Come here go away poor raggedy Pappa Nothing in my hands but crumpled paper.* Andre had recognized the borrowing but chosen to ignore the meaning as in their most intimate moments he held himself just perceptibly from her, in the most subtle opposition, perhaps it was a fear of being engulfed by her terrible ravenous need, or by his own.

She'd begged of him *Why.*

She'd begged of him *Please don't do this.*

She'd begged of him *But there is your son, you must love him even if you don't love me.*

Dreamily she has opened her legs—her legs are bare, she is naked beneath the soiled terry cloth bathrobe she'd found in one of the bedroom closets, must've belonged to the woman who lived in this house whose name Serena has forgotten, she has opened her legs to the sun's sudden warmth and she is reckless, eager. There is Andre Gatteau looming above her, his dark battered beautiful face taut with love, his eyes fixed upon hers, how fleshy and solid the man's chest, how soft his berry-colored nipples, and the wiry gray tangle of hairs covering his torso like a pelt, the small dinning voice of irony at the back of Serena Dayinka's head is silenced, the sneering nasal voice that has so exhausted her, she is stricken now with silence, dumbness; his body is scalding, something molten is being poured into her. It is the great happiness of Serena's life, for which Serena has been waiting all her life This man is her savior.

Yes this is true. It is a bare raw truth. It will be the fatal truth of Serena Dayinka's life.

Except the child wakes her, whimpering and squirming. What is wrong with this child! From little Andre she has caught a chest cold, a fever, her stomach swirls with nausea though she has not eaten anything but stale cornflakes dashed with rancid-smelling milk in recent memory. And the over-sweetened orange juice she has been giving the child laced with aspirin. When she'd been taking the lorazepam she'd nodded helplessly off into a sour dreamless sleep and awakened hours later with a start, sweating and panicked and terrified that something had happened to the child who'd slipped away from besde her. At that time they'd slept in one of the beds, in fresh clean sheets that quickly became soiled, smelly from their bodies. Serena remembers a shameful scene in the glaring-bright bathroom, Serena naked and sweating on her knees groping for the last of the small white pills, she'd dropped the pill and it had rolled behind or beneath the lilac-colored ceramic toilet and she was desperate to retrieve it for otherwise a night of insomniac hell lay before her like the Sahara vast and uncharted and with no visible horizon. *Oh God help me. I can't continue like this.*

She'd been wounded, and she'd been anxious, months ago seeing one of Andre's poems in the *New Yorker* which he hadn't shown her, a Zen poem it seemed to be, sharp and bright and aimed for the jugular, in a terse elliptical style unlike Andre Gatteau's characteristic style. (Andre had claimed that he'd shown her a draft, but Serena was sure he had not. How could she have forgotten any poem of Andre's? She was avid for his poetry as for his most secret innermost life, withheld from her.) The speaker in the poem broods about his raging sexuality, his "poor, blind, stunted desire"—as if it were a sickness to be overcome; she'd been humiliated seeing such a poem in this prominent magazine which all their friends read, knowing that everyone who knew her and her relationship to Andre Gatteau would think of her in terms of the poem, and feel pity for her: that Serena Dayinka's revered lover considered his desire for her as something to be healed.

How she hated Zen Buddhism! All pseudo-mystical Eastern religions, Serena hated! Her father had never spoken disparagingly of his Hindu relatives in India but he'd considered himself a "rationalist"; her mother had but the vaguest Protestant-Christian beliefs; Serena had come of age amid a defiantly Americanized *mixed-blood* generation born in this country of foreign-born parents, her allegiance was to secular America, her best poems were cast in the idiom of the American colloquial, startling at times in their use of slang, even obscenities. She hated the solemn pieties of religion, especially the austerity, asceticism, lunar chill of Zen. As Andre was drawn to Zen, so Andre was turning away from her, she knew. From her, and from the child.

Wanting to be a monk, as once he'd wanted to be a Jesuit priest. How ridiculous her lover was, sitting *zazen*. At his age, coiling his legs into the lotus position! Through Andre's study doorway late one night when he hadn't come to bed she'd observed him, her heart thudding with scorn, and resentment. Andre Gatteau the most sexual of men, the most needy of men, and the most vain, seeking Nirvana; seeking transcendence, and escape from all desire; escape from the *merely personal and petty and finite*.

She'd wanted to laugh at him, to shame him. But she knew better, she dared not offend him even playfully for he would not speak to her for days to punish her; he would be cold with little Andre, he would stay away from the house. In silence Serena retreated to their bed.

That was the beginning, she thinks. The first clear sign.

Which of the knives will she use?—Serena has not yet decided. The steak knife is unwieldy, so long. The chef's knife is a chopper! The paring knife is small and practical. When she'd first seen the knives on the magnetized band quickly she'd turned away, suffused with a kind of excited horror. For as soon as the woman welcomed

Serena and the child into her beautiful house, speaking so kindly to her, touching her gently as you might touch a convalescent, it had been a death sentence to Serena. This house! Fifteen-foot ceilings, walls of glass, skylights and a redwood deck and bright-colored sofas, pillows, rugs; original works of art on the walls, shelves of books, here was a long-settled life, a married life, the woman and the man equals in their relationship. Envy struck Serena with the force of nausea, her soul was extinguished. Knowing then that she, Serena Dayinka, would never inhabit a house like this. She would never inhabit a life like this. Never a marriage like this. The places to which Andre Gatteau brought her were always temporary. Rented houses, apartments and flats owned by friends, university residences. These were furnished places, owned by others. She did not inhabit a house of her own with Andre Gatteau because Andre Gatteau did not wish to inhabit a house with her and now it seemed that Andre Gatteau did not wish to inhabit any place with her nor did Andre Gatteau wish to acknowledge her existence.

"Just until things get settled, Serena. I think that you and little Andre will be very comfortable here . . ."

This chattering woman, kindly/condescending so that Serena had all she could do to keep smiling, tugging at little Andre's hand to keep him by her side, saying *Yes thank you Mrs. Nichelson how kind you are thank you!*

It was a death sentence. The jeering voice that had persecuted Serena through adolescence spoke now so vividly it seemed to Serena that the chattering white woman must hear. *You will never have this. No man will ever provide you with this. How contemptible you are, how pathetic. You are not even a good poet. You are not even young any longer. He will love other women. He will have sex with other women. Since he's been your lover, he has had sex with other women. You know this. Did you think that having his child would make a difference? Did you think that he would love you, and marry you? He will outlive you, he will outlive the beautiful son.*

Not the first time Serena has cut herself, she'd begun at the Quaker school at age fourteen. Fine razor-strokes on the insides of her slender arms, where her sleeves would hide the feathery little wounds. Meant to sting, and to comfort. Blood sprang forth so readily, like a caress. She would press her tongue to the scratch, lick the salty secret blood.

Later, she began to cut the insides of her thighs (that seemed to her, no matter how she fasted, *thick, heavy, flabby, ugly*), inside her curly black pubic hair the pale soft skin of the groin.

Cutting herself as a girl Serena had used a razor, never a knife. Now, she could not have said why, though in a poem she might have explored the subtlety of such distinctions, the thought of using a razor is repellent. A knife is required, but not an ordinary knife: a knife that is a work of art, savage, gleaming in the late-winter sunshine. "This one. Andre?" Serena lifts the chef's knife, which is surprisingly heavy. A chef working with such a knife must develop strong wrist muscles, this is a serious instrument.

"Yes, Andre. Good! I thought this would please you."

Serena only now recalls, it's a measure of her dazed-fever state of exhaustion and exhilaration that she only now recalls, Andre Gatteau has a brilliantly unsettling sonnet in his first collection of poems *Enchanted Voyager*, about the ritual *seppuku* suicide of the Japanese novelist Yukio Mishima in 1970, at the age of forty-five. *He will understand. It has been his will all along.*

It is 11:55 A.M. And now it is 11:59 A.M. She is no longer waiting—is she waiting?—is her heart pounding absurdly, in childlike anticipation?—no longer waiting for the call on the cell phone, or for the car turning into the long graveled driveway, or for a firm knock on the door and the man's uplifted voice *Serena? Little Andre?* No longer waiting Serena has shuttered her heart, in her mouth there is a cold stony taste that is the taste of the poem, the purest of poems, which the poet recognizes only when she has uttered the final words, the final syllables, and placed in position the final punctuation mark. For much of the morning close by on Edgehill Lane a chain saw has been in use. Serena hates the high-pitched shrieking but sees the logic that, if the child begins to scream, if Mummy can't control his screaming, the din of the chain saw, and an accompanying wood chipper, will mask the sound, neighbors won't hear. (If there

222 * JOYCE CAROL OATES

are neighbors within earshot. Serena isn't sure but she doubts that there are neighbors within earshot of the Nichelsons' house, these expensive properties on Edgehill Lane are so large.) Meticulously Serena has planned, her fever-dream of the previous night will guide her: she will hold little Andre down by straddling him and with both her knees pinioning his little body, he will protest, and squirm, begin to kick, thrash and cry, for he can be a mutinous child, strong as a panicked cat despite his illness and the drug she's been feeding him, Bayer baby aspirin mashed in orange juice. Without hesitation she will cut—swiftly, she will *slash*—the veins and arteries in little Andre's left arm, soothing him *Hush! Hush baby! There is no pain* just below the elbow; she will slash the veins and arteries in the right arm, just below the elbow. So swiftly this will be accomplished, the child will think it is some sort of game, he is not a suspicious child and will be utterly bewildered. And truly Serena believes, there will not be much pain. Truly Serena believes, for Serena loves the child more than life itself, far more than her own life, she would never wish to hurt him.

Canny Serena has thought to have a supply of baby diapers, a pillow from a sofa, a roll of toilet paper to absorb some of the blood. For she is fearful that the sight of the child's spilling blood will unnerve her.

"Mum-*my*?"

"Hush, sweetie. Mummy hasn't gone anywhere."

Critically Serena examines her own arms, looking for veins, arteries. Slender pale-skinned arms, how many times he'd kissed the insides of her arms with not the slightest awareness of the feathery-thin faded scars from her girlhood, wrists so small he could circle them with his thumb and index finger gripping each of her wrists above her head as he eased himself into her, always tentatively at first, as if fearful of hurting her, for she was so small, she weighed at least ninety pounds less than Andre, always he held himself back, she could not draw him deeply enough into her, deep, deep . . . never deeply enough.

Always he'd murmured to her *Beauty, my beauty. My beauty* in an ecstasy of desire, possession. Always he'd sated himself in her body though he would not penetrate her deeply enough, he never sought her soul.

Nor did he sleep close beside her. Never in her arms. Often restless, waiting until Serena slept, or he believed she slept, then slipping away to another part of the house. Or slipping from the house altogether.

Though they'd made a baby together. Somehow, that had happened.

In the mountains he is sitting *zazen*. He is observing her, she is convinced that he can see her though his figure is hidden from her, her eyes are not strong enough to perceive him. *He thinks I can't do it! I can do it, I am stronger than he is.*

It is 12:12 P.M. It is the very last day of March but Serena has forgotten the year. Serena has forgotten where she is, exactly. Whose (borrowed) house this is. Close by, the wood chipper has abruptly ceased. The wood-grinder has ceased. But the lawn crew truck has not departed, Serena will wait for the noise to resume. Adjusting the shawl around the feverish child, wiping his runny nose, his clammy-damp forehead, tenderly Serena kisses each of his eyelids and his parched panting lips. "Sweetie? Daddy is on his way."

At Lost Lake the Heart Sutra is being chanted. Another incense candle is shrinking to a stump. It is past noon, their break will be at 12:30 P.M., others have given up and slipped away from the *sesshin* room but Andre Gatteau wracked in arthritic pain and his bladder (yet again) urging him to stumble away to urinate is determined to continue until the Zen master releases them, it has become a matter of pride. If anyone knows Andre's identity, he must protect his pride. He will push himself to the limits of his endurance. How far he has come already on this journey! Less than forty-eight hours, less than five hundred miles yet how far, unfathomable. He is a poet, he seeks purity. You cannot be a poet if your mind is muddled, muddy. You cannot be a poet if you are distracted. Recalling how as he'd approached Lake Schroon the other afternoon he'd passed a dismaying *literalness* of man-made artifacts: taverns and gas stations and automobile/truck/motorcycle dealerships adorned with fluttering banners, house trailers propped up on cinder blocks in the pine woods, bungalows, habitations that appeared to be no more than concrete foundations in the rocky earth, like bomb shelters. There were bait shops, yet more taverns, roadside wood-frame churches, bullet-ridden road signs, lakeside cabins, small boats on trailers, junked vehicles in the ditch by the side of the road, mattresses at the roadside, abandoned furniture as if families had thrown off their chains in a frenzy of repudiation and loss. The poet finds little poetry in such sights only the residue of irony which leaves a bitter taste on the tongue. The poet has come to this place to escape irony.

In Zen there is no irony. In the mountains there is no irony.

This fifth hour of *zazen*, or is it the sixth? Through the strain of concentration the poet has glimpsed the merest glimmer of bliss, fleeting as a flash of heat lightning in a summer sky, in that instant his soul is flooded with hope, with something like strength, the thought comes to him *I will call her. At the break. I can do this. I will do this!* It is the revelation for which the seeker has come to Lost Lake Mountain though it is not the revelation he has expected. As the Heart Sutra continues in the reedy chanting voices of the earnest young *No color sound smell taste touch object of mind no realm of eyes and no realm of mind No ignorance and also no extinction of ignorance There is no path There is no way that is not the path.* On the altar the candle begins to gutter, the pale flame quivers as from an expelled breath.

Part Two

Dear Joyce Carol,

Oct 1 2006

Dear Joyce Carol,

If you knew me youd be amazed, that I would write a letter to a Stranger "out of the blue"—it is not my nature, Joyce Carol as one day you may learn.

The occassion is, your visit here to Boise last week. In the paper it is said that you are a Known writer, that must make you very proud Joyce Carol. I was not able to attend your Talk at the University but it has come to my attention in the library here, in the *Boise Journal-Times* there was a picture of you which picture I have very carefully ript out, and am sending to you here, for your Autograph.

And now I have akcess to your books, there are four in this library, and your Address at the publisher where I am sending this letter requesting that you will Autograph this picture of you and return it to me. Thank you Joyce Carol! Also it is my hope that you will wish to know my lifestory that it might be first a Novel then a Movie. It is QUITE A LIFE Joyce Carol, I promise you!

Except he is too old now Clint Eastwood would be the actor to
play me. I wonder Joyce Carol, do you know him?

I must go now, it is that time when Darkness will prevail.
Here I am sending this picture, Joyce Carol and this letter hoping
to here from you very soon.

Sincerely, your friend

Esdra

Esdra Abraham Meech
P.O. Box 338746
TFMMSF Twin Falls ID

Oct 17

Dear Joyce Carol,

I have not yet rec'd your letter & am wondering if my letter sent
16 days ago has been rec'd by you? It will be a loss to me, if your
picture from the Boise newspaper is not returned. Joyce Carol, I
did not wish to embarass, to say how special that picture was, tho'
we are Strangers across a thousand miles, and more, & how
anxious I am, to hear from you.

This time I am sending a Drawing of you, that I have done
myself. This likeness is taken from a picture of you on the back
cover of a Novel of yours here, that I have been reading with
much amazement & certitude, that you are the writer to tell the
lifestory of Esdra Abraham Meech, like no other. Joyce Carol, it is
our destiny! I am sure of this.

I hope that this Portrait will not be offenseful to you, Joyce
Carol. It has been said of me that I have Artistic skills, & certain
persons I have drawn Portraits of, are very complimentary especially
women & girls, for which I have more skill, than for men. Why this
is, I dont know! Except where the Portrait is a beautiful likeness, as
in this Drawing of you, Joyce Carol, it is like a Stranger's hand takes

hold of mine, to guide the pencil. For in you, Joyce Carol there is a special Soul. In your eyes which I have tried to render, so "firey" it is like sparks fly from them. In your picture on the book here it seems that your eyes are very dark as my eyes are very dark & tho' the picture on the book is not in color it is clear that your skin is a very pale skin & you are a Lady not a corse type of female like the kind prevvalent in this State & in the State of Utah which is my home State. It may be that we are not the Perfect ages for each other Joyce Carol but that is for another time, to think of.

Hoping to hear from you very soon, your Special Friend

Esdra

Esdra Abraham Meech
P.O. Box 338746
TFMMSF Twin Falls ID

P.S. (Later!)
I have courage now to speak of the feeling in my heart, Joyce Carol of a True Love beteen us. Now it is said, I am glad to have said it. It is very hard for me to speak of such feelings, it is like cutting a vein & blood-drop oozing out. & to show you how my feeling for you is, I will sign this in blood. In this way Joyce Carol, you know my heart.

E

Oct 19

Dear Joyce Carol,

I feel that our letters will "cross" in the mail, that is my hope!

Since writting to you 2 days ago, I have contined to read your Novel, & am more than ever convinced, we are Soul Mates. From

first seeing your picture in the Boise paper, it seemed that my
heart was "caught" like a bird that has flown into a building &
cant see that the windows are glass. People who know me here,
have noted this. I have done a dozen Drawings of you Joyce Carol,
& am hoping to send another soon, for you to Autograph to me, if
you would be so kind.

Youd be amazed if you knew me, to realize that Esdra Meech
is saying such things to a Stranger, that many women have craved
to hear in vain, & were brokehearted at this denial. & these very
young goodlooking & "sexy" women. But if you keep this Secret
beteen us, Joyce Carol & not tell them! (Joke)

Hoping to hear from you soon, your Loving Friend

Esdra

Esdra Abraham Meech
P.O. Box 338746
TFMMSF Twin Falls ID

P.S.
Joyce Carol, forgive me, I am known as a Joker. From when I was
a boy, this was my nature. My pa did not like this friviliss attitude
& "cuffed" me but my mother just laughed saying Esdras is the
one to make a joke being dragged down to Hell by Satan himself,
& this is so. & in our platoon in 'Nam, so I was known. Would
you be surprisd, Joyce Carol to learn that Esdra Abraham Meech
served his country in Vietnam 1964–1967 & was a "decorated war
veteran" & rec'd the Purple Heart & the Silver Star & yet was
fucked over by the VA at the hospital in Provo, treated like shit
after serving my country? & am not well to this day, with bad
headaches where there are metal filings in my head, that the VA
will not acknowledge? You would be surprisd, I think. Even so, I
have been a Joker since childhood. If you cant laugh at this Life,
you will cry & that will really fuck you up, is my wisdom. In
confiding in you my lifestory, Joyce Carol this will be explained to
you with "no holds barred."

Again this Special signing for you Joyce Carol, no one will share our Secret.

$\mathcal{E}$

Oct 21 2006

Dear Joyce Carol,

Still have not rec'd a letter from you, Joyce Carol. I am thinking that our letters will "cross" in the U.S. mail—

In the night not able to sleep, I have worried that my last letter might be offenseful to you, Joyce Carol. For you are a Lady, not a corse female to be joked with. Truly I did not mean to offend with any profanity, I am very sorry for this. Tho' it is true, there is some grief in my heart at the VA & certain doctors, who treated "Esdra Abraham Meech" like s—t. In my lifestory which I hope to share with you, Joyce Carol you will learn the injustice of this. You will find it in your heart to tell my lifestory, I believe.

Tho' Clint Eastwood is not the age to play "Esdra Abraham Meech" yet Clint Eastwood might direct this movie, do you think? Joyce Carol, I promise my lifestory could also be a TV movie of that kind that is broadcast for many weeks. It is that kind of life, Joyce Carol. Like people you have known, that must be your family etc. you have written about & have rec'd much Praise.

Joyce Carol, I am hoping our letters have "crossed" in the U.S. mail! It would be hard for me, to lose my Drawing of you, that requird many hours as I think you can see, & the love that has gone into it, Joyce Carol I think you can see can't you

Hoping to hear from you very soon, your loving friend

Esdra

Esdra Abraham Meech
P.O. Box 338746
TFMMSF Twin Falls ID

Oct 23 2006

Dear Joyce Carol,

This is a new Drawing of you, I hope you will see the love that has
gone into these eyes I have "enlarged" to show the special soul,
that abides inside. Joyce Carol, in the night your eyes shine upon
me, I am warmed by your Soul that is like none other, in my life.
This is truthful in every way, Joyce Carol. I swear.

    This precious Drawing, another time I am entrusting to the
U.S. mail, please will you AUTOGRAPH & RETURN.
THANK YOU JOYCE CAROL!!!

Sincerely, your loving friend

Esdra

Esdra Abraham Meech
P.O. Box 338746
TFMMSF Twin Falls ID

Oct 27 2006

Dear Joyce Carol,

<u>I am a light come into the world that whosoever believeth in me
should not abide in darkness</u>.

    It is a fact as Jesus has said. Tho' some of us dwelling in
darkness cant reach to Him, we have hope in our heart, one day
we will.

    This picture of "Joyce Carol Oates" that has been ript from
the back cover of your Novel, I am sending to you for you to

Autograph. I promise it is the last time, Joyce Carol. I am not begging for I am a man of Pride. I do not harbor ill will against any man or woman, with the help of Jesus I hope that will prevail when I am released & a FREE MAN which will be soon: 73 days.

Sincerely,

Esdra

Esdra Abraham Meech
P.O. Box 338746
TFMMSF Twin Falls ID

Nov 1 2006

Dear Joyce Carol,

Why you have betrayed me, Joyce Carol? My gift of Love, you have spat back into my face?

Sincerely,

E

Nov 7 2006

Dear Joyce Carol,

Now it is known, Joyce Carol. Now it has been revealed.

You UGLY BITCH did you think you could fuck with Esdra Meech's head & not be detected? You are a stupid cunt like any other.

Yesterday it was brought to my attention, Joyce Carol that you have stolen from me, in April 2003. How this was so, I cant comprehend. You are not a Lady but in your inner heart, a corse type of female. You will be punished for your deception.

Your mistake was, you would not think that in this place,
I have akcess to the Internet. For I am not a Trustee (tho'
qualified as anyone here & now that I will soon be maxed out,
I dont give a fuck.) Yet my friend is a Trustee & he has lookt up
your name & downloaded certain materials for me. This "fiction
story" you have written that is dated April 2003 that was in a
magazine, I did not give permission to you, to steal from me.
This is not my lifestory that was to be shared with you, Joyce
Carol but certain private things known to no one living except
me. You have changed names & places but the story is taken from
my life 15 yrs ago in Provo without my permission. Certain facts
pertaining to the female you have called "Wanda" & this man
who is tall & weighs 220 lbs & red-haired streaked with gray & a
"bristling beard like static electricity" you have called "Elisha"
living in "Camden, Maine"—these facts are not in the police
record or would have come out in court but did not. My lawyers
did not know. & across the state line where I was living at
Sawtooth Falls, you have taken that & changed certain facts, to
make a story of them that is a theft, In that place too, my lawyer
did not know. & did not wish to know. Yet somehow, Joyce Carol
<u>you knew</u>.

Now it is too late for you to reply to me. Now you cant be forgiven
for this betrayal. This woman you have called "Wanda" & the other,
you did not seem to know of, it was wrongly said that I had hurt them
but this has not been proven & will not be proven because both are
<u>alive</u> & <u>well</u> & hiding away in another state as my lawyers argued.
Why have they done this, the one in Provo, that was my "common
law wife" (as the God damn newspaper said) & the other one, you
have called "Wanda," it was to make trouble for me & fuck up my life
that is why. A female revenge. None of this was proved against me. I
think it is called <u>Habas corpis</u>—my lawyers said, if they dont have the
damn bodies they do not have a Case which is why my sentence was
11 yrs. & would have been paroled after 7 yrs except for some things
that happened, that could not be prevented. & now in the New Year
2007, I will be maxed out & emerge a FREE MAN.

Joyce Carol, you had your chance & fuckt it. That's tough shit for you Joyce Carol, soon youll know how much.

Sincerely,

Nov 15 2006

Dear Joyce Carol,

This is my last letter to you, Joyce Carol. I am warning you & you will know why.

As I cant prove you have stolen from me unless to "confess" certain crimes, & cant prove that you have profitted from my suffering in this place of Darkness. As you have profitted from the suffering of many others in your books & "fiction stories" bringing you Fame & Wealth not giving one penny back to those you have stolen from. Joyce Carol, I am the one to see into your heart, that is evil.

10 yrs 11 months I have been lockt up here & 6 yrs previous at Moab for crimes I did not commit; & it was not proved that I committed. I know your asking like all of them do you have remorse Esdra, well remorse for what? Do YOU have remorse, Joyce Carol?

Maybe I never did enough, Joyce Carol! To warrant 11 yrs at Twin Falls & 6 yrs at Moab both maximum security & everywhere you look, mexes & mud people fouling the air. Maybe I needed to do more & that is what I am remorseful of, I could not tell the court.

It is not too late, I will be a FREE MAN soon. I would know that I really offered society something in return for my soul. Id know I made my mark, like you.

It is not hard to kill somebody, the human skull is no harder than a clay pot & cant protect what is inside. The brain is pus,

I have seen such pus & next time would not feel a thing. A head wound is bloody tho' & will splatter, onto your legs & feet & if you are not aware, up onto the ceiling (!). This is not something known, you think of in the night.

This Drawing of you, Joyce Carol is for your safekeeping. You may Autograph this if you wish!

UGLY BITCH your too old for me, its a laugh you might think any man would wish to love *you*. Yet females are stupid & vain enough, to believe such a joke, every day.

It would be a joke, Joyce Carol if you had not ever rec'd any letter of mine. If the Address for you was not right, or the letters were not forwarded. & now you would not know, that Esdra Meech has seen into your heart as my friend has downloaded your lying "fiction story" stolen from my life. There are many Jokes in our lives, you cant guess. For example a joke that a certain "witness" did not appear, on a certain day & has never been seen again. My "last meal" I had dreamt of & had drawn in such a "lifelike" way, at the court hearing it was marveled at by all who saw it & I said, it was like I had already eaten this meal & it was a good meal (of a cheeseburger & all the French fries you would wish & chocolate milkshake that was my favorite as a kid but they dont give you any choice of beer for alkohol "spirits" are not allowed in the death chamber) (now theres a joke—they dont want you to be drunk, on your way to Hell). You would not know, Joyce Carol how good a meal like that would taste as you would not know that Wrath may come to you like a tornado, from afar.

It is people like you Joyce Carol, who do not comprehend that Jesus is a firey light in the darkness & Jesus bears a sword, not peace. Few comprehend this, that the Wrath will come upon them when least expected.

In my lifestory I was to tell you, Joyce Carol there was a fox cub found by me when I was 10, & slept with sometimes, & was supposed to shoot one day with my .22, Pa said it is grown too big & has killed chickens but instead I took him out into the hills & let him go & was beaten by pa in his place & did not regret it. & other things I was to tell you, Joyce Carol you have scorned. & now it is too late for Jan 12 2007 is my Release date & I will "max out" & be a FREE MAN for this time there will be no need to register at the county courthouse & no parole officer hanging over me like a vulture & you must abide by the parole dept laws like having to piss in a cup each week & be tested for drugs & not "consorting" with certain persons, or your parole will be revoked. It is better to "max out" for if you "max out" you are OUT. You are a FREE MAN to leave the God damn state & travel anywhere you wish, thousands of miles you may travel & there is no one to track you, Joyce Carol. Not even you.

Sincerely,

ε

Suicide by Fitness Center

Suicide by cop, you'd think. Since this is Jersey. The aggrieved party takes a hostage or two, or three—for convenience usually his own family since they're the ones likely to be already in the house with him; he dials 911 to report a "hostage situation"; as the street in front of his house is cordoned off by police, and his house surrounded by SWAT officers armed with high-powered rifles, and overhead TV news helicopters hover with the drone of demented giant mosquitoes, the suicidee might "negotiate" with a police officer via telephone, or might simply display himself in the doorway of his house making threatening gestures with what appears to be a weapon—a toy gun, or a hammer, or a bread knife, or, in one recent case, a hairbrush; he might cock his finger suggestively at police officers and shout "Bang! Bang!" while allowing sharpshooters a clear "head shot." Thirty cops, each getting off five shots, you have a minimum of 150 bullets tearing into the aggrieved party, any one of which might be fatal.

Or, say the aggrieved party doesn't have a hostage at hand, or doesn't have a house, suicide by cop can be as easily executed by speeding on the Turnpike, refusing to pull over onto the shoulder when adrenaline-charged New Jersey State Troopers give chase, and waving out the window any object that resembles a gun: toy gun, hammer, etc.

Though it's true, Jersey cops are slower to be summoned in recent months. Too much strain, the economy being what it is. Suicide by cop may not be so reliable an option.

Suicide by Turnpike! Without relying upon Jersey cops, suicide by Turnpike requires just the aggrieved party and his vehicle. He drives recklessly at a very high speed and aims his vehicle like a missile at a concrete wall and—that's it.

Except for cleanup. And "survivors" if any. Suicidees don't wish to think of mitigating factors.

But in our part of New Jersey, suicide by cop or by Turnpike is rare. You might say, nonexistent. In the Village of Halcyon Mills no resident has ever been mowed down in a fusillade of bullets, nor has anyone crashed his Land Rover into a concrete wall. Our option is Suicide by Fitness Center.

And so, this darkest-day of the year, December 21, I have taken myself to the Halcyon Mills Fitness Center on Route 31, just north of the Halcyon Mills Mall.

The Halcyon Mills Fitness Center is a large windowless slab of cream-colored stucco in a pseudo-semi-rural setting on a formerly "country" road that intersects with busy state highway 31. Behind the Center are several tennis courts, unused in winter; to the side, an unused cinder track. In winter, activity is indoors. These dreary days, there are few of us at the gym. Few vehicles in the parking lot and of these, most belong to the staff. Even the dun-colored Dumpster looks forlorn. Overhead the Jersey sky looks like a carelessly scoured kitchen utensil. Inside, the place has a sepulchral air. You feel that, having stepped inside, you've had to push a boulder away. The lighting is a faded tea-tint. Fluorescent, with a humming sound. Or maybe this is the sound of sluggishly pulsing blood. Of course, the young staff workers play popular music on the radio, which is piped into all of the rooms: loud furious tribal music, harsh black ghetto music incongruous with the Halcyon Mills citizenry, maybe with the laudable intention of stirring up the atmosphere, like running inert matter through a blender. "Is that rock music?" I'd once overheard a gentlemanly older man inquire, meaning to be friendly, and not at all critical or sarcastic; and Andy, dark-skinned and beautifully sculpted in muscle, said, with a toothy smile, "Naw-sir, that's hip-hop. Like it?"

Like it? We hate it! But we can't bring ourselves to complain. None of us wishes to be registered as prim-reproachful old-fart Caucasians by the vigorous young staff.

Who belongs to the Halcyon Mills Fitness Center?—I've often wondered, and I have been a member myself for more than a calendar year. (Last year the winter malaise in our household by late November was such that we—this indefinite "we" is purposeful—decided impulsively to sign up at the Halcyon Mills Fitness Center. That's how desperate we were.) There is a much larger singles-oriented Gold's Gym near Mammoth Mall on Route 1 where the average membership age is reputedly thirty-two; here, the average membership age must be fifty-two. It's rare to see anyone younger, except the attractive staff workers who double as trainers and would not ever be mistaken for paying members. Most days when I'm here, most rooms at the Fitness Center are mostly empty, so far as I've been able to discover. One fairly attractive room with mirrored walls contains rows of stationary bicycles that are never in use. At least, I've never seen any of them in use and I have poked my head into that room numerous times out of idle curiosity. There are terribly claustrophobic squash courts, a gymnastics room with the most melancholy of imperatives in an arterial red banner on the wall: YES YOU CAN!, a strangely-echoing basketball-practice room, a nightmare-mustard-colored karate-class room, and a shadowy-sinister massage room: all of which are usually empty. In the corridor beyond the reception desk are offices for a resident chiropractor, a resident "herbalist," a "geriatric specialist," even a "fully accredited" physiopsychotherapist (Center for Advanced Psychological Inquiry, J.J. Pittman, Ph.D.) but these offices are usually darkened, and shades pulled down over their windows. (Once—only once!—at the onset of my winter malaise, which traditionally begins at Hallowe'en, intensifies at Thanksgiving, and reaches a crisis of stasis as Christmas approaches, I did linger in the twilit corridor outside Dr. Pittman's office; but his/her door was shut, and all that I could see beyond the edges of the drawn blind at the window was but an obscure darkness.) At the reception desk, membership cards are kept in files in drawers and I seem to remember, when we were first applying for membership—though the term "applying" is a misnomer, for the Fitness Center was energetically campaigning for new members—having seen suspicious red stickers—*deceased*?—on a number of the cards; but many more members must be inactive, for virtually no one is ever here. Sometimes the reception desk is without a receptionist. You are greeted by a machine: when you swipe your plastic membership card in front of the electronic eye it clicks and releases a chirrupy female voice: "Have a good workout!"

To which some of us trained to respond to social cues can't help but meekly murmur, "Thank you."

Though the resident trainers are young and enthusiastic and, like Andy, in enviable physical condition, sometimes if you peer covertly when they have no idea you are watching them you can discern expressions of fatigue and worry in their faces. For surely, if membership in the Fitness Center is down as it appears to be, and continues to fall, their jobs are endangered? More than once, when I've lingered late in the Fitness Center reluctant to brave the wintry twilight outside, I've encountered Carla vacuuming in the women's locker room, and Jorge and Andy mopping floors. Yet good-natured Dominican Republic–born Andy makes it a point to call out, "How's it goin, ma'am!" whenever he sees me; his smile couldn't be wider, toothier or more genuine; he is the most fervent and evangelical of the resident trainers. Once when I was struggling with one of the diabolical "free-motion" machines Andy came up quietly beside me to reposition my hands, readjust the straps and reset the weight, and explained what I was doing wrong. "I'm so embarrassed," I said, for it's true, I am easily embarrassed, "having to struggle so to lift a mere twenty pounds..." but with an air of reproach, as you'd chide an exasperating but endearing child, Andy said, "Ma'am, we all got to begin somewhere! 'Every gain is good.'"

It is mesmerizing to (covertly) watch Andy work out among us in the gym as if in some benign Disney-cartoon way we are equals. Running effortlessly on the treadmill without breaking a sweat; lifting iron weights the size of wagon wheels, with no more strain than if they were made of papier-mâché; cheerily making his way through the gauntlet of free-motion machines with weights set at two hundred pounds, and never once gasping for breath or chuffing... (What does the average male at the Halcyon Mills Fitness Center set these weights at? Somewhere between forty and eighty pounds, and that involves gasping and chuffing. The average female? About half these figures.) I think that Andy is a Christian of some kind for he wears a small gold cross on a chain around his muscled neck; and though he excels at all the machines at which we can only aspire, Andy never gazes upon us with anything like scorn, only just affable kindness, sympathy, and patience.

When, from time to time, I've come to the Fitness Center with a companion, Andy is likely, to call out to both of us, "Good to see you! Let me know if you need assistance! 'Every gain is good.'"

Another feature of the Fitness Center is the "gym cat." This is a heavyset graceless creature the size of an Airedale with coarse tufted fur the color of spilled oil, large spatulate feet, spongy pads, a blunt pugnacious face, stiff whiskers and green-glassy feral eyes. So far as I can determine, the gym cat has no name. It may not even be an official gym cat, only just the most opportunistic of a colony of feral cats that lives in a field behind the shopping mall and scavenges from Dumpsters; this cat has made his way into the Fitness Center for cunning reasons of his own, and reveals himself only to certain privileged individuals. At least I want to think that we are "privileged" and not—well, something else. Sighting the gym cat isn't always a pleasant experience, for you are most susceptible to seeing the coarse-furred creature in a mirror you are facing during a vigorous workout, at which time the gym cat appears crouched on a raised ledge behind you like something on the Internet that has popped out of cyberspace and into your head: the glassy-green eyes catch fire in the fluorescent lighting that, so unflattering, has cast shadows downward onto your face so that you resemble an animated skull, and these glassy-green eyes seem to pierce your very soul. "Oh—kitty! Nice kitty." You speak feebly to the gym cat through the mirror, fearful of turning too abruptly to him, and startling him into leaping at your head. "Handsome kitty." The gym cat—nameless, though I have tried to name him—continues to stare from his perch only a few feet away; he is impassive, inscrutable, his sword-like tail twitches with malicious feline glee; yet, when you turn, the ledge is empty.

It's a shuddery sensation. Turning to see the graceless tufted-fur tomcat who has been staring at you, and there is no cat in sight.

"Kitty? Kitty? Where . . . ?"

I have asked Andy about the gym cat, and Carla, and Jorge, and none of them has seen the gym cat, not ever. Once in a weak moment, I may have asked Carrot Top (of whom, more later) if he'd seen the gym cat, and Carrot Top mumbled an evasive reply without meeting my gaze which allowed me to think that yes, Carrot Top had seen the gym cat but wasn't certain that he'd seen the gym cat or what it might mean if he'd seen the gym cat and so he was hedging his bets. (Only one of numerous disappointments with Carrot Top, I may as well admit.) Though there is a colony of feral cats living out behind the Dumpster, Andy conceded, and it's plausible to think that an aggressive tomcat might slip into the Fitness Center for purposes of his own.

The gym cat appears to those who will die. He is our totem.

This thought came to me a few weeks ago. I shared it with no one, of course.

In these rapidly waning days of the year when the sun sets at ever-earlier hours, and shadows dart upward from the snow-carmelized earth like malevolent elves, it is a mystery why each day is in fact longer than the preceding day by as many as forty unbearable minutes; and why, since we are not idiots, we continue to Endure.

And so this morning as I became acutely aware of time-not-passing while reading the *New York Times*, my avid eyes descending each column of print mesmerized by the procession of letters and numerals that constitute "the news" and my brain calculating *Why, this is an addition of zeros! No matter how many zeros, the sum total is zero!* it seemed to me hideously clear that time had ceased to move at its normal speed; at even its normal sluggish speed; that in each room of the house in which there was a clock—expensive antique clocks from yesteryear when we'd gone gaily "antiquing" in quaint old shops along the Delaware River, functional modern electric clocks, wind-up clocks and battery-operated clocks, ticking clocks and digital clocks—that time had maliciously slowed: what had formerly been "five minutes" had become twenty minutes, "twenty minutes" had become sixty minutes, "sixty minutes" had become ninety minutes, and so to—Infinity. And that I would never finish the *New York Times* for always there would be an unread column on an obscure page, a minuscule "corrections" paragraph tucked in beneath an unread column on an obscure page, an entire section ("Styles"—"Dining In"—"Dining Out"—"New Jersey"—"Escapes") yet to be dealt with.

And so the thought of Suicide came to me. Though not for the first time, I must concede.

Have a good workout!

This afternoon, I bite my lip to keep from saying *Thank you*.

It is December 21 and by 5:03 P.M. darkest night. If I don't succeed in Suicide by Fitness Center today, I'm afraid that I will lose my courage and never try again.

In a blast of snarling hip-hop music I enter the gym in lilac sweatshirt, sweatpants, ill-chosen chalky-white gym shoes. I am feeling edgy, nerved-up. And annoyed: the workout room isn't deserted as I'd hoped it might be at this hour of the afternoon. This, the largest room at the Fitness Center, is a vast sepulchral space with a high ceiling, cruelly bright fluorescent lights, and mirrored walls as in a malignant fairy tale; here the air is never entirely fresh but smells of stale sweat, anguish, and disinfectant. To the left are two rows of treadmill machines, several elliptical machines, NordicTrack, StairMaster, MasterMan, and of these one is in use by an individual I've sometimes encountered in the gym in the late afternoon: Big Gus. (Which is not his name! I have not the slightest interest in this person's true name.) Big Gus is a lurid ruin of a man in his mid-sixties, nearly bald except for dank grass-like tendrils of hair he has combed across the dented dome of his head as in a parody of male vanity; he has fierce sunken eyes and a lockjaw look to his flushed lower face as if he'd been, in his former life, a "dynamic" and "difficult" business executive; packed inside a tight-fitting T-shirt his torso is fleshy-muscular and seems to be cascading down into his belly and groin; he is covered in sweat, grimly "jogging" on the treadmill and every now and then expelling a loud hissing sound as of a valve about to blow. (This sound will permeate every corner of the workout room, there's no escaping it.) In the center of the room are rows of free-motion machines and at one of these, to my dismay, is another familiar sight—Chuffer: younger than Big Gus by a decade, and in minimally better physical condition, but as usual Chuffer has set himself tasks that demand enormous effort for him and so invariably he pants, gasps for breath, grunts, moans and "chuffs" in a way that makes me fear for his life, even as I try discreetly to ignore him.

And there, on the far side of the gym, struggling to lift a pair of dumbbells while staring glumly into a wall mirror, is an equally exasperating individual I've taken to calling Eggplant Man for his flushed, blood-heavy face that is frightening to behold as he strains himself lifting weights in a grim and unvarying routine to which he appears indentured, like a slave.

Yet more annoying, Eggplant Man has a perky little wife who sometimes accompanies him to the gym. This wife, clumsy with weights and on the machines, yet has the showy confidence of a long-ago cheerleader though now her face is creased as a prune and her tinted-russet hair is frizzed in an unbecoming perm; while the rest of us struggle gamely if futilely with the machines, Mrs. Eggplant Man merely plays at them, not caring how poorly she performs; most days, she finishes her unadventurous routines well before her husband finishes his and drifts about the gym gazing at herself in the wall mirrors, makes calls on her cell phone, and finally tiptoes to Eggplant Man to kiss him on his bald spot—like a monk's tonsure, at the back of his head—and tell him in a stage whisper, "I'll be waiting for you upstairs in the lounge, honey! Don't strain yourself."

Except for his purplish-flushed face and anguished eyes, Eggplant Man is not unattractive, by the standards of the Halcyon Mills Fitness Center. He's relatively youthful—in his early fifties, if not his late forties—with a rotund little belly no larger than a football, and respectably developed upper arm muscles. His legs are not impressive, like the legs of most older members of the Fitness Center, but in another lifetime he might have been a high school athlete in some non-contact sport like soccer or basketball. If I were to guess at his employment I might guess high school math teacher, or maybe, since from time to time he exudes an unmistakable air of vexed authority, high school principal. Between Eggplant Man and me there has been—this was long ago, and fleeting—a frisson of a rapport. Altogether by accident when, new at the gym, I dropped a ten-pound dumbbell onto my foot, and cried out in pain, and Eggplant Man immediately laid down his own dumbbell and hurried to me, to see if I was all right. (I was. Oh, I was! Though deeply embarrassed.)

Since then, there continues to be an indefinable something between us, not quite what you'd define as a rapport, but let's say a kind-of awareness of each other, though we don't greet each other in any formal or even informal way, and I would not dream of casting a sidelong smile at him just to signal *Yes, here I am! I am here*.

What a relief: today, Mrs. Eggplant Man doesn't seem to be on the premises. When I collapse, I will be spared the silly woman's cries for help.

Before going to the treadmill or any of the machines, you are supposed to Stretch. This I was earnestly instructed when I first joined the Fitness Center. And so now I approach a bar, stretch on my toes and take hold of it, and manage to lift myself, as if to fling my (surprisingly heavy, leaden legs and feet) into the air, as I'd done as a young girl in another lifetime; and at once as if in mockery of my childish effort a lightning-like pain shoots through my arms and shoulders and my head falls backward as if the vertebrae in my neck have snapped. My vision goes dark. Blood pounds in my ears. Is this it?—so quickly? My right hand slips, my left hand gives way, I fall to the hardwood floor with a soft thud. Am I dead—already?

"Ma'am? C'n I help you?"

Not Eggplant Man, who fortunately hasn't seemed to notice me, or Big Gus, or Chuffer, but Jorge, one of the smiling young trainers. Courteous Jorge helps me to my feet and explains to me another time how to "stretch" without straining myself. Deeply embarrassed I limp away explaining that I don't want instruction right now, thank you.

My arms feel as if they've nearly been yanked from their sockets. I'm dazed with pain and yet exhilarated, encouraged. Death by Fitness Center is no idle fantasy.

Next I go to a treadmill machine. My preferred machine, in a remote corner of the gym, as far from the noisy struggles of Big Gus and Chuffer as I can get. I set my treadmill speed at two. Anyone who can get to the gym without crutches can walk on a treadmill at two. At the end of the row of treadmills there is Big Gus hurtling onward at an advanced speed of—could it be five? Five miles an hour, an older man in Big Gus's condition? Not for the first time I'm concerned that Big Gus will suffer a coronary on the treadmill and if he does—what are the rest of us supposed to do? Long ago in a previous lifetime as a summer camp counselor in the Adirondacks I'd had a course in emergency first aid and CPR but the practice sessions made me queasy and light-headed and if

I passed the course, I don't know how I did it. (Right now, I'm not even sure what "CPR" means. There must be a "cardio" in it somewhere.) All I can do is try to ignore Big Gus's explosive exhalations of breath—as I try to ignore Chuffer's exhalations and grunts—I am too far away to be an eyewitness to Eggplant Man's heroic/quixotic dumbbell straining. Boys, you are on your own! I am not going to rush to your aid. With gay abandon I raise my treadmill speed to three, to four; four and a half; five. . . . Five! Now I am actually running, my arms flailing at my sides like slightly misshapen flippers and my breath coming quickly. My small fist of a heart is beginning to beat quickly as if bang! bang! banging on a door shut unjustly against me. If I run at this speed for—how long?—a half-hour, an hour?—will I keel over in exhaustion, or will my heart simply give out? Is that how it happens—with a pop? Recklessly I raise the speed to six. Six! Six-and-a-half! This isn't running, this is galloping. Never in my months of membership in the Halcyon Mills Fitness Center have I dared even to consider running at six.

A soupçon of perspiration, at the nape of my neck. The lilac sweatshirt is beginning to feel a little warm. I wonder—I won't glance over, of course—if any of the boys have noticed the advanced pace I am running at, or whether Andy, Jorge, or Carla is observing with astonishment and admiration.

I know—I have not described myself. It's a grim task I will not attempt.

In a wall mirror a few feet away, there's a clenched-faced individual running on a treadmill, a female of some blurred and indeterminate age—could be a girlish-gawky thirty-nine, or forty-nine—maybe, almost—in the right blurred light—twenty-nine. (Well, maybe. In the right blurred light she might pass for twenty-nine.) This individual must be five feet ten inches tall and can't weigh more than 112 pounds. Lanky, flat-chested and narrow-hipped, long-legged and big-footed. Her hair is a dark scribble streaked with flashes of silver—"premature"—and her pebble-colored eyes—her "best feature"—shine with a just-perceptibly fanatic myopic intensity. Her eyelashes turn downward as if she's been crying. (She has not been crying! She has given up the effort of tears.) Her thick eyebrows would grow together at the bridge of her nose except she takes care, with the dispatch of one whose basic nature is not to take care, to pluck the exasperating hairs out one by one. Her fingers are gawky-girl fingers chafed from winter and her nails are broken and split. Her gym shoes are size 10 AA.

She has been: (a) a librarian (b) a poet (c) a flautist (d) an ardent young wife. (All of these? None?)

(But—is this portrait truly "me"? Maybe it's just something I've grabbed at blindly the way, if you're only partially dressed and hear someone ringing your doorbell, you grab at whatever clothes you can find before hurrying to answer the door.)

Well, I am still running at six-and-a-half. And my heart is beating like the wings of a frantic butterfly to keep pace. And I am giddy thinking How sad. For didn't Physical Fitness used to be Fantasy Time? Like Sunday morning church services? Any kind of boring and repetitive activity—Girl Scout hiking, knitting-and-purling, fence post digging, chicken-defeathering and—gutting. What's sad is that there is a time inevitably in a life when Fantasy Time is played out because your Fantasy has been fulfilled.

For instance, in a Fitness Center like this, where male and female fitness-seekers interact, to the vague degree to which we interact, the most natural Fantasy is romantic. (For females, that is. For males, the most natural Fantasy is luridly sexual. Let's be frank about this.) Dreamily the female seeker thinks while pounding away entranced on the treadmill Will someone love me? Will someone stride into the gym just now, and notice me, and make some excuse to come over to meet me, and fall in love with me, and—whatever comes next? But if this Fantasy comes true? If you have actually been in love with, and been married—"happily" in fact—there is no margin for Fantasy ever again.

You have to imagine that it's the same with all wished-for achievements. With the Nobel Prize, for instance. Once you've won, you can't ever again mope about not winning. You can't console yourself with maudlin-drunken complaints. Sure I'm miserable. And I have a damned good reason to be miserable—I haven't won the Nobel Prize, or in fact any damned prize. You'd be miserable, too. But once you've won the Nobel, that solace is finis. You can't annul the Nobel Prize the way an ambitious politician can annul a marriage.

Once, at the Fitness Center, where I'd come without my companion, entangled in the macabre abdominal-press machine, I was crying.

That is, I wasn't *crying*. Not actually. I'd gotten myself twisted at a lateral angle, my left wrist in a strap and my left knee turned out, and tears spilled out of my eyes like hot bits of volcanic ash dribbling down onto my cheeks, and there stood Carrot Top above me looking concerned in the stiff way of one who, while looking concerned, wants to communicate to the object of his concern that this is an impersonal, not-to-be-protracted, *acte gratuite* sort of concern, and not anything binding. "Are you all right? Can I help you?" Gallantly Carrot Top helped untwist the strap, helped me to my feet and, though I hadn't requested this, readjusted the weight on the machine, from twenty-five pounds to fifteen. "This should work for you now. Take care!"

Carrot Top—of whom I'd been obliquely aware, from time to time—was one of the more fit of the Fitness Center civilians. He might have been as young as forty-five; he was freckle-faced like a brash American boy in a painting by Norman Rockwell; his carrot-orange hair sprang from his scalp in feathery-curly tufts receding at his temples but thick at the crown of his head. Usually he was cheery. He whistled to himself, he did not grunt or chuff but made his way through the gauntlet of machines without alarming observers or calling attention to himself. He was lean, except for wobbly love handles at his waist; his leg muscles were impressive, and covered in carrot-orange hairs like flickering flames. It must have been that Carrot Top frowned a good deal, unconsciously, for his boyish face was furrowed above his eyebrows; he had the look of a father whose children clamored for his attention.

In fact, Carrot Top drove a battered S.U.V. in which, in the rear seat, there appeared to be children's toys and scattered clothes. (In the Fitness Center parking lot, I'd seen Carrot Top's S.U.V. I did not stand gazing into it but yes, I was aware of it occasionally.)

Once in the parking lot at the SuperFresh on Route 31 where we'd met by accident—Carrot Top and me—what a surprise!—he'd stared at me with a quizzical smile, then saw who I was, "I know you, don't I?—from the Fitness Center?" We struck up a conversation. We talked, we laughed. We jangled our car keys, inched away to suggest that really we had to get to our respective vehicles, then paused, and talked further, and laughed some more. And Carrot Top was about to ask *Should we get some coffee?* or possibly *Let's have a drink, in T.J.'s*—for T.J.'s was an Italian restaurant in the Halcyon Mills Mall with a liquor license, rare in Halcyon Mills—which caused me to panic mildly and say in a mumble that I guessed I had to leave, my husband was waiting for me back at the house, and Carrot Top said yes, he had to leave, too. And walking to his S.U.V. Carrot Top waved and called back, "See you at the gym, maybe—tomorrow?"

Next day at the Fitness Center, no Carrot Top.

Nor the next day, nor the next.

Unless Carrot Top was coming deliberately at another hour, unguessable by me.

Oh—there was Chuffer, faithful Chuffer; and there was Big Gus, and there was Eggplant Man and for a mercifully brief while Mrs. Eggplant Man, and there were cameo appearances by Porkpie (female, of my approximate indeterminate age, heavier than me by thirty pounds though shorter by at least five, a miracle of animated cellulite and Botox-blank suburban-rich-wife face) and Pumpkin Head (don't ask), but no Carrot Top!

Was I hurt? Was I crushed? Was I angry? Not at all, I was amused. *I was untouched.*

So, Carrot Top is a mystery. But only as suburban-husband-males are mysteries. Truly I didn't want the mystery explained. (Well, maybe I did: I trailed Carrot Top's S.U.V. at a very discreet distance out of the Fitness Center parking lot one afternoon, followed him out onto Route 31 and south into the Harmony Woods Luxury Homes sub-division where in an exhausting maze of lanes, drives, cul-de-sacs and vistas he vanished. But I didn't really care enough about his identity to ask one of the staff what his name was, *I did not.*) It's the same way with magic—you don't really want magic tricks explained, for they are always banal and disappointing. If explained, it isn't magic. And we can't live without magic.

Some weeks later: I sighted Carrot Top in the Halcyon Mills library shepherding three young children and our eyes snatched at each other's with a kind of bittersweet regret for we had no time to speak just then; though in the parking lot I lingered beside my vehicle and when Carrot Top emerged from the library with books and videos in his arms, and three small children chattering and tangling with his legs, we smiled at each other—Carrot Top indicating the children, and me with an airy ambiguous gesture that might have signaled Yes I'm busy, too. But maybe see you soon, at the Fitness Center?

Yet, next time we saw each other, at the Fitness Center, Carrot Top was lifting weights in a strained and heaving manner like a beached whale and a flush came into Carrot Top's freckled face, and seeing me watching him in the mirror he did not smile; he broke off eye contact; demonstrably, he was rude.

What was this? Why was this? Carrot Top had initiated the flirtation—hadn't he? (I certainly had not.) In the lounge upstairs, where Fitness Center members are urged to "socialize"—purchase coffee, soft drinks, skim milk—it happened that I overheard Carrot Top on his cell phone, a fascinating one-sided exchange: "I can't, yet. I will—but not just yet." Carrot Top listened. His forehead contracted and furrowed like an accordion. His dun-colored eyes glistened with inchoate rage. "I can't, I said." He listened. He sighed. He said, ramming a finger against the base of his nose as if he'd have liked to break the cartilage, "Oh, all right. Fuck it, *I will.*"

A wife? Was Carrot Top speaking to a wife? Was their marriage in trouble? Were they—about to be separated? Were they separated?

Like a hungry mosquito hovering near a victim-to-be, I must have been buzzing too loudly. For Carrot Top put away his cell phone, saw me looking at him with a faint smile and said, with the chill precision of one firing a stapler gun, "Are you stalking me? Don't."

"S-S-Stalking? M-me? I—I am not—"

"Whatever it is, then: don't."

Carrot Top was glaring at me now. Carrot Top was the ugliest man I had ever seen. Carrot Top so frightened me, I turned away limping and in the corridor nearly collided with Carla as tear-blinded I retreated, in deepest chagrin I stumbled away to the women's locker room to lick my wounds.

Needless to say, I never attempted to speak to Carrot Top again, nor even to smile at him. Never waved at him! Not even in a wall mirror.

Though the last time I'd seen Carrot Top red-faced and panting at the seated chest press machine, over his shoulder on a ledge there was the ghostly outline of the gym cat just emerging out of the fluorescent haze. As I watched in (covert) fascination, pretending to be wholly engrossed in the squat cable cross machine, I saw the outline of the gym cat taking shape on a ledge beside Carrot Top; saw his fur the color of spilled oil materialize, and his eyes glistening glassy-green, and with a thrill I thought Carrot Top *doesn't see!*—or is *trying* not to see. And I thought Carrot Top is doomed but doesn't know it.

Damned if I would tell him. I would not.

After Carrot Top, days began noticeably to darken at ever earlier hours. As I'd noted above, though "daylight hours" were said to be shorter, yet time itself passed with enormous reluctance, like motor oil oozing uphill on a suburban driveway.

On the treadmill where I am running—panting—at this amazing advanced speed—something compels me to raise the speed

254 * JOYCE CAROL OATES

another notch, and there is a click, and a snap, and the treadmill suddenly rushes beneath me—not at seven but at—could it be seventeen?—"Oh my God—oh!"—fluorescent tubing spins and careens overhead like demented comets veering too close to earth—there's a terrible pressure pushing me backward—glassy-green eyes hovering in mid-air, in malicious glee—*Why do you want to die, you silly woman? You will die soon enough in any case*—and all the points of the compass seem to intersect in me, hurtling me backward against the concrete wall which is a bland-beige wall, against which I bounce harmless as a cloth doll.

"Hey!"

At once Big Gus leaps off his machine, to come to my aid. A man in his sixties red-faced and exhausted yet eager to help me to my feet, sympathetic and uncritical: "Have to watch out, treadmills can be treacherous."

Gingerly I'm on my feet. So embarrassed to be thanking Big Gus! Here's a man of whom I have been contemptuous, now Big Gus is being kind to me, asking if I'm sure that I am all right (Yes! I am) and suggesting that I quit the treadmill for now.

"Just a brief concussion. I'm fine!"

I escape to the women's locker room before anyone else can swoop upon me. Especially I don't want Andy's sympathy, or Jorge's; nor do I want anyone to guess what my mission is. In the mold-smelling locker room I am close to tears. I am close to despair. I am close to rage. If I hadn't keeled over dead on the treadmill, or had a brain hemorrhage having been flung against the wall, there is the possibility that I am invincible.

Like She of *She*. Can't die, and can't be killed. Only when the spell is broken can She be released, in a kind of spontaneous combustion.

The women's locker room! I hate this, and I hate having to describe it! No more depressing place. It's even more dreary, I'm sure, than the men's locker room since it is always deserted. Not once—well, maybe once—a long time ago, when my companion and I first joined the HMFC—have I seen another woman in this room—poor fretful Porkpie staring at a yellowed poster on the wall BE AWARE: ONE IN FIVE WOMEN BETWEEN THE AGES OF FIFTY AND SIXTY WILL SUFFER THINNESS OF BONES SCHEDULE A BONE DENSITY TEST NOW SEE RECEPTIONIST. But I haven't seen anyone in the locker room in months. I never come in here except to use the lavatory and leave as quickly as I can.

Three walls of lockers and not one locker in (evident) use. Of course, most women don't change their clothes here. Most women don't come anywhere near breaking into a sweat at the Fitness Center. I wear my "gym clothes" here, and I wear my "gym clothes" when I leave. There is a shower room, the most depressing shower stalls, you can see mold and fungus growing in the drains, a murmurous sound of fungal breathing. Who would ever shower here? Strip off her clothes and venture into a shower stall, here? The thought makes me shudder and yet: I examine the shower stalls to see if there might be a—well, no—of course there isn't—the thought is ridiculous—some sort of way to "hang" oneself by a shower head—an idle thought, a silly fantasy, let's strike this. Anyway, you would need a rope of some kind, to make a "noose." None of this is remotely plausible. Strike this.

Before leaving the women's locker room I open as many doors as I can, and discover just a few left-behind items: an old pair of Lady Champ gym shoes, a broken and disreputable comb, a wadded tissue (ugh) and a Visa card—no, only just a plastic HMFC membership card, the kind you flash at the electronic eye.

This card is the property of Brooke Harness. Out of pure meanness I don't turn it in at the reception desk but shove it into a pocket of my lilac sweatpants.

When I return to the workout room—face splashed with cold water, mad-scribble hair tamped down with damp fingers—to my relief I see that Big Gus has departed. This is good! No more explosive exhalations and unseemly grunts from that corner of the gym. And if Big Gus imagines that he and I have forged some sort of bond here this afternoon, Big Gus is sadly mistaken.

After Carrot Top, no more misunderstandings.

After Carrot Top, finis.

But here is Mrs. Eggplant Man tripping about the machines—in her aged-cheerleader bubbly mood, playing at such terrifying torture machines as the quad cross, the hamstring, the NordicTrack and StairMaster. Mrs. Eggplant Man sets her weights at ten to fifteen pounds—I have checked them—and seems scarcely to care that she's a figure of folly here in the gym. Like a show-offy schoolgirl she chants aloud—"One!"—"Two!"—"Three!"—"Four!"—as if any of the rest of us could possibly care about her diligence; sometimes Mrs. Eggplant Man gives up abruptly, releases her grip on a weight and lets the weight fall with a jarring clatter.

Eggplant Man must be damned embarrassed of her but he's too gentlemanly to let on.

Eggplant Man has become alarmingly purple-faced, struggling with the same old dumbbells. What is he trying to lift?—scarcely one-third of what Andy lifts with such ease. Once in SuperFresh I saw Eggplant Man and almost didn't recognize him since his face wasn't so floridly flushed but an ordinary suburban-Caucasian sallow; he was wearing a nice-looking overcoat and, over his thinning sorrel-colored hair, one of those Aran Island tweed caps of the kind I'd once bought for my husband, on a long-ago trip to Ireland. Such a cap can transform the most ordinary suburban male into an object of romance . . . In the steamy fresh-produce mirror our eyes met, but quickly I glanced away, and pushed my shopping cart away. I am not a lonely suburban wife. I am not one of you but someone else. Don't follow my shopping cart!

Eggplant Man, a gentleman, though saddled with an impossible wife, did not follow me.

For today, I have had enough of the treadmill. A vigorous workout, a mile-run at least, and I am feeling both bone-tired and exhilarated, the way long-distance truckers must feel having smoked—injected—snorted?—enough crystal meth to propel them from one coast to the other. As soon as Mrs. Eggplant Man gives up on the free-motion machines, and drifts over to the corner where her panting husband is working out, to plant a kiss on the hapless man's bald spot, I take my place at the seated two-arm-row press, which, in the wake of Mrs. Eggplant Woman, is set at a very comfortable ten pounds. With deft fingers I change the weight to—sixty pounds! I slip my hands into the grips, take hold and—pull—try to pull—strain myself trying to pull—my arm sockets, sore from my first exercise, throb with sudden pain—a sob escapes my throat—as I struggle with the weight (which won't budge, as if it is cemented into place) I see how, only a few feet away, poor Chuffer is struggling with his weight—must be twice mine—and how huge veins have pushed out on the man's forehead and the backs of his hands. Chuffer is still chuffing—grunting—shiny-red-faced like a roasting tomato that is about to burst—and I feel a tug of sympathy for the man, even a kind of—is it affection?—for Chuffer isn't at all a bad-looking man, with bulldog-jowls, droopy bulldog-eyes, a flaccid sinking chest like uncooked pancake dough, but his shoulder muscles are reasonably developed, his leg muscles are respectable, he has a dogged, earnest, diligent manner you would have to find endearing, as in an overweight golden retriever you see the perplexed grieving eyes of the frisky puppy-that-was; from time to time, Chuffer has, in fact, smiled at me; if Chuffer has not struck up a conversation with me it is because I have not encouraged it; but now—unless I am imagining it—Chuffer is signaling to me, trying to speak.

With cool composure I say: "Yes? Is something wrong?"

Oh, dear: Chuffer's sweaty face collapses in pain. This is the very sight I have most dreaded seeing at the Fitness Center! And on a ledge beyond the Cable Cross Quad there is the faint outline of the malicious gym cat . . .

"H-Help me—"

A moan—a groan of pain—surprise and pain—and Chuffer has sunk to one knee. And Chuffer has fallen. And Chuffer is whimpering for help. And in that instant I am beside him, and pressing my fingers against a pulse in his neck: erratic heartbeat! Heartbeat like a kick! Eggplant Man and his wife have departed. No one is in the gym at this moment except Chuffer and me. What a nightmare!

258 * JOYCE CAROL OATES

Though I am terrified, I try to remain calm. I hear my voice urging Chuffer to lie on his back and to lie very still, not to thrash about, not to try to sit up, like a schoolteacher I instruct Chuffer to breathe as evenly as he can, even as I call "Help! Help us!"—and here comes Jorge at a a trot—except, seeing a man fallen on the floor, Jorge reacts in a way I would not have expected—is Jorge going to faint?—as I scream at him, "Call 911! He's having a heart attack!" I am furious with Jorge who is surely more recently trained in CPR maneuvers than I am, I who can barely recall what the initials CPR mean, cardiopulmonary something?—damned Jorge is practicing first aid on himself, stooping over, bringing his forehead against his knees to bring blood back into his brain—but by this time poor Chuffer has lost consciousness, he has fallen limp, his face is a ghastly papery white, I am the one to administer first aid to the stricken man, speaking to him in a soothing voice, seeing that Chuffer's eyes have rolled back into his head and his face—a huge moon-face, with roughened skin as wrinkled and creased as an old glove—has gone clammy, and his lips are flaccid and blue, in my desperation I press the palms of both my hands on Chuffer's chest—gingerly!—not with the panache you see in TV medical emergencies—and lean daringly over Chuffer's face, lower my lips to his and force my breath into his mouth, and into his lungs; me, who would no more kiss a stranger than she would kiss, well—a friend—flush on the mouth like this; oh, this is awful! This is so awful!—trying to establish a rhythm I lean back, push—again, gingerly!—and then less gingerly—with some actual force—on the fallen man's chest, which is a fatty-muscled chest covered by a cotton T-shirt through whose thin damp fabric some wiry gray hairs have sprung, like weeds; I am panicked that I can't seem to feel any heartbeat but I continue to lean over poor Chuffer, press my mouth against his clammy and unresponsive mouth and breathe—force my breath—into his mouth, and into his lungs; and in this now stronger rhythm, it seems to me that Chuffer has begun responding; at any rate, I can taste something like coffee on his mouth, or on his breath; Brazilian mocha roast; poor Chuffer's tongue is inert

and cold like something on a cold meat platter. By this time Jorge
has recovered from his panic-fainting fit, and has been shouting for
help; it will turn out to be Carla at the reception desk who calls 911
and by the time the Halcyon Mills Medical Emergency team bursts
into the gym to take over from my aching arms and mouth, Chuffer
seems to be breathing again—is he?

In a haze of exhaustion and excitement, I drive home. Just beyond
Pheasant Hill, where Holly Drive intersects with Route 31. This
very long day whose origins are shrouded in mist like prehistory.
It is nighttime-dark now, and wet snow has begun to fall. Slick-
treacherous pavement but I am a cautious driver and arrive home
within twenty minutes. Our house—for it is "our" house, in which
"we" live—is mostly darkened. Only a few downstairs rooms are
lighted for my husband has been working through much of the day
at the rear of the house. Lights in that room are on, I discover him
seated at his desk with his head in his hands brooding over a spread
of financial records, receipts, canceled checks. My husband is preparing a quarterly payment for IRS that must be postmarked by
December 31. Otherwise we will be held liable for—exactly what, I
don't know. Such details, I don't want to know. Silently I tiptoe
into his study, and kiss the bald spot emerging at the back of his
head through his feathery graying hair.

"Where've you been all this while? At the Fitness Center?"

The remainder of this shortest-day-of-the-year passes without
incident. True night comes, when it comes, quickly.

The Glazers

She had known him for several months and she had been in love with him, in secret, for most of that time when, with disarming casualness, and the dimpled smile that sliced at her heart like a razor blade, he said: "Will you come home with me this weekend? I'd like you to meet my family." And she was excited and flattered by the invitation—for surely this indicated that Glenn Glazer's feelings for her, though unstated, were sincere.

Her first love. Though she was twenty years old. Though she was a junior at a highly competitive Ivy League university, a serious student, mature for her age. Calmly she told Glenn Glazer that yes, she would like that very much: "To meet your family. Of course!" She squeezed his hand, in affection. She brushed her lips against his cheek. She did not tell him, Please don't take it for granted that I will share a bed with you at your house. She did not tell him, There is something about me you should know: a secret.

In fact, more than one secret. But Penelope would not confide in Glenn Glazer until she was certain that his feeling for her was as deep and sincere as her feeling for him.

"My Dad! He's an unusual character, I guess . . ."

And: "I hope you like him, Penelope. I hope you like each other and I think you will."

It was a two-hour drive to the Glazers' sprawling French Normandy house on a large, partly wooded and professionally landscaped lot in the Village of Fair Hills, New Jersey. During this time of protracted intimacy, the longest time they'd been alone together, Glenn did most of the talking, and Penelope was content to listen. In their circle of friends at the university, as in his classes, Glenn Glazer was one of those individuals to whom others deferred, a young man who spoke earnestly and sincerely and who seemed to have something of value to say. Alone of the boys Penelope had gone out with at school, Glenn had what might be called a political consciousness; he was majoring in economics with a minor in politics; he was a "registered independent" with "serious qualms" about all political parties. His father, he said, was a "long-time Republican"—what you'd call a "moderate conservative." They'd been arguing about politics since Glenn was in high school: "Not serious arguments, I don't mean that. Our essential ideology, our grasp of what's called 'human nature,' is pretty much the same, I think." How rare it was, Penelope thought, among other boys who spoke ironically, or bitterly, or with bemusement or disdain, of their fathers, Glenn Glazer so clearly loved and respected his father, as, Penelope thought, she loved and respected her father. This was an encouraging sign, wasn't it? That Glenn Glazer and Penelope Whittlesley were temperamentally compatible? Only when they arrived at the Glazer home on a gravel road posted with the warning PRIVATE ROAD NO OUTLET did Penelope realize that Glenn had been speaking repeatedly of *My dad*, and, less frequently, of *My brothers*; not once had he said *My parents*, still less *My mom*.

Uneasily Penelope thought, I will wait for him to tell me why.

"'Penelope'! Hello, dear."

There came Glenn's father to greet her on the front walk of the

house, as if he'd been awaiting her and Glenn just inside the massive
oak door. He was an older, burlier, more mirthful version of his son,
heavier than Glenn by perhaps thirty pounds, with a high broad sunburnt forehead and short-trimmed brushed-aluminum hair, Glenn's
hazel eyes bizarrely bloodshot and crinkled at the corners from years
of squinting and smiling, and a wide warm eager glistening smile.
"Glenn has told me: 'Penelope' not 'Penny'! I can see that, Penelope:
you are not a 'Penny.' You are a dazzling silver dollar and not a penny,
and very pretty, and I hope that you will call me 'Douglas'—'Doug.'"
Mr. Glazer, who appeared to be in his early fifties, struck Penelope
as an aggressively cordial man accustomed to getting his own way. It
was a warm sunny April afternoon and he was wearing a madras
jacket in wanly festive colors, that fitted his thick torso tightly, and a
lime-green sport shirt with a tiny golfer stitched on the front pocket,
pleated linen trousers and sporty shoes that looked as if they were
woven of hemp, with thick sponge-like soles. At Mr. Glazer's collar,
opened to mid-chest, metallic curls bristled alarmingly; his wrists
were thick, covered in bristly hairs; he was almost exactly Glenn's
height, a tall looming man who looked as if he'd once been taller and
was beginning now to settle, like a monument on its foundation. His
breath smelled of something sweetly alcoholic and yet astringent,
like mouthwash; across his fleshy nose was a scribble of broken capillaries like tiny red cobwebs. It was unnerving for Penelope to see
Glenn and his father together, one so clearly very closely related to
the other: where Glenn's strong-boned face was flushed with boyish
vigor, Mr. Glazer's flaccid face was leathery and creased; the charming little dimple in Glenn's right cheek was, in Mr. Glazer's fleshier
cheek, a sharp crease like something made with a knife blade. Mr.
Glazer's grasp of Penelope's small hand was so uncomfortably warm
and encompassing, Penelope had to resist the impulse to ease away,
in fear that her hand was being swallowed up in another's avid flesh,
as in the gullet of a boa constrictor.

"My dear, it's a pleasure to be meeting you at last. Glenn has
been telling me wonderful things about you and that is not, repeat
not, my son's way. Of my sons, Glenn is the least effusive. Plays his

hand close to his breastbone not like his dad, as you can see. Let's go inside and Rita can bring us something to drink . . . Shall we sit out back on the terrace, and have a quick drink? You must be exhausted from the drive—"

Deftly Glenn intervened, saying that Penelope would probably like to be taken up to her room and have some time to herself before having something to drink, for which Penelope was grateful; she was feeling overwhelmed by the exuberant Mr. Glazer, for whom she felt a pang of affection, though she couldn't help glancing around, into the interior of the lavishly decorated house, and toward the showy spiral staircase, in the hope that a Mrs. Glazer might appear. Penelope was accustomed to the more restrained, formal manners of men like her own stockbroker father who would no more have been waiting just inside the front door of his house to spring out at visitors than he'd have worn a tight-fitting madras jacket with a lime-green golfer's shirt and smiled so eagerly at a stranger as if he'd have liked to crush her in an embrace.

Mr. Glazer would have accompanied Glenn and Penelope upstairs except again Glenn deftly intervened, in the practiced way of an agile young athlete (in fact, Glenn Glazer was on the university's varsity soccer team) outmaneuvering an older athlete, taking up Penelope's suitcase and hurrying her up the stairs as his father gazed after them with a look of yearning. "I'll call your brothers, Glenn. We've been waiting all afternoon . . ."

On the second floor, in an airy, attractive bedroom decorated in yellow chintz, with a four-poster canopy bed and white organdy curtains, that looked as if no one had ever disturbed it, like a feature in *Better Homes and Gardens,* Glenn kissed Penelope in his quick way, that reminded Penelope of punctuation in a sentence, saying, in a tone of embarrassment commingled with pride, "My dad overdoes it, I know. Every friend I've ever brought home—and my brothers, too—I don't mean girlfriends but guys, mostly—Dad tries so hard to make them feel welcome, it can be overwhelming at first. See, Dad is just the most generous, kindhearted man you'd ever encounter, except he's kind of lonely for female companionship. It's been a long time since"—Penelope sensed how Glenn steeled himself not to flinch or to allow his voice to turn maudlin—"a woman has lived in our house, except for housekeepers."

Lived in our house. A strange way of phrasing it, Penelope thought. "Do you mean your mother, Glenn? Or—a stepmother?"

Another time, though more forcibly this time, Glenn kissed Penelope on the lips, so hard that she felt the impress of his teeth. At such moments his maleness excited her even as it intimidated and disconcerted her, like his smile, that reminded her now of his father's smile, though with nothing mirthful in his eyes, as he said: "Take your time freshening up, Penelope. There's no hurry about joining us downstairs. Dad will be grilling me about classes and soccer and 'plans for next year.' And you are looking a little exhausted."

Left alone in the cheery-chintzy room, Penelope felt the sting of a rebuke.

He wants me to look pretty. To show off to his family.

Secrets! Penelope Whittlesley was a girl with secrets.

For instance, at the age of twenty, which seemed to her as to others of her generation, born in the late 1980s, no longer really young, she was (yet) a virgin. (By her own choice. Or had it been circumstances?) Though she gave no sign, or very little, of which she was conscious, she was the daughter of rich parents, as she was the daughter of a very rich grandfather, her father's father; but she'd been taught, and by nature was so inclined, to be concerned with educating herself, "making her own way." Her least romantic secret, which she dreaded revealing in a weak or maudlin moment, was that, at the age of sixteen, after a series of inexplicable falls and mishaps, and an alarming numbness in her legs, she'd been diagnosed with a "neurological deficit" resembling, though not identical to, multiple sclerosis; her symptoms had been relatively mild and had not worsened and, since the summer preceding her freshman year at college, when she was eighteen, she'd been in that precarious state known as *remission*.

These secrets were of unequal significance of course. Very likely it was known among Penelope's friends that she was (probably) a virgin. And certain of her classmates at the university who'd known her in prep school probably knew something of her family background. But no one, Penelope wanted to think, knew of her medical history, for she'd never collapsed in public, she'd never had a severe attack of muscular weakness in the company of anyone except relatives; for several years now she'd glided along like a skater on ice suspected to be thin, waiting for it to crack and shatter—and yet, it had not. (The "neurological deficit" was said to be of genetic origin and there was no treatment for Penelope's condition, yet; but the neurologists to whom her parents had sent her were optimistic about research in their field.) And so she would have to consider, Penelope thought, whether she would confide in someone who loved her, and whom she loved, as she would make love to this individual. "What I admire in you, Penelope, is something missing in most people: integrity." Glenn Glazer spoke sincerely for he, too, was an individual of unusual integrity, Penelope thought. You couldn't spend time with Glenn Glazer without seeing that there was something special, something truly singular, about him.

Maybe soon, Penelope would tell Glenn Glazer her most jealously kept secret. Maybe this weekend.

From a window of the cheery-chintz guest room Penelope could see a lavishly landscaped lawn, an edge of what appeared to be an Olympic-sized swimming pool, covered in a shiny blue tarpaulin; a gazebo on a hill; and a tennis court flanked by juniper pines so beautifully uniform they might have been artificial. It was clear that the Glazers were well-to-do: the French Normandy house was large, and impressive; Glenn had hinted, without exactly boasting, that his father was a "self-made business success" whose real interest was in "cutting-edge" science: molecular biology, genetics, biomedicine. ("Dad is too modest to talk about it but he has endowed fellowships at the New Horizon Institute for Biological Research and there's a 'Glazer Distinguished Professorship' at Yale. Since he won a National Science Fair prize in seventh grade, his first love has been 'pure' science but he had to 'make his fortune,' as he says, in business.") Penelope would have felt as strongly about Glenn Glazer if he'd been from a less prosperous background but it was consoling to her, she had to concede, that Glenn wouldn't have to be concerned about finances as his father had been, and was free, as he said, to "follow his dream": a year's travel after graduation, volunteer work of some kind in Africa, then law school where he intended to study biomedical law—"An entirely new field of law just opening up."

Penelope had met Glenn Glazer in a seminar in bioethics taught by a world-renowned professor whose columns appeared frequently on the Op-Ed page of the *New York Times*. Very possibly she'd fallen in love with Glenn Glazer for the way in which he spoke in the seminar, engaging the professor in passionate discussions of the ethics of euthanasia, genetic engineering, cloning; of the twenty or so students in the seminar, Glenn Glazer had been outstanding. (Penelope had been grateful to earn a B+ in the course. Though Glenn hadn't told her his grade, she had reason to suspect that it was a high A.)

On the terrace below, of which Penelope had a partial view from one of the windows, someone was standing: not Glenn, but one of his brothers. Voices lifted to her, boys' voices. Badly Penelope wished that a Mrs. Glazer might yet appear, but somehow she knew that this wouldn't happen. For Glenn hadn't mentioned his mother, Penelope realized, in the several months she'd known him.

There was some trauma here, very likely. At the least, a divorce. And the father had been granted custody of the children, which was unusual, and troubling.

Unless the mother had died. Or had disappeared from her sons' lives, without a trace.

Insane? Criminal? A suicide?

Penelope supposed that she would learn, eventually. But maybe such knowledge would not be to her benefit.

Her few things she'd unpacked and hung most of them in an empty cedar closet. Even the wire hangers looked pristine, untouched. In a heart-shaped mirror above a white wicker dressing table like something designed for the pampered adolescent daughter of an affluent household she saw that her skin was looking sallow, her hair lank and windblown, her lipstick worn off. She must not come downstairs looking "exhausted"—she'd been warned. Maybe middle-aged Douglas Glazer had gazed at her with admiration, and had gripped her hand a little too forcibly, but Penelope had no reason to consider herself beautiful, especially among other girls her age at the university. Her face was just perceptibly asymmetrical, her eyes darkly rueful, hopeful. Her nose seemed too long, and her forehead too low. Though if she made an effort, as she would do now, vigorously brushing her hair, that fell straight to her shoulders, until it shone as if burnished, and reddened her somewhat thin lips, and darkened her somewhat indistinct eyebrows, she could manage to look "striking"; if she wore bright, bold colors, unlike the neutral colors she favored—this dazzling bright-aqua Issey Miyake tunic given to her by a fashion-conscious aunt, with stylish raised shoulders, lacy ruff and sleeves, and cream-colored silk trousers, that flattered her petite, unexceptional figure—she could pass as eye-catchingly chic.

And so maybe Glenn Glazer would desire her, and love her. At least, as far as Glenn Glazer could know her.

As in a disjointed rapid-paced film Penelope was introduced to Glenn's several brothers, on the flagstone terrace at the rear of the Glazer home, as Mr. Glazer firmly gripped her hand—"Boys, here is Glenn's new friend Penelope, who does not wish to be called 'Penny.'"

First was twenty-six-year-old Craig, who'd been practicing tennis serves when Penelope had first come outside, and who bore an unnerving resemblance to his twenty-one-year-old brother Glenn except that his hair straggled past his collar, he wore rakish dark-tinted glasses and had a whiskery-wiry beard that looked as if it had been clamped onto his chin like a disguise: "H'lo, Penelope! Welcome to the Glazer household." Next, eagerly pushing forward, was ten-year-old Terry, a fleshy, ruddy-cheeked replica of

Mr. Glazer, with a wide beaming smile and a precociously firm handshake of his own: "Please to meet you, Pen-el-ope." And there was five-year-old Sam, a sweet-faced, diminutive version of Terry, with a shy smile and a mumbled greeting that provoked Mr. Glazer to nudge him, annoyed: "Speak up, Sam! Penelope will think you're slow."

Terry laughed with little-boy gusto at this cruel remark of their father's, as if to distance himself from his stricken little brother.

Penelope would have liked to assure Sam that certainly she wouldn't think such a thing, but little Sam gamely cleared his throat with adult vigor and like a smiling wind-up toy managed to articulate: "H'lo Penelope please to meet you."

Next, with sharp breathless barks, wriggling their furry, somewhat fat terrier bodies in an ecstasy of excitement, came Mick and Mike trotting across the terrace to press their cool noses against Penelope's knees, and to lick avidly at her hands. "More Glazers than Glenn prepared you for, maybe, 'Penelope,'" Craig said, so pointedly pronouncing Penelope's name that she had to wonder if he might be mocking her, or, in his oblique way, purposefully to annoy his brother Glenn, flirting with her; even as Mr. Glazer said in a booming voice, "Hope we're not too much for you, dear"—as if other young women, brought to this very spot at the rear of the Glazers' French Normandy house, overlooking the lavishly landscaped rear lawn, had been intimidated, and fled. Quickly Penelope said that she was delighted to be meeting Glenn's family, of whom she'd heard such good things; though she could not recall having heard that Glenn had an older brother, only just the two younger brothers of whom he seemed fond. In the corner of her eye she saw Glenn standing a little apart from his father and brothers, a glass of beer in his hand, baseball cap pulled low over his forehead so that his eyes were obscured, looking on with an irresolute smile. It was the smile of a young man who is undecided, who is moving toward making a decision. In the dazzling aqua tunic and cream-colored silk trousers, at the center of such an intensity of masculine attention, Penelope was feeling like a nervous actress blinded by spotlights who is beginning to sense the enthusiasm and support of her audience.

Only Mr. Glazer, Craig, and Glenn were drinking, tall glasses of "our favorite imported Belgian beer"; Penelope and the younger Glazers were drinking pink grapefruit juice. It was a festive occasion, like a homecoming: Penelope found herself basking in the attention, now smiling at a witty remark of the rakishly bearded Craig, who'd removed his dark glasses to reveal warmly bemused hazel eyes uncannily similar to Glenn's eyes; now laughing at a comical antic of Terry's involving the terriers Mick and Mike, who so closely resembled each other that only Terry, allegedly, could tell them apart; now listening, with a gravely inclined head, to Mr. Glazer expounding on the shortsightedness of the present administration's policy regarding stem-cell and other "cutting-edge" biomedical research, and what he saw to be the "global market of the future." Little Sam had overcome his initial shyness to invite Penelope to come see his termite colony, for which he'd won first prize at a school science fair, which Penelope promised she would do, shortly. And there was Glenn casting glances at her, Penelope wished to interpret as admiring, approving. So many times he'd said *I hope you like my dad and my brothers*, Penelope had come belatedly to realize that Glenn was also saying *I hope my dad and my brothers like you.*

Repeatedly Penelope exclaimed, "What a beautiful house, and what a beautiful setting"—feeling suddenly giddy with hope.

Mr. Glazer said, beaming, "We like it, yes indeed. We're pretty happy here, Penelope." As if by accident allowing his heavy warm hand to brush against Penelope's arm as he loomed over her. Penelope had to resist the impulse to step away, preserving a bright daughterly sort of smile as she asked, "And how long have you lived here, Mr. Glazer?"

"Now, dear: 'Doug.' You must call me 'Doug.' 'Mr. Glazer' is what my employees call me."

Dutifully Penelope said, "'Doug.'" Yet how awkward she felt, addressing Glenn's father whom she scarcely knew so informally.

"Unless you'd rather call me 'Dad,'" Mr. Glazer said with a wink, nudging Penelope and making her blush.

Though it was late afternoon, and dinner was scheduled for early evening, there was much to eat and drink on the terrace, platters of appetizers prepared by the Glazers' housekeeper Rita, and imported Belgian beer on ice; Penelope saw that all the Glazers were eating hungrily, and the unbidden disturbing thought came to her that, one day, lean lanky athletic Glenn Glazer would be thirty pounds heavier, like his father whom he so closely resembled; very likely, all the Glazer sons, even diminutive Sam, would put on weight, in time, and come to resemble their fleshy ruddy-faced father.

Penelope wondered what the boys' mother had looked like. Visibly at least, the mysterious woman seemed to have had little genetic influence on her children. Unless she and Mr. Glazer resembled each other: eye and hair color, facial features, body type. Penelope wondered if in fact there had been but one mother for these four sons, spread across so many years. *That* was the puzzle.

She calculated: Craig was twenty-six, little Sam only five. Twenty-one years! A lengthy period of childbearing for one woman, at least in the social class to which the Glazers belonged.

Penelope shuddered, considering.

She was noting how as the smiling Hispanic housekeeper in a white maid's uniform moved about the terrace serving the Glazers, and taking away their dirtied plates and crumpled napkins, none of the Glazers, even sweet-faced little Sam, so much as glanced at her: as if, in her meekly subordinate role, the woman wasn't an individual but a mere function. Though sensing that Mr. Glazer would stare after her disapprovingly, and that Glenn would be disapproving, too, Penelope boldly volunteered to help Rita, accompanying the housekeeper as she re-entered the house, and following her into a spacious white-walled kitchen. There, Penelope said brightly, "What a good cook you are, Rita! Have you worked long for Mr. Glazer?" and Rita, clearly embarrassed, smiling nervously, murmured almost inaudibly, "One year, I have worked here."

Penelope asked if Rita had ever met a Mrs. Glazer, and Rita shook her head ambiguously: was this no, or yes? Clearly Rita wished this intruder in her kitchen gone, but Penelope persisted: "Have you ever met the boys' mother? Or—mothers?" as Rita began to rinse plates noisily at a large aluminum sink. She was much shorter than Penelope, a plump, compact woman in her late forties with wavy dark hair parted neatly in the center of her head and knotted in a chignon at the nape of her neck. In the Whittlesley household in Kent, Connecticut, where Penelope had grown up, she had been taught to consider household "help" as "family"; but the Glazers didn't seem to share this sentiment, for Rita behaved as if fearful of being overheard by her employer, visibly reluctant to speak with Penelope. "I don't mean to pry, Rita, but I'm just so curious—Glenn has told me so little about his mother—have you ever met a Mrs. Glazer? Or heard about her? Or—seen photographs of her?"

Over the noisy water, the housekeeper's murmured words were barely audible. "No. No 'Mrs. Glazer.' Only 'Mr.'"

"So many Glazer sons—you must get confused at times?" Penelope spoke lightly to suggest that she wasn't altogether serious in this inane remark, but the frowning woman at the sink ignored her; and at that moment Craig Glazer—yes, it was Craig, and not Glenn—twenty-six-year-old Craig Glazer with straggly hair, tinted glasses and a whiskery beard affixed to his boyish-Glazer face—bounded in the kitchen to fetch Penelope.

"Dad is wondering where you are, Penelope. We all are!"

Returning to the terrace, his fingers lightly on her back, Craig steered Penelope along a corridor illuminated with incandescent lighting from invisible fixtures in the dark walnut paneling, where rows of framed photographs were displayed. Penelope had a confused impression of repeated Glazer faces as in a surreal wallpaper of repetition with minimal variation, the elder Douglas Glazer and his sons, boys with soccer balls, hockey sticks, tennis racquets, individual portraits, family scenes, school graduations, camping trips; no glimpse, so far as Penelope could see, of any woman, except in school photographs. "Is this Glenn?" Penelope asked, pointing to a boy of about fifteen with a deep-dimpled smile, tennis racquet brandished in a victory gesture, and Craig laughed derisively. "You kidding? That's not Glenn, that's me. Just won the Tri-State Junior Tennis Tournament, at Lake Placid." As Penelope murmured words of admiration and interest, uncomfortably aware of the young man looming over her, Craig pointed out several other photographs of himself: "Graduation day, Harvard. (Glenn didn't get admitted, he tell you? He wouldn't!) And here, my graduation from Yale Law. (That's Dad next to me in the black cap and gown, received a 'Distinguished Alumnus Award' at the same commencement.) Here, Morocco, that's me perched on the camel; here, on the Yangtze River with some Fulbright fellows; and here, West Africa, that's me with the guitar with some of my 'boys'—outside an AIDS hospital in Gabon where I was a volunteer for a remarkable—profound and life-altering!—three months, just last year. (Glenn probably hasn't told you about his big brother in Africa, eh?) The kind of law I'm practicing now, just hired by one of Dad's business associates, it's dealing with this cutting-edge new field—'synthetic biology.' Ever heard of that?" Penelope felt Craig's fingers drifting against her hair, and his warm beery breath against her face; her heart began to beat rapidly, as if the young man was Glenn, the young man she loved; Penelope stepped away, alarmed. Seeing the deep-dimpled smile on Craig's face, unsure if it was mocking, or yearning, Penelope thought *They are fairy-tale brothers, this is a test of some kind.*

"Penelope, dear: my son Mark. My 'beat' son."

"Dad, geez. Not 'beat'—'goth.' 'Beat' is your era."

Penelope was astonished to be meeting yet another Glazer son, who'd arrived belatedly at the terrace gathering, having provoked paternal annoyance on Mr. Glazer's part, though clearly Mr. Glazer was very fond of this son, too: for here was, in Penelope's eyes, the most striking of the Glazer brothers, exactly her height, very lean, lanky, sulky and contemptuous in theatrical "goth" attire, a grungy black T-shirt with a faded iridescent skull on its front, worn black jeans that emphasized the weasel-like thinness of the boy's hips and pelvis, black leather boots. Here was seventeen-year-old Mark—"home for the weekend from the Hun School"—who'd shaved his somewhat bumpy, diminutive-looking head so close to his skull he appeared bald, and those exposed ears were pierced with studs and cruel-looking clamps. Mark's boyish-Glazer face would have resembled Glenn's to an uncanny degree except for the numerous silver piercings in his nose, eyebrows, lower lip. So glittering was the boy's face, Penelope had the impression that he was winking at her from a dozen covert eyes.

And Mark's warm bemused beautiful hazel eyes—so like Glenn's eyes, Penelope felt a tinge of vertigo.

She thought *Another fairy-tale brother! But he is the princess's true love.*

All this was ridiculous, Penelope knew. She was feeling dizzy, disoriented. The younger boys Sam and Teddy—no, Terry—were tugging at her hands, pleading with her to come with them to see their "special projects"; Craig and Glenn were going to play a set of tennis, and would have been disappointed if Penelope didn't come watch them, for at least a few minutes. And Mr. Glazer was zestfully draining his second or third glass of pungent Belgian beer, and inviting Penelope to an "audio guided tour" about the Glazer property before dinner. Yet Mark, who hadn't troubled to shake Penelope's hand when they were introduced, and who'd mumbled a dismissive greeting as if he couldn't be bothered with meeting his brother's girlfriend, remained close by her side, glancing covertly at her; at last volunteering that he played electric guitar—a "fantastic" Schecter C-2 Hellraiser he'd bought online—and composed his own "post-heavy-metal" music. Mark boasted to Penelope that he was "blowing off" the remainder of his junior year at prep school and had no intention—"Repeat: *no* intention"—of appying to any college, anywhere, as his older brothers had slavishly done, and as his father wished. When Penelope, casting about for something to say to the edgy, appealing teenager, chanced to remark that she badly wished she'd learned to play a musical instrument as a child, Mark gazed upon her blinking as if she'd touched him; now grave-faced, not at all sullen or contemptuous but with boyish ardor inviting Penelope to listen to his music: "There's this kind of weird piece I was working on all last night, nobody's heard yet. C'mon up to my room—" even as Glenn advanced upon his glittery-faced younger brother with an air of menace Penelope had never seen before in him, genial good-sport Glenn Glazer who, having been tripped on the soccer field, got quickly to his feet blushing, laughing away his chagrin; except now Glenn wasn't laughing but pushing Mark belligerently in the chest saying, "She doesn't want to hear your puerile 'goth' bullshit, any more than the rest of us do," and Mark flared up, "Fuck you, Ivy League asshole," and Glenn cursed him and pushed more forcibly at Mark who, shorter than Glenn, and at least fifteen pounds lighter, staggered backward and nearly fell; regaining his balance, and trying to knee Glenn in the groin; there came Craig to intervene—"Break it up, assholes"—whether to push the brothers apart or to goad them into further antagonism; suddenly, a fistfight broke out, on the terrace amid showy white wrought iron furniture; a glass-topped table was overturned, shattering glass on the flagstones; food and drink went flying; the terriers began barking hysterically; there came red-faced Mr. Glazer pulling at the struggling, wildly punching brothers, as the younger boys—Terry, Sam—came running; underfoot Mick and Mike snapped at ankles; grunting with effort, Mr. Glazer nearly tore his seventeen-year-old son's black T-shirt off his shoulders: "Boys! I have told you, there is zero tolerance in this household for violence."

Glenn stepped back, panting and wiping at his face, and Penelope made a move to come to him, except a look in his face, of fury and sheer brotherly hatred, stopped her cold. Craig was laughing as if he'd never witnessed anything so funny while Mark, who'd had the worst of the fight, bleeding from his nose, and from a wound in his eyebrow where one of the piercings hung torn and dangling, turned on his father with a look of fury: "You! 'Dad'! What a hypocrite! You're to blame!" In tears Mark stumbled away shame-faced; Mr. Glazer tried clumsily to restrain him, whether to comfort him or to rebuke him further wasn't clear; tangled in their legs was little Sam, who fell heavily to the ground, and began crying; Mr. Glazer, short of breath, had slipped to one knee, and had dirtied his trousers; he was tearing at his shirt collar as if he were having difficulty breathing. Rita appeared on the terrace, to comfort the weeping little Sam, and Penelope helped Mr. Glazer to his feet as his older sons stood staring at him, alarmed and seemingly helpless. With the lofty gesture of a stricken king Mr. Glazer waved them away, as if his disgust with them went beyond speech. He leaned heavily on Penelope's arm as she helped him make his way into the house. "Some quiet. Please, dear: I must have quiet." So red-faced had the older man become, and so quickly, his coarse skin giving off a throbbing heat, Penelope understood that his blood pressure was dangerously high, and she must try to calm him.

Inside the house, in a dimly lighted room paneled in dark walnut, that appeared to be Mr. Glazer's study, Penelope succeeded in getting Mr. Glazer to lie back on a leather sofa; in an adjoining bathroom she soaked a washcloth in cold water, brought it to him and pressed it against his burning face. Though still breathing audibly, an ooze of perspiration on his broad sunburnt forehead, Mr. Glazer shut his eyes and made an effort to relax. Penelope helped him remove the madras jacket that was sweated through beneath the arms; Penelope removed Mr. Glazer's heavy hemp shoes, that weighed on his swollen ankles like hooves. How strange it was, that Penelope Whittlesley should be doing such things, performing such intimate acts, with a man she scarcely knew: a man who seemed now to have forgotten her name. "Just a touch of brandy from the cabinet there, dear. Please." Dutifully Penelope brought the brandy snifter to Mr. Glazer and a glass into which, like a nurse, she poured an inch or so of the strong-smelling liquid.

"Thank you, dear! Now close the door."

Penelope understood that, though Mr. Glazer might not recall her name, or who she was, exactly, her presence was crucial to his well-being. In lunges and surges he spoke, by turns distressed, angry, self-pitying, baffled and hurt: ". . . think sometimes that my life has turned out wrong, for all my calculations! I mean—that this is the wrong life I am leading. Like some 'alternative universe' you hear of—my son Terry speaks of, yet what does 'alternative universe' mean if you are *here*, and can't get *there*? Some of us were brought up to respect order, honor, control, discipline—'noblesse oblige.' That never changes! Nothing is so repulsive as lax morals— mongrelization—'open borders'—'amnesty' to criminals—promiscuous mixing of DNA—" On Mr. Glazer's desk was a state-of-the-art computer with one of the thinnest screens Penelope had ever seen. Also on the desk were printouts of financial statements, copies of *Financial Times, Wall Street Journal, Economist, Journal of the New Horizon Institute for Genetic Research, American Heritage Quarterly*, among other titles; in the built-in walnut bookshelves were numerous books on science, finance, history, politics. Many of the books were in pristine dust jackets as if they had never been opened.

In the corridor outside the closed door were voices; boys' voices; muffled, hissing as if somehow inside the walls; so many Glazer sons, like rats in the walls; there were thuds, exchanges of curses, or blows; footsteps on the stairs, and overhead; a pack of marauding youths out of some epoch before the human, at all times close to mutiny against the father. Did this sort of incident happen often in the Glazer household? Would Rita simply clean up the mess on the terrace, prepare and serve dinner as planned? In Penelope's home in Kent, Connecticut, such an outburst between family members would never occur; if it did, relationships would be forever altered, if not ended; yet somehow, in the Glazer household, Penelope had a feeling that the upset would blow over, and be forgotten. *For they have no one but one another, there is no choice.*

As Mr. Glazer continued to speak, now in a slower, slurred voice, his puffy eyelids drooping, Penelope was thinking of how, at the university, Glenn Glazer had been so attractive a figure, because so singular; with his frank, friendly manner, and the direct way in which he looked at you; the ease of his dimpled smile; his way of speaking with deliberation, as if choosing his words with care. Especially he'd been attractive to Penelope for the subtle, fleeting shadow of melancholy in his face in repose, that only Penelope noticed. (Or so she'd believed.) But now, in the Glazer household, amid the pack of Glazer males, so clearly the son of the wheezing red-faced man on the sofa, Glenn no longer seemed singular, and no longer very attractive.

As if sensing her thoughts, Mr. Glazer peered at her with bloodshot hazel eyes. Sternly saying, "Don't judge us harshly, my dear girl! You don't know us. My boys are damn good boys, if sometimes emotional. 'Boys will be boys.' My sons are absolutely devoted to one another. All Glazers are loyal to the death, to the family lineage. Such loyalty *is* our lineage. A proud family, six generations of Glazers in America... Even Mark, who is going through his 'rebellious phase'—like Craig and Glenn at his age— indeed, like his dad—in my time. But Mark will snap out of it, as we all did. When he learns that credit cards can be cancelled with a snap of the fingers. And Mark will do his old dad proud by enrolling in a first-rate university, like his brothers. You see, dear, not having a mother—a female presence in this household—has been a problem at times, but we persevere."

Penelope took advantage of this remark to inquire what had happened to the boys' mother, or mothers; and Mr. Glazer said, "The boys' 'mother' has not been with us. There has not been a—'mother.'" The word "mother" was uttered with fastidious precision, like a clinical term. "My dear, it is a curse to be a perfectionist. To have 'high standards' in an epoch of mongrelization. You may call perfectionism a blessing or a curse, but I have persevered, I have not been defeated. I have sired five sons of whom I am very proud—I have not yet sired a daughter—but that may come. I have not had good luck with women—'stepmothers'—for my boys. A succession of nannies and housekeepers has not been sufficient, I'm afraid." Mr. Glazer gazed at Penelope with sudden longing, as if she'd been brought to him, as in one of those horrific Biblical tales of a young virgin brought to an impotent old patriarch to stir

278 * JOYCE CAROL OATES

his sluggish blood and revive his manhood; but without success. Clumsily, Mr. Glazer signaled for Penelope to come closer, and sit beside him, for she was sitting on a chair some feet away, hands clasped in her lap like a schoolgirl. Fortunately, Mr. Glazer had grown very sleepy, and his eyelids were closing. His wheezing breath slowed, and became rhythmic. Cautiously Penelope settled a pillow behind his heavy head, and quietly left the room.

Only 6:05 P.M.! She had been at the Glazers less than two hours, and felt as if she'd been there for days. So utterly drained of energy, her blood might have been pumped out of her body.

In the corridor outside their father's study just the younger boys Terry and Sam remained, eagerly awaiting news of their father; or perhaps they were eagerly awaiting Penelope, whose hands they tugged at, pleading with her to come see their "special projects." Outside on the tennis court, Craig and Glenn were walloping tennis balls at each other, with grim ferocity, Penelope saw through a window; they appeared to be evenly matched; badly she hoped that Glenn would win, for a loss to his brother would plunge him into a very bad mood. On the terrace, Rita was just finishing her cleanup, having swept away a pile of broken glass. Penelope allowed herself to be led into a computer room by Terry, who was chattering excitedly about a computer program he'd designed for which he'd won a National Science Fair prize in his age category: " 'Transaction.' It *is not* a dumb old game but a 'virtual experience' inside your head. There is an alternative world—'mentally driven'—not an 'action game'—but it's cool 'cause people get killed—'deleted.'" Ten-year-old Terry was now speaking in the pedantic and argumentative way in which his father spoke, tugging impatiently at Penelope's hand as she tried to focus on the computer screen before her, that seemed to shift and dissolve before her eyes; gamely she tried to make sense of Terry's boast of what he'd accomplished, that even his teacher couldn't comprehend; his hope was, his father would file "Transaction" with the U.S. Patent Office, and provide the capital "up front" for manufacture. Wistfully little Sam was asking if Penelope was going to stay with them, as the other "step-mommies" had stayed, or was she going to leave again, as the other "step-mommies" had left, and Terry said derisively, "Retard, she can't stay. She isn't *may-reed* to Dad." Terry pronounced *may-reed* as if it, too, were a clinical term whose definition he didn't know, even as he cast a furtive glance at Penelope, to see if somehow this might be so, that Penelope was *may-reed* to their father.

Next, Penelope accompanied Sam into another part of the house, to be shown his "termite colony" for which he'd won a Science Fair prize at his school. The termite colony had been established in an aquarium-like glass structure in a warm room smelling strongly of earth and rot. Penelope stooped to stare at, or into, the colony through one of the glass sides, hoping not to be sickened by what she saw. Insects repelled her, especially insects with a propensity to squirm, or swarm. Sam said excitedly, "People think that termites are all alike—like ants—but they're not. And ants aren't, either. With magnification, you can see how different and special they are." Sam insisted that Penelope observe several individual termites through magnification. Dutifully she peered at the ugly things, feeling a shudder of revulsion as they loomed gigantic in her eye. One of them seemed to be staring back at her, its sardonic, beadily-metallic eyes bulging from its blunt head, and with a sharp little cry she drew back fearing the termite might crawl through the glass and up her arm. Sam seemed disappointed in Penelope's reaction saying it was "silly" to be afraid of termites because they weren't "carnivorous insects"—not like the "giant jungle ants" of the Amazonian rain forest: "Those ants—*Formicidae lupus*—can march on a village and eat everything—animals, people—that don't get out of their way. There's ant armies a mile long, and a mile wide." It was clear that Sam's sympathies lay with the giant jungle ants and not with their hapless victims. "That's horrible," Penelope said, with a shudder. "I don't want to hear anything more about ants, and I don't want to see any more termites."

There was a sharp little dimple in Sam's right cheek as he

smiled, or smirked: "Dad says women don't 'get' science, 'cause they are *ear-rationell*."

Through a sudden headache haze Penelope glanced at her watch: only 6:28 P.M.

She would have helped Rita in the kitchen preparing dinner except the Hispanic housekeeper so clearly didn't want her, so Penelope had no choice but to retreat. Making her way then, not very quickly, or with much enthusiasm, to the pristine clay tennis court where Glenn and Craig were playing furiously, each grim-faced, jut-jawed, determined to beat/humiliate the other, Penelope was waylaid by Mark—"Hey!"—who touched her wrist and signaled for her to join him at the edge of the terrace where they couldn't be seen from the tennis court or the interior of the house. This seventeen-year-old Glazer brother had washed his face and changed his blood-splattered black T-shirt and was looking now young, abashed and resentful; in his hand was a bottle of imported Belgian beer from which he'd been drinking; his breath smelled of beer. The hand was identical to Glenn's hand except for the broken, dirt-edged fingernails: Penelope had held that hand, that had closed over hers in a gesture of tenderness, or of appropriation. And there was Mark's mouth so like the mouth Penelope had kissed, except downturned now, sulky and defiant. In a quavering voice Mark said: "There's a s-secret about our family, you should know."

"A secret?" Penelope tried to smile. Mark was crowding close, fixing her with hazel eyes that brimmed with emotion. On his unshaven jaws a downy boy's beard was only just perceptible and in his right eyebrow a small fresh wound glistened with coagulated blood like a misplaced comma.

"Wonder where our 'mother' is?"

Uneasy, Penelope nodded yes.

"There is no 'mother.' There never was."

"'Never was'—?"

Mark took a swig from the bottle of Belgian beer, offered the bottle to Penelope who stared at him uncomprehending. "We aren't brothers, that's the secret. Dad isn't 'Dad'—we are 'Dad.' I mean, we are 'Douglas Glazer.'"

"I don't understand . . ."

"I'm called 'Mark'—but I'm really Douglas Glazer '90 because I was generated in 1990."

"'Generated'? You mean—born?"

"Not *born. You* were born. Ordinary people—and animals—are born." Mark spoke with bemused disdain, as little Sam had spoken a few minutes before, chiding Penelope for being silly about his termites, and about science. "The Glazers, except for Douglas Glazer '56, who came first, have been cloned."

"'Cloned'—?"

"You sound like a parrot, Penelope," Mark said, laughing. Again he lifted the bottle, and swallowed a large mouthful of beer. His eyes were so very faintly bloodshot, you could not have seen from a distance of several feet. "Our secret is, Dad's 'sons' are all clones of his, not 'sons.' We were cloned at different times which is why we're different ages and I think we were cloned at different places, cloning of *Homo sapiens* is against the law at the present time, in the U.S. Except for Dad coming first, and providing DNA for the rest of us to be generated from, and being older, and being our financial support, you could say, and providing a 'home' for us like a normal 'family'—we are not different from him. We have different names—'Craig,' 'Glenn,' 'Terry,' 'Sam,' and me, 'Mark'—but really, we are identical individuals." Mark smiled broadly, and now Penelope could see the sharp little dimple in his right cheek. The boy's face so glittered and winked with silver piercings, Penelope felt a wave of vertigo, as if she were about to faint. Quickly Mark touched her wrist again, in concern.

"Hey. Just kidding."

On her cell phone, in the cheery-chintz guest room with the door shut, Penelope called home. Fortunately, her father answered. Trying to remain calm Penelope explained that she was at Glenn Glazer's home in Fair Hills, New Jersey, from which she needed to escape immediately, and would he please help her; at once Penelope's father asked if she'd been hurt, if something had happened to her, and Penelope assured him no, she had not been hurt; *hurt* being a code for sexual molestation, rape; Penelope insisted it was nothing like that, nothing "physical" or "threatening" but a situation from which she needed to extricate herself immediately. Penelope paused, short of breath. She would never be able to explain the Glazers to her father, or to anyone: she would not have been believed. She'd been feeling ill since arriving at the house, now there was a growing numbness in her legs that terrified her. Elsewhere in the house were uplifted voices. Boys' voices, and Mr. Glazer's voice booming over the rest. In another minute Glenn would come for her, to summon her to dinner. Penelope was close to tears: "I need to come home, Daddy. Please help me, Daddy, I need to come home."

"You're leaving? *Now?*"

Mr. Glazer was astonished, and hurt. Hurriedly Penelope explained that a car was being sent for her—"A family emergency. My mother just called on my cell phone. My father is ill."

A heart attack, it seemed to be. He'd been taken to a hospital.

Solemnly the Glazers gathered to see their anxious guest off. Terry and little Sam appeared stricken. Craig was frowning doubtfully. Hanging back, there was Mark staring at Penelope with a look of guilty chagrin as if after all he'd been *just kidding*, and Penelope had taken his words literally. Glenn was the most surprised and Mr. Glazer was the most emotional. His words were rushed and slurred. "This is terrible news, dear. You must be with your father of course. But promise me you'll come back to visit us soon." Penelope shuddered at the touch of the man's hand, that had seemed so warm and protective initially. And his warm damp smile that had seemed so good-natured, so paternal, was horrible to her now.

Glenn carried Penelope's suitcase to the limousine. At such

short notice, the Fair Hills car service could provide only a stretch limousine, a black hearse-like vehicle with tinted windows and freezing air-conditioning, which Penelope hated. Yet how appropriate, this ghastly vehicle, to bear Penelope away from the Glazers. "Penelope, please call me as soon as you get home," Glenn said urgently, and Penelope assured Glenn that yes, she would, though she knew that she would not. Scarcely could she bear being touched by Glenn Glazer, still less kissed, as Glenn took hold of Penelope's shoulders and kissed her hard, with an air of hungry desperation. Penelope broke away, gasping for breath.

Glenn flushed a deep angry red. "It's my father, isn't it? One of my brothers? Did someone say something to you? Something—rude?" Penelope assured him it wasn't anything like that, truly there was a medical emergency at her home, and Glenn said, bitterly, "There's something wrong with our family, some reason people don't like us, and we don't understand. We don't know what it is. Craig's girlfriends never stayed either." Penelope protested feebly, "People like you, Glenn! They do," even as she slid into the cushioned rear of the limousine, eager to depart. Glenn said, "If you don't like my dad, and don't like my brothers, Penelope, I guess you don't like *me*."

Again Penelope tried feebly to protest. Yet she could not force herself to lift her eyes to Glenn's face, that had meant so much to her only a few hours before.

"Goodbye, Penelope."

Glenn spoke coldly now. On the front walk of the house stood the rest of the Glazer family gazing after Penelope, unsmiling.

In the rear of the limousine bound for Kent, Connecticut, Penelope collapsed in tears. She was exhausted, and hoped that she could sleep; that, sleeping, she might sink into oblivion; and, by the time she reached home, she'd have forgotten the Glazers altogether.

Mistrial

Years awaiting a sign, now God sent a sign.

Jury duty! The summons came in the mail.

Amid the usual pile of bills, flyers and hobby-catalogues for my brother Hubert McSwann was the letter from the Mercer County Courthouse stamped DENISE McSWANN. With a shiver of dread and excitement I picked up the envelope for it was rare that any actual mail came for DENISE McSWANN, 73 Hurdle Avenue, Trenton, N.J. On her aluminum walker my elderly mother clattered into the room muttering Denise? Is that the mail? Is there anything for me? and quickly I hid the letter saying No Mummy. Just for me.

In the courtroom, at one of the tables at the front of the room he was seated.

From a distance I saw him, yet clearly. A sensation of such weakness flooded my veins I thought I might faint. Which is not like me for I am scarcely a weak-minded woman. I am a former librarian and skilled in dealing with the public yet at the sight of this person designated as *the defendant* I felt as if a tightness had been released from my heart—or a darkness, inside my skull—and I stopped short, and stared.

Ma'am? Something wrong? one of the sheriff's deputies inquired of me and quickly I said No! Not a thing is wrong officer, thank you.

Dared not look at him further. Dared not reveal my emotion.

Blindly took a seat. Oh!—my heart pounded like a trapped sparrow fluttering its wings.

He was accused of such cruel behavior, I knew it could not be true. I knew it had to be rumors and false witnesses borne against him. There was such an appeal in his eyes in that first instant—*There passed between us an understanding!*—unlike anything I had experienced in my life until then.

Though certainly I'd been vexed and anxious at being summoned to downtown Trenton, it seemed to me now that there was a purpose to it, God was leading me to see.

Please don't smile: I am not a weak-minded religious woman not at all. This was utterly unknown in my life, such a conviction. How I saw that in this ridiculous courtroom he alone was designated as *the defendant*; and the staring eyes of all others latched onto him as a *criminal* who would be made to *stand trial*; but such paltry evidence as would be brought against him would not convince me, I knew from the start.

Scorn filled my heart like the sweetest balm. *You will never convince me!*

I think I will not disclose his full name. His initials only: *R.S.*

You will wonder how with such certainty I knew, that R.S. was innocent of the crimes for which he was charged, and the answer is I have always been one to trust intuition and instinct and have rarely been mistaken in my judgments. In my career as a librarian in constant confrontation with the public soon I had come to rely upon this *inner light* which has never failed me.

Nor was I a stranger to the process of *jury selection*. DENISE McSWANN had been summoned to the Mercer County Courthouse several times in the course of twenty-five years and each time summarily dismissed as a juror in the *voy deer* when questioned by the presiding judge. This time, I vowed it would be otherwise.

It was the judge's task to choose a jury of fourteen persons—twelve "active" jurors, two "alternates"—how badly I wished, and inwardly prayed to God, that DENISE McSWANN would be called.

Very straight, I sat in the hardwood seat of the bench amid fellow jurors. I am forty-six years old and a woman of a very good Trenton family and yes, I am a virgin; and do not regret the inviolable integrity of my body.

During the tedious procedure of *voy deer* covertly I watched the *defendant*. A man in his mid-thirties he appeared, seated with dignity at the defense table beside his attorney, from time to time restively shifting his shoulders that were broad and muscular inside a tight-fitting dark suit coat; unable to resist turning to glance over his shoulder at the rows of jurors, with a look that tore at my heart . . . His hair was trimmed short for this occasion, stiff-tufted and tar-colored and his eyes *haunted eyes* so very dark, the irises must have been black.

Like a captive creature, the *defendant R.S.* You felt pity for him, yet a shiver of dread that, if he were freed, he might be dangerous.

Of the charges the judge had listed it was *voluntary manslaughter* that was the most severe. Of course the defense was contending *self-defense* yet you could see how unwise it would be to provoke such a man: the unfettered male animal. For here was no sniveling hypochondriac bully like my brother Hubert whose food must be prepared just so—his white cotton "dress" shirts ironed just so—his every wish and whim catered-to by his doting mother and his indentured-servant sister but an *alpha male* to whom the morality of the commonplace does not apply.

On the wrist of R.S.'s right arm, a tattoo of some kind. And on the underside of his heavy chin and jaws, a delicate tracery of scar tissue, or another tattoo, I could not see clearly from my position in the courtroom.

A blush rose into my face, by chance R.S. had caught me watching him! The beautiful *haunted eyes* narrowed in surprise and something like animal alertness. Daringly I smiled—a twitch of the lips—quickly lowering my gaze—for the prissy judge might be observing—a moment glanced back, my heart hammering beneath my breastbone and with all my power willing the man to know *I! I am your friend! Trust me, in all of this courtroom of strangers it is I who have been sent to aid you.*

And so it seems to me: all things are from God. As God is the arbiter of chance, fate, destiny. And so it must be, God has arranged for this, that is seemingly pure chance: that Denise McSwann had been summoned to *jury duty* on this day of all days, when the trial brought against R.S. by the State of New Jersey was scheduled to begin.

There can be no coincidences. Mere chance is but a form of destiny.

Have I mentioned, the judge in this case was female? Earnest and plain-featured and of about my age if not older in her silly black judge's robe like a Hallowe'en costume rousing some envy in me, it is true, but primarily scorn *Who does she think she is just a homely woman in disguise.* As if addressing a roomful of slow-witted individuals repeating her statements to an exasperating degree but DENISE McSWANN in the second row most cannily did not reveal anything of the impatience she felt.

Tediously we were warned, and again warned: not to communicate with any officers of this court nor with the defendant for the duration of the trial. Not to exchange greetings in the courtroom corridors with any of these individuals and not to seek knowledge of the case in the news media and above all are not to seek out the defendant or any member of the defendant's family nor any acquaintance of the defendant under pain of *contempt of court*. Jurors were forbidden to speak of the trial even to family members under pain of *contempt of court*.

Pleasantly I nodded Yes! Yes of course.

As in a lottery prospective jurors' names were being selected at

random and these presented to the judge to enunciate in her
nasal-grating voice. Each time I prepared to hear DENISE Mc-
SWANN and like a child felt a stab of disappointment when a
stranger's name was called in my place. So frustrating! As the hours
passed eight, ten, and finally eleven jurors were chosen and there
were just three places remaining in the jury box, and of these two
were *alternates* without votes. By which time I was inwardly de-
spairing thinking *Has God misled me? Is God teasing me? To bring me into
his very presence and then to deny me—why?*

The several times I'd been summoned to *jury duty* in the past, I
hadn't been chosen of course. Carefully it was explained that such
rejections are *not personal* and yet you would have to be quite a fool
to suppose that they are not. When in the *voy deer* I was asked the
usual questions, I answered honestly as you are supposed to do,
and with what results?

A pompous (male) judge intoned *Mz. McSwann do you comprehend
the principle of "innocent until proven guilty"—are you capable of forming an
objective opinion on the guilt or innocence of the defendant after due deliberation
without being influenced by the fact that the defendant has been indicted and
charged with these crimes* and unhesitatingly I replied *No Your Honor*
and there was a hush in the courtroom as the judge stared at me as
if he had not heard correctly and so I explained *Your Honor anyone
with any common sense can reason, if a criminal has been arrested by police and is
standing trial, he must have done something to deserve it; especially in this
crime-ridden city of Trenton, where nobody is ever caught for anything, and there
are break-ins and robberies every night, if on a rare occasion the police do manage
to catch someone we can assume he has committed many crimes beforehand—and*
in great alarm and with a reddening face as if now the judge suspected that I was joking or taunting him rudely he interrupted
saying *Mz. McSwann you are excused, you may leave the courtroom.*

Like a naughty child banished from the courtroom and in my
wake—I'm sure I was not imagining this—titters of laughter.

Vowing this time *Such rejection will not happen another time.*

I knew that I was making an excellent impression not only on
the judge but on the young woman prosecuting attorney and the

defense attorney, a man of premature middle-age with a furrowed face. For it is easy to mistake Denise McSwann for a meek "librarian-type" female lacking a strong will of her own—a female to be impressed and manipulated by others. I was the only woman among the jurors to be wearing a hat and white gloves; one of very few women not in slacks or slovenly jeans but a dress, beneath a good black wool coat with a Persian lamb collar; in good leather shoes, and stockings. My hat was a sky-blue wool cap, which I removed. Though the world sees a plain-featured middle-aged woman with a slight overbite, a sagging lower face and thin lips, the type of female to be ignored by most men, near-invisible in fact, my secret is *I am a very different person inside, how astonished you would be!* for it has never been Denise McSwann's nature to "suffer fools" gladly, in judicial robes or otherwise. As a librarian for eighteen years at the Merck branch of the Trenton Public Library, I was sorely tested by the slow-witted and obtuse among the citizenry, not to mention unruly children and "teens"; at the age of thirty-nine I was transferred to the downtown branch of the library, removed from *Circulation* and given a desk in *Cataloguing*; at last, at the age of forty-five, granted *early retirement.*

It was humiliating to me, to be forced into retirement at such a young age, since I'd had excellent grades in library school and knew myself to be a damned good librarian; but frequent clashes with my ignorant supervisor, and certain others, took their toll on my nerves, and so I accepted the offer made to me by the district. Taking some spiteful pleasure in knowing that my brother Hubert was envious of me. For it will be at least fourteen years before Hubert McSwann can retire as chief administrative assistant at the New Jersey State Historical Museum on State Street to have free time to pursue his myriad "hobbies"—ridiculous activities of which an adult man might rather be ashamed, than eager to "rejuvenate." (As a young adolescent Hubert had ranked surprisingly high in the Northeast Junior Chess League, or so was his and Mummy's claim. Now it was Hubert's fantasy to return to chess, among other follies.)

All this while I observed the *defendant*. As the drone of *voy deer*
continued. With a stab of tenderness I saw that his dark socks did
not appear to be a match, one a solid color and the other with a
faint pattern. I saw that his suit fitted him awkwardly, as if it belonged to a slightly smaller man. I saw how nervously he stroked
his oiled hair. In profile his face was blunt as carved rock. His forehead was low with a look of brooding. Though surely he'd shaved
that morning in preparation for court, already by mid-afternoon
his dark beard was beginning to emerge like buckshot on the lower
part of his face.

Restless the *defendant* turned to glance back at me. It seemed
that "vibrations" emanated from me, to be registered by him. His
expression was grave, frowning—his gaze moved swiftly across
mine—badly I wanted to signal him but of course dared not—if
the judge saw, she would expel me from the courtroom and all
would end abruptly.

Voy deer is a procedure like running a clumsy and unwieldy
substance—rags, young tree limbs—through a grinder. So slow! So
exasperating! When at last the judge called a recess there was muttering among the jurors, for they were hoping to be sent home for
the day: it was 4:05 P.M. Stiffly we stood. Stiffly made our way out
of the courtroom. My head rang with fatigue. My knees were weak.
I dared not glance back at R.S. to see whether he would be free to
leave the courtroom as well.

Outside the ten-foot windows of the courtroom the wintry
New Jersey sky was of the hue of tin and porous-seeming as leaky
insulation.

Quickly I made my way to a women's restroom on the first
floor landing of the creaky staircase. Despite my "meek" demeanor
I make it a point to be first in line whenever I can, as other females
drift dazedly in my wake. Such a strange state I was in, part dreamy,
part alarmed, there came to me the stern admonition *If you leave now
no one will know. If you slip away, great harm will be averted.*

Naturally Hubert had tried to discourage me from obeying the
summons. Counseling me to plead *poor health* to the jury manager

and be excused from this ordeal. You are a nervous woman, Hubert said in his kindly/sneering voice. And you know you are needed at home to care for Mummy.

You are a nervous man, and *you* are needed to care for Mummy.

So boldly I retorted, trembling with audacity as I'd done since girlhood confronting my big-bully-brother.

It was not true, that I was a nervous woman, intrinsically. Nor was it true that our mother required anything like twenty-four-hour surveillance. For a woman of eighty-one with arthritis, high blood pressure, "fluttery" heart and "blotched vision" Mummy was in very good health and rarely complained except jokingly in the way of her favorite TV comedians; you would be impressed, seeing how Mummy could make her way with her aluminum walker like an upright, antic crustacean scuttling across a room! It was like Hubert to exaggerate Mummy's medical state, out of a crude wish that Mummy would pass away soon.

Because Hubert will inherit the "bulk" of Mummy's estate! I have not seen Mummy's will, but this I know.

Returning from the restroom I was surprised to see R.S. in the corridor, standing with his lawyer. So he was "free"—perhaps "free" on bail bond?—and could return to his home afterward? With a hard-beating heart I managed—unobtrusively—to pass close behind the men in hope of overhearing their conversation. Though it was not a true conversation, as the lawyer—who was shorter than R.S. by several inches—did most of the talking while R.S. listened glumly. I saw how the *captive animal* was watched over by deputies stationed only a few yards away. Brute uniformed bullies weighed down with gear—leather holster and belt, revolver, billy club, two-way radio.

Out of a nearby alcove designated PROSECUTION WITNESSES ONLY spilled a slovenly family of fat disheveled mother, young children with runny noses and frightened eyes, and so it happened that I was obliged to pass close behind R.S. as the thought came to me swift as lightning *If he took me? As a hostage? But he would need a gun.* I was smelling R.S.'s scent—an odor of cigarette smoke, tarry hair

oil—his skin was swarthy and coarse as if pitted on his cheeks and
forehead—yet his *haunted eyes* were beautiful eyes, thick-lashed and
sensitive. On the underside of his jaw was indeed a tattoo, and on
his right wrist the tattoo of a silver dagger with crimson roses
twining around the blade . . .

Ma'am? Are you all right?

Must've stumbled. There was a roaring in my ears. My heart
had kicked—and stopped—and then began again—a terrible heat
rushed through my body.

It was one of the guards who'd come forward to offer me assistance. He was a young deputy courteous to his elders and did
not betray any disrespect. My face was so very flushed, I felt that
my cheeks must be flaming. Oh this was so embarrassing, to one
with my dignity! The *defendant* and his lawyer moved quickly from
me with but sidelong looks at me, for further communication was
forbidden.

Thank you, officer. I am . . .

But the young deputy firmly took my arm, to escape me back
into the courtroom, and to my seat. As if I were an infirm woman!
An older woman! And not at forty-six in the prime of my life.

Yet I had passed close by R.S., and might have reached out to
touch him.

And he'd seen me. And he knew me. *Now my luck will change* I
seemed to know, and so it was when the final name was chosen by
lot that afternoon to be pronounced in the judge's nasal-grating
voice this name was DENISE McSWANN.

Here, Your Honor! I am here.

Shrewdly answering the judge's questions. *No Your Honor I would not
be prejudiced. Yes Your Honor I would be objective. No Your Honor I had not
read of this case nor heard of it. Yes Your Honor I believe in the principle of innocent till proven guilty. No Your Honor I would not value the testimony of a
law enforcement officer over the testimony of a civilian. Yes Your Honor I comprehend the principle of "beyond a reasonable shadow of a doubt . . ."* Clasping

my gloved hands in my lap and my voice just slightly quavering and my demeanor that of an utterly ordinary not-very-bright middle-aged female resident of Trenton, New Jersey, no one could guess the exultation in my heart as the judge declared *Mz. McSwann you are hereby accepted as juror number twelve.*

In this way as I foresaw the jury to deliberate the case of the *State of New Jersey vs. R.S.* was completed. In this way the lives of R.S. and Denise McSwann were entwined together like tattoo-roses about the blade of a tattoo-dagger, forever.

Not five minutes home that evening, my overbearing brother could not find it in his heart to congratulate me for once. Staring at me with his jeering smile.

Denise, *you!* There has got to be a mistake.

I began to tremble. Fearing that Hubert would sabotage my chance for happiness.

Stammering I said that yes it was so, I was a *juror.* The trial was starting at 9 A.M. the next morning.

How is this possible, Denise? You know that you aren't capable of *objectivity.* You're emotional, easily upset, angered—

No. I am not.

Denise you *are.* Certainly, you *are.*

No! I will make an ideal juror in this case. I was carefully interviewd by the judge in the *voy deer* and neither the defense attorney nor the prosecutor objected to her seating me on the jury.

Voy deer?—do you mean *voir dire?*

My face reddened. Hubert laughed. Hubert never missed an opportunity to show up my inferior local--New Jersey education.

At the courthouse it is called *voy deer.* That's exactly how the judge pronounced it, Hubert—*voy deer.* And I've been chosen, and that's that. I am juror number twelve and I've been sworn in with the others, I've taken an oath to uphold the law *so help me God.*

Hubert shook his head as if this was all too much for him. A man of utmost rationality, in a household of weak-minded women.

For it was true, in the months leading to my retirement as for some time afterward I had not been altogether what you would call a *well person*. But all that was past, I never gave any thought to it now except when Hubert prodded me so cruelly, as you might prod a terrified animal with a stick. He had succeeded in riling me and causing me to speak with a stammer. The fear pervaded me, this cruel man who took such pride in his paltry employment at the state history museum might, with a single strategic telephone call to a fellow government-employee at the Mercer County Court-house, ruin my chances to serve on R.S.'s jury.

Just what kind of trial is this, Sissy?

(*Sissy!* So Hubert addressed me when his mood began to shift from annoyance to exasperated affection, as you might speak to a recalcitrant child or family pet.)

It is—a criminal trial.

I swallowed hard. My mouth had gone dry. Badly I wanted to protest *But the defendant is not a common criminal!*

Really? And what is the crime?

Hubert, I can't discuss it. You know that.

Well—who is the criminal?

There is no *criminal*. The man to be tried is a *defendant*. We have all pledged to regard him as *innocent until proven guilty*.

Sissy, come on! Don't be obtuse. D'you think that "innocent" citizens are arrested and tried for crimes, especially in Trenton? What's he been charged with?

Hubert, no. I can't talk about it.

Certainly you can tell me, Sis. It's hardly like telling Mummy. I would never violate any confidence.

No! The judge gave us our instructions.

It will be in the *Trenton Times,* probably. I can look it up.

The way Hubert was regarding me, I had to think that he must be speculating how to sabotage my plans. He could sense my excitement and see the glisten in my eyes, he could not know of R.S. but with the shrewdness of the predator he could sense a new radiant presence in my life.

Wanting me to confide in him, I thought. So that he could betray me. That is his game.

Quietly I said taking care not to allow my voice to quaver, Really Hubert I can't discuss the case. Please understand.

Such integrity, suddenly! Sissy I am impressed.

This was a sneer. I knew. Turning on his heel to walk away from me rudely but I was determined not to succumb to a tantrum of sisterly fury and rush after him beating at him with my fists and screaming at him to upset Mummy and throw the household into a commotion just before supper, not at this crucial hour of my life.

This scene with Hubert, I have inscribed in my journal. A handsome notebook with a marbled cover in which I'd written a few entries years ago, in recovery from my *breakdown*.

Pitiless and honest will be all entries in this journal. A distillation of all that I hate, loathe, and bitterly resent about my brother Hubert.

I suppose, you might define it as *classic feminist injustice,* what I have endured from him. Except in my years as a librarian surrounded by *feminist-type females* I came to loathe these individuals, too.

Here was the issue: since my retirement from the library it seemed to have been decreed—not with my consent!—that I was to remain at home full-time and care for Mummy and for the house—which is not a small house—like an indentured housewife of the 1950s while Hubert was the sole member of the household with a career, a profession, an income and *a life outside the family*.

Hubert: pronounced *Huu-beart* in pretentious nasal-French.

Since childhood Hubert had been my big-brother protector outside the house and my big-brother tormentor inside. We were Mummy's only children, and Mummy was our only (living) parent.

If I harbor a (secret) loathing of Authority—a wish to sabotage and do (secret) harm—it is because of Hubert.

When we were children Hubert tormented me by claiming that he alone could recall the days—years—when our father lived with us in the spacious English Tudor house on Hurdle Avenue, at a time when the neighborhood was still "exclusive"—"not yet 'integrated.'" (My beloved father Timothy McSwann died suddenly of a heart attack when I was just seventeen months old, & Hubert was six. He had been part-owner of a family business McSwann Ball Bearings Inc. in Trenton, long since sold.) Hubert claimed that our father had taken him—*Not you Sis you were just a baby always crying*—to the state fair and the planetarium and the New Jersey Historical Museum where one day Hubert McSwann was to be chief administrative assistant and that our father loved *him* best and had confided in him, he hadn't wanted a *second child* at all.

What a cruel thing to say to this *second child*! Feebly I protested that Hubert was mean and nasty and I did not believe him.

Gleefully Hubert cried Yes! It's true! Daddy and Mummy were *not getting along* at that time. Having you was *Mummy's idea* and not Daddy's.

It was not! I don't believe you! I hate you . . .

When I began to cry my big-bully-brother might relent. If he could take gloating pity on me, he would leave off this torment.

Already as a child of eleven Hubert had acquired the air of a predator bird, a vulture or a turkey buzzard, with small shrewd glaring-yellow eyes and a way of baring his teeth in a "smile" that made smaller children shudder. His cruel bullying nature he hid from teachers and other adults-in-authority who mistook him as mature and reliable and to be entrusted with extra responsibilities and privileges. Our mother adored him as did other (female) relatives. His hobbies (chess, model sailing ships, stamp collection, etc.) were indulged while mine (flute and recorder, tap dancing, astronomy etc.) were barely tolerated. Hubert was sent to the Pennington School while I went to the local public school. Out of a mysterious "trust fund" Hubert was sent away to Yale where he received both a B.A. and an M.A. (American history) while I commuted by bus to Ryder College and later to the New Jersey State Library School in New Brunswick. And out of this same trust fund Hubert was able to travel to Europe several times while

I remained at home taking care of our widowed mother's needs and commuting to my job at the Merck branch of the Trenton public library.

Not that I am complaining, *I am not*.

For yes—there were romances. Even—once—almost!—when I was twenty-eight—an engagement.

(About which Hubert had no more sensitivity than to tease me though he had to know that my heart was broken and that for months I cried myself to sleep waking in despair and famished in the night to tiptoe downstairs to the refrigerator helpless to withstand the terrible craving to devour ice cream out of the package ravenous as a beast.)

(And possibly it was at that time nearing my thirtieth birthday when I resolved to hurt him. Seeing my life stretching out before me like the New Jersey Turnpike littered with debris and the knowledge came to me that somehow, someday—I didn't yet know how—God would infuse me with the strength to exact justice from my cruel brother, at last.)

Now it seemed to me, so long awaiting a sign *God had sent a sign*. As juror number twelve pledged to uphold the law and grant to the defendant R.S. all *presumption of innocence unless proven guilty*, I would see my life so scorned by individuals like my brother and so taken for granted by all others *redeemed*.

All rise!

You would think that this command would be infuriating to me, who so chafes at unwarranted Authority, yet there was something thrilling in it, each day of the five days of the trial *All rise!* like a summons in a place of sanctity.

At the start of each court session a pork-faced sheriff's deputy opened the door behind the judge's bench and through this doorway as onto a stage stepped the judge in her silly black robe—plain-faced and sallow and with a self-important smirk—*no ring* on her left hand, which was not surprising—and all of us—mere commoners!—were obliged to rise to our feet in deference to her power. And so quickly I did. As through the tedious and unconvincing presentation by the prosecutor that lasted for hours I maintained this air of calm, courtesy, deference. For this was the strategy of juror number twelve DENISE McSWANN.

The trial was short: just five days. There was very little for the defense to argue except *self-defense* and so, unfairly it seemed to me, as surely to other jurors, most of the trial was taken up by the prosecutor. As Hubert had anticipated it was covered in the *Trenton Times* but not very thoroughly covered, relegated to inside pages which was disappointing. Nor did local TV news run any footage. (Though I had insisted to Hubert that I would not discuss the case nor look it up in the news, of course I did. It was not likely that anything I read about the case would influence *me*.)

The charges brought against R.S. were: *voluntary manslaughter, obstruction of justice, resisting arrest & assault against a police officer*. These charges were pronounced by the young female prosecutor and vigorously contested by the defense attorney. Each side presented witnesses, many more for the prosecution than for the defense, and each side argued that its witnesses were telling the truth and that the other witnesses were not. The prosecution argued that R.S. was *guilty*, the defense that R.S. was *not guilty* for he had acted without premeditation in the heat of an argument and had wished only to "unarm" an angry woman who was attacking him.

In essence, this was the case. No matter the hours of testimonies by prosecution witnesses—relatives of the deceased, Trenton police officers, an old-goat forensics "expert" like someone on TV—this was the case. In my heart I felt scorn for the prosecution and a citizen's resentment that such a vast entity as the State of New Jersey could be mobilized against a lone individual like R.S.—who, as it was revealed, had served in the U.S. military at the time of the Persian Gulf War of 1991 and had been "honorably discharged" and was now thirty-seven years old. Badly I yearned to smile at this persecuted man seated a short distance away, that I might offer him solace. *Don't give up hope! Their case against you is not convincing at all.*

In the first row of seats behind the defense table were relatives of the defendant. Over the course of the five days these individuals would vary but always there was a dazed-looking older woman with limp gray hair like used Brillo pads & a morose set to her mouth that resembled R.S.'s mouth. His mother, I supposed.

From time to time, R.S. would glance back at his relatives. With a look of tenderness and concern he would smile at the gray-haired woman as if to signal *I am all right! I love you.*

Not an attractive woman yet there was something wistful and yearning about her. In a grocery store Mrs. S. would be the annoying older customer pushing her cart slowly and blocking the aisle until at last impatiently I would murmur *Excuse me! Please!* and push my cart around her. But in the courtroom, I felt some sympathy for her. How painful it must be, to see her son on trial! Mrs. S. had to be at least ten years younger than my mother but walked in that wincing way that suggested arthritis like poor Mummy and seemed often on the verge of tears when the prosecution spoke most harshly of R.S. enumerating his alleged *unconscionable actions* on the night of the alleged *voluntary manslaughter* and calling him *a careless brutal man.*

To Mrs. S. I wanted to send a signal as well. *Have faith! Don't despair. You have a friend on this jury.*

In my car which is a five-year-old pearl-gray Nissan, for some minutes I sat exhausted and strangely elated in the lot on Broad Street designated JUROR PARKING MERCER COUNTY COURTHOUSE. This was following my first day as a juror. This was following hours of testimony by prosecution witnesses. Though I was expected home to prepare supper for Mummy and Hubert yet I could not bring myself to leave, just yet.

At the courthouse I had lingered on the stairs hoping to catch sight of R.S. Not that I would have spoken with him, of course I would not. Nor with his lawyer, or with anyone in R.S.'s family. For all that was forbidden to jurors and I dared not risk expulsion from the jury. Though in some private place casually together, for instance a women's restroom, if Mrs. S. chanced to be inside, and by chance I entered, I would have smiled and nodded at her in a friendly manner but not exchanged actual words.

But I saw none of these people. Not R.S. nor any of those individuals I believed to be his relatives.

Ma'am? C'n I help you with anything?—a female deputy sighted me on the staircase landing, and spoke sharply to me.

Politely I thanked her and said no.

I was just leaving, I said. I am a juror in a trial, and I am just leaving for the day.

Feeling ice pick eyes on me as I descended the stairs. My face burned but not unpleasurably.

Always you think in the presence of such brute bullies armed and prepared to shoot *The power to kill resides in them. But in me, the power to provoke!*

In my state of heightened nerves I could not bring myself to drive directly home, to the drafty old house on Hurdle Avenue to prepare our evening meal as usual. As I had arranged for a neighbor woman to visit with Mummy until either Hubert or I arrived home, I was not greatly concerned about her. As for Hubert's disapproval *He can go to hell! The tyrant.*

After fifteen minutes or so in the car in the parking lot—it was twilight now and a feathery light snow falling—that melted as soon as it touched the pavement—slowly I drove from the near-empty lot and along Broad Street past the courthouses and beyond to State Street; and north on Stuyvesant Avenue and at Mott Street turning east, as I had never done before in my life, and proceeding to the 900-block of Mott—this, a section of Trenton unknown to me—and so to 941 Mott which was a weatherworn brownstone duplex like others on the block—darkened windows upstairs and down—litter on the front walk—and a faintness came over me as I stared at the house *There is no one inside now. What has happened, has happened and is over.*

This was *941 Mott* where the woman had died. In an upstairs bedroom of that brownstone. Now a darkened room no one would wish to enter. Soaked into the mattress of the bed, on the floor bloodstains of the woman who had bled to death through that night.

So the prosecution claimed. And witnesses who were R.S.'s enemies. Wishing to portray R.S. as a drunken brute. But R.S. had only protected himself for the woman had wakened him from sleep to lunge at him with a knife, he had tried to disarm her and in the desperate struggle by accident he had stabbed her.

Nine times, he had stabbed her. For once begun, in a kind of trance he had not been able to stop. So it would be argued. *A classic case of self-defense* his lawyer argued.

And R.S. was a Gulf War veteran. That fact, jurors must never forget.

Rudely a horn sounded behind me. A vehicle had driven close up nearly striking the rear of my car. Blinding headlights in my rearview mirror.

Nowhere to go now for Denise McSwann, but home.

And how is your trial, Sis? Boring, eh?

So Hubert wished to provoke me. That first night, and subsequent nights. Stiffly I replied that I could not speak of it, as he knew. As a juror bound to confidence. Seeing my prim pursed expression Hubert laughed. *As a juror bound to confidence!* You are very funny, *Den-ise.*

Even my name was a source of amusement to my insufferable brother! But I refused to be drawn into an exchange and cast our suppertime into disarray.

Mummy too was eager to know of the trial. Firmly I explained that I could not discuss it until its completion.

They were jealous, I think. This new radiance in my face and a certainty in my manner. My old nervousness and quick-irritation like an edgy cat had vanished. Unknown to Hubert and Mummy each night on my way home from the courthouse I would stop at a 7-Eleven to purchase copies of all Trenton newspapers I could find, and eagerly read through them for news of the trial—disappointing, there was so little—in the *Trenton Times* just minimal coverage on an inside page—though on the third day of the trial a double column and at the top a photo of R.S. unsmiling and somber in military uniform and a photo of the deceased female, thirty-two years old and pretty in a superficial way with plucked eyebrows, a stubby nose, arrogant mouth *Bernadette Enzio, thirty-two at the time of her death.* It was the first likeness of the alleged victim I had seen, quickly I tore it out of the newspaper page and crumpled it in my fist.

No: I did not wish to contemplate *Bernadette Enzio.* At the trial there was far too much made of this female with whom R.S. was said to have lived intermittently the previous winter and spring until the time of her death. This female who had surely provoked R.S. to behave as he had. *I am not jealous of her. Yet there is justice, she is no longer a presence in R.S.'s life.*

Meaning to be friendly, the 7-Eleven clerk who was a woman of my age said to me, seeing what I was reading, That's a nasty trial isn't it! Makes me sick to read about it people like that, their kind of lives so careless. Saying he *blacked out* and didn't know the woman was bleeding to death and he's in the same bed!—had to be drunk or high on drugs—makes me sick to think about it. The clerk is shaking her head and I am careful to say quietly the defendant is a Gulf War veteran under medication and how can that be his fault? It was the woman who stabbed at him first, with a knife. And the clerk frowned and said well yes, maybe that was so.

I thought, if you were on the jury with me! We would see that justice was exacted.

Outside the parking lot I took care to dispose of the newspapers. All I retained was the *Times* story with the handsome photo taken so long ago, almost I would not have recognized R.S.

The final days of the trial it was my practice to arrive early at the courthouse. In this way hoping to avoid a long shuffling line at the security check that straggled out onto the sidewalk. If I came at the right time there was the chance of encountering R.S. I would observe R.S. on the street walking with the older gray-haired woman and some others—the surprise was, R.S. walked with a stiffness in his left leg, and his left shoulder carried just slightly lower than his right. To pass close by him I quickened my steps. In the cold air my breath steamed. My lips were fixed in a small smile like something stitched in my skin. Daring to cast a sidelong look at him seeing that he wore dark-tinted glasses in the glare of morning and there was a stiffness in his face, like one who hopes not to be seen. The thought came to me *They have shamed him in the eyes of the world, he must be avenged.*

Quickly I hurried by. R.S. and his mother were joined on the sidewalk by another individual, unknown to me. I entered the courthouse that was a relief, after the cold rushing wind of Broad Street. My eyes watered with tears and my heart was a-flutter and how Hubert would laugh at me in scorn, as a weak-headed female who could not manage her own financial accounts, for all her librarian-training, but would have to be managed by *him*. In the security line, I fumbled to place my handbag and tote bag on the conveyor belt. Ma'am? Anything in your pockets? Keys? Cell phone? Out of the tote bag spilled a package of Red Zinger herbal tea, yogurt containers, two small McIntosh apples and a small plastic knife—that made the older black deputy laugh. Ma'am, you have come prepared for a lengthy day!

There was an address given in the *Trenton Times,* on Drexell not far from Mott.

In the Nissan driving slowly past 1291 Drexell which was a single-story wood frame house set back from the street in a small yard stippled with snow like sand dunes strangely beautiful in the reflected light from the windows. At twilight and again at dark for forty minutes circling that block of 1291 Drexell where the S. family resided and I had reason to think, if he was freed on bail, R.S. must now be living.

At the curb I parked. Like the buzzing of a giant insect the engine ran. A sickly sort of heat spilled from the vents of the car and a stupor of happiness came over me, just to sit here and gaze at the windows of the S. residence, drawn blinds warmly lighted from within.

The house was a small bungalow of shingle wood. The front porch listed to one side in need of propping and repairing. This was a run-down section of Trenton far from our house near Academy Woods Park. Yet, in the driveway beside the house there was a new-looking vehicle, I thought must be an S.U.V.

On the jury, I was cunning and quiet. This was my strategy. In the courtroom you are not allowed to take notes but in the jurors' room you are allowed and so when we were sent from the courtroom I sat by myself with my herbal tea taking notes in this journal while the others chattered noisily of TV programs, families and vacation plans.

It was a matter of outrage to me, that these fools had been selected to pass judgment on R.S.

So long as the trial continued we were not allowed to discuss the case and yet I could sense by certain remarks overheard and by the self-righteous air of the jury foreman—a man of Hubert's type, taking up more space than he deserved—that some of my fellow jurors were doubtful of the defendant's claim of self-defense.

At my corner of the table I kept to myself, writing in this journal. *None of you will sway me. I know what I know and will never change my mind.*

At the curb in front of the shadowed bungalow in my parked car, I waited. From time to time vehicles would pass by for the street was wider than Mott. A half-hour, I waited. I could not have said why I waited and yet it would not have been possible for me to leave.

At last the door opened. Hesitantly a figure—a female—stood in the doorway. The Nissan's headlights were out but the engine continued to run and sickly-smoothing heat lifted into my face. It was not R.S.—I did not expect that it would be R.S.—but the gray-haired woman who was his mother, in a coat hastily thrown on. Mrs. S. was in her sixties with a sagging body, sad-sagging face.

That morning outside the courthouse she had taken note of me and in the courtroom saw that I was seated in the juror box. In the unsparing light of early-morning the woman's face was revealed as a ruined girl's face wanly pretty but now faded, and a look of bafflement in her eyes.

Now she was calling to me. I lowered my car window, to hear her query.

Excuse me? Ma'am? Are you looking for someone?

Yes. I am looking for—

Stating his name. Calmly, and boldly.

Quickly she said, He is not here.

If you are the mother of R.S., we could talk.

The woman had come closer, to peer at me. She was clutching the collar of her coat, shivering. Her frizzed-gray hair was disheveled from the wind. Why, she asked. Why should we talk ma'am.

Worriedly casting her eyes about, to see if other vehicles were parked in the area. What did Mrs. S. expect, that I would be conspiring with the Trenton Police Department, to entrap her! This was so far from my motive, I had to laugh, sadly.

Please will you trust me Mrs. S. I am your friend.

A look of cunning came into the woman's face. Yet she was wary, suspicious.

Ma'am I don't think so. No.

May I come inside your house and we can talk.

Ma'am no! I don't think that is a good idea ma'am. If you are who I think you are, you are not supposed to be here.

Not supposed to! Now I was laughing, in contempt. Saying I am a free citizen of the United States, God damn I will visit where I wish. I will make friends where I wish. No one can order me about.

This blunt statement made an impression on Mrs. S., I saw. She had to see, that I was serious. I was her friend. Though sucking at her lips in anxious indecision as forcefully I said, Then will you give a message to your son for me, Mrs. S.? This is crucial.

Ma'am that is not a good idea. I think, I have to go back inside now ma'am.

Don't you trust me, Mrs. S.? I am sorry.

Goodnight!

Nervously the woman backed away. Clutching her coat closed, at the throat. Laughing suddenly, and her breath steamed.

All right then goodnight! I said laughing.

I put the Nissan in gear and drove away and Mrs. S. who had retreated to the listing porch of the bungalow stood watching the red taillights disappear and I felt such happiness knowing that she would hurry then to call her son, in a breathless voice of alarm and wonder *That woman! That juror! I think she is our friend! She has just been here to see me.*

Hubert had a fiancée, but the poor woman came to her senses in time.

It was an irony of our lives, that Hubert's friend Hedda was a librarian, like me. Yet unlike me, a librarian in a (mere) junior high school in Ewing. Her narrow horse-face and mournful eyes revealed that desperation, I saw immediately. And felt some sympathy for her as to a lost sister.

It was a kindly time in my brother's life, when he was cordial to me and most attentive to Mummy. As if the fact of *having a fiancée* had wakened Hubert to generosity, to a degree. This I have to concede.

Hubert at age thirty-five! Before his fair brown-blond hair began to thin, and the hard little pot-belly to protrude above his belt like a kettledrum.

Yet Hubert's cordiality was false, I knew. The predator-bird awaited inside those yellow eyes, and at the slightest provocation the *Yale degree* was a scimitar to swipe at Denise, at will.

One afternoon by chance encountering Hedda in a store at the Ewing mall. Where several times I shopped in the hope of such an encounter, at an hour when a school librarian would be on her way home.

I was so friendly then! I was not pretending, such a warm

sisterly feeling for poor Hedda. For I knew her to be a deluded woman, who must be warned against a terrible error.

It was pathetic to me, how this horse-faced woman could imagine herself *loved* by any man, even my brother Hubert. Finding any reason to glance at the engagement ring on her hand, that had been a ring of Mummy's mother, a family heirloom Mummy was foolish enough to give to Hubert, and to smile at the ring which was a beautiful antique ring, a square-cut diamond set amidst smaller diamonds in a gold setting. *What right does Mummy have to give such a ring to Hubert, and nothing to me?*

Though I was not jealous. Hardly!

Hedda and I had coffee in a food court there. Coffee and pastries, which were my treat. For I had a shock to reveal to this poor deluded woman, and wanted to soften the blow somewhat.

After some exchange of complaints—good-natured & laughing for the most part—about our respective library-jobs, bluntly I informed my prospective sister-in-law: My brother is a fetshist.

A what?

Fet-shist.

Hedda stared at me blankly. She had taken a small bite of a pineapple pastry at my urging and her jaws slowed, chewing. Her beautiful thick-lashed horse-eyes blinked in utter bafflement.

Hedda, a *fet-shist* is a depraved man who craves sex-stimulations and release through some weird thing like a woman's shoe. It is a very shameful pathology said to be *resistant to any form of therapy*.

Still Hedda stared. Hastily she brought her napkin to her mouth.

In a grave lowered voice I leaned across the table to confide in the poor woman the terrible shock it had been for me to first discover my brother's *secret cache* in a box in his closet, tied with twine, some years before when I had been hardly more than a girl, in experience. And how, that time, I had quickly put the box away, not wanting to open it. Then, there was *a thing* that happened at the History Museum, a few years ago, I told Hedda it had not gotten into any newspapers and was *hushed up* and so this time when I was alone in the house one day daringly I returned to Hubert's room, and there was the box, in fact now a bigger box, hidden at the rear of the closet, and with a thudding heart I pulled this box out and slipped off the twine and inside this box—a terrible shock, it made me sick to recall—were women's high-heeled shoes, not pairs but single shoes, and little girls' shoes, smelly dirt-stiffened socks Hubert must have found in the park, or in the trash somewhere. As I told Hedda of my discovery, my eyes moistened with tears and I laid my hand on hers, to comfort her.

Oh! Denise I c-can't believe you . . .

Hedda it's true! How can you think that I would invent such a disgusting fact about my own brother!

Poor Hedda bit her lower lip, to keep from crying. Her voice was weak and wavering and the several times I'd overheard Hubert speaking with her, in the parlor of our house on Hurdle Avenue, I had scarcely heard Hedda at all, only just Hubert's loud voice. Here was a nervous woman who'd become a librarian as I had surely out of a mistaken belief that there was a kind of solitude in a library and in books that would protect us from the cruelty and vulgarity of the world, that was a world of *men*.

At a small table in the food court Hedda and I were sitting. Our handbags were at our feet. I was rummaging in my pink plastic tote bag as Hedda stared. What are you doing, Denise? What is—?

Hedda was frightened, as I pulled out of the tote bag a smaller plastic bag, in which there was a little girl's black patent leather shoe, a woman's ridiculous high-heeled "sling-back" sandal glittering with some kind of faux gold dust and a single black silk stocking, badly torn and stiff with filth. These are just a few items from Hubert's *cache* I said.

Hedda staggered to her feet. Hedda stumbled away. Hedda looked as if she would be sick to her stomach.

That was nineteen years ago. Since then, Hubert has not "dated" any other innocent woman, to my knowledge.

And so, on the evening of the fourth day of the trial, when Hubert asked in his sneering voice *How's the juror?* even as I hurried to serve the meal I'd hurried to prepare, as Hubert and Mummy took their places at the dining room table, and my nerves were raw in the aftermath of the day's courtroom session, I heard myself counter Hubert's query with, What has become of that poor homely fiancée of yours, Hubert?—The junior high librarian . . . Knowing that it would provoke him, and deflect his attention from me. And so this was, for a flush mottled Hubert's face as he said, in as steady a voice as he could manage: Who?

As if, *who?* I had to laugh.

Calmly I continued to serve the meal. (You would wonder what I could so quickly prepare having returned home—late—from the courthouse: meat loaf, made with the very best quality of beef, pre-prepared and frozen the previous weekend. Delicious meat loaf baked with lavish dollops of ketchup that is an old favorite recipe and served with fried potatoes. *Yes I am a good cook!*) Saying, You know exactly who I mean, Hubert. Her name was Hedda.

As Hubert drew breath to speak harshly to me Mummy interjected quickly, Now Denise now Hubert! Children, it is our suppertime. Please.

Mummy is an elderly woman and yet: at such times her eyes are alert and vigilant and the worrisome vagueness of her manner vanishes. Casting her look of dismay on her grown daughter and son. At such times I felt sympathy for Mummy, and a tinge of shame for myself, for there have been forty years of bickering in this household, at mealtimes at this dining room table most of all. Overhead our glass crystal chandelier that is a precious antique, in which glaring bulbs have been set, for the practical purpose of lighting our meals but banishing all residue of elegance and romance from our household. In a pleading voice Mummy said, Denise you know it's a sore point with your brother. The fickle behavior of certain women.

This was funny! Mummy's innocence provoked me to laugh.

And Hubert too, recovering from his fit of fury. Red-faced trying to laugh saying, As if I care! I don't even remember her name.

I said, her name was Hedda.

Well, I don't remember. I'd forgotten.

"Hedda Denticatt." You remember very well.

I do not. "Hedda Denticatt" is a ridiculous name not known to me.

Liar! I laughed, I was angry. Mummy put her hands over her ears, though Mummy is hard-of-hearing. Neither Hubert nor I would retreat from supper for that was not our way on the occasion of such outbursts, that took place from time to time unexpectedly. Neither Hubert nor I would wish to deprive ourselves of our evening meal. Sometimes truly it does not seem that I am forty-six years old and my brother is fifty-one. *It seems that we are children again, he is the bully and I must protect myself against him for he would suck away my life.*

It was in the concluding hours of the trial, R.S. testified at last.

Taking the witness stand as it is called. To speak openly and in anguish.

In halting speech to all the courtroom describing the events of that night. Wakened from a stupor sleep by the woman and he had no choice but to defend himself.

Conceding yes, he had ingested alcohol—as she had, earlier that night—and a certain drug, Percodan which was prescribed for him.

R.S.'s lawyer questioned him for some time politely and respectfully. The conclusive fact in this case was, the deceased woman's fingerprints were discovered on the knife, with R.S's prints. This was such unshakable proof, there seemed to me little need to listen further.

In the front row of spectators Mrs. S. sat with downcast eyes and a mouth of bitter sorrow. Yet some motherly pride, in hearing her son speak to the courtroom at last, with such conviction. Naturally we had not acknowledged each other in the courtroom and would not, to the very end of the trial. While his lawyer questioned R.S. in a kindly voice taking care to emphasize how this is a man who had been willing to sacrifice his life for his country and who had sacrificed his *health & mental well-being* you could feel that the sentiment of the courtroom was with him, and I was sure that my fellow jurors felt as I did, but then, such a rude change of tone!—as with unseemly eagerness the young-female prosecutor leapt to her feet to approach the witness, to query him in a voice laced with sarcasm. This was shocking to many in the courtroom, that R.S. should be subject to so harsh an interrogation—a veteran of the Gulf War!—after forty minutes of this abuse lapsing into a sullen silence, his mouth working. On his knees, his fists were clenched and tremulous. And the cruel judge had no sympathy for him, prodding in her nasal-grating voice, Please answer the question, Mr. S. And the thought came to me *He would smash their faces with his fists, if he could. If he had but the freedom!*

So offended by the bitch-prosecutor subjecting R.S. to this ordeal, I blocked off her yammering voice for the remainder of the trial, and paid not the slightest attention to her hysterical summing-up in the end. And there was the judge admonishing us, like children she could not trust: You must judge by the evidence and you must come to a unanimous verdict. And I thought gloating *I have come to my verdict in my innermost heart, and I will never change my mind.*

There came the first vote, by secret ballot.

Eleven *guilty* and one *not guilty.*

The jury foreman stared through bifocals at the lone paper ballot held in his hand as if he didn't know where to place it.

We were in the windowless and airless *jurors' room* down the hall from the courtroom. Locked away to *deliberate* and to *reach a unanimous verdict.*

Hours had passed, it was believed fruitfully by these fools and now they might vote led by their "foreman" and believed they might reach their *unanimous decision* to be taken to the judge by 5 P.M. But this was not to be. For when the foreman asked for a show of hands, unhesitatingly eleven jurors raised their hands for *guilty* and only one, juror number twelve, for *not guilty*.

In surprise they stared at me. The fool-foreman, exactly like Hubert when he is thwarted, fixed me with a smile of ghoulish insincerity. Mz. McSwann is it! Would you like to explain to us, your line of reasoning? If this bully wished to goad me, he could not; for I am too cunning to be goaded by such provocation. Quietly and with seeming shyness of the kind you would expect in a middle-aged retired librarian I explained why I believed as I did, I had listened carefully to all the evidence presented by the prosecution, and to the testimony presented by the defense, and after searching my conscience, I simply did not believe that the prosecution had proven its case *beyond a reasonable shadow of a doubt*.

More hours would pass, in the effort to "reason" with me. That afternoon and again the next morning in the windowless and airless *jurors' room* on the second floor of the Mercer County Criminal Courthouse. At all times Denise McSwann listened politely to the arguments of fellow jurors yet remained unmoved; nor would she smile abjectly or in apology as men expect of women in such circumstances, only just reiterating *I must vote as the evidence directs me. I have prayed, to find justice*.

And so the session continued, through the second day. And the fool-foreman insisted upon another ballot, and another "show of hands"; but always there was one *not-guilty* vote amid the eleven *guiltys*. Initially the discussion was composed and not rancorous but by quick degrees tempers began to flare up, both female and male jurors were becoming exasperated with me, which I acknowledged I understood: But I could only vote following my conscience, as the judge had instructed. A request was made to the bailiff to bring us transcripts of several testimonies, including that of R.S., and the old-goat forensics expert, and several hours passed in the fruitless perusal of this material while I sat with clasped hands and a calm-beating heart, like the stillness at the core of a tornado. For, to me, there was no other evidence that yielded the full truth except the fact that *the deceased woman's fingerprints were on the knife, with those of the defendant*. This was a point I would never concede, I said.

And what would it take to change your mind Mz. McSwine, the foreman asked of me, with his ugly big-toothed smile, Oh! Excuse me, Mc*Swann* I meant to say. Red-faced and sweating inside his white cotton "dress" shirt as he was made to realize he could not bully juror number twelve who replied to him without rancor, There is nothing that can change my mind.

So three full days passed, in what the newspapers call a *deadlock*. And since juror number twelve could not vote *guilty* on the main charge of voluntary manslaughter, she could not vote *guilty* on any of the lesser crimes for these followed from the first, by which time several of the (female) jurors had broken down into tears, and several of the (male) jurors were speechless with dismay and disgust, and at the close of the third day of deliberations the exhausted foreman sent notice to the judge that we could not agree on a unanimous verdict; and the judge summoned us into the courtroom and spoke sharply to us as to disobedient children. As if she could force us to become *unanimous*! I saw her disgruntled eyes drift over me, in search of the *holdout juror*.

Sending us back to the windowless and airless *jurors' room* another time. How weary we had grown of one another! Yet, I would not budge. And in the end, on the final ballot another juror had joined me, with a vote of *not guilty*.

The judge had no choice but to dismiss the jurors and to declare a *mistrial*.

Not that evening but the next I drove to Drexell Street.

Parked the Nissan at the curb at 1291 Drexell and went to the door of the bungalow and knocked and there was a face at a window peering at me and the door opened, it was Mrs. S. gazing at me with some of the stunned relief she had shown in the courtroom, when the judge declared a *mistrial*. Saying, You! God has sent you! seizing my hand in hers as if she might kiss it, and looking at me with such giddy joy, as if she might embrace me. Her breath smelled of whiskey, her sallow skin was flushed.

A faintness came over me. I could not have said if I was very happy at last—or shivering with dread. (It was a cold windy evening, bits of snow like mica flung against my heated skin.) My mouth had gone dry. I said, Is he here? Your son?

And Mrs. S. said, Yes he is here.

Uneasy and yet courteous calling me *ma'am*. Saying how grateful he was to me, for he knew, it had to have been me; the other jurors had looked at him as if he was an animal.

God had sent me a sign, I said. That was all.

We were drinking. Mrs. S. had brought us a bottle of whiskey and two drinking glasses and left us alone together. In another part of the bungalow were TV voices and laughter.

I am not accustomed to drinking. And never hard liquor. But this was a special occasion, it would have been priggish of me to decline. I said, They had no evidence really. You served your country in war, it was wrong of them to betray you.

He said, The fuckers! That's what they want, to fuck you over. He drank. He said, wiping his mouth on the edge of his hand, You gave me my life back, ma'am. I owe you.

I laughed. My face heated pleasurably.

It was a magical time! There have not been many such magical times in my life, and none like this.

When I'd touched Hedda's hand, that day in the food court, and dared to grip it, in sisterly feeling—that had been a time. But none since, and that was nineteen years ago.

My brother, I said.

I began to cough. The whiskey flamed in my mouth and throat and flared at my eyes, making me laugh. But I was anguished, too. To speak of the cloud that hangs over me.

Ma'am, your brother—what?

My brother is an evil person. A cruel person who has threatened me.

Pronouncing these words with such vehemence, I was surprised by myself. And yet, I was proud of myself. As somberly R.S. regarded me not knowing what to make of me, I suppose. The tattoo on the underside of his jaw was shadowy and mysterious as a caressing hand. Tell me about your brother, ma'am, he said.

Dear Husband,

Dear Husband,

Let no man cast asunder what God hath brought together, is my belief. And so I have faith that you will not abandon me in my hour of need. Dear husband, you will forgive me and you will pray for me as you alone will know the truth of what has happened in this house, in the early hours 6:10 A.M. to 6:50 A.M. as you alone have the right to condemn me. For it was my failure as a wife and the mother of your children that is my true crime. I am confessing this crime only to you, dear husband for it is you I have wronged. Our children were to be beautiful souls in the eyes of God. You led our prayers: Heavenly Father, we will be perfect in Your eyes. And in the eyes of Jesus Christ. "With men it is impossible but not with God: for with God all things are possible." Our firstborn son named for you, dear husband, was most beloved of you, I think. Though you were careful not to say so. For a father must love all his children equally, as a mother must. Loell, Jr. was meant to be perfect. And Loell, Jr. was a very happy baby. That he would not be a "fast learner" like some in your family was hurtful to him, for children can be cruel, but he did not cry overmuch in his crib. It is true, your mother fretted over him for her grandson did not "thrive" as Mother McKeon would say. Loell, Jr. had such warm brown eyes!—a sparkle in his eyes though he came late to speech and could not seem to hear words spoken to him unless loudly, and you were facing him. It was God's wish to cause our firstborn to be as he was. And then God sent us twin daughters: Rosalyn and Rosanna. Bright lively girls with white-blond hair so much prettier than their mother's hair which has grown darker—"dirty blond"—with each year. The twins were closest to Mommy's heart, when they were not misbehaving. And little Paul, with his Daddy's sharp eyes and wavy hair, and little Dolores Ann: Dolly-Ann, our "sudden gift" from God, born within a year of your second son. All of my life here in Meridian City has been our family, dear husband. You said, I will make a home for us. Like a city on a hill our family will be, shining in the sun for all to behold. You are praised as a draftsman and the plans you work with, blueprints out of a computer, I can't comprehend. It is like a foreign language to me, that you can so easily speak. Though in high school I took algebra, geometry, trigonometry, one of the few girls in Meridian High in Mr. Ryce's class, I did not do badly. Each semester my name was on the honor roll and I was president of Hi-Y in senior year and a guard on the girls' basketball team and at the Christian Youth Conference in Atlanta, I was a delegate in my senior year. You would not remember for you were three years older than "Lauri Lynn Mueller" and a popular boy on the football team, yearbook staff, studying mechanical engineering and one of those to receive scholarships at Georgia Polytech. It was unbelievable to me that Loell McKeon would wish to date me, still less to marry me, I must pinch myself to believe it! Dear husband, this letter I will be leaving for you on the kitchen table, where I have cleared a space. My handwriting is poor, I know. My hand is shaky, I must steady it as I write. I will dial 911 when it is time. Within the hour, I think. On the counter, there are three knives. Who has placed them there so shiny-sharp, I am not certain. The longest is the carving knife, that has been so clumsy in my hand, you would take it from me to carve our roasts. I have swallowed five OxyContin tablets, you did not know that I had saved out of my prescription, and there are twelve more I am to swallow when God so instructs me, it is time. I am so grateful, each step has been urged on me, by God. No step of our lives is without God. Upstairs, the children are peaceful at last. They have been placed on our bed in the exact order of their age for it is this order in which God sent them to us, there is Loell, Jr., and there is Rosalyn, and there is Rosanna, and there is Paul and there is Dolly-Ann and you would believe Those children are beautiful children, so peaceful! Dear husband, when the "bad feelings" first began, before even I went to that doctor you believed to be Pakistani, or Indian, from the health plan, I would have a dream while awake and my eyes staring open driving out on the highway and my hands would turn the wheel of the car to the right—quick!—quick as a lightning-flash!—before any of the children could perceive it, we would crash into the concrete wall at the overpass and all would be over in an explosion of flame. This dream was so searing, dear husband, my eyes have burned with it. It is the purest of all flame, all is cleansed within it both the wickedness and the goodness of humankind in that flame annihilated for as Reverend Hewett has preached to us out of the pulpit *Unto every one that hath shall be given, and he shall have abundance: but from him that hath not shall be taken away even that which he hath.* This was long ago it seems when Rosalyn and Rosanna were still in car seats in the back, and Loell, Jr. was buckled in beside me, fretting and kicking. A later time, when Paulie was in back with the twins, it was the station wagon I was driving, on Route 19 south, and the children were fretting as usual, for a kind of devil would come into them, when Mommy was behind the wheel and anxious in traffic, little Paulie would shriek to torment me, his cries were sharp like an ice pick in my brain! Mother McKeon said, she did not mean to be harsh but was kindly in her speech, Can't you control these children, Lauri Lynn? It should not be that hard, you are their mother. Your mother looks at me with such disappointment, I do not blame her of course. Your mother has a right to expect so much better of Loell McKeon's wife, all of the family has a right to expect this for you are their shining son. Now in her face there is disappointment like a creased glove someone has crushed in his hand. Mother McKeon had no difficulty raising her three children. You, and Benjamin, and Emily May. You are perfect, God has blessed you. To some, it is given. From others, it is taken away. Why this is, Reverend Hewett has said, is a mystery we must not question. At Thanksgiving, I was very anxious. You said, why on earth are you hiding away in the kitchen washing dishes before the meal is concluded, why do you behave so rudely, what is wrong with you?—you were on the honor roll at school, you won the *Meridian Times* essay prize, $300 and publication in the paper—"Why Good Citizenship Is Our Responsibility in a Democracy." Little Dolly-Ann had diarrhea and the twins could not be seated together for their giggling and squabbling and Loell, Jr. ate so fast, with his head lowered, and was so messy, and Paulie sulked wanting to play his videos and shoved at me saying Go away Mommy, I don't love you Mommy. The children eat so fast, and are so messy, Mother McKeon crinkled her nose saying, you'd think these children are starving, and nobody taught them table manners, look at the messes they make. It is sweet things that make them so excitable, out of control. Always at family meals there are many sweet things. Even squash, and cranberry sauce, your mother laces with sugar. Dear husband, I have tried to keep them bathed. It is hard to fight them sometimes, for they kick and splash in the bath knowing how fearful I am, the floor will get wet, and the tile will warp, and water will drip down through the dining room ceiling. I have tried to keep this house clean. You would laugh at me, your angry laugh like silk tearing, dear husband, but it is so, that I have tried. When the police come into this house this morning, I am ashamed to think what they will see. Of the houses on Fox Run Lane, you would not believe that 37 is the house of shame for from the street, it looks like all the others. Of all the "Colonials" in New Meridian Estates, you would not believe that this is the house of shame. The bathrooms are not clean. The toilets cannot be kept clean. Beneath the cellar steps, there is something so shameful, I could not bring myself to reveal it to you. You have been so disgusted, dear husband, and I know that you are right. I know that it is not what you expected of this marriage, and what was promised to you. And you are working such long hours, and you are away more often at Atlanta. I know that I am the mother, and I am the wife. I do not need anyone to help me. Mother McKeon is right, it is a dangerous idea to bring strangers into our homes, to carry away stories of us. Such wrong stories as are told of Loell, Jr. at his school, that he bites his own fingers, and arms, it is in frustration with the other children teasing him. Yet, as a baby, his eyes were so happy, and unclouded, your mother said what a blessed baby, look at those eyes. For in Loell, Jr.'s eyes, your mother perceived your eyes, dear husband. None of this is your fault, dear husband. At Christmastime you bought me an excellent vacuum cleaner to replace the old. It is a fine machine. I have seen it advertised on TV. It is a heavier machine than the other, which is needed in this house. It is difficult to drag up the stairs, I am ashamed of what the police officers will discover. The boys' rooms are not clean. The boys' bedclothes are stained. There is a harsh smell of the baby's diapers and of bleach. The twins' hair cannot be kept free of snarls. They push at my hands, they whimper and kick, when I try to comb their hair. And so many dirtied clothes, socks and sneakers, and towels. Worse yet are certain things that have been hidden. I am so ashamed of what will be revealed to you, after I am gone. It was my fault, to provoke you to say such things. I know that such terrible words would never erupt from your mouth, dear husband, except for me. And never would you strike a woman. My jaw still hurts but it is a good hurt. A waking-up hurt. You said, Lauri Lynn what the hell do you do all day long, look at this house. You have nothing to do but take care of the children and this house and look at this house, Lauri Lynn. You are a failure as a mother as you are a failure as a wife, Lauri Lynn. Tricked me into marrying you, pretending to be someone you are not. You were right to say such things, dear husband. Many times I have said them to myself. In a weak moment, when little Paulie was just born, I asked you could the Morse girl drop by after school to help me sometimes, I would pay her out of my household money. I was not begging from the neighbors, dear husband! I was not telling "sob stories" as you have accused. I did take counsel with Reverend Hewett, as you know. Reverend Hewett was kindly and patient saying God will not send us any burdens greater than we can bear, that is God's promise to mankind. I began to cry, I said I am a failed mother. I am a failed wife. My children are not good children, Reverend. My children are flawed and broken like dolls, like the dolls and toys they break, the stuffed animals they have torn. I am so tired, Reverend Hewett. It was held against me that at Sunday services, I slept. I could not keep my eyes open, and I slept. Our church is the most beautiful of all churches in New Meridian, we are very proud of our Church of the Risen Christ which is only three years old. Like an ark it is built with its prow rising. Two thousand worshippers can gather in our church and sing praises to the Lord, it is like a single voice so strong you can believe it would rise to Heaven to be heard. In such joyous sound, Lauri Lynn was but a tiny bubble and what sorrow there is in a tiny bubble, is of no consequence. I am the Way, the Truth, and the Life so Jesus has promised but Jesus was disgusted with Lauri Lynn, you could not blame Him. If I could sleep, I would be happy again. I do not deserve to be happy ever again, I know. It is for this reason, I think, that this morning at last I acted, as God has instructed. For now what is done, is done. For now it cannot be undone. Mommy! Rosanna cried but I did not heed her, for the strength of God flowed through my limbs. When we were first married, dear husband, I weighed 126 pounds but after the babies, these past few years my weight has been 160, I am so heavy, my thighs are so heavy, the veins are blue and broken in my flesh like lard and my breasts are loose sagging sacs, you would not believe that I am twenty-eight years old which is not old. I stand in front of the mirror gripping my breasts in my hands and I am

322 * JOYCE CAROL OATES

so ashamed, yet there is a fascination in it, what I have become. For I am not now Lauri Lynn who was a plain girl but known for her smiles, to make others feel welcome. And in some snapshots, I am almost pretty. Where that girl has gone, I do not know. Truly she was not a "trick" to beguile you, dear husband! You will say, Lauri Lynn will abide in Hell. But Lauri Lynn is not here, the children scarcely knew her. In the 7-Eleven if there are teenaged boys outside, I am ashamed to walk past. These boys jeering and mocking as boys had done with my friend Nola who weighed 150 pounds when we were girls. Look at the cow, look at the fat cow, look at the udders on that cow, moo-cow, moo-cow, moooo-cow like hyenas the boys laughed for nothing is so funny to them as a female who is not attractive. We must not pay attention to such crude remarks, and yet. And yet in your eyes, dear husband, I see that scorn. It is the scorn of the male, it cannot be contested. In the mirror, in my own eyes, I see it. In Jesus' eyes, I see it. I am a bad mother, and now all the world will know. It is time, all the world should know. It was very hard to force them, dear husband. Like you they are not patient with me any longer, they have smelled the weakness in me. In animals, weakness must be hidden. For a weak animal will be destroyed by its own kind. There is a logic to this. I began with Loell, Jr. for he was the oldest, and the biggest. Loell, Jr. I had to chase for he seemed to know what Mommy wished to do, to make things right again. Loell, Jr. is named for you, he is your firstborn son though he has been a disappointment to you, I know. For Loell, Jr. cannot comprehend arithmetic, the numerals "fly" in his head he says. He fought me, I was surprised. When I chased him in the upstairs hallway he ran screaming and squealing like one of our games except when I caught him he didn't giggle—I didn't tickle him—the "spider tickle" he used to love—he fought me, and bit my fingers, but I was too strong for him, and carried him back to the bathroom and to the tub where the water was just warm the way the children like it, and now there is so much water on the floor, it is leaking through the floor and through the dining room

ceiling, you will be so disgusted. Some parts of what happened, I
don't remember. I remember laying Loell, Jr. on our bed, his
pajamas so wet, the bedspread became wet. Next was Rosanna,
for she had wakened, and Rosalyn was still sleeping. (This was
very early, dear husband. At the Days Inn in Atlanta, you would
still be asleep.) Jesus said to me, It is true that you are a bad
mother but there is a way: "If thine eye offend thee, pluck it out."
There is a way to be forgiven, and cleansed. Dear husband, I wish
that the toilet was not so stained but the stain is in the porcelain
and cannot be scrubbed out. And the tub, I have scoured with
cleanser so many times tearful and in a fury but the stains will not
come out. Even steel wool would not clean it, please forgive me.
After Loell, Jr. the others were wakening and God instructed me,
Lauri Lynn! You must act now. A feeling of flames ran through
the upstairs hall, I could see this flame like heat waves in the
summer and from these flames which were the flames of God, I
drew strength. From these flames, I understood what was or-
dained. For he who hath not, from him shall be taken away even
that which he hath, I had not understood until now is God's
mercy, and God's pity. It is not God's punishment for God is a
spirit, who does not punish. So swiftly this truth ran through me,
I cried aloud in joy. The little ones believed, it was their bath
time. And the promise of bath time in the morning is breakfast,
and if they do not misbehave, they can have their favorite cereal
which is Count Chocula, that is covered in chocolate. It was so
very early—not yet dawn! The house is quiet before the start of
the long day. The children must be scrubbed if they have soiled
themselves in the night and they must be readied for school
except for Paulie and the baby and then there is the return from
school, noise and excitement, it is a very long day like a corridor in
a great motel where you cannot see the end of it, for the lighting is
poor, and the rooms are strangely numbered. Mommy is so tired!
Which of those doors in the corridor is Mommy's door, is not
certain. For the day has no end. My sister said chiding, You look
so tired, Lauri Lynn, you should see a doctor. I was furious with

her poking her nose in our business, I said, I am not tired! I will
not break down and cry. I will not be ridiculed, or pitied. I will
not be laughed at. I am not a TV woman, to spill her guts to
strangers, to reveal such shameful secrets, to receive applause. I
have done a good job, I think, to hide from them. From the
McKeons especially. But it is too hard, I am so tired, one by one I
drowned them in the tub, it was not so very different from
bathing them, for always they kicked, and splashed, and whimpered, and whined, and made such ugly faces. Some parts of what
God instructed me, I can recall, but others are faded already now,
like a dream that is so powerful when you are asleep, you would
wish to keep it, but when your eyes open, already it begins to fade.
It was a hard task but needed to be accomplished for the children
had not turned out right, that is the simple fact. As at birth, some
babies are not right, malformed, or their hearts are too small, or
their brains, or the baby itself is too small, and God does not
mean for such babies to survive, in His infinite wisdom. These
children, who did not show their deformities to the eye, except
sometimes Loell, Jr., when he twisted his mouth as he did, and
made that bellowing sound. I am a bad mother, I confess this. For
a long time I did not wish to acknowledge this fact, in my pride.
But the flames cleanse us of all pride. Even Reverend Hewett
would not know, for in his heart he is a proud man, that pride is
but a burden, and when it is taken from you, what joy enters your
heart! In your eyes, dear husband, I hope that this is restitution. I
hope that this is a good way of beginning again for you. The baby
did not suffer, I promise. Like the others Dolly-Ann thrashed and
kicked with surprising strength for a five-month infant but could
not fight her mother as the others tried to do, and beneath the
water little Dolly-Ann could not scream. How many times you
have pressed your hands over your ears, dear husband: Why does
that baby scream so? Why is it our baby that screams? It is a
cleansing, now. God has instructed me, and Jesus Christ has
guided my hand. As I am a bad mother I will be punished by the
laws of man, I will be strapped into the chair of infamy, and

flames will leap from my head, but I will not be punished by God
for God has forgiven me. Dear husband, you will be called at
work, in Atlanta. You will be asked to return home. In Heaven,
the children will be at peace. They will no longer be dirty, and
squabbling, but they will be perfect as they were meant to be.
Always you will know from this day forward, your beloved
children are with God, and are perfect in His bosom. There will
be strangers in this house that has been a house of pride too long.
To the police officers who are men like yourself you will say with
your angry laugh, there is not a clean glass in this house, if one of
the police officers requests a glass of water. And the broken toys
on the floor. Ugly Robo-Boy that Mommy could not fix, for the
battery did not fit right, that provoked Paulie to scream It won't
walk! It won't walk! Mommy I hate you! The twins, I have
wrapped in their new plaid coats, to lay on the bed. I brushed out
their snarled hair like halos around their heads. The others are in
their pajamas, that are wet, and I have hidden their faces with a
sheet. These are not beautiful children, I am afraid. For their
mother was not a beautiful woman. My big girl, you called me. My
breasts filled to bursting with milk, you held in your two hands in
wonder. My big-busty girl you moaned making love to me, lying
on top of me and a sob in your throat, your weight was heavy upon
me, often I could not breathe, and your breath was sour in my face
sometimes, a smell as of something coppery, I hid such thoughts
from you of course. Now you are released from our wedding vows,
dear husband. In the place where I am going, I will not have
children. If I had been strong enough, the fire would consume
me. But the fire has burnt down now, I am very tired, it is all that
I can do to swallow these pills, and take up the carving knife, at
the kitchen sink. You will find another woman to honor and to
cherish and to bear your children and they will be beautiful as you
deserve, and they will be perfect. Lastly dear husband, I beg you
to forgive me for the heavy casserole dish hidden beneath the
cellar stairs, that is badly scorched and disgusting for not even
steel wool could scrape away the burnt macaroni and cheese, now

in cold water it has been soaking since Thanksgiving. I could not hide it in the trash to dispose of it for it is a gift from your mother, it is CorningWare and expensive and might yet be scoured clean and made usable again, by another's hand.

Your loving wife,
Lauri Lynn

About the Author

JOYCE CAROL OATES is a recipient of the National Book
Award and the PEN/Malamud Award for Short Fiction.
She has written some of the most enduring fiction of our
time, including the national bestsellers *We Were the Mulva-
neys, Blonde,* which was nominated for the National Book
Award, and the *New York Times* bestseller *The Falls,* which
won the 2005 Prix Femina Étranger. She is the Roger S.
Berlind Distinguished Professor of the Humanities at Princeton University and has been a member of the American
Academy of Arts and Letters since 1978. In 2003 she received the Common Wealth Award for Distinguished Service in Literature, and in 2006 she received the Chicago
Tribune Literary Prize for lifetime achievement.